Marion Lennox has written more than one hundred romances, and is published in over a hundred countries and thirty languages. Her multiple awards include the prestigious RITA® Award—twice—and the *RT Book Reviews* Career Achievement Award for 'a body of work which makes us laugh and teaches us about love'. Marion adores her family, her kayak, her dog—and lying on the beach with a book someone else has written. Heaven!

Christine Rimmer came to her profession the long way around. She tried everything from acting to teaching to telephone sales. Now she's finally found work that suits her perfectly. She insists she never had a problem keeping a job—she was merely gaining 'life experience' for her future as a novelist. Christine lives with her family in Oregon. Visit her at christinerimmer.com

Also by Marion Lennox

Christmas Where They Belong
The Earl's Convenient Wife
His Cinderella Heiress
Stepping into the Prince's World
Stranded with the Secret Billionaire
Reunited with Her Surgeon Prince
The Billionaire's Christmas Baby
Finding His Wife, Finding a Son
English Lord on Her Doorstep
The Baby They Longed For

Also by Christine Rimmer

The Nanny's Double Trouble
Almost a Bravo
Same Time, Next Christmas
Switched at Birth
Carter Bravo's Christmas Bride
James Bravo's Shotgun Bride
Ms. Bravo and the Boss
A Bravo for Christmas
The Lawman's Convenient Bride
Garrett Bravo's Runaway Bride

Discover more at millsandboon.co.uk

CINDERELLA AND THE BILLIONAIRE

MARION LENNOX

HER FAVOURITE MAVERICK

CHRISTINE RIMMER

MILLS & BOON

First Published in Great Britain 2019
by Mills & Boon, an imprint of HarperCollinsPublishers,
1 London Bridge Street, London, SE1 9GF

Cinderella and the Billionaire © 2019 Marion Lennox
Her Favourite Maverick © 2019 Harlequin Books S.A.

Special thanks and acknowledgement are given to Christine Rimmer for her contribution to the *Montana Mavericks: Six Brides for Six Brothers* continuity.

ISBN: 978-0-263-27251-2

0719

MIX
Paper from
responsible sources
FSC™ C007454

This book is produced from independently certified FSC™ paper to ensure responsible forest management.

For more information visit: www.harpercollins.co.uk/green

Printed and bound in Spain
by CPI, Barcelona

CINDERELLA
AND THE
BILLIONAIRE

MARION LENNOX

To our friends, Neil and Dale,
and to all the intrepid islanders who make their homes
and/or their livings on the islands of Bass Strait.

It's a harsh and unforgiving place to love,
but it gives back in spades.

PROLOGUE

THE LACEWORK ON McLellan Place's gatehouse looked almost perfect. From the helicopter, Matt and Henry saw the last piece being fitted into place. Once they landed they admired the result, agreeing with the foreman that it had been a major storm. The damage wasn't the fault of workmanship.

If Matt had come by himself he might have headed straight back to Manhattan, but he was entertaining a seven-year-old. He and Henry therefore walked across the vast sweep of lawn to the main house beyond.

'It's big,' Henry whispered as Matt led him into the massive kitchen and through to the butler's pantry to find juice and cookies. The place was always stocked, even though Matt was lucky to arrive once a month.

The house *was* big, Matt conceded. With eight bathrooms and ten bedrooms, it was far too large for one semi-reclusive bachelor. But the East Hampton home, two hours' drive or a short chopper ride from Manhattan, had been in his family for generations. Its upkeep kept a team of locals employed, its seclusion gave wildlife a precious refuge and it was as much a home as he'd ever known. It had been his refuge as a child from being dragged from one international hotel to another by his jet-setting parents.

Henry should have somewhere like this, he thought. McLellan Place was a far cry from the Manhattan legal offices where Henry seemed to spend half his life.

The seven-year-old was now sitting at the vast stretch of granite that formed the kitchen bench, seriously concentrating on his juice. He was nothing to do with Matt, but there was a part of Matt that connected with him.

Henry's mother, Amanda, was one of Matt's employees, a lawyer and a good one. Nothing got in the way of her work, including her son. When he wasn't at school she left him in her office and often, somehow, he ended up in Matt's office, reading or playing computer games.

The call today, to tell Matt of the storm damage, had come through when he'd had an unexpected break in appointments. Matt hadn't been near McLellan Place for weeks. His chopper was available. It was time he checked on the place.

He'd looked at the silent kid and made a decision. A call to Amanda had given slightly stunned permission—she couldn't believe her boss had time for the boy.

Thus Henry was here with him, quiet and serious.

'It has beautiful furniture,' the little boy ventured.

It did. His mother's interior designer would be pleased.

'Those stairs are really long.'

'When I was your age I used to slide down the bannisters.' The bannisters were an ode to craftsmanship, the oak curving gracefully at the end to stop a small boy coming to grief. 'Would you like me to show you how?'

'No, thank you.'

Probably just as well. He hadn't slid down for maybe twenty years.

'We have time for a swim,' he suggested. The horizon pool by the house was kept warm all year round.

'I didn't bring my swimmers.'

'We could swim in our jocks.'

'No, thank you,' Henry said again, politely, and Matt felt like banging his head. This kid had been schooled to be seen and not heard, to fade into the background.

'Then let's go for a walk on the beach,' he told Henry.

And then his personal phone rang. Uh-oh.

Matt's secretary knew what he was doing and when he'd be back. She'd only contact him if it was urgent.

'Helen?'

'Matt?' And by the tone of her voice he knew something was wrong. Seriously wrong.

What the…? 'Tell me.'

'Matt, it's Amanda. You know…she went out to lunch. Matt, they say she was texting and she walked… Matt, she walked straight into traffic. Matt, she's dead. That poor little boy. Oh, Matt, how are you going to tell him?'

CHAPTER ONE

'You employed me to act as a fishing guide. Now you want me to act as a glorified taxi driver? *And in* Bertha? Four hours out and four hours back, with overnight stays? Is she even safe?'

'She's safe as houses.' Charlie's voice was smooth as silk as he patted the reservation book with satisfaction. 'This is a last-minute booking, *Bertha*'s the only boat available and Jeff's rung in sick. Have you any idea how much this guy's prepared to pay? Never mind,' he added hastily, no doubt figuring Meg would up her wage demands if she knew. 'But it's enough to give you a decent bonus.'

'Charlie, I've been out since dawn on a fishing charter. I'm filthy. I'm off for the next three days. I have five acres of grass to slash and it's almost fire season. If I don't get it done now the council will be down on me like a ton of bricks.'

'Sell that place and move into town,' Charlie said easily. 'I know it was your grandpa's, but sentimentality gets you nowhere. Look,' he said placatingly. 'You do this job, and I'll send Graham out to slash the place for you.'

Charlie's son. Not in a million years.

'You're kidding. Knowing Graham, he'd slash the house before he touched the grass. Charlie, I'm not about to drop everything and spend the next three days ferrying some cashed-up tourist with more money than sense. Why does he want to go to Garnett Island anyway? No one goes there.'

'I do.'

The voice made her jump.

She'd been leaning over the counter of Rowan Bay's

only charter boat company, focusing on Charlie. Not that Charlie was anything to focus on. He was flabby, florid, and he smelled of fish.

The guy who'd walked in was hitting six feet, maybe even more, lean, ripped, tanned. Sleek? The word seemed to fit. In the circles Meg O'Hara moved in, this guy was... well, a fish out of water.

Or a shark? His smart chinos, his butter-soft leather jacket, his brogues all screamed money. His hair looked as if it had been cut yesterday, conservative and classy, every jet-black wave knowing its place.

And his eyes...

Dark as deep water, they were watching her and asking questions. She found herself getting flustered just looking into those eyes.

'I'm Matt McLellan,' he said softly, but there was a growl underneath, an inherent threat. Was it...*don't mess with me*? 'You're booked to take me to Garnett Island. Is there a problem?'

Charlie stood up so fast his chair fell over behind him. He grabbed a grubby notepad from beside the phone, wrote a figure on it and shoved it across the desk at Meg.

She glanced down at it and turned bug-eyed.

'That'd be my cut?' she asked incredulously. What had this guy offered Charlie?

'Yes,' he said hurriedly and surged around the desk to take the stranger's hand. 'There's no problem, Mr. McLellan. This is Meg O'Hara, your skipper. She'll take you out, anchor until you have the little one settled and then bring you back.'

'Little one?' Meg asked.

'He's taking a boy out to his grandmother,' Charlie said, talking too fast. 'That's right, isn't it, sir?'

'That's right.' The man dropped Charlie's hand and glanced at his own. She saw an almost-instinctive urge to wipe it.

She didn't blame him. Charlie's hands… Ugh.

Though she glanced down at herself and thought…
I'm almost as bad.

'But you have reservations?' he said. He'd obviously overheard. 'The boat?'

'We had the boat in dry dock just last week,' Charlie said. 'I checked her personally. And Meg here is one of our most experienced skippers. Ten years of commercial fishing and another two years taking fishing charters. There's nothing about the sea she doesn't know.'

'She doesn't look old enough to have done any of those things.'

'Is that a compliment or what?' It was time she was part of this conversation, Meg decided. She knew she looked young, and her jeans, baggy windcheater, short copper curls and no make-up wouldn't be helping. 'I'm twenty-eight. I started fishing with my grandfather when I was sixteen. He got sick when I was twenty-five so we sold the boat and I took a part-time job helping Charlie with fishing charters. My granddad died six months ago, so I can now take longer charters.' She glanced at the note Charlie had given her. This amount… She could even get the leak over the washhouse fixed. 'The boy… Is he your son?'

'I don't have a son.'

Hmm. If she was going to be forthcoming, so was he.

'I'm not about to let you take a kid I know nothing about and dump him on Garnett Island.' She planted her feet square and met him eye to eye. 'Garnett Island's four hours off the mainland. As far as I know, Peggy Lakey lives there and no one else.'

'Peggy's Henry's grandmother.'

'Really?' Local lore said Peggy had no relatives at all. 'How old's Henry?'

'Seven.'

'He's going on a holiday?'

'To stay.'

'Is that right? Are you his legal guardian?'

'It's none of your business.'

'If you want my help it's very much my business.' Behind her she could see Charlie almost weep. The figure he'd scrawled represented a month's takings and that was only her cut. But she had to ignore the money. This was a kid. 'You're American, right?'

'Right.'

'Henry's American, too?'

'Yes.'

'Then you must have had documentation allowing you to bring him out of the country. Giving you authority. Can I see?'

'Meg!' Charlie was almost wringing his hands but Charlie wasn't the one being asked to leave a child on an almost-deserted island.

'You can see,' he said and flipped a wad of documents from an inside pocket and laid them on the desk. Then he glanced outside, as if checking. For the child?

'Where's Henry now?' she asked.

'We just had fish and chips. He's feeding the leftovers to the seagulls.'

'Greasy food before heading to sea? Does he get seasick?'

That brought a frown. 'I didn't think…'

She was flipping through the documents. 'These say you're not even related.'

'I'm not related,' he said and then obviously decided the easiest way to get past her belligerence was to be forthcoming.

'I'm a lawyer and financial analyst in Manhattan,' he said. 'Henry's mother, Amanda, is…*was*…a lawyer in my company. She was a single mother and no one's ever been told who Henry's father is. Henry's quiet. When he's not in school he sits in her office or out in the reception area. He reads or watches his notepad. Then two weeks ago,

Amanda was killed. She was on her phone, she walked into traffic and suddenly there was no one for Henry.'

'Oh…' And her head switched from distrust to distress, just like that. Her own parents… A car crash. She'd been eleven.

Her grandparents had been with her from the moment she'd woken in the hospital. She had a sudden vision of a seven-year-old who sat in a reception area and read.

There was no one for Henry.

But she wasn't paid to be emotional. She was paid to get the job done.

'So…your relationship with him?' She was leafing through the documents, trying to get a grip.

'I'm no relation.' His voice was suddenly bleak. 'Sometimes he sits in my office while I work. It was term break, so he was with me when we heard of his mother's death. The birth certificate names the father as Steven Walker but gives no details. We haven't been able to track him down and no one else seems to care. Apart from Peggy.'

And just like that, her bristles turned to fluff.

'Garnett Island?' she said, hauling herself—with difficulty—away from the image she was starting to have of a bereft seven-year-old sitting in a lawyer's office when someone came to tell him his mum was dead.

'As far as we can find out, Peggy Lakey's now Henry's only living relative,' he told her. 'Peggy's his maternal grandmother. Unless we can find his father, she has full say in his upbringing.'

'So why didn't she get straight on a plane?' The solitude of Henry was still all around her.

'She says she turns into a whimpering heap at the sight of a plane. I've talked to her via her radio set-up. She sounds sensible, but flying's not an option. She made arrangements for an escort service to collect Henry and bring him to her, but, at the last minute, I…'

'You couldn't let him travel alone.'

The last of her bristles disintegrated. For some stupid reason she felt her eyes fill. She swiped a hand across her cheek—and felt an oil streak land where the tear had been. Good one, Meg.

'So is that enough?' Matt McLellan's tone turned acerbic, moving on. 'Can we leave?'

'After I've double-checked *Bertha*,' she told him with a sideways glance at Charlie. He'd checked her personally? Yeah, and she was a monkey's uncle. She could at least give the engine a quick once-over. 'And when you and Henry have taken seasickness tablets and let them settle. Bass Strait, Mr McLellan, is not for pussies.'

What was he doing here?

The Cartland case was nearing closure. He had to trust his staff not to mess things up.

He checked his phone and almost groaned. No reception.

'There's not a lot of connectivity in the Southern Ocean.' The skipper—if you could call this slip of a kid a skipper—was being helpful. 'You can use the radio if it's urgent.'

He'd heard her on the radio. It was a static-filled jumble. Besides, the boat was lurching. A lot.

The boat he was on was a rusty thirty-foot tub. 'She's all that's available,' Charlie had told him. 'You want any better, you'll have to wait until Monday.'

He needed to be back in New York by Monday, so he was stuck.

At least his instinct to distrust everyone in this tinpot hire company hadn't gone so far as to refuse the pills Meg had insisted on. For which he was now incredibly grateful. His arm was around Henry, holding him close. Henry was almost deathly silent, completely withdrawn, but at least he wasn't throwing up.

They were almost an hour out of Rowan Bay. Three hours to go before they reached Garnett Island.

He thought, not for the first time, how much better a helicopter would have been.

There'd been no helicopters. Apparently there were bush fires inland. Any available chopper had been diverted to firefighting or surveillance, and the ones remaining had been booked up well before he'd decided to come.

Beside him, Henry whimpered and huddled closer. There had been no choice. The thought of sending him here with an unknown travel escort had left him cold.

Dumping him on an isolated island left him cold.

He had no choice.

'Boof!'

He glanced up. Meg had turned to look at Henry, but she was calling her dog?

They'd met Boof as they'd boarded. He was a rangy red-brown springer spaniel, turning grey in the dignified way of elderly dogs. He'd given them a courteous dog greeting as they'd boarded but Henry had cringed. Taking the hint, the dog had headed to the bow and acted like the carvings Matt had seen on ancient boats in the movies. Nose to the wind, ears flying, he looked fantastic.

Now…one word from Meg and he was by her side.

Meg was fishing deep in the pocket of what looked a truly disgusting oilskin jacket. She produced a plastic packet. Then she lashed the wheel and came over and knelt before Henry.

'Henry,' she said.

Henry didn't respond. Matt felt his little body shake, and with that came the familiar surge of anger on the child's behalf.

In anyone's books, Amanda had been an appalling mother.

Henry had been lonely when Amanda was alive and he was even more alone now.

Meg had obviously decided to join the list of those who felt sorry for the little boy. Now she knelt with her dog beside her, her bag in her hand, and she waited.

'Henry?' she said again.

There was a muffled sniff. There'd been a lot of those lately. Matt's hold on him tightened and slowly the kid's face emerged.

They were both wearing sou'westers Meg had given them. Henry's wan face emerging from a sea of yellow made Matt's heart lurch. He was helpless with this kid. He had no rights at all and now he was taking him…who knew where?

'Henry, Boof hasn't had dinner,' Meg said and waited.

The lashed wheel was doing its job. They were heading into the wind. The boat's action had settled a little.

The sea was all around them. They seemed cocooned, an island of humanity and dog in the middle of nowhere.

'Boof needs to be fed,' Meg said, as if it didn't matter too much. 'He loves being fed one doggy bit at a time, and I have to go back to the wheel. Do you think you could feed Boof for me?'

There was an almost-imperceptible shake of the head.

Unperturbed, Meg opened the packet. 'I guess I can do the first bit. Boof, sit.'

Boof sat right before her.

'Ask,' Meg said.

Boof dropped to the deck, looked imploringly up at Meg, then went back to sitting. He raised a paw. *Please?*

Matt almost laughed.

That was saying something. There hadn't been any laughter in the last two weeks.

But Meg's face was solemn. 'Great job, Boof,' she told him and offered one doggy bit. Boof appeared to consider, then delicately accepted.

And Henry was transfixed.

'Does he do that all the time?' he whispered.

'His table manners are perfect,' Meg said, giving Boof a hug. 'Boof, would you like another one? Ask.'

The performance was repeated, with the addition of a sweep of wagging tail. This was obviously a performance Boof enjoyed.

There were quite a few doggy bits.

But Meg glanced back at the wheel. 'Boof, sorry, you'll have to wait.' She headed back to the wheel, and Boof dropped to the deck, dejection in every fibre of his being.

'Can't you give him the rest?' Henry ventured, and Matt could have cheered.

'If I have time later.' Meg's attention was back on the ocean.

And Matt could feel Henry's tension.

From the time he'd heard of his mother's death, he'd been almost rigid. With shock? Fear? Who knew? He'd accepted the news without a word.

Social Services had been there early. Talking to Matt. *If there's no one, we'll take care of him until we can contact his grandmother.*

Matt hardly had the time or the skills to care for a child, but in the face of Henry's stoic acceptance his voice had seemed to come from nowhere.

I'll take care of him, he'd said.

Almost immediately he'd thought, *What have I done?*

To say Matt McLellan wasn't a family man was to put it mildly. He'd been an only child with distant parents. He'd had a few longer-term lovers, but they'd been women who followed his rules. Career and independence came first.

Matt had been raised pretty much the same as Henry. Care had been paid for by money. But he hadn't been deserted when he was seven. His almost-visceral reaction to Henry's loss had shocked him.

So Henry had come home to Matt's apartment. The place had great views overlooking the Hudson. It had the best that money could buy when it came to furnishings and art, but Matt pretty much used it as a place to crash. In terms of comfort for a seven-year-old there was nothing.

They'd gone back to Amanda's apartment to fetch what Henry needed and found almost a carbon copy of Matt's place. The apartment was spotless. Henry's room had designer children's prints on the walls but it still spoke sterile. His toys were arranged almost as if they were supposed to be part of the artwork.

Henry had taken a battered teddy and a scrapbook that Matt had had the privilege to see.

He'd wanted nothing else.

The scrapbook was in his backpack now. There was panic when it was out of reach, so the backpack had pretty much stayed on for the entire trip. And Teddy... When Matt had put on his oversized sou'wester, Henry had tucked Teddy deep in the pocket, almost as if he expected someone to snatch it away.

A kid. A scrapbook. A teddy.

There'd been nothing else. And Matt had had no idea how to comfort him.

'Maybe we could feed the dog,' Matt said and waited some more.

'Boof likes boys more than grown-ups,' Meg said from the wheel. 'Though he likes me best. The same as your teddy, Henry. I bet your teddy likes you best.'

So she'd seen. His respect for her went up a notch.

Actually, his respect was mounting.

Even though it had annoyed him at the time, he'd accepted—even appreciated—her checking his authority to take Henry to the island. And her skill now... The way she turned the boat to the wind, her concentration on each swell... They combined to provide the most comfortable and safe passage possible.

She was small and thin. Her copper curls looked as if they'd been attacked by scissors rather than a decent hairdresser. She'd ditched her oilskin and was now wearing faded jeans and a windcheater with the words *Here, Fishy* on the back. Her feet were bare and she seemed totally oblivious to the wind.

Her tanned face, her crinkled eyes… This woman was about as far from the women he mixed with as it was possible to get.

And now she was focused on Henry. He saw Henry's surprise as Meg mentioned Teddy. Henry's hand slipped into his pocket as if he was reassuring himself that Ted was still there.

'Ted likes me.'

'Of course,' Meg agreed. 'Like Boof likes me. But Boof does love friends giving him his dinner.'

She went back to concentrating on the wheel. Boof sat beside her but looked back at Henry. As if he knew what was expected of him. As if he knew how to draw a scared child into his orbit.

Had there been kids in the past, scared kids on this woman's fishing charters? He couldn't fault the performance.

But there was no pressure. Maybe it was only Matt who was holding his breath.

Boof walked back over to Henry, gazed into his face, gave a gentle whine and raised a paw. Matt glanced up at Meg and saw the faintest of smiles.

Yep, this was a class act, specifically geared to draw a sucker in. And Henry was that sucker and Matt wasn't complaining one bit.

'Can I have the doggy bits?' Henry quavered.

Meg said, 'Sure,' and tossed the bag. Matt caught it but she'd already turned back to the wheel.

No pressure…

He could have kissed her.

He needed to follow Meg's lead. He dropped the bag

on Henry's knee. 'You might get your fingers dirty,' he said, as if he almost disapproved of what Henry might do.

'I can wipe them,' Henry said.

'I guess.'

Henry nodded. Cautiously, he opened the bag.

'Sit,' he said to Boof, and Boof, who'd stood with alacrity the moment the bag opened, sat.

'Ask,' Henry said and the plan went swimmingly. A doggy bit went down the hatch. Boof's tail waved and then he raised a paw again. His plea was obvious. Repeat.

It was such a minor act, but for Matt, who'd cared for an apathetic bundle of misery for two weeks without knowing how to break through, it felt like gold. He glanced up at Meg, expecting her to be still focusing on the sea, but she wasn't. Her smile was almost as wide as his.

Did she know how important this was? She'd seen the legal documents. He'd told her the gist of the tragedy.

Her smile met his. He mouthed a silent thank you with his smile, and her smile said, *You're welcome*.

And that smile…

Back at the boatshed she'd said she was twenty-eight. He'd hardy believed her, but now, seeing the depth of understanding behind her smile…

It held maturity, compassion and understanding. And it made him feel…

That was hardly appropriate.

She turned back to the wheel and his gaze dropped to her feet. The soles were stained and the skin was cracked.

She'd said she'd been fishing since she was sixteen. She was so far out of his range of experience she might as well have come from another planet. There was no reason—and no way—he could even consider getting to know her better. That flash of…whatever it was…was weird.

He went back to watching Henry feed Boof, one doggy bit at a time. The little boy was relaxing with every wag of the dog's tail. Finally the bits were gone. He expected

Meg to call Boof back, or that the dog would resume his stance at the bow. Instead, the dog leaped onto the seat beside Henry and laid his big, boofy head on Henry's lap.

Matt glanced up at Meg and, surprised, saw the end of a doggy command—the gesture of clicked fingers.

Part of the service?

She grinned at him and winked. *Winked?*

Henry was feeling Boof's soft ears. He wiggled his fingers, and the dog rolled his head, almost in ecstasy.

Henry giggled.

Not such a big thing?

Huge.

His hold on him tightened. This kid was the child of a business connection. Nothing more, but that giggle almost did him in.

He glanced back at Meg and found her watching him. Him. Not Henry. His face. Seeing his reaction.

For some reason that made him feel…exposed?

That was nuts. He was here to deliver a child to his grandmother and move on. There was no need for emotion.

He didn't do emotion. He hardly knew how. That Meg had somehow made Henry smile, that she'd figured how to make him feel secure… How did she know how to do it?

Matt McLellan was a man in charge of his world. He knew how to keep it ordered, but for some reason this woman was making him feel as if there was a world out there he knew nothing about.

And when Henry snuggled even closer, when Henry's hands stilled on the big dog's head, when Henry's eyes fluttered closed… When he fell asleep against Matt with all the trust in the world, the feeling intensified.

Once again he glanced at Meg and found her watching. And the way she looked at him…

It was as if she saw all the way through and out the other side.

* * *

She shouldn't be here. She should be home, slashing her grass, doing something about Grandpa's veggie patch. If he could see the mess it was in, he'd turn in his grave. That veggie patch had been his pride and joy.

She'd let it run down. She'd had no choice. The last months of her grandfather's life he'd been almost totally dependent. She didn't begrudge it one bit but she'd come out the other side deep in debt. She now had to take every fishing charter she could get.

The veggie patch was almost mocking her.

She should sell the whole place and move on. It'd cover her debts. She could go north, get a job in a charter company that wasn't as dodgy as Charlie's, make herself a new life.

Except the house was all she had left of Grandpa. All she had left of her parents.

Stop it. There was nothing she could do to solve her problems now, so there was no use thinking about them. She was heading out to Garnett Island. The money would help. That was all that mattered.

Except, as the hours wore on, as *Bertha* shovelled her way inexorably through the waves, she found herself inexplicably drawn to the man and child seated in the stern.

They'd exchanged niceties when they'd first boarded: the weather, her spiel about the history of this coast, the dolphins, the birds they might see. The guy… Matt…had asked a few desultory questions. Other than that, they'd hardly talked. The child had seemed bereft and the guy seemed as if he didn't want to be here.

And then she'd convinced Henry to feed Boof and something had happened. She'd seen them both change. She'd seen the kid light up. She'd seen him pat Boof and then snuggle into the side of the man beside him.

And she'd seen Matt look as if he was about to cry.

What was it between the pair of them? What was a

Manhattan financier doing carting a kid down into the Southern Ocean to dump him on Garnett Island?

Except the guy now looked as if he'd cracked wide open. He cared. Something had shifted inside him, and when he'd smiled at her…

Um…not. Let's not go there. This was a seriously good-looking guy being nice to an orphan, and if that wasn't a cliché for hearts and violins nothing was.

But that smile…

Was nothing to do with her. She was doing a job, nothing else.

They were getting close to Garnett now. She could see its bulk in the distance. There were a couple of uninhabited rocky outcrops in between, the result of some long-ago volcanic disturbance. She needed to watch her charts, watch the depth sounder. Not think about the pair behind her.

And then, suddenly, she had something else to think about. *Bertha* coughed.

Or that was what it sounded like, and after a lifetime spent at sea Meg was nuanced to every changing engine sound. She checked the dials.

Heat?

What the…? She'd checked everything obvious. How could the engine be heating? And almost as she thought it, she caught her first faint whiff.

Smoke.

CHAPTER TWO

SMOKE?

Oh, dear God.

Meg had a sudden flashback to a couple of days back. She'd been bringing in a fishing charter and she'd seen Graham, Charlie's son, coming out of the inlet. He'd been in this boat.

Rowan Bay was a marine reserve, a fish breeding ground. It was tidal, shallow, full of drifting sand and water grasses. It was a good place to add to your catch for the day—if you weren't caught by the fisheries officers.

And if you didn't care about your boat.

She was suddenly hearing her grandpa's voice.

You go in there in anything bigger than a dinghy, you're an idiot. Operating in murky waters can cause blockages in the cooling-water intake. That can lead to engine overheating.

Graham was an idiot.

But now wasn't the time for blaming. Almost instinctively, she shut the motor down, grabbed the fire extinguisher and headed below.

The whiff of smoke became a wall.

Meg O'Hara was not known to panic. There'd been dramas at sea before. She'd swum to shore when a motor died. She'd dived overboard to clear a fouled propeller. She'd even coped with a punter having a heart attack as he'd caught a truly excellent bluefin tuna.

But fire at sea, this far out…

Fire extinguishers had limited volume. It was useless to simply point it at smoke and pull the trigger. But how to get to the seat of the fire?

She hauled her windcheater over her face and tried to open the hatch over the engine…

Flames.

'Get out.' The voice was harsh, deep, and then repeated, a roar of command. She hesitated, shoving the extinguisher forward, trying desperately to see…

'Now!' And a hand hooked the collar of her windcheater and hauled her upward.

She dropped the extinguisher and went. He was right. The speed of this fire…

There was a bag at the entrance to the galley. Heavy. Lifesaving. She grabbed it and lugged it upward.

'Let it go,' the voice roared, and the hand on her collar was insistent.

Pigs might fly, she thought, clinging like a limpet as the hand hauled her higher. And then she was out on the deck, clinging to her precious bag.

'The tender…' A condition of charters in these waters was that a lifeboat was with them at all times and she'd checked the inflatable dinghy before she left. Thank God. The deck was now a cloud of smoke. If the fuel went…

She had to get the tender into the water and get them all into it. Now!

She grabbed the lifeboat's stern pulley. Matt was beside her, seeing what she was doing, matching her at the bow. Lowering it with her.

It hit the water. Almost before it did, she grabbed Henry and thrust him into Matt's arms.

'In. Now.' She grabbed one of the lines from the tender and thrust it into his hand. 'Don't let go. If you fall in, shove the tender away from the boat and pull yourselves in.'

'You take him,' Matt snapped.

'Don't be a fool.' The engine could go up at any minute. 'Take care of the kid. Go.'

She copped a flash of concern but the decision was

made. Henry had to be his first priority. He lifted the stunned Henry onto the side of the boat, steadied for a moment and slipped downward.

Thank God she had them both in lifejackets. Getting into an inflatable from a wallowing boat was fraught at the best of times. But he had Henry in, tucking him into the bow. Then he was standing, holding on to the boat. 'You!'

It was the kind of order her grandfather would have made. A no-nonsense order, the kind you didn't mess with, but she still had stuff to do.

'Boof!' she yelled and the big dog was in her arms. She thrust him downward and somehow Matt caught him.

'Get down here,' he yelled.

She could no longer see him. The smoke was all around her.

One last thing…

She grabbed her bag and slid over the side. Strong hands caught her, steadied, but she allowed herself a mere half a second for that steadying. Then she was at the tiller of the tender. The little engine purred into life. *Thank You, God.*

Without being asked, Matt was shoving with all his might, pushing the tender as far from the boat as he could.

Into gear… Full power… Away.

And maybe twenty seconds later the fuel tank caught and *Bertha* erupted into a ball of flames.

She kept the tender at full throttle. The danger wasn't passed yet. Burning fuel could spread across water.

A minute. Two. The distance between them and the flames was growing. She could breathe again.

Just.

She did a quick head count. Not that it was necessary but she needed it for her sanity.

Matt. Henry. Boof. Bag.

They should survive.

* * *

'Wow, that was exciting. We're safe now, though, Henry. We're okay.'

He couldn't think what else to say. Matt sat in the bow of the little boat and held Henry. Tight. He was giving comfort, he told himself, but the feel of the child against him, the solidness of the little body, *the safeness of him…* It was a two-way street.

The charter boat was now a smouldering wreck. The flames were dying. It was already starting to look skeletal.

They'd been so lucky. From the time he'd seen Meg's head jerk around, heard her cut the engine, from the time he'd caught the first whiff of smoke himself… A minute? It must have been more but it didn't feel like it.

He felt stunned to numbness.

They were safe.

Meg was at the tiller. She was coughing, but she was in control. She'd been hit by a wall of smoke as she'd gone below and she'd fought him for that stupid bag. When she'd got herself together, he was going to have words with her about that bag. Like passengers on an airliner trying to save their carry-ons after a crash landing, she could have killed them all. His and Henry's baggage was now ashes, and he wasn't grieving about it one bit. For her to fight to get her bag…

Mind, there was nothing unprofessional about the rest of the way she'd performed. She'd moved seamlessly. All he'd done was follow what she was doing. She'd made them safe.

Safe was a good word. A great word.

He held Henry and let it sink in.

And then he thought, Where are we?

Maybe they weren't so safe.

Meg had pointed out Garnett Island to him a few moments ago. It was still in the distance, surely too far to head for in these seas, in this little boat. The tender was sitting low already. The swells didn't cause a problem but the wind was causing a chop on the top of the water. Meg was steering into the wind, minimising water resistance, but if one of those waves veered sideways…

He looked ahead and saw where she was steering.

A rocky outcrop rose, almost like a sentinel, straight up from the ocean floor. Maybe half a kilometre from them? Maybe less. It looked rough and inhospitable, but part of the rock face seemed to have slipped, forming what seemed a little bay. A few hardy plants must have fought their way to survival, because there was a tinge of green.

'That's where we'll land,' Meg said, watching his look, and then she had to stop and cough again. And again.

She buckled, fighting for breath. She'd copped so much smoke.

'We're swapping places,' he said.

'I'm not moving anywhere.' Every word was a gasp.

Time to be brutal.

'No choice. Your breathing's compromised. Think about what happens if you collapse at the tiller.'

'You can't…'

'I can handle a boat.'

And he saw her shoulders sag, just a little. Relief? She was only just holding herself together, he thought, and with that thought came another. She'd gone down below, to try to fight a burning engine.

'The flames… Is your throat burned?'

'Only…only smoke. Not…burned.'

'Good, but you're still moving. When I say go, move.'

She didn't reply, fighting another paroxysm of coughing.

'Meg needs help,' he told Henry. He was torn. Henry needed to be held, but the tiller had to be priority.

Boof was on the floor of the boat, crouched low, almost as if he knew stability was an issue. He took Henry's hand and guided it down to the dog's collar. 'I want you to hold on to Boof,' he told him. 'He'll be worried. Hold him tight. Don't let him move, will you?'

And to his relief he got a silent nod in response. Excellent. Not only would Henry's hold anchor him to the big dog, it'd keep him low, as well.

Right. Meg. The tiller.

He watched the sea, waiting for his chance. The next swell swept by. No chop.

Now.

One minute she was holding the tiller, trying to stop the coughs racking her body, trying to keep control. The next…

Matt seemed to come from nowhere. Keeping his body low, he was suddenly at her end of the boat, though with enough sense to keep his weight back as far as he could. Crouching low, he tugged her hard against him, pulling her forward. For one long moment he held her still, checking balance, checking the waves.

Another swell passed—and then she was swung around and propelled onto the central seat.

And then Matt had the tiller and she was no longer in control.

His hold had been swift, firm to the point of brutal, a hard, strong grasp that had left her with nowhere to go. In any other circumstance it would have been terrifying, but right now she'd needed it. It was the assurance that responsibility wasn't all hers. That she wasn't alone.

It was a feeling that made her almost light-headed.

Though maybe that was the smoke.

She was still struggling to breathe. Matt might be in control, he might have reassured her that the boat was being cared for, but she needed air.

Smoke inhalation…

She'd done first-aid training. Grandpa had insisted and he'd also insisted on her updating over and over.

'The bag…' she managed and then subsided again. Oh, her chest hurt.

Matt was handling the tiller, watching the sea, but in between she could see him coming to grips with controls. He was also watching Henry, but he flashed her a glance that told her he was almost as worried as she was about her lungs.

He looked down at the bag. She'd seen his reaction as she'd tossed it down to him—*what, you're worried about luggage?* Now, though… He wasn't a fool. He had the bag opened in seconds, and, still with one eye on the oncoming sea, he started checking the contents.

The first-aid kit lay on top.

What she needed apart from a canister of oxygen—which she didn't have—was a bronchodilator. Albuterol. It was in the first-aid kit to cope with possible asthma attacks.

'Alb…alb…' she gasped but he got it. He had the small canister clear, and she clutched it as if she were drowning.

'You know how to use it?'

She did. She'd used it once on an overweight fisherman with a scary wheeze. She held it and inhaled, held it and inhaled.

Matt was steadied the little boat and turned her slightly away from the outcrop they were heading for, making a sensible adjustment to their path so it was more of a zig-zag. It would stop the sideways swell.

He knew boats, then.

Maybe panic had as much to do with the coughing as smoke did, she thought. As she felt her breathing ease…as she watched Matt turn the tiller to avoid a cresting chop… as she twisted in the boat and saw Henry, crouched over Boof, holding his collar and even speaking reassuringly to him…her world seemed to settle.

For now they were safe. Moving on.

They needed help.

Radio…

'There's a radio in the bag, too,' she managed. The coughing wasn't over but at least she could talk. 'And a GPS tracker. In the side pocket.' She subsided and coughed a bit more while she watched Matt delve into the bag again.

And come up with nothing.

'There's nothing in the side pocket.'

'There must be.'

No charter boat went to sea without an emergency radio and tracker beacon. It was illegal to leave port without them. Every boat in Charlie's Marine Services therefore held a bag such as the one Meg had rescued. The presence of the bag was one of the things she checked, every time she boarded. She hadn't checked the contents today, though. There'd been no need. The contents were standard, always in there.

But *Bertha* wasn't usually used for charters.

No!

'What?' Matt went back to looking at the sea but she could tell by the rigidity of his shoulders that he'd sensed something was wrong. Seriously wrong.

'My idiot boss.' She buckled and coughed a bit more, and maybe that was caused by panic, as well. She was trying to make herself think.

Radios and GPS trackers had batteries that ran out. Charlie ran a regular schedule of checking, because it was sensible, but also, if any marine inspector found a charter boat without a working GPS beacon, or a radio with a flat battery, he'd be down on them like a ton of bricks.

But if such an inspector had come…say, last week… and Charlie had panicked and realised one of the sets was flat…

Why not grab the set from *Bertha*'s bag? *Bertha* wasn't being used for charters. She wouldn't be checked.

All these things were flying through her head like

shrapnel. Her head felt as if it might explode. For one awful moment she thought she might be sick.

And then Matt's hand was on her head. He was leaning forward, propelling her downward.

'Head between your knees until it passes,' he said. 'And there's no need to panic. We're safe. One step at a time, Meg.'

She had no choice but to obey. She ducked her head and started counting breaths. It was a trick her grandpa had taught her after her parents had been killed.

When all else fails, just feel your breath on your lips, lass. That's all that matters. One breath after another.

It felt wimpy. It felt as if she'd handed total responsibility to a stranger but she put her head down and counted.

She was up to about a hundred and twenty before she heard Henry, his thin little voice piping up from the back. 'Where are we going?'

She should answer. She should…

'We're going over to that big rock you see in front of you.' And Matt sounded totally in control, as if he were stranded at sea after fire every day of his life.

'Is that Grandma's island?'

'Nope.' Matt's voice sounded almost cheerful. 'We're going to this island first. Garnett Island's a bit far away for us to get there in this little boat.'

'But how will we get to Grandma's?'

Good question, Meg thought. Right now she didn't have an answer. Luckily Matt did.

'We might have to wait awhile,' he conceded. 'But I've been checking this interesting bag our skipper's brought with us. Apart from muesli bars and bags of nuts and sultanas, there are some cool things that look like flares. When you light flares you can be seen for miles. So my guess is that we'll land on this island, we'll eat our muesli bars and our sultanas, and we'll wait for Meg's boss to realise she's no longer in radio contact. I imagine they'll send a helicopter to find us. If we need to, we'll light our flares to help him find us and then we'll all be rescued. Even Boof. Is that a good plan?'

'We might need a drink,' Henry said cautiously.

'There's a water carton under the seat you're sitting on,' Meg managed and then turned and checked herself. All the tenders carried fresh water. At least that was there.

'And what if it gets dark?' Henry quavered.

'I'd imagine Meg's boss will send help before that, but if he doesn't then we'll build a fire with driftwood. I can see matches in Meg's Marvellous Bag. We'll sing songs and tell each other stories and then we'll lie on these…yep, thermal blankets…and we'll wait until they come. Is that okay with you, Henry?'

'I…guess…'

It was okay with Meg, too. It sounded like a workable plan—the only hiccup being…

Charlie.

We'll wait for Meg's boss to realise she's no longer in radio contact…

Charlie's charter boats were supposed to check in every hour, acknowledging to Charlie that boats and punters were safe. Meg couldn't remember the last time she'd seen Charlie monitor those calls. The calls were made—most of his skippers were punctilious—but they were made to an empty control room.

Charlie was always on the pier, chatting to the locals. He watched his boats come in every night. If Meg was due in tonight and didn't show, Charlie would notice. The trouble was, Meg wasn't due back tonight. Or tomorrow.

She closed her eyes.

'Bad?' Matt asked sympathetically.

And she thought, *He's not going to be sympathetic when I tell him I work for one of the world's shonkiest charter companies.*

But it was no use telling him now, especially not when he'd just reassured Henry.

'I'm okay,' she muttered and lowered her head again. It must be the smoke still making her feel sick. 'We'll all be okay. Eventually.'

CHAPTER THREE

FIFTEEN MINUTES LATER they reached their destination.

The combination of medication and salt air had worked their magic. Meg's lungs felt almost clear.

She still wasn't in control, though. Matt had taken over. The letterhead on the documents she'd read had been embossed with the words *McLellan Corporation*. Matt's name? Her first impression had been wealth and command, and she was now adding skill to the mix. Wherever he'd learned it, he'd acquired knowledge of the sea and small boats. He was now in charge, and the feeling was almost overwhelming.

How long had it been since anyone had taken charge of her world? Not since her grandpa had got sick. Even as a child Meg had learned to be leaned on. Her grandparents had been gutted when her parents had been killed. If she cried, they couldn't handle it. She'd had to act cheerful even when things were dire.

When she was sixteen her gran had died, too, and Grandpa had pretty much fallen to pieces. That was when she'd decided to quit school and go fishing with him. She'd cajoled him back to enjoying life.

It was only when he was gone that she realised how restricted her own life had become. She could heave craypots. She could count punters in and out of charter boats and she could cope with boats in heavy seas.

Was that what she wanted for the rest of her life?

At twenty-eight, what other choices did she have?

Oh, for heaven's sake, why was she thinking that now? They'd reached the outcrop. Matt was steering carefully—because the boat was inflatable and the rubber could rip on any one of these sharp rocks—into the tiny cove. There was a stony beach.

She needed to stop thinking of the complications of her life. More immediately, she needed to stop thinking how good it was to let this guy take over—and how good he looked while he did it—and start being useful.

She hauled up the legs of her jeans, checked the bottom and jumped out into knee-deep water. Beaching the tender wasn't an option on these sharp stones.

The cove was sheltered from the prevailing winds, and she could see to the bottom.

'I didn't mean you to do that,' Matt said, sounding displeased. 'I thought we'd run her up on the beach.'

'And rupture the membrane?'

'Instead of your feet? Yes. And we won't have any more use for her. We're hardly here to reprovision and set off for the mainland.'

'But why wreck a perfectly good inflatable?' She wasn't about to tell him it might well be needed again. *Focus on now.*

She clicked her fingers. Boof jumped into her arms and she carted him to shore. Ouch, these stones were sharp! Her shoes were…with the remains of *Bertha.*

Henry next. 'Will you let me carry you to Boof?' she asked him.

'I'll take him,' Matt said but she shook her head.

'Can you stay at the tiller until we're unloaded? If we get an unexpected swell the boat might be damaged.'

His eyes had narrowed. 'So that matters?'

'That matters.'

He got it. But he glanced at Henry and didn't comment. 'You're not fit enough to…'

'Lift Henry? Of course I am. Henry, I bet you don't weigh as much as Boof. Will you let me carry you? You could jump in and walk, like me, but the water's a bit cold.

I think I saw a seal somewhere round the back of these rocks. Boof might show you if you ask.'

But the strangeness of their situation was taking its toll. Henry clutched his seat and held. 'Our boat burned,' he said flatly.

'It did,' Matt told him. 'It was a bad accident and we're lucky Meg brought this little boat along. Now we need to stay here for a bit.'

'Will you stay?' Henry demanded and Meg heard raw fear. Matt, then, was more than just his mother's employer to this little boy. He was the only link Henry had to his past, to an unknown future.

And Matt obviously got that, too. 'I'll stay with you,' he said solemnly, and Meg thought what choice did he have? But Matt didn't waste time explaining. He simply promised. 'I said I'll stay with you until you're with your grandma and I will. No question, Henry. Now, will you let Miss O'Hara...?'

'Meg,' said Meg.

'Will you let Meg carry you to the shore?'

There was a moment's thought. Then: 'Yes,' Henry said. 'Yes, please, Miss O'Hara.'

'Meg,' Meg said again.

'Yes, please, Meg,' Henry said and looped his arms around Meg's neck and allowed her to carry him.

And why that made her feel like bursting into tears, she had no idea.

She was amazing.

Half an hour ago she'd been coughing so hard she'd been retching. Now it was as if this were nothing out of the ordinary.

He couldn't fault her.

While he kept the boat steady she gathered the bag and carted that to shore, as well. Finally she agreed to allow him out of the boat.

'We need to take the motor off and cart that up the beach, then the water and the bench seats, and then carry the tender itself,' she told him. 'I don't know about you, but I'm not strong enough to cart it with the motor attached.'

'We can't just anchor?'

'Too risky—these rocks are sharp. Leave your socks on by the way.' She was already disconnecting the motor.

'So we're being careful of the tender…why?' Henry was out of earshot now. Boof had met him on the shore and they were both tentatively looking for seals. With his hand on the dog's collar, Henry seemed to have found courage.

'If we can get it onto the sand it'll make a comfy place to sleep,' Meg told him. 'With the thermal blankets, we'll be snug as bugs in rugs.'

'We're not expecting rescue tonight?'

'No.'

'I would have thought,' he said almost conversationally, 'that a burned boat in the middle of Bass Strait, with three stranded passengers and one dog, might mean immediate search and rescue.' He kicked off his shoes, hitched his trousers and was over the side. 'You hold the boat. I'll cart the motor in.'

She was more than happy to let him. Someone had to hold the boat. She'd heaved an outboard motor before, but she was five feet four and slightly built, and even a lifetime of heaving craypots wouldn't have prevented her from staggering.

So she could only be grateful as Matt disconnected bolts, heaved the motor into his arms and strode through the shallows to the beach.

What sort of New York financier and lawyer was this? One who worked out, obviously.

She'd given them both sou'westers and lifejackets as they'd boarded the boat. Henry was still wearing his, but Matt's was on the floor of the tender with his shoes. She thought fleetingly of his gorgeous leather jacket, replaced with the sou'wester. It'd be ashes by now, but he wasn't worrying about a jacket.

He'd hiked up his trousers and rolled his shirtsleeves. He'd taken her advice and was still wearing socks. Another guy might look naff in bare legs and socks, but not this man. He was all hard muscle, lean, toned, ripped. He carted the motor as if it were nothing and, as she held the boat steady, Meg had a sudden fantasy of what it'd be like to be carried by such a man. To be held in those arms... against that chest...

Um...not.

'Earth to Meg,' Matt said as he returned, hauling her back to reality. 'You were explaining why rescue isn't imminent.'

Time for confession. Just say it.

'The radio's not in the bag, nor is our emergency transmitter,' she admitted. 'Someone's head will roll for that.' Probably not, though, she thought. Charlie was her boss and she was hardly in a position to complain. 'Our phones don't work out here. We have no way of saying we're stranded.'

'I'd imagine your boss will be checking your position, though. If you don't make it to Garnett tonight, surely he'll notice.'

And there was no way she could sugar-coat this. 'Don't bet on it. Monitoring the radio takes staff or work, both of which Charlie keeps to a minimum. The reason you were able to hire *Bertha* at such short notice is that we're not a flash operation. In fact—' *go on, say it* '—Charlie runs on the smell of an oily rag. If there's a corner to cut, he'll cut it. *Bertha*'s due back to port by Monday. On Monday night he'll start wondering.'

'But not before.'

'Probably not.'

He didn't comment. Instead he heaved the water container from under the seat and carried that to the beach as well, then did the same with the removable seats.

A lawyer with muscles.

She thought, suddenly, idiotically, of fairy tales she'd read as a kid, and romance novels since. It had seemed to her that a hero would be rich and handsome. She'd thought mistily that a hero might even heave her craypots for her.

And here he was, rich—presumably, if his name headed a prestigious Manhattan law firm. Handsome… Yeah, tick that. Now he was carting the motor and water as if they were featherweights.

Fantasy plus. She almost grinned but then he was striding back, gripping the boat's bow, readying to lift it and carry it to shore.

He couldn't do this alone. It wasn't the weight; it was the sheer size of the thing.

'So we're dependent on Peggy,' he said, almost conversationally.

She'd already thought of that, with some relief. Peggy Lakey. Henry's grandmother.

'I assume you told her your travel plans,' she said.

'I did. She knows we landed in Melbourne this morning. She knows we were using this charter company and she's expecting us by dark.'

'And she has a radio.' They were heaving the boat upward, out of danger of scraping, working as a team. Once again she had the impression that this guy was used to boats, used to the sea. Used to work?

'It was a shaky connection this morning,' Matt said. He was moving backward. She had the easy option of walking forward. 'But I'd imagine if we're not there by dark then she'll call Charlie.'

'And if Charlie doesn't answer?'

'Is that possible?'

'The local football team's reached the finals,' she said dryly. 'Yes, it is.'

'And you work for this man?'

She couldn't defend herself. She didn't even try. They had the boat out of the water now, carrying it over the rocks to the strip of sand beneath the cliff. They set it down with care and Meg breathed a sigh of relief. The boat was safe. They had water and supplies. This wasn't a total disaster.

'So Peggy?' she ventured. She knew a little about Peggy Lakey, an elderly woman who'd bought Garnett Island years ago. She was said to be reclusive—she'd have to be to live on Garnett—but the fishermen who carted her supplies over had always been impressed with her.

'She seems no-nonsense,' Matt told her. 'Charlie assured me—and I assured Peggy—that we'd be there before dark. I'm thinking she'll contact the rescue services soon after. This is her grandson, after all.'

'Does she want him?' Her gaze moved to Henry. The little boy had found a shallow rock pool. He was pointing to something in its depths and Boof, bless his doggy heart, was paying attention.

It'd be minnows. The thought almost made her smile. Years of devoted hunting, and Boof had never caught one.

She watched kid and dog watching the fish darting below the surface. Matt was watching, too.

'Does his grandmother want him?' she asked again.

'I think so.'

'You think so?' That jolted her. What the…? 'You bring him all the way here—and you *think so*?'

'There's no choice,' he said, heavily now. He wasn't taking his eyes off the child. 'Amanda's will left him in the care of his grandmother. Peggy's expressed willingness to take him.'

'But she wouldn't fetch him.'

'No.'

'Does he even know her?'

'They write,' he said. 'He tells me he gets a letter every week, old-style, in an envelope with a stamp. She sends Polaroid pictures of the island. That's what's in his backpack—letters and pictures she's been sending for years. I've seen them. She also makes radio telephone calls when she can. He feels like he knows her and there's no doubt she cares.'

That was something at least, but she hadn't finished probing.

'Has he ever met her?'

'Will you cut it out?' His voice was suddenly laced with anger. 'The paperwork's in order. It's your job to get us there safely, and might I remind you that you're doing an appalling job of it.'

'And so are you,' she snapped back. 'Your job's to get him to his grandma, so we've both failed. Get over it.'

'I'm over it. Just don't make me responsible...'

'For what?'

'For bringing him here.' He closed his eyes and ran his fingers through his hair, a gesture of total fatigue. 'Look, this is a no-win situation,' he said. 'Amanda was an excellent lawyer but an appalling mother. According to office gossip, when she turned forty she decided she wanted a child like some people decide they want a puppy. She's been paying as little as she could get away with for child care. During term breaks Henry would be alone in her office for hours. Now she's dead and she has no friends close enough to care. Henry has a grandma he's never met and no one else.'

'So how come he's never met her?'

'Because Peggy hasn't seen Amanda for years, either,' he said wearily. 'Peggy told me the outline when I contacted her. She's Australian. She was married to an American. He died a couple of years back, but the marriage broke up when Amanda was in her teens. Peggy came home to Australia. She says she tried to keep in contact, but Amanda wasn't interested. When Henry was born Peggy doubled her efforts. Maybe she knew what sort of mother Amanda would make. I gather Amanda allowed Peggy to write to him and speak to him occasionally via her not very satisfactory radio connection, but that's all. Now she's all he has.'

'He has you, though,' Meg said, thinking what she was hearing wasn't weariness. This was desolation for a child left with nothing.

Desolation from a high-flying businessman who'd dropped everything to bring a kid to his grandma.

Her first impression of this guy had been arrogance. He'd reacted with astonishment when she'd questioned his right to bring Henry to the island, and what he was paying Charlie was astounding. He was obviously accustomed to throwing money and watching minions jump.

But now... Yes, the need to control was still there, but despite it she was starting to like what she saw around the edges. Even before the fire she'd been sensing helplessness in the way he was caring for Henry. Now he was stranded, shaken from his controlled world, his desolation was exposed, and it touched something deep within.

'It's okay.' Her hand went to his shoulder, a touch of reassurance. 'I bet Peggy's lovely. Writing real letters every week... That's awesome. We'll land on the island, she'll love him to bits and they'll live happily ever after.'

'Yeah,' he said. She'd tugged her hand back but the look he gave her... It was as if he couldn't figure her out. 'But meanwhile...'

'Meanwhile we collect driftwood before it starts getting dark,' she said. 'A fire will cheer us up. It's a warm night. With the seats removed from the boat we have a comfy bed, and we have thermal blankets. We have the means to make a fire and we have food.'

'Muesli bars?' he said dubiously, stooping to check her bag.

'Yes, but some of them have chocolate coating. Yay.' She investigated with him. 'Plus, here's a fishing line and a lure. By the time you have the fire going, I'll have fish to cook.'

'Right,' he said dryly.

'You doubt me? I may not be able to deliver you to your island without sending you up in flames but I was born with a fishing line in my hands. Watch this space.'

'And we'd cook it how?'

'Seaweed and ash,' she said. 'Don't they teach you anything in law school?'

'Apparently not,' he said faintly. 'Henry,' he called. 'Do you want to help me make a fire, or watch Meg fish?'

And that was a no-brainer. Henry headed straight for Meg. And as dog and boy clambered over the rocks toward them, Matt thought, *He looks almost happy.*

He'd never seen Henry look happy.

It was almost enough to make a burned boat and a night on a deserted island worthwhile.

CHAPTER FOUR

THE ROCKS AROUND the cove looked as if they'd been a drift-wood catchment for years. Matt lit a fire and then went down to the rocks to watch what was happening. Henry was riveted, and as soon as he arrived, so was Matt.

As Matt settled on a rock beside them, Meg seamlessly included him in a fishing lesson.

They'd been catching fish too small to keep, she explained. She was teaching Henry how to throw them back.

'Barbs damage their mouths,' she told him. 'They often don't survive. An unbarbed hook rarely does lasting damage but it needs skill. The trick is to feel the moment the hook's taken. If you keep the pressure steady on the way in, the fish won't get off. Henry, there's one on the line now. Here it comes. You know what to do.'

There'd been a netting insert on the inside of the emergency bag. He'd seen Meg tie it to driftwood sticks to make a net. Henry had ditched his shoes and socks. Now he waded into the water and scooped the fish like an expert.

'It's nearly big enough,' he announced. He stared into the net at the flopping fish and then he glanced at Matt's foot. 'Meg says it's got to be as big as your foot before we eat it. I don't think this is.'

'Not quite,' Meg said, inspecting their catch. 'It's a good one, though. Do you want to try to get the hook out yourself this time? Remember what I showed you.'

'Yes,' Henry said, and while Meg held the fish he cautiously removed the hook. A surgeon couldn't have taken more care.

'Can I let it go?' he asked.

'Of course.' She manoeuvred the slippery fish into Henry's hold and Henry waded back out into the water.

'Goodbye, fish,' he said solemnly. 'Meg says your mouth won't hurt for long. Don't go near them hooks any more.'

He slid the fish into the water and Meg tossed the line back out. Pretty far for a girl, Matt thought, and grinned to himself at his blatantly sexist thought. Pretty far for a fisherman? Fisherwoman? Whatever, that was what she obviously was.

They settled down again. Meg and Henry were side by side on the rock. Boof had been sniffing seaweed. He came back to them now and Henry's spare arm wrapped around the dog's neck.

And Matt thought, What a gift.

For the last two weeks Henry had been limp with shock and with fear. He'd hardly spoken during the journey here. He'd been totally self-effacing and then he'd had to cope with the fire. Matt had done what he could to reassure him but it had been Meg who'd hauled him out of his frozen acceptance of things a child shouldn't have to face.

The sun was sinking but there was still enough warmth in it to give comfort. Henry was dangling his feet in the water. He was watching his line, intent, fascinated.

What looked like a tiny stingray drifted near his toes. Henry lifted his feet in alarm but Meg reacted by showing him the beauty of the little creature. She explained how it steered with its 'wings'. How the fins on its tail, the only part breaking the surface, made it look a bit like a Loch Ness monster in miniature.

'Or a diplocaulus,' Henry ventured and Matt thought… What?

But the conversation continued without a pause. 'It could be a very small diplocaulus,' Meg said, appearing to consider. 'Some pictures I've seen have fin-like feathering on their tails like this.'

'What's a diplocaulus?' he asked, and both Meg and Henry looked at him as if they were astounded someone wouldn't know.

'It was a kind of shark,' Henry said with patience. 'It lived about three hundred million years ago, and it had a head like a boomerang. That made it hard for other things to swallow it.'

'Which seems a good reason to have a boomerang-shaped head,' Meg said, and she grinned.

And he thought, *She's beautiful. No, more than beautiful. She's stunning.*

She wasn't his kind of woman. Not in a million years.

The women Matt associated with were part of his corporate world, socially elite. There'd never been anyone special enough to make him think of long-term commitment, but at some time in the future he imagined one of these women could become his wife. She'd be a woman who fitted seamlessly into the world he moved in, with her own career, her own identity, but who understood the needs his high-pressured job put on him.

Meg was so much out of that mould that maybe it was like the... What had they been talking of? The diplocaulus. With her bare feet, her torn jeans and stained windcheater, with her freckled nose, her badly cut copper curls, her wide green eyes... It was as if she'd come from a different planet from the one he inhabited.

But she was, indeed, beautiful.

'What?' she said and he realised he was staring.

'I... Sorry. It's just...the women in the circles I move in don't fish.'

'Is that a rule?'

He gathered his wits—with difficulty. 'We don't have a lot of places to fish in Manhattan.'

'And yet you know your way round boats.'

'My family's always had a home in the Hamptons.'

'Where's that?

'It's on the South Fork of Long Island.' He reached for his phone to show her a map. And remembered. There wasn't a lot of internet access here.

She saw the motion and her smile returned. It really was dazzling. Her nose was snub. She had the remains of zinc on her nose—she'd insisted they use expensive sun lotion on the boat but she obviously preferred the old-fashioned kind. It must have its limitations, though. Her eyes crinkled at the edges, presumably because of too much exposure to water-reflected sun. A fault?

No. She was definitely beautiful.

'So the Hamptons are where your mum and dad live?'

'We use it for holidays.'

'Gorgeous. Did you have it when you were a kid?'

'We've had it for generations.'

'There are holiday cottages like that in Rowan Bay,' she said. 'They look like they're held up with string, but generation after generation arrive, summer after summer. A stovetop, bunks, a cold shower and the beach at the door. They love them. Is that what your place is like?'

'Um…no.' McLellan Place?

'It does run to hot water,' he admitted.

'Luxury.' The smile seemed irrepressible. 'We have hot water at our…at my place, too.'

He got the *our* versus *my*. He saw the cloud.

'Is that the place you shared with your grandfather?'

Where had that come from? Asking personal questions of someone he'd hired as a marine taxi driver wasn't his style. She wasn't a taxi driver now, though. She had her arm around Henry while he was concentrating on his line. What did you pay for making a kid relax? Personal interest seemed the least he could do, and, besides, he genuinely wanted to know.

And she told him. 'I did live with my grandpa,' she said. 'I told you back at the office. He died six months ago and I

miss him. I guess you feel exactly the same, Henry, missing your mom and all.'

And that pretty much took his breath away.

Henry hadn't talked about his mother. Not once. Henry
had been drawing dinosaurs before they'd left the office
the day his mother had died, big dinosaurs on a huge
sketchpad his mother had left him. He'd kept drawing in
the days that had followed, but the dinosaurs had become
very small.

So now Matt expected Henry to close down, as he'd
closed every time his mother had been mentioned. But he
was still encircled by Meg's arm. Boof was nestled on his
other side. They were watching the float above the hook
on the end of the fishing line. No pressure.

'I miss her at night,' Henry whispered. 'She always
comes in to say goodnight, even if it's really late. I make
myself stay awake. Me and Teddy. Now we stay awake
and stay awake and she doesn't come.'

There was a gut clencher.

His heart seemed to close down in sympathy. Empathy?

Suddenly he was remembering years of waiting for his
socialite parents to come home. Their steps on the stairs.
Goodnight, darling...

The flashback hit hard. He winced. This was not about
him. He hadn't lost his parents when he was a child. His father had died three years ago, of a coronary probably brought
on by years of too much wine, too many cigars. His mother
was still in his orbit although rarely coming close, expend-
ing her energy in keeping her place in New York's social
hierarchy.

He struggled to think of something to say. Anything.

But Meg was before him. 'I bet your mom still says
goodnight to you,' she said, almost conversationally.

'She's dead.'

'So's my grandpa. At night, in bed, knowing he's not in
the next room, it hurts so much sometimes I feel like my

chest is about to burst. But if I close my eyes, if I sing to myself, a song Grandpa taught me, or if I think of something we both liked—like dinosaurs—then I know that somehow Grandpa's still with me. Not really, of course, not in the way he was there when he told me off for wearing muddy shoes in the house. Just…it feels like he still loves me. I feel him when I need him. Henry, I reckon you could feel your mom like that.'

'My chest hurts, too,' Henry whispered.

Matt thought, Ditto.

'Your grandma will tell you stories about your mom,' he managed. 'Your grandma loves your mom, Henry.'

'And I wouldn't be the least bit surprised if your grandma says goodnight to you every night, as well,' Meg added. 'But meanwhile, Henry, that float's wobbling. I reckon there's a fish about to bite.'

'Yes!' said Henry, lighting up again. Fish were immediate. Fish were now. He stared intently at the definitely wobbling float. Conversation over.

Matt expected Meg to turn her attention to the float as well. Instead she turned her gaze to him and her look was…thoughtful? Speculative?

More. The way he was feeling about Henry… In Meg's eyes he could almost read the same, but for some reason it didn't seem like sympathy toward Henry. Her emotions seemed directed to him.

How much was she seeing?

This was crazy. It was ridiculous to think this woman could sense the emptiness he shared with Henry.

And he didn't share it. Not any more. It was simply that Henry's loneliness had struck a chord.

But had that loneliness killed something? He'd tried his best over the last couple of weeks to find some way to comfort Henry, to give him time out from his grief, but his approaches had been stilted. He knew they had. Henry had become more and more exhausted with his fear of an unknown future, and Matt had found no way to break through.

This woman, though… From the time she'd grasped Henry's hand and shaken it, adult to adult, to now… She'd been giving Henry time out, and she'd been doing it almost instinctively. How did she do that?

And what was with the way she looked at him? As if he needed sympathy, too?

'I'll check the fire,' he said, a bit too roughly, and her smile came back. But this time her smile was different.

'You do that,' she said. 'We'll need it to stay warm tonight.' And then she turned back to Henry as the float plunged underneath the water. 'Henry, we've got one. Ooh, look at him. Trevally! Careful, hold steady but no tugging. Hooray, Henry, we might be about to meet our dinner.'

CHAPTER FIVE

Given the circumstances, it was an excellent dinner.

Meg was obviously an old hand at cooking fish. She wrapped it whole in damp seaweed, then buried it in hot ash. Half an hour later she dug it out and lifted the charred seaweed away. They used their fingers to lift away chunks of the succulent flesh and Matt thought he'd never tasted such fish.

Even Henry, who'd eaten birdlike portions over the last couple of weeks, enjoyed his. It might have been because he was sharing with Boof. The fish they'd caught was big enough for them all, but Meg discussed rules with Henry before they ate.

'Boof eats doggy kibbles. You fed him on the boat so he shouldn't be hungry. Sometimes, though, I give him me-food as a treat, but he's not allowed to ask. I eat three bites and give him one. Then three more bites and one for him.'

It sounded an unlikely rule. Matt raised an eyebrow and Meg smiled. As Henry started on his first bite, Meg sent him a conspiratorial wink.

She had him entranced. He watched Henry do the three-one rule and he thought, How clever was that? She'd seamlessly persuaded Henry to eat three pieces of fish before he could feed Boof. The fish went down, then Henry shared his muesli bar.

With Henry fed, safe, warm, the little boy leaned against Meg and listened as she told him about the evening star, just starting to appear as the light faded.

She told him of an Aboriginal legend: two beautiful sisters, escaping danger, one flying all the way into the night sky to become the evening star, then using her powers to watch over her earthbound sister and keep her safe.

Meg was sure she was also watching over them.

Yep, he was definitely entranced.

The dark descended and Henry fell asleep. Meg went to lift him, to carry him to the tender but Matt was before her.

'Give me a break,' he told her. 'I've watched you save us from fire, provide us with a campsite, catch our dinner. I need at least one opportunity to be manly.'

'Or one excuse to give Henry a hug,' Meg said as he lifted Henry into his arms and that made him blink, too.

She made him transparent.

She made him feel…vulnerable?

That was dumb, but as he carried the sleeping child to the tender, as he settled him on its air-filled base and tucked a thermal blanket around him, making sure Teddy was close, his feeling of vulnerability increased.

Why?

It was obvious, he told himself. He was somewhere in the Southern Ocean, stranded after a fire that could easily have killed them.

Matt McLellan was a man to whom control was everything. He'd been born to inherited wealth, and his financial acumen had seen that wealth increase tenfold. He was one of Manhattan's movers and shakers.

But this situation wasn't frightening. Yes, they were stranded but Peggy would contact the authorities. They had fresh water, they had fire and they had food. Thanks to Meg and her blessed bag.

And that was where his thoughts paused. Meg.

Meg, who worked for a company that had nearly killed him.

Meg, who made a little boy chuckle.

Meg, who looked at him as if she saw inside.

That was being dumb. She didn't see anything, or, if

she did, maybe it was just that shock had meant his face was less than impassive.

But the thought still had him unnerved. He spent longer than he needed making sure Henry's blanket was tucked around him, giving himself space. He needed to focus on imperatives. Making contact with the outside world.

But for some reason his thoughts were stalling there as well. For the time being they were safe. The weather was kind. Something about this situation—or was it something about Meg?—was helping Henry put aside the trauma of the last weeks. To be honest, Matt was feeling the same. He wouldn't mind a little longer...

Or not. Was he thinking? He needed to hand Henry to his grandmother, make sure he was safe and then get back to the world he knew. He didn't need to get any more involved. The last two weeks had hauled him out of his comfort zone, facing emotion he didn't know how to deal with.

Meg knew how to deal with it. She was warm, funny, empathic. She was all the things he wasn't. She provided things he'd been trained since birth not to need.

He turned back to the fire. Meg was sitting on a driftwood log. Her face was lit by the flames. She looked...

It didn't matter how she looked. It didn't matter that something within him was telling him to ignore what he needed to do and go sit beside Meg.

Moving on. He rose and headed for her blessed bag, stooping to forage.

'What are you looking for?' she asked. 'Don't you dare eat the orange-and-chocolate muesli bars. I've saved them for breakfast. If you eat them now, we'll be reduced to the bran-and-oatmeal ones.'

'I'm looking for something to save us from bran and oatmeal. Yes!' He tugged flares from the base of the bag.

'I already thought about the flares,' she said diffidently. 'But it seems unsafe.'

'Because Peggy might see them from Garnett?' He guessed her thinking on this one. Peggy seeing was one thing. What Peggy did with that knowledge was another.

'Our rescue's not urgent,' Meg explained. 'We're within sight of Garnett Island. It's still maybe half an hour away in a decent boat, but a flare could well be seen over there. But Peggy'll have been expecting her grandson and by now she'll be terrified something's happened. I'm hoping she'll have contacted the authorities, which means they'll be organising a search, but that won't start until dawn. If she sees a flare now, it could be from a sinking boat. If she thinks that… If it was my grandson, I'd be in a boat, heading out, no matter how elderly I am or what condition my boat is in.'

'I agree,' he said, setting the flares in a row. 'Twelve flares. Excellent.'

'So what I just said?'

'Factored in, but my plan is to try to stop her spending the night out of her mind with worry. I've been trying to put myself in her shoes. If I were Peggy, I'd have radioed the authorities but I wouldn't stop there. I'd be scanning the sea, waiting, hoping. So my current plan is to use more of this excellent driftwood to light three burning fires along the top of the cliff. Spaced so they look as if they've been deliberately lit and they can't be mistaken for a burning boat. I imagine they'll still be hard to see from Garnett, but if we light the flares, I hope she'll see a flash and focus. The fires should be spots of light visible by the naked eye and easily seen with field glasses. She sounded sensible when I talked to her. I imagine she'll figure where we are, which means tomorrow we'll be rescued without the need for an expensive search. And she'll sleep…not easy but maybe she won't be in total meltdown.'

There was a moment's silence. A long one. And then, for some reason, Meg's eyes welled. She swiped a tear away with what seemed anger, and when she spoke again her voice was choked. 'That's…that's a great plan. And kind.'

'Self-preserving. We'll be rescued sooner.'

'You know we'll be rescued. But to think of Peggy... Matt, that's brilliant. I'll help you collect driftwood. We just need to climb...'

'No,' he said forcibly. 'Meg, there's not a snowball's chance in hell that you're doing more tonight. I can still hear the smoke in your lungs. There's no way you're climbing cliffs.'

'I'm responsible,' she said miserably. 'You paid me, and I got you into this mess.'

'I paid your boss, and your boss was paying you to be at the wheel of an unseaworthy boat. We're in the same mess, except you've been injured and I haven't. Also... Meg, Henry's asleep and if he wakes, do you think I want him alone? He needs one of us here and you're elected.'

And then, because he could see a tear tracking its way down her smoke-stained face in the firelight—he didn't know what that tear was about but he was stopping it regardless—he cupped her chin and wiped it away with his finger.

'Put the albuterol in your pocket in case you need it,' he told her. 'Then get into the tender with Henry and stay there. Tug another thermal blanket around you. Hug Boof. Hug Henry if he needs it. But see if you can sleep. I'll keep the fires going, Meg, and I'll keep watch.'

'In case of werewolves?' She was struggling to sound light.

'Yep. No werewolf will get past me and my trusty...' He searched the ground for something weapon-like and found a flare. 'Me and my trusty flare. And I have twelve of 'em.'

And she chuckled. It was a choked kind of chuckle but it sounded...okay.

'Take Boof,' she managed. 'He's good at werewolves.'

'Really?'

'In all the years I've had him, I haven't been troubled by a werewolf once.'

'That's a huge recommendation,' he said. For some reason he was still cupping her chin. Smiling down at her.

'But you know what? I'll cope with my own werewolves. Boof's staying here to cope with yours.'

She followed orders and it felt wrong.

Or maybe not wrong. Strange. Someone else was in charge of her world.

She should feel terrible. She'd lost the boat. She'd almost killed her paying customers and she knew already that Charlie would put the blame squarely on her. If this guy was to sue—and he was a hotshot US lawyer so that was well within the realms of possibility—she already knew she'd be thrown to the wolves.

To Matt's werewolves. Unaccountably, she found she was smiling.

He'd given her a job: snuggle down in the tender and take care of Henry.

She did just that. She hauled a thermal blanket around her. Henry muttered a little in his sleep. She settled beside him, moved closer and put her arms around him.

Boof jumped in on her feet. Um, maybe not. 'Out,' she murmured and he obligingly jumped out. She clicked her fingers to the side of the boat and he settled as close as he could. She could reach out and touch him if she wanted.

Matt had stoked up their camp fire before he left. Its flames were still easing the dark.

'We're warm and we're safe and Matt's looking after us,' she murmured to Henry and she felt him nestle closer still.

Matt's looking after us.

It was a good thought. Maybe it was even a great thought.

She closed her eyes and felt herself drift into sleep.

Peggy noticed.

Bless her.

Thirty minutes after he lit his fires, after his first flare lit the night, just before he was about to use his second, he saw an answering glow from Garnett Island. She must have heaved combustibles together fast. He had no field glasses and Garnett was some way off but he saw the faint, answering glow and he relaxed.

It was the most primitive communication he could think of but it was enough. Peggy had seen his fires. She'd know where they were and her answering fire meant she'd send help. He wished he could let her know they were all safe, but he hoped she'd assume it.

He wouldn't light more flares—they could be seen as a plea for immediate help. He'd done all he could. He could head back to the tender and see if he could get some sleep.

He made his way carefully down the cliff, thinking how glad he was he hadn't needed Meg's help. The rocks were small, shifting, unstable. He wanted her where she was, snug in the tender. Their camp fire was a glow below him and as he climbed down he was aware of a surge of something strange.

As if...he was heading home?

It was a weird feeling, and it didn't ease when he reached the bottom. Boof lifted his head and gave him a token tail wag as he neared the little boat. He kept his flashlight on, but low and turned aside so he wouldn't wake the occupants.

Meg was cradling Henry, even in sleep. She had him tucked into the crook of her arm. Taking comfort or giving it? He couldn't be sure.

They were huddled against the tender's side and there was space left beside her. Boof could have fitted, he thought, but with a flash of insight he realised what Meg had done.

She'd left space for him.

A hero wouldn't climb into the tender with them, he thought wryly. A hero had no need for that sense of comfort. Surely he should stay awake, tending the camp fire, keeping watch over his charges, keeping werewolves at bay.

But there was nary a werewolf, and suddenly Meg stirred. She was on her back, one arm around Henry, and now her spare arm reached up toward him.

'Hey,' she murmured, half-asleep. 'Time to rest?'

'Peggy saw our fires. She lit one herself to show us she's seen.'

'Excellent.' Her voice was still slurred. 'So come on in, Matt McLellan.'

There was hardly room. Widthways, yes, but lengthways his feet would either have to rest up on the sides or they'd have to squash.

She smiled up at him. That hand still reached up.

He smiled back down and decided to squash.

She woke and she couldn't breathe.

Her first thought was that she was choking. Her second was that she couldn't wake Henry. She choked into her sleeve, fighting for breath. Her whole body was trembling.

She mustn't wake…

But Matt's arm was suddenly around her, tugging her to sit upward. Henry was waking beside her, jerked into alarm.

She sat and buckled and coughed and fought for breath, and then Matt was lifting her up, out of the boat, cradling her in his arms.

'Henry, it's okay,' he said. 'Meg got smoke in her chest today but she'll be okay. She just needs to cough it out.'

She wasn't okay. She felt as if she were dying. Somehow, almost by instinct, she forced herself to snap her fingers to Boof, make a gesture…

Boof was a great dog. He looked up at his mistress, his head on one side while he figured what she was trying to tell him—and then he stepped carefully into the tender. He plonked down beside Henry. Henry's arm came around him and the little boy settled again into sleep.

Which meant Meg could concentrate on breathing. Which wasn't happening. She was fighting, her breath coming in sharp, short rasps. Her chest hurt. Her whole body was shaking.

Matt was carrying her over to the embers of their fire, swearing.

'It's okay, sweetheart. The albuterol's in your pocket? Right, let's get you breathing.'

He settled on a rock and held the albuterol to her lips.

She sucked like she was drowning. It wasn't helping. It wasn't...

And then Matt was grabbing one of the bags of muesli bars. The bars were unceremoniously tipped and the bag held to her lips.

'Meg, I'm thinking this is a panic attack. Let's treat it as that. Breathe into the bag.'

Panic attack? She'd never had such a thing. This was a heart attack or worse. But Matt was holding the bag to her lips. 'Breathe,' he said. 'Fill the bag and then take it in again. Slow as you can. Do it, Meg.'

And his authority cut through her terror. He was still holding her, cradling her like a child, but his voice brooked no argument.

She breathed.

The bag forced her to slow. She had to make it inflate. She was trying so hard...

'Great job, Meg. Keep going. One after the other.'

He held her while she breathed. She just...breathed.

And slowly, miraculously, the panic eased. The pain in her chest backed off.

She was still shaking. If Matt let her go she would have sobbed with distress but he did no such thing. He held her close until finally the shakes subsided. Until finally she was brave enough to put the bag down, to try to talk. She was mortified.

'I can't... I don't...'

'It's okay,' he said, gently but firmly. 'You're okay. Meg, I don't think it was the smoke. I've seen a full-blown panic attack before. It was a colleague when she'd realised she'd forgotten to register a share transfer. Half a million lost in an instant. You, waking up to the memory of a burning boat, with lives at stake… That's so much worse. You have every right to panic.'

'I don't… It felt…'

'Like you were suffocating? We called the paramedics for Donna. They said with the bag you're forced to focus on breathing. You can see what's happening with the rise and fall of the bag, and you don't have room for the rest of the stuff. Neat, huh? I love it when a plan works.'

She didn't reply. She couldn't yet, but his steady voice, his calm, had her world settling. The tremors hadn't completely eased but the panic had.

Had she had a nightmare? She vaguely remembered waking to the memory of flames, of choking smoke, of looking out of the hatch and knowing the lives entrusted to her were in peril.

It was over. Past. Why should she be shaking now?

'I think it's adrenalin,' Matt said, as if he could hear what she was thinking. 'In an emergency adrenalin kicks in. You responded brilliantly. You got us here safe. You comforted Henry, you made him feel like all was well with his world and then you flaked out with exhaustion. And the adrenalin dropped and the fear found its way to the surface.'

'It was my fault. I should have—'

'What, inspected every part of the boat for faults? Nothing's perfect, Meg. Even luxury limos break down.'

'They don't burst into flames.'

'I bet they do. I bet somewhere in the echelons of motoring history someone's standing beside a half-million-dollar car while the engine puffs smoke.' And then as she relaxed, just a little bit, he hugged her tighter. 'You did great, Meg, and it's all great from here on. Peggy will have contacted the authorities. I wouldn't be surprised if we have helicopters hovering over us at dawn, so how about we sleep now?'

And before she realised what he was about, he lifted her and carried her bodily back to the tender.

Henry, reassured by Boof's solid presence, had drifted off to sleep again. The big dog was still lying beside him, taking up the entire floor space. Now he opened one eye and gazed up at them suspiciously. As well as he might. 'Boof, out,' Matt said and Boof did exactly that.

'He only does…what I say,' she managed.

'He only does what's good for his mistress.' Matt lowered her onto the rubber and tucked a space blanket around her. 'Now, sleep.'

'Matt?'

'Mmm?'

'There's room for you.'

'I'll sleep by the fire.'

'No.' The panic was still in the recesses of her mind. It was because the tender was more comfortable, she told herself. He'd sleep better on the inflatable surface.

But she knew it was more than that. He'd held her and the terror had receded. If he could just…hold her…

And he got it. He stooped and touched her on the cheek. It was the gentlest of touches and why it should send a frisson of pure heat through her…

There was no reason, but as he smiled and slid into the tender beside her, as he tucked her under his arm, as he pulled the blanket over the two of them…

She smiled, too.

And then she slept.

Matt didn't sleep.

There was no reason why he shouldn't. The tender was comfortable enough. Sure, his feet had to rest on the side but it was more comfortable than a bed on the rock-strewn sand. He did a bit of recreational hiking. He was used to sleeping rough.

Their problems had been solved. Rescue was on its way.

There was no reason at all why he should lie with Meg tucked into the crook of his arm and stare at the dark and think…

Meg.

He could understand why he should lie in the dark and think of the fire. But Meg?

It was the circumstances, he told himself.

But it was more than that. It was the sight of her at the wheel of the boat, handling the boat in the tricky seas as if she'd been born to it. Which obviously she had.

It was her insistence on seasickness pills. It was the way she'd persuaded Henry to treat Boof as a friend.

It was her competency and courage in the face of fire.

She'd saved them. That thought was overwhelming enough, but she'd done it with a warmth and empathy he could hardly comprehend. So many times since Amanda had died he'd felt helpless, and now this woman was making him feel even more as if there was an entire life skill set that had passed him by.

The way she looked. The way she smiled.

The way she felt…

Circumstances…

He was emotional, too, he told himself, and as she murmured in her sleep, as he instinctively held her closer, as he felt the warmth of her body against his chest he thought…

Circumstances?

He needed to get a grip because the way he was feeling, circumstances didn't come into it.

She woke in the small hours. Something must have woken her, but there was nothing but the hush of the waves against the sand and rocks in the sheltered cove.

The starlit night, the warmth, the peace…

And then she heard it, the faintest of whimpers.

She wiggled a little, so she could hold Henry. He'd been deeply asleep when Matt had lowered her into the tender

and she'd been careful not to disturb him. Now, though…
Matt's arm had been cradling her against him, forming
a pillow. It took a wrench but she slid out of his hold and
tugged the little boy to her.

'Hey, Henry, it's okay, we're here.' He was barely
awake, maybe trapped in the same nightmare she'd had.
But how much worse? His mother was dead. She was remembering the barren grief after her parents were killed,
the fear, and all she could do was hold him.

'Matt's here, Boof's here and I'm here. And your
grandma's waiting. She lit a fire on her cliff to say she's
seen us. Hey, I wonder if she has a dog. And I bet she
can fish, too, though if she can't, now you can teach her.'
She was muttering inconsequential things, or maybe they
were important. She wasn't sure he was hearing, but all
that seemed important was to hold him close and let him
know he was…loved?

Loved. That was the ingredient that was missing, she
thought. She'd had her grandparents. Did this little boy
know that he was loved by someone?

'We've got you.' It was Matt's voice, firm, soft but in-
arguable. 'Meg and Boof and I are here for you, Henry.
We're not going to let you go until we're sure your grandma
will cuddle you. Sleep now.'

'You and Meg…' Henry's voice was a quavery whisper.

'And Boof and your grandma Peggy. We're a team.
We're the caring-for-Henry team. Hey, Henry, how about
we shift so we're a sandwich?'

And before Meg knew what Matt was about, he'd risen
and lifted Henry over her, so the little boy was wedged
between them.

'You're a Meg and Matt sandwich now,' Matt said sleepily, the suggestion inherent that this was simply part of a
dream. A warm, safe, dream. And then, because the tender was very narrow—and because…okay, maybe he even
missed the contact with Meg that she'd been valuing so

much—his arm slid behind her head again, tugging her close. In the process it made a snuggly, warm V for one frightened child.

'Now,' Matt said firmly, 'everyone comfy? Everyone safe? Let's sleep again.'

Henry's sleep was almost instantaneous. Meg, though, lay and looked up at the stars.

'They're spectacular, aren't they?' Matt whispered. How *did* he know what she was thinking? 'You don't get these in New York. But, Meg, you need to sleep, too. You're as safe as Henry. I promise.'

Because this man was holding her?

It made no sense but that was the way she was feeling.

She hadn't liked him on first sight. Even on the boat, he'd responded to her attempts at conversation with the politeness of someone who moved in a rarefied atmosphere far from hers. She'd thought he was kind, but that kindness was overlaid with an arrogance that was almost innate. He'd thrown money at Charlie like water. He was accustomed to getting what he wanted from life, accustomed to getting his own way.

But he was holding her now and it felt…amazing.

She drifted back toward sleep but the feel of Matt, the thought of his words, his voice stayed with her.

It felt as if something had changed within her—and it felt wonderful.

CHAPTER SIX

RESCUE DIDN'T COME by helicopter. Instead, an hour after dawn, a cabin cruiser arrived. It was a boat that looked as if it had seen better days and those days were long behind it.

At the wheel was an elderly lady wearing men's trousers, an ancient fishing guernsey and huge black boots. Her hair was a mass of white curls, tied, incongruously, with a scarlet ribbon. She steered the boat expertly to within thirty yards of shore, cut the engine, tossed the anchor and hailed them.

There was no need to hail. They'd been watching her approach for the last fifteen minutes, Meg with growing incredulity.

This boat looked less seaworthy than *Bertha*. The skipper looked as if she was in her seventies. There was a dog standing at the bow—a dachshund, for heaven's sake.

This wasn't what Meg had hoped for.

Henry was beside her. She could hardly say, 'What on earth…'

She could think it, though, and as she saw how decrepit the boat looked she glanced at Matt and saw her dismay reflected.

Had Peggy decided to do the rescue herself?

'Ahoy.' Peggy's yell cut across the water. 'Is that a tender? Can you come and get me? Or just bring yourselves straight out. I can't get any closer because of the rocks.'

'Is anyone else coming?' Matt called.

'Just me.' Peggy sounded joyful. 'Henry, love, is that you?'

'Grandma.' Henry was on his feet. 'Grandma!'

'Yep, it's me and Stretchie. Stretchie—say g'day to Henry.'

And the little dog on the bow wagged her tail and gave an obedient woof.

The dog was cute, Meg conceded. And it was lovely to see Henry reacting with such joy to seeing Peggy. These were good points. But...

'That thing doesn't even look seaworthy,' Matt muttered, echoing her own dismay. Henry was out of earshot. He was standing on the shore, every fibre of his small being looking as if he needed to be out there hugging his grandma. Matt and Meg were carting the tender to the water, but doubts were everywhere.

'Don't take Henry out.' That part seemed obvious. 'Matt, she might be planning to take Henry back to Garnett herself and leave us for the authorities to collect.'

'That's not happening,' Matt said grimly. 'I'm seeing him safe all the way. That's what I promised.'

Promised who? Meg thought. Promised Henry? She glanced across the cove at the little boy. His whole body language was joyful. His grandma had come to fetch him. He wouldn't be holding Matt to any promise.

But the knowledge came to her, sure and strong. This was a promise Matt had made to himself and Matt was a man who kept his promises.

It made her feel...solid. As if some things in life were right.

As if she'd found something good?

That was a dumb thing to think. Or maybe it wasn't, she conceded. Matt seemed honourable, dependable, caring. After a couple of days she'd never see him again, but it was good to know there were people like him in the world.

Except...after a couple of days...

Oh, cut it out. Just because he'd held her in the night... Just because he'd cared... This man was so far out of her orbit he might just as well belong to another species. Thinking about him...as she was thinking...

Fantasy.

'What's wrong?' he asked, and she hauled her head back to the here and now. To the sensible.

'Just worrying about Peggy.'

'It's okay. Even if she hasn't organised the authorities to come and get us, we'll use her radio to contact them ourselves.'

'It's not that.' She'd forced her mind to move from where her thoughts wanted to be—like centred around the guy at the other end of the boat—to where they should be. To an elderly woman taking her seven-year-old grandson to an island as remote as Garnett. She'd had qualms before. Now, looking at Peggy's rusty excuse for a boat, they surfaced again. 'It's just…'

'I know.' Once again she knew Matt got her thoughts. 'Meg, I have no control over this. I'm not family. I have no legal right to interfere. If I have any grave concerns, like the prospect of ill treatment or neglect, then I can contact the authorities, but you can see there's love between them. We can't interfere.'

'He's not going back to Garnett in that boat.'

'No,' Matt said with the same firmness she was feeling. 'I'll bring her to shore and then we all wait. How many muesli bars do we have left?'

'Enough, but we ate the chocolate ones for breakfast. We're down to bran.'

'Then let's get this organised fast,' Matt told her and then he smiled. 'Hey, Meg, cheer up. Peggy's the forerunner to rescue. If Peggy hasn't explained to the authorities that our situation is dire then we'll have to recontact. I want helicopters, skydivers, paratroopers, whatever it takes, but I'm a man who hasn't had coffee since yesterday. Things are indeed dire.'

It wasn't worth fixing the motor back onto the tender, so Matt rowed out. He used the excuse not to take Henry.

'You'll get in the way of my arms,' he told him. 'And I need room to bring your grandma to you.'

Meg stood at the shore and held Henry's hand. Henry clutched Teddy and waited.

Boof stood at Henry's other side. It was almost as if the big dog thought Henry was in need of protection.

Maybe he was.

Not from the little dog on Peggy's boat, though. The dachshund was greeting Matt with exuberance. Her body language was unmistakeable—*finally, something exciting's happening in my life.*

Just how isolated was Peggy?

Meg had heard of her—of course she had. Peggy had lived briefly at Rowan Bay before she'd bought the island, but that had been before Meg could remember. Peggy had been on her island for so long now that interest had faded.

Matt had climbed aboard. They were talking. A lot.

'Why are they taking so long?' Henry was jiggling at her side.

'I guess your grandma is showing Matt her boat.'

'But I want Grandma to see me.'

Finally Matt helped Peggy into the tender, handing her the dog. Peggy sat in the bow while Matt rowed, looking ahead at Henry, her eyes misty, her smile beatific.

Matt, not so much. His body language was…grim.

As the tender reached the cove Meg waded in and caught it. Peggy, though, was over the side, wading straight to Henry, catching him in her arms, holding him close.

'Oh, Henry.' Her voice broke on a sob and she buried her face in her grandson's hair. Henry clung right back.

And part of Meg relaxed. The biggest question—was Henry going to someone who loved him?—was being answered.

Matt had climbed out of the tender. He went to the stern. Meg was at the bow, preparing to lift the little craft yet again.

But Matt's face…

'What?' she said. Peggy and Henry were caught up in their hug. The dogs were sniffing each other. Meg and Matt could talk without anyone hearing.

'She doesn't have a radio.'

'On the boat?' Was he kidding? Who'd put to sea in Bass Strait without a radio?

'Worse than that,' Matt said. 'There's no radio on Garnett, either. It seems she's let her batteries run down and forgotten to reorder. She says the shock of her daughter's death made her forget everything, including that she'd swapped to backup batteries when the initial contact was made. My last contact with her kept dropping out and now I know why.'

'So she has no radio at all?' Meg stared across at Peggy in incredulity. 'To be on that island by herself with no way of contact…' Her mind was racing, not just to their immediate situation but to what lay ahead. 'Matt, if she can't be depended on to keep radio contact… To keep a child…'

'There's no use thinking that now,' he said roughly, and she knew his concern matched hers, maybe tenfold. 'But what to do?' He hesitated. 'Surely Charlie will try to contact you.'

'I'm surrounded by idiots,' she said bitterly. Frustration was threating to overwhelm her. She glowered up at him. 'Which hasn't been helped by hiring me to stay until you were sure Henry was settled. And offering Charlie that ridiculous amount on a daily basis. He'll be rubbing his hands with glee when I don't return. There's no way he'll be worrying.'

'You're blaming me?'

'It was ridiculous money.'

'But that's why you took the job.'

She glowered some more. The truth of his statement didn't help. 'I need a new roof,' she muttered.

'And I need security for Henry. So your justification is greater than my justification?'

'All right,' she threw at him. 'You're the hero and I've been a dope. Moving on…'

'You're not a dope. When we get back to Rowan Bay I'll personally organise you a new roof.'

Her eyes widened. 'You're kidding.'

'I'm not kidding.'

They'd been poised to carry the tender back up the beach. Now they were standing in shallow water, staring at each other from opposite ends of the boat.

'You don't even know how much a roof costs.'

'It doesn't matter.'

'Your offer of money got us into this mess in the first place.'

'My offer of money got Henry reunited with his grandma.' He motioned to Peggy, who was cradling Henry as if he was the most precious thing. 'You're saying that's a bad thing?'

'But you can't just buy me a new roof. Why should you?'

'Because I'm wealthy,' he told her. 'To be honest, Meg, I'm very wealthy. One roof, no matter how large, couldn't possibly dent my income. And you've been put to enormous inconvenience.'

'It's not my boat that sank. And I'm still being paid by the day, remember?'

'And those days might now stretch. Realistically, Meg, is there any way you'll be missed before Monday?'

'Maybe not,' she conceded. 'But Monday… I'll definitely be missed then. Charlie has a charter booked and I'm skippering. He'll have twelve angry corporates—it's a team-building fishing trip—demanding their money back. Also, I phoned Maureen, my next-door neighbour, before I left. She's feeding my chickens but by Monday she'll be asking questions.'

'So three days.' He stared across at Meg's bag. Oat-and-bran muesli bars. Not many.

He also looked at the water container they'd hauled from the tender. Four people and two dogs.

There was silence as they hauled the tender up the beach. Meg's mind was racing and, it seemed, so was Matt's.

'Mrs Lakey,' he called and Henry's grandma released her grandson—just to arm's length—and turned.

'Call me Peggy,' she said, and Meg could hear tears in her voice. 'Thank you for bringing me my grandson. And you put yourself in harm's way…'

'Our boat burned, Grandma,' Henry told her, sounding awed, and Peggy tugged him tight again.

'And I didn't even know. Last night I was terrified. If I hadn't seen your fires…'

'Peggy, do you have water on your boat?'

'I have a thermos,' she said, sounding confused. 'Half-full. It'll be cold now, though.'

'And that's all?'

'There's plenty of water on Garnett.' She didn't sound bothered. 'I guess your friends will send a boat for you soon enough. We should all go home and wait.'

Meg turned and stared out at Peggy's tub of a boat. So did Matt.

'It's a risk,' Meg said at last. 'But while this weather holds… I think we should attach the tender behind Peggy's boat and head to Garnett.'

'It doesn't even *look* seaworthy,' Matt muttered.

'I'll need to check the engine. And I mean really check. I want a couple of hours in the hull.'

'You know enough about engines to do that?'

'It's my splinter skill,' she told him. 'Holding old engines together with pieces of string. Mostly I win.'

'You didn't check *Bertha*.'

That brought a glower. 'Charlie assured me she'd been checked. You were in a rush. I was dumb enough to take his word.'

'Meg…'

'What are our choices?' she asked. 'Send Henry with Peggy without us? No way. Stay here? In three days we'll be seriously dehydrated. I'll check and double-check.'

'My boat's fine.' Peggy was listening, starting to look offended.

'She might seem fine,' Meg retorted, 'but look what happened to the *Titanic*. I'm checking.'

'She's checking,' Matt said, sounding bemused. 'There's a new order on this island. Rule of Meg.'

'Are you saying I'm bossy?' she demanded.

'I'm not saying you're bossy,' he told her. 'I'm saying you're awesome.'

Three hours later, filthy beyond belief, a greasy, oil-spattered Meg decreed the boat was as sound as she could make it.

'It hasn't been serviced for years,' Meg told Matt as they loaded the dogs into the tender. Peggy and Henry were already aboard Peggy's boat. 'Matt, how can Peggy care for a child with this sort of attitude toward basic safety?'

'I'm starting to think she can't,' Matt said. 'But legally I have no choice but to take him to Garnett.'

'And if it turns out he's not safe?'

'There's a bridge we cross when we reach it.'

'Not a bridge,' she said grimly. 'Just a nasty piece of water known as Bass Strait.'

CHAPTER SEVEN

THEY MADE IT and Garnett Island was okay.

Garnett Island was safe.

The first few hours were busy: securing the boats, trying—and failing—to figure out a way to get the radio working, checking and using Peggy's pantry to make scratch meals—tinned spaghetti and sauce, and some herbs Meg found in Peggy's riot of a garden—chopping wood to get heat into the house, and coming to terms with the fact that Henry wouldn't be able to stay on the island. Safe or not.

After dinner Peggy tucked her grandson into his specially prepared bedroom and read him a story. Matt checked after half an hour and found the two of them asleep.

He left them there, huddled together, and came back to the kitchen to find Meg poking hopelessly at the wood-stove.

'There's a hole in the flue,' she told him. 'There's no way it'll stay damped down overnight. I also suspect the chimney's blocked. Every time there's a gust of wind outside I get a back blast of smoke.'

'Peggy can hardly chop wood anyway. Meg, they can't stay.'

She wiped her hands on her truly disgusting jeans. She'd been dirty when he'd first met her, he remembered, just off an early-morning fishing charter. Since then she'd coped with a fire on the boat, taught Henry to fish, slept in her clothes and spent hours tinkering with the engine of Peggy's ancient boat. She'd had a wash when she got here but making the stove hot enough to heat dinner had undone what little improvement there'd been.

But she turned from the stove and looked at him thoughtfully, and once again came that almost ridiculous thought... *She's beautiful.*

'Want a walk on the beach?' she asked. She was smart as well as gorgeous, this woman. The message between them didn't need to be spoken—they needed to talk out of earshot of the two upstairs, and the old ceilings were thin and cracked.

So they walked down the track to the cove, where the boat was tied at Peggy's jetty.

The night was still and warm. The moon was almost full. It was low tide. The wet sand was a shining ribbon. The place *looked* like paradise.

'We've been so lucky,' Meg said. They'd walked almost in silence until they'd reached the cove. Now, as he helped her down an incline where the sea had washed away steps, there was no need for silence, but still it seemed wrong to break the peace of this place. Meg's voice was almost a whisper, as if she agreed with him.

'Bass Strait's one of the wildest pieces of water in the world,' she told him. 'This jetty...' She motioned to the wooden structure where Peggy's boat was tied. 'It looks okay from the top but I checked when you were lifting Henry and the dogs off. The wood's rotting underneath. One big sea could smash it. Matt, the weather we've had over the last few days has been extraordinary. I need you to understand that.'

'Why?'

'Because you're thinking of all the reasons Peggy can't stay here and I'm adding another. Or more. The place is ramshackle. Peggy's supposed to get supplies once a fortnight but there'll be times when a boat can't land. If this jetty goes it'll be impossible. Her shopping list is on the fridge and it's all over the place. Items written three times. No fresh fruit. Despite having no backup batteries for the radio, she hasn't written them down. She's using solar power with battery storage, but even those batteries need replacing. And tonight, fixing dinner…she hardly seems to know what's in the pantry. I know her daughter's just died and she's stressed but this is survival stuff.'

'I get it,' he said heavily. She was saying nothing he hadn't already figured.

'I'm so glad you brought him yourself rather than sent him with a paid travel escort. To have dumped him here… it doesn't bear thinking of.'

'No.'

She glanced up at him, and then away, as if she didn't want to watch what was happening on his face. He didn't want to think about that. This situation was doing his head in.

'I made enquiries,' he said heavily. 'Peggy's not too old to take care of a grandchild. She owns the freehold of this island. She seemed to have regular suppliers. I asked about schooling and she had that nailed, too. School of the Air and occasional trips across to Rowan Bay to integrate with the kids there. She sounded competent, in charge…'

'And desperate to have her grandson,' Meg finished for him. 'There's no doubt she loves him.'

'And he, her. Have you seen that scrapbook? Every single week, a letter. You know, I should have twigged at that. Letters instead of emails. No internet. Intermittent telephone calls via her radio. I didn't ask enough questions.'

'But you came,' Meg said gently. 'You can hardly beat yourself up now.'

'So what the hell do I do?' It was almost a groan.

'Contact Social Services?' Meg was watching him, her expression thoughtful. 'After all, he's no business of yours.'

But it wasn't a statement. It was a question, and both of them knew it.

Henry was no business of his.

Meg was right, he wasn't. But for so many years…

'He sits in my office.' The words were almost an explosion, breaking the peace of the night. 'I remember the first time she brought him into work. He was four and she had a business lunch. "Sit there and don't bother anyone," she told him. I heard her as I passed on the way to a meeting. She told her secretary to keep an eye on him, but an hour later I found him sitting exactly where she'd left him, with two picture books and a computer game. He was watching neither, just staring ahead, trying not to cry. Luckily I had an understanding client. We all ended up making paper planes while we talked about the complexities of bitcoin transfer for a property settlement. But Amanda didn't get back for another hour and that was just the start of it. I almost sacked her, but I realised if she left my company then Henry would be in the same situation somewhere else. To be left like that…'

He broke off, appalled at the emotion in his voice. He hadn't realised quite how much he cared until right now.

Meg didn't comment. She was letting himself pull himself together, he realised. Giving him the space he needed.

They walked a bit more along the ribbon of sand. She was a peaceful woman, he decided. She hadn't jumped in with words of outrage. She hadn't even commented. And finally, when the next question came it was strangely out of left field.

'So tell me about you.'

'What…?'

'I'm hearing empathy,' she explained. 'You and Henry. Am I right?'

'That's got nothing to do with—'

'How you're feeling. I think it does. Did you ever get left like that?'

'My parents are wealthy.'

'Yeah, like that answers questions,' she said dryly. 'If Amanda was a lawyer in your firm then I imagine she didn't lack money, either. Money doesn't prevent loneliness. So, your childhood—'

'It's none of your business.'

'Of course it's not,' she said cordially. 'It's just, I'm feeling ties all over the place, emotion, need, empathy. I'm trying to sort it in my head.'

'I'm paying you to bring us to this island, not practise amateur psychology.'

'Ouch,' she said but she didn't sound offended. 'But you can't blame me. Social niceties are for others. I'm guessing you went to the best schools. Me, I left school when I was sixteen. It's a wonder I know how to use a knife and fork.'

She was smiling. Laughing at herself. Taking the tension out of the situation.

Making him smile?

His prickles settled. She was asking personal questions. Two could play at that game—and he really wanted to know.

'So how come you left school at sixteen?' he asked. 'And don't tell me it's because you're dumb. I don't believe it.'

'How can you be smart with no education?'

He could hear a note of regret behind the light words. 'You were born smart.'

'Yeah,' she said dryly. 'Thanks, but…'

'But tell me. Why?'

'Because isolation sucks.'

It was a blunt answer, harsh even. They were walking slowly along the moonlit sand. They were looking out at the night-time seascape instead of each other.

It was a good time for revealing…all?

'You were lonely at school?' he asked cautiously.

'I loved school.'

'Then why…?'

'Because Grandma died.' She sniffed, almost defiantly biting back emotion. 'Okay, brief history. My grandpa was a fisherman and so were Mum and Dad. We shared a big old house up on the headland overlooking Rowan Bay.

Big garden, enough land to run a few cows. Gran kept chooks. Her veggie garden was the best. Mum and Dad were sad they couldn't have any more kids after me, but I had the best childhood. I had four grown-ups who loved me. Then, when I was eleven, Mum and Dad were killed in a car crash and our world sort of folded. I was okay. I was still loved, but Dad was Gran and Grandpa's only child. Gran never got over it. She used to sit on the front porch and wait for them to come home, but of course they never did. And then she got cancer. She died the day after my sixteenth birthday and it was awful.'

'I'm so sorry.'

'Yeah, well, I was still…okay. I was a kid. I had mates in Rowan Bay. Life went on. But after Gran died, Grandpa started sitting, as well. He stopped going out in the boat. He just sat. And one day I came home from school and looked at him and I thought he's not even seeing me. I got the biggest fright. I suddenly thought, he'll get cancer, as well. I know it's illogical but I couldn't shake it.'

'So…' he said cautiously, seeing her as she'd been then—alone, terrified.

'So the next day I didn't go back to school. I made Grandpa take me out fishing and we fished ever since. And it worked. We were a great fishing team. We had fun. Then two years back, he got sick. I've spent most of the last couple of years looking after him. Which was expensive to say the least. I had to sell the boat but I didn't care. We were together all the time. He died six months ago and I don't regret a single moment of the time I had with him.'

She paused then, obviously regrouping, and she managed a smile. 'So if you ask me to say g'day in French or solve some sort of fancy equation I'm not your woman, but I can strip a mean engine and if you want a fish dinner I'll get it on the plate for you. So that's me, done. How about you?'

He didn't answer.

He felt winded.

And ashamed?

He was smart enough to read the gaps in her story. He was also smart enough to hear the loneliness. A kid with lost parents. A teenager dealing with an old man with what sounded like chronic depression and then terminal illness. A young woman putting her life on hold…

'Come on,' she urged as they kept walking. 'Your turn.' Amazingly she was back to being cheerful. 'Fair's fair.'

'Mine's boring in comparison.'

'So tell me.'

After that, he hardly had a choice.

'I was a lot luckier than you,' he told her. 'I'm an only child, too, but I had both parents and grandparents. My grandparents are gone now, and Dad died three years ago but for my childhood I had an intact family. My mother's still hosting society lunches, travelling, lording it over the ladies of Manhattan. She keeps in touch. I might be heir to the family dynasty but she sees herself as the McLellan matriarch. Even the most remote cousin knows its worth.'

Meg frowned, as if she was detecting undertones. As well she might. She was dissecting his words, looking for the parts she didn't understand.

'Family dynasty?'

'Historically a line of hereditary rulers.'

'I know that.' She glowered. 'I may not be educated but I'm not thick.'

'Sorry.'

'So you should be. So in the US… I figure the Kennedys are a dynasty. How does the description fit the McLellans?'

He smiled ruefully. She was smart, this woman. And… insightful? Seeing what was at the core of what he was saying. He took time to think of an answer that'd respect her.

'In Manhattan? A family succession playing a leading role in the financial world. My grandfather explained it to me when I was six. Our family has power.'

'So you rule Manhattan.'

'Not quite,' he said dryly. 'But we do have influence.'

'Hmm.' She cast him a thoughtful look, then moved on to the personal. 'So your mum and dad… They didn't live in the house you were telling me about?'

'My father was living in Sweden when he died. My mother hasn't been near McLellan Place for years.'

'They divorced?'

'They'd never have divorced. That doesn't mean they didn't have partners but partners came and went. They both…bored easily.'

She thought about that, too, and then cut straight to the bone. 'So did you bore them, as well?'

Ouch. What was he revealing?

'Maybe,' he said neutrally, trying not to feel as if she'd just nailed him, that she was seeing him as a kid alone apart from staff. His parents had indeed found parenthood too boring for words.

She walked a little way into the shallows, kicking up water before her. She was still barefooted—none of Peggy's shoes came close to fitting her.

She was giving him space.

'So this house in the Hamptons…' she said at last when the silence started to get oppressive. 'The cousins…family… You get together there for Christmas and stuff?'

'Not there. When my father died I bought the place from the estate so it's mine. I go there occasionally.'

'By yourself?' And then she caught herself and peeped a grin across at him. 'Whoops, sorry. I'm not inquiring about your legion of lovers.'

'So I shouldn't inquire about yours?'

She chuckled. 'I might even tell you.' She left the water and came up the beach to join him again. 'I've just knocked back one of the most romantic proposals you could imagine. Graham, Charlie's son, thinks I'll make a fine wife. He's seen me pulling an engine apart and putting it back together, and his passion's for expensive, stupid cars. He's eaten some of the cookies I bring into the office and he's seen me fish. He's also seen me clear a drain, chop wood and cart a drunken punter off the boat, all by myself. A woman who can cook, clean, gut a fish, keep his car on the road and put him to bed when he's drunk... I'm his wet dream. He says I can sell Grandpa's place, pay off his mortgage, plus the money he owes his ex-wife, and we can live happily ever after.'

'And yet you knocked him back?' he said faintly and she chuckled again. It was a great chuckle, soft and sexy.

'I know. I'm so fussy. Graham says I'm doomed to be an old maid.'

'I'm sure you're not.'

'I don't think I'd mind.' She paused, turning to stare out to sea. 'There are a lot worse things to be. To have a marriage like your parents'...'

'It suited them. They had money, the family name, the prestige of power.'

'Power?'

'Money means power,' he said simply. 'And there's a lot of money.'

'So this dynasty thing... When you offered to pay for my roof...'

'I suspect one day's power might more than pay for your roof.'

'And you have a lot of...power?'

'Yes. Financial juggling... It's in my blood.'

'Wow,' she said but strangely she didn't sound impressed. She almost sounded sympathetic. 'But no one shares your house?'

But then she caught herself and the laughter returned. 'Sorry, I forgot. Your litany of lovers.'

'One a week and two on Sundays.'

'Now, why don't I believe that?'

Why? He didn't have a clue. She was starting to seriously unnerve him.

Or was *unnerve* the wrong word?

It was the setting, he thought. The place. The events of the last two days.

If he saw this woman in Manhattan he wouldn't look twice at her, he thought. He wouldn't even see her.

Or maybe he would. Grease stained, barefooted, her short, copper curls tousled and stiff with salt and smoke… He'd glance twice.

Because she was out of place?

Because she was lovely.

'We'd best get back to the house.' He was starting to think he needed to be sensible where this woman was concerned.

'Yeah, we get to sleep on Peggy's living room floor.' She sighed. 'I'm thinking if we carted the tender up to the house it'd be more comfortable.'

'You can have the settee.'

'Have you sat on the settee?' she demanded. 'It has springs where no settee should have springs.'

'We'll manage,' he said and then, before he could stop himself, he reached out and took her hand. 'We've been through a lot together. Sleeping on a threadbare rug seems the least of it.'

'Yeah,' she said, but faintly, because suddenly she was looking down at their linked hands.

Because suddenly something was happening.

'Matt…' she said and her voice was uncertain.

'Meg.'

Meg. It was a name. A word. Why it hung…

Something indeed was changing.

The night was still. The beach was deserted. The sky was a glorious panorama of stars, the like of which he'd never seen before, making the night seem almost magic.

Which was pretty much how he was feeling now. Unreal. Time out of frame.

This woman was nothing to do with him, nothing to

do with his world, and yet she was standing before him, looking up at him, her gaze a question.

And her question was the same as his.

And her chin tilted, just a little, as if her part of the question had been resolved. It was up to him…

And the night, the peace, the warmth…and, being truthful, his need, answered for him.

He cupped her face gently with his hands and drew her to him.

He kissed her.

What was she doing?

This guy had paid for her services. He was one of Charlie's punters. He was a customer, a fancy New York lawyer. He had absolutely nothing to do with her.

His hands cupped her face and she melted. Sense was nowhere.

His mouth touched hers and her willpower…everything…disintegrated in the need to be closer. His mouth claimed hers, and she felt as if her bones were melting. Her arms linked around him and it was as if she needed them to hold her up.

It didn't make sense but part of her was thinking she was merging. Becoming one? If she wasn't part of him she'd fall…

How stupid was that? But stupid was ignored. Everything was ignored. There was only the feel, the taste, the glorious wonder of being…cherished?

Loved.

There was a dumb word. She'd known this guy for less than two days. She was twenty-eight years old and she was sensible.

But sensible had gone the way of stupid. Irrelevant. The part of her brain doing the deciding decided the only available option was to concentrate on this kiss. To disappear into it, because it was magic.

She'd been kissed before—of course she had. She was twenty-eight years old and there'd even been some guys she'd seriously considered. A partner could have complicated her life with Grandpa but it wouldn't have made it impossible. She'd never ruled out falling in love.

But not one of the guys she'd dated had made her feel like this.

Desired. Beautiful. As if the cocoon she'd built around herself was shredding and what was emerging was someone she didn't know. She was someone who held this gorgeous, hunky, tender, strong, clever, amazing man close and who was claiming him.

Because that was what this kiss was. She wanted him, simple as that. Every fibre of her being was tuned to this overpowering need.

The kiss deepened and deepened again. His hands tugged her hard against him and she knew his desire was as great as hers.

But maybe they weren't separate desires. Maybe they were the same, because that was how she was feeling. As if her body were fusing. One kiss…

It was so much more.

One body?

She loved the feel of him. His strength. The rough texture of his thick, dark hair as she ran her fingers through. The roughness of the stubble on his jaw. The sheer, arrant maleness of…Matt.

'Matt…'

And somehow, through the passion of the kiss, she heard herself say it. And she heard in her voice her desire, the release of every vestige of self-control.

And he heard it, too, and somehow, appallingly, it made a difference. She felt his body stiffen, just a little. Just enough to matter.

He broke away. His hands still held, but as he gazed down at her in the moonlight she saw shock.

It was enough to send the same sensation through her. She tugged away and he let her go. They were left staring at each other, disbelief reflected in both their eyes.

It was Matt who pulled himself together first. Who managed to speak.

'I don't suppose,' he said in a voice she hardly recognised, 'that when we jumped off our burning boat you thought about packing condoms?'

It was enough. It made her laugh, even if the laugh came out choked.

'I… No. I don't know what I was thinking. And what sort of emergency bag doesn't contain condoms?'

'It's a problem,' he said, gravely now. 'Though, Meg, maybe it's just as well.'

'Maybe it is.' She was still having trouble getting her voice to work. 'Matt, this situation is complicated enough. We do not need sex.'

'No?' And astonishingly there was laughter in his voice.

She looked up into those gorgeous eyes and found herself smiling in return. This situation was absurd. They'd been thrown together by the most appalling of circumstances. Emotion was everywhere.

Sex might even have been good.

Great?

'We both need to take cold showers,' she said, trying for astringency.

'Have you seen Peggy's hot-water service? That's exactly what's in store for us.'

She knew that. She'd had to heat water on the stove to give Henry a meagre bath.

Henry. The future.

'We both know he can't stay here.' She said it deliberately, not just because it was important but also because it took their minds—and their hands—off each other.

Laughter died.

'I know that,' he said. 'Okay, Meg O'Hara. Let's head

back to the house and draw straws as to who gets to sleep on the lumpy settee or the hard floor. Reality starts now.'

It did.

But as they turned, Matt took her hand. Maybe it was because it was dark and she could trip on the rough track.

Maybe it was because he thought she needed protection.

Maybe it was because…they both wanted it?

Regardless, his hand held hers and she left it there. She even gripped his back.

It might be time for reality but she wouldn't mind fantasy for just a while longer.

Meg slept on the settee, buffered from broken springs by a quilt and exhaustion.

Matt tried to sleep on the floor. Since he was a kid and a friend's family had introduced him to hiking, he'd used camping, the wilderness to break the pressure of the stresses of the financial world. He was used to sleeping rough. A carpeted floor, cushions, quilts, didn't stop him sleeping.

Meg within arm's reach was a different proposition. He lay and stared into the dark and listened to her breathing and wondered what had just happened.

He'd kissed her.

He'd kissed women before. This was more than that. Much more.

It was the situation, he told himself. The emotion surrounding Amanda's death, Henry's bereavement. The long flight over here, jet lag, worry for Henry, then the fire on the boat and the adrenalin charge that had gone with it. The layers of sophisticated protection that he'd built around his emotions had been pierced and the kiss was the result. So it was the place, the situation.

The woman.

He lay and listened to her soft breathing and a part of him wanted to move across and take her into his arms.

To feel her softness against his chest. To feel her mould against him, to need him…

Maybe that was it. The women he dated never needed him. He dated women who matched his world, sophisticated, intelligent…

Meg was intelligent.

And warm. And caring. And funny.

And the way she'd responded to his kiss…

Yeah, he wanted to be on that settee with her. Which was a joke. She was sleeping around broken springs as it was.

If he gathered her to him, if he said…what he wanted to say…how much more would be broken?

She was twenty-eight—old enough to protect herself, and old enough to know the rules in chance encounters. And yet the way she looked at him, the way she smiled, the sound of her chuckle…

She wasn't old enough. She wasn't savvy. If he took this further…

Did he want to?

For heaven's sake, he'd known her how long? What was he doing, thinking further?

He didn't do commitment. One day maybe? The McLellan billions demanded an heir and there were plenty of women in his orbit who knew how his world worked, who'd fit pretty much seamlessly into his life. But Meg…

What the hell was he thinking?

It was late. He was tired. What he was thinking was just plain stupid.

Close your eyes and go to sleep.

It wasn't about to happen.

CHAPTER EIGHT

THE NEXT DAY was so glorious Meg could imagine living on Garnett herself.

'But this weather won't hold,' she told Matt. 'Believe me.'

Peggy had taken her grandson fishing. They could see them down on the jetty, the white-haired grandma coaching her grandson as Meg had coached him the day before.

They'd gone off happily, although there'd been one dispute. 'You can't use barbed hooks, Grandma,' Henry had been explaining as they left. 'It hurts their mouths.'

That had made Meg smile. She'd turned to Matt, expecting to find him smiling as well, but instead she'd caught him looking at her. Just…looking.

He'd glanced away and made some innocuous remark about Henry's broadening education, but the expression she'd caught had her unsettled.

Henry was wearing one of Peggy's windcheaters, the sleeves rolled up, the hem hanging to his knees. He seemed cheerfully oblivious.

Meg and Matt had both decided their filthy jeans and trousers would have to keep on keeping on, but Matt's shirt and Meg's windcheater were currently flapping on the line. Meg was wearing one of Peggy's T-shirts, far too tight.

Matt was wearing…nothing at all.

Apart from his trousers, of course. Not that that helped. He was naked from the waist up.

Meg had tried not to watch as he'd chopped enough wood to keep them warm for a week. She'd failed. The sight of that naked chest, the delineation of muscles… A New York financier had no right to look like that.

And now… She'd been sitting on a log overlooking the cove, watching the pair below fish. Matt came and sat beside her and he brought his naked chest with him and she thought… She felt…

Like a sensible woman had no business thinking or feeling.

'So, plan,' he said, and she had to haul her thoughts away from an entirely inappropriate path and focus on… What had he said?

'Plan?'

'You know what I mean.'

She did. While Matt had chopped wood this morning she'd tried to distract herself by investigating the contents of Peggy's fridge and her pantry. The results had left her horrified.

'It's a wonder we survived last night's dinner,' she told him. 'There's stuff in that fridge that's about to walk out on its own.'

'You don't think it's the shock of losing her daughter, of trying to plan for Henry? Grief can make you fuzzy-headed.'

He got that, then. Impressive. This man was smart— that had never been in question. He was kind. He was also…empathetic?

'It can,' she agreed, thinking of the things her grandparents had done while in the throes of grief. 'But the pantry's full of weevils and she hasn't noticed. That's long-term.'

'Ugh.'

'And the battery thing… If I lived here, I'd have half a dozen sets of rechargeable batteries for extra solar storage and for the radio. If she were to get sick… If Henry was to fall and cut himself…'

'I know,' he said heavily. 'So where do we take it from here?'

'Let me talk to her.'

'You…'

'I'm good with oldies,' she said hesitantly. 'I could talk my grandpa into letting me help him shower. If I can do that, the next step's world peace.'

'But if she leaves the island…where do you propose they go?'

'Is that up to you and me to decide?' Meg asked. 'Matt, one thing I've learned from living with my grandparents is that age shouldn't take away choice. Yes, Peggy's struggling and maybe she might need help, but it's her life we're talking about. Seeing her this morning, watching Henry… I suspect we'll be pointing out stuff she already knows. She might even have a plan. Let's give her the respect of making a choice herself.'

Except Peggy didn't have a plan. They found that out after dinner. Fish caught by Henry, seared to perfection. Potato crisps made from potatoes Meg had dug from a neglected vegetable patch. A stir fry of greens from the same source.

Matt could have walked into the best restaurant in New York, eaten that meal and come out happy.

As soon as dinner was done, Henry crashed. He'd spent the day fishing, exploring the island with the dogs, doing stuff he'd never done in his life. He was exhausted.

Peggy also looked grey with fatigue, but she found enough energy to read him a bedtime story without going to sleep herself. Then she came down and sat at the kitchen table and faced them both. They all knew it was time for things to be brought into the open.

'I know what you're going to say,' she said heavily before either Matt or Meg could find space to comment. 'I can't keep him here. I hoped I could, but when the battery failed… It was my stupid fault, but it's a sign. I'm not as sharp as I should be. This was my lifestyle choice but I thought today, what if Henry gets something like appendicitis? When I heard Amanda was dead, the shock… Losing Amanda…

All I wanted was to have him here. I know now it's impossible. I should have faced it before but I'm facing it now. So...' She looked helplessly at the pair of them. 'What do I do about it? Will you help me? Please?'

Matt flashed Meg a look. Peggy had known... His respect for Meg was increasing by the moment, but her face didn't show for an instant that she was satisfied with her call. Her face was pure concern.

But she left it for him to speak first.

'Peggy, we're sorry,' he said. 'But if you can't keep Henry here...do you want to be evacuated with him?'

'Yes.' There was no hesitation. 'You know Amanda's father was American? I was born on a farm south of Rowan Bay. Amanda was the result of my one stint at trying to be a city girl. I even ended up with American citizenship, but look where that left me. Both Amanda and her father despised the lifestyle I longed for. Finally, I had to walk away and I've been a loner ever since.' There was a wealth of sadness in her voice, a wealth of regret.

She sighed and looked around at the peeling paintwork, at the obvious signs of neglect. 'I've loved this island but now I can't even afford to fix the house. I'll need to find somewhere to rent in Rowan Bay, though what with... It'll take time to sell this place even if I can find a buyer. No one wants rocky outcrops in such a climate. And I can't... I can't...'

She stopped. A tear rolled down her wind-weathered cheek and Meg reached out and took her hand.

'Hey, Peggy, don't cry. Let's take one step at a time. What we need is a plan.'

'A plan...' Peggy looked at her as if such a thing was unthinkable.

'A plan,' Meg said firmly. 'Something to give us breathing space.'

We? Matt thought blankly. Us? He'd hired Meg to skipper a boat. What was she doing, offering to be in the mix?

But the *we* was continuing. 'Why don't we spend tomorrow packing?' she suggested. 'We can pack essentials and things like Stretchie's favourite ball, your favourite pillow, your best fishing rod. Precious stuff we can take with us when we're evacuated. When you're settled, I can bring you back in one of our bigger boats and we'll collect the rest.'

'But where will we go?' Peggy's voice was muffled, grief mixed with despair.

And Meg's grip on her hand tightened. 'I've been thinking of that, too,' she said. 'I have a big old house on the headland south of Rowan Bay. I've lived there with my grandparents but sadly now I'm on my own. So I have four bedrooms, lots of squishy old furniture, lots of space. It's not grand but it's comfy. I have a huge garden—well, it used to be a garden, now it's sort of wilderness because I don't have time to care for it. I have chooks. I have five acres of coastline where you can fish or walk or just get to know your grandson. Peggy, you're very welcome to come and stay with me for as long as you want. While you get your breath back. While you plan. It sounds sensible to me but what about you? What do you say?'

It obviously took Peggy's breath away. She didn't answer, just stared at Meg, astounded.

It pretty much took Matt's breath away, too. He'd been ready to swing into action, find them a hotel until he could organise a rental property, foot the bill himself. He opened his mouth to say it—but then he closed it again.

He was due back in the States. He had massive financial contracts hanging on his return. He'd spent a lot of today worrying that he couldn't simply dump Peggy and Henry and leave.

But now, with one extraordinary offer, the responsibility had been lifted from his shoulders. By one extraordinary woman.

'But…' Peggy was gazing wide-eyed at Meg, as if she couldn't believe what she was hearing. 'But for how long?'

'For as long as you want,' Meg said soundly. 'To be honest, my place is lonely. Boof will love company and so will I. How are you at gardening?'

'I love gardening. I've struggled to keep this one going but if I had a bit of help…'

'There you are, then,' she said, smiling. 'I spend my days skippering charter boats and my garden's rubbish. We'll fix it together. If you can push a mower and pull weeds, there's your rent taken care of. And Henry can go to the local school. I imagine it'll take him time to settle but it's a good school.'

She really was talking long-term. Matt was growing more and more astounded.

'Meg…' he started and she flashed him a warning look.

'You have any objection to our plan?'

And there it was again. *Our.* She'd incorporated herself into this situation, she'd taken responsibility, she was one of them.

One of…*us*?

No. Because suddenly he was the outsider. He was the one going back to the States while Meg took over.

That should be fine. He couldn't think of a better solution. He wasn't convinced Peggy's confusion was solely down to grief and shock, but Meg would be there, keeping an eye on them both. Caring.

And then he thought, why did that make him feel empty? Bereft?

There was no reason. After all, Henry was the child of an employee, nothing more. The problem of what to do with him had been solved. He could head back to the States, conscience clear.

'There will be some money coming through from Amanda's estate,' he said, deciding to go down the professional route. The much less emotional path. 'Not as much as you might expect. To be honest, she seems to have led a fairly flamboyant lifestyle.' He'd been at her apartment, a penthouse overlooking Manhattan. He'd seen the wardrobe overflowing with shoes even he recognised as extraordinary. 'But there will be enough for you to rent for a while once we find you a place.'

'I'd rather stay with Meg,' Peggy said, casting him a scared look. Like a child about to have a treat snatched away.

'You could put Amanda's money into trust for Henry,' Meg suggested. 'When Peggy sells the island, we can make a decision whether living with me is working. She can buy her own place then if she wants.'

'Meg, do you realise…?'

And he got a flash of anger. A look that definitely said, *Butt out.*

'I think it's a good plan,' she said. 'No, I think it's a great plan. I get a free gardener. Boof and Stretchie will have each other and so will Peggy and Henry. And me… I'll get to come home after a day's charter and the lights will be on. It'll be home again. Any objections, Matt McLellan?'

Any objections? Strangely the biggest was that he wasn't included. That was dumb. He really did need to get back. But before he realised what he was about to say…he said it.

'Can you put me up for a few days, as well? I need to assure myself that Henry's safe.'

'Henry will be safe,' Peggy growled. 'I'm not a total incompetent.'

'Neither am I,' Meg said, and astonishingly she grinned. 'But let's humour him, shall we, Peggy? Blokes like to be in charge and I suspect someone like Matt McLellan likes that even more than most blokes. So let's give him the illusion of control. It's a very good plan, Matt McLellan, but you're welcome to come stay in my house and see for yourself.'

And then she hesitated, appearing to think about what to say next.

'But Peggy and Henry's invitation is open-ended,' she told him when she'd thought about it. 'Yours is a few days only. I have a big house but it still doesn't feel big enough for the two of us. And now... I don't know about you two, but it's time I hit the sack. We have a heap of packing to do tomorrow, Peggy, and we have a plan.' Her grin returned. 'I do love a plan, don't you?'

She lay on the decrepit settee.

He lay on the floor.

It was barely ten o'clock. He never went to bed before midnight.

How could he sleep?

Meg's breathing was soft and regular. She was within arm's reach.

She was...

Meg.

He was starting to feel as if he'd never met a woman like this. A woman who faced the problems of the world and embraced them, solved them her way, without a thought to consequences.

Peggy was elderly and confused. Henry was seven years old and needy. She'd taken them under her wing as if such a commitment were no more than inviting house guests for a couple of days.

She knew it was more than that. He'd seen it in the look of defiance she'd flashed at him, like butt out, this is none of your business.

Peggy needed support. Henry needed love.

Once ensconced in Meg's house, could she ever ask them to leave?

Was she planning to?

'This is my responsibility.' To his horror he heard himself say the words out loud. What was he doing, talking to himself? And Meg heard. She stirred and rolled over to face him. The moonlight was streaming in the window and he could see the mound of her on the settee. A small mound. A power-packed mound.

A mound of decision, of warmth and of kindness.

Also profanity. She hit a broken spring as she rolled and her expression was pure sailor.

'Where's a pair of wire clippers when you need them?' she said bitterly. 'I went looking for them today and the only ones Peggy has are rusted closed. Now... What did you say?'

'I didn't.'

'Yes, you did. If I'm right... This is your responsibility? How so?'

'I never in a million years wanted to land them on you.'

'You didn't. Amanda's death did. You and I were simply conduits to get Henry to Peggy. You go home. I get to share my too-big house. Problem solved. Yikes, there's another b...'

He grinned. Her lightness was infectious.

But she'd almost scuttled to bed when Peggy retired and now... He had a feeling her swearing was out of character. Was she purposely reminding him of the gulf between them?

He didn't want a gulf, and right now even six feet felt like a gulf.

'You know, if we hauled your quilt and cushions onto the floor we could have one half-comfortable bed between us,' he ventured.

'Matt, I've checked Peggy's bathroom cabinet. There are no condoms there, either.'

'I didn't mean...'

'Yeah, you did. Or if you didn't it'd occur to one or other of us sooner or later. Probably sooner. And neither of us want...'

'I suspect that's the problem,' he said. 'Both of us want.'

'Then neither of us can have,' she said firmly. 'I'm heading back to my life running fishing charters from Rowan Bay. You're heading back to your life as a billionaire or whatever you are in Manhattan. Are you a billionaire, by the way?'

He had to tell the truth. 'Yes, I am.'

'There you go.' There was not the least hint of resentment in her voice. 'Poles apart. So you're heading back to your life, and you're not taking my broken heart with you.'

There was a big statement. 'Would it be broken?' he asked, cautiously, and he heard her gasp as she realised what she'd said.

'I… No. Of course not. We've known each other two days. But there is this…thing between us and if it gets any stronger…'

He got that, too. He didn't understand it but it left him wanting.

He wanted this woman.

She was being sensible. He had to be, too.

'You're stuck with the springs, then.'

'I can cope.'

'Meg, the money side…'

'Yeah?'

'There'll be all sorts of costs involved in having Peggy and Henry. I already promised you a new roof. Whatever else you need…'

'You want to pay?'

'Of course I do.'

'Okay, then,' she said, as if it didn't matter one way or another. 'If you really are rich and you really want…'

He did want, but it was more than helping out financially. He wanted to be involved.

But he wasn't needed. There was no place for him in this scheme and why that made him feel bereft…

It was too strong a word, he thought. He wasn't bereft.

Suddenly Meg's words came back to him.

I'll get to come home after a day's charter and the lights will be on. It'll be home again.

He found himself thinking… To come home from work late at night and find the lights on… To have this woman waiting for him…

Fantasy.

'Goodnight, Matt,' Meg said firmly and rolled over on her springs and swore again. 'I think we have things sorted. Sleep.'

Right. How was a man to sleep after that?

Things didn't feel sorted at all.

CHAPTER NINE

Two DAYS LATER they came, in a helicopter, with all the bells and whistles a small boy could possibly require. It said a lot for the security Henry was now feeling that he could hold Matt's hand and watch the chopper land with fascination. And when the guy in charge, a yellow-jacketed member of the state's emergency services, walked across to the chopper to meet them, smiling his relief, saying, 'Well, are we pleased to see you! What happened to your boat?' Matt was stunned to hear Henry answer.

'It got burned,' he said, almost proudly. 'Meg tried to put it out but she coughed and coughed and then we had to get into the little boat and we were stuck on an island that was all rocks. Meg and me caught a fish and then Grandma came to find us. Only her radio's busted and Meg says everyone will be worried but you don't have to worry because Meg and Matt and Grandma and Stretchie and Boof looked after me.'

It was the most words Matt had ever heard Henry say. He found himself grinning, and his grin was matched by the guy in the yellow jacket's. Relief all round.

They'd all come out of the house as they'd heard the chopper. They were grouped together. Mum and Dad and Grandma and kid? For some reason that was what it felt like. Family. His pride in Henry seemed almost as deep as if the kid were his own.

He glanced at Meg and saw a shimmer of tears in her eyes. She was feeling the same?

'Got it in one,' the guy was saying in satisfaction and he went straight to Henry and gripped his hand. Henry shook it without blinking. 'I wish all our rescues were as straightforward. Well, young man, how can we help? Was anyone burned? No one injured at all?'

'Meg still coughs a bit,' Henry volunteered.

'She was in the cabin when the boat caught fire,' Matt said. 'She copped a fair dose of smoke inhalation.'

'I'm better,' Meg said and the guy nodded. He'd been joined by a couple of teammates now, all looking just as pleased. A boat missing at sea, especially with a child on board, was everyone's nightmare.

'We'll get our doc to check you out as soon as we reach the mainland,' the guy said. 'How about the rest of you? You need evacuation?'

And it was up to Peggy. She took a deep breath, took a firm hold of Henry's hand and nodded.

'Yes, young man, we do,' she said. 'I can't… We can't stay here any longer.' She cast a quick, fearful look at the helicopter and then looked deliberately down at Henry. 'How…how long does it take to get to Rowan Bay?'

'Less than half an hour, ma'am,' the guy said, gentling as if he sensed her fear. 'You'll be safe as houses.'

Safe. It was a good word. No, it was a great word and Peggy responded. She exhaled, all her fear of flying, all her love for her grandson combined in one long sigh.

'Then I can do it,' she managed. 'If Henry holds my hand all the way. Thank you, sir. Yes, please. Can you take all of us?'

What followed was a chopper ride that Peggy managed, eyes squeezed shut, Meg gripping one hand, Henry the other.

Henry, though, enjoyed the flight immensely. Life was suddenly an adventure. He coped okay with the reception at the little Rowan Bay airport. He became quiet again— some things didn't change—while official questions were asked, while the emergency services doctor took Meg into the office and did a fast examination, while the dogs checked out the little-used airstrip for rabbits. But he still seemed deeply contented.

Finally, Meg emerged, smiling. 'The doc says I need to take steroids for a few days until my lungs are clear,' she told Matt and Peggy. 'But I'm fine. The guys have organised taxis. Are we ready to go home?'

Home. It was a strange concept.

Matt had never felt less at 'home' in his life.

They made a fast stop at the general store and the pharmacy on the way. Matt and Henry needed pretty much everything, but half an hour later, armed with packages of new clothes, they reached Meg's place.

The house looked almost as ramshackle as Peggy's. Maybe not quite, Matt conceded. It was old and in need of paint. It definitely needed a new roof, but it wasn't actively falling down. With ancient settees on the wide veranda, a decent veggie patch, even if the rest of the garden looked in serious need of attention, and a view right out over the bay, it looked warmly welcoming.

A middle-aged woman, plump, aproned, beaming, came out of the front door to meet them.

'Meg,' she said in satisfaction. 'I knew there was something wrong. You should have heard what I said to Charlie when I realised he hadn't been in radio contact. I think the safety authorities will be having words. I was never more glad of anything when word came through you were safe. Your chooks are fine. You have a fridge full of eggs. I've just been in and put a casserole and apple pie in the oven. Now, who's this?'

Maureen was introduced to them all. She greeted Peggy and Henry with warmth but she eyed Matt with caution.

As well she might, Matt thought. He hadn't seen a razor for days and his new clothes were still in their wrapping. To say he was unkempt was an understatement. But with the way this woman looked at him came the odd, irrelevant thought. He was the one in this picture who didn't belong.

And maybe that was right. His job was done. He could organise a car to take him to Melbourne Airport, get on a plane and be back in the States tomorrow.

But he'd asked to stay and Meg had agreed. Didn't he have a responsibility to Henry?

Henry no longer needed him.

He couldn't just land this all on Meg and walk away.

But Meg was practically bouncing, showing them inside, opening bedroom doors, hauling open a linen cupboard and distributing sheets, filling water bowls for dogs, showing Henry where the dog toys were kept.

Peggy and Henry were happily following. So was Matt, but as he followed his feeling of dislocation deepened—as well as thinking he'd landed Meg with a life-changing set of circumstances and she'd taken them on as if it were nothing.

She was amazing.

'Lunch first and then I bags first bath,' she said. 'Peggy, is everything fine?'

'Everything's great,' Peggy said. 'Oh, Meg, if you're sure…'

'I'm sure,' Meg told her. 'This'll be fun.'

Fun. Once again Matt felt…hornswoggled.

And as if he had no place here and it mattered.

Back in the land of telecommunications, his phone was crammed with messages. Of course. He'd abandoned complex negotiations to bring Henry to Australia, and his world hadn't stopped because of it.

When he finally had time to check, it was four in the afternoon, which was midnight New York time. It was hardly the time to return business calls.

There was, though, one caller whose need for a response seemed more urgent than the rest. Helen, his personal secretary for years, was intelligent, competent and unflappable. But now she sounded…flapped.

She'd left ten different voicemail messages at various times over the last few days, each increasingly pressing.

'Matt, you need to ring me. Please, Matt, this can't wait. I need to speak to you, now.'

If it was anyone but Helen, he wouldn't ring at this hour but he could hear the increasing worry. For him to be out of range for this long was unthinkable. It was a wonder she hadn't organised a search party herself.

She answered on the second ring. He imagined her in her neat New York apartment, cool, collected, part of his ordered business world, but there was nothing ordered about the way she answered. 'Where the hell have you been?'

He explained but she hardly listened.

'Well, thank heaven you're okay,' she said, interjecting over his last words. 'But, Matt...something's happened. We've located Henry's father. Steven Walker. You know you asked me to keep looking? After you left I thought of searching through Amanda's client files from eight years ago, just on a hunch. And there he was. Of course, I wasn't sure—how many Steven Walkers do you think there are in the States? But on the off chance I took the liberty of ringing, ostensibly to let him know his lawyer had died and to check there was nothing outstanding we needed to cover. And at the end...I ventured. I sort of casually dropped that Amanda had a seven-year-old son. Matt, there was a silence on the end of the phone, almost like he expected what was coming. So I went for it. I said the father's name on the birth certificate was Steven Walker and we hadn't been able to find him. Could that possibly be him?'

And then Helen hesitated, seeming to gather herself for what needed to be said next.

'And then he said yes, it could. He was almost cool about it, maybe as if he'd suspected. He asked what was happening with Henry. I told him and he thanked me and disconnected. He went away and obviously did some investigation. A few hours later he phoned back. He has a family of his own—actually children from three marriages. He says he'll want a DNA test but as long as that proves positive he'll accept responsibility.'

'That's…good,' Matt said cautiously.

'Maybe,' Helen told him. 'But there's more. He says it depends on the DNA result, but if it's positive…he says he's damned if he's letting a son of his live on some forsaken island in the middle of nowhere. He's wealthy. He sounds sensible but he also sounds tough. He says he'll provide housing, a nanny, "anything the kid needs", but he has to come home. Matt, I've done some preliminary investigation and checked with a couple of the other lawyers here. As the named father, he'll have priority over Henry's grandmother, even if there is a custody dispute. I don't know where that leaves you, Matt, but the lawyers in the office say you'll need to bring Henry back.'

Henry fell asleep before he finished his apple pie. He'd had a huge day. He had his grandma and his teddy, he had the dogs and he had Matt. Life was okay. Did Matt realise just how much Henry adored him? Meg wondered as Matt lifted the little boy and carried him to his bedroom.

And did Matt know how much he'd become attached to Henry? She'd watched him watching the child and she thought, for all his talk of detachment, the bond tied both ways.

And Peggy was bonded with Henry, too. She was exhausted, she'd coped with a helicopter flight that had clearly terrified her, but she'd spent the remainder of the afternoon making sure Henry was happy. She'd abandoned her beloved island for him. She was sitting cradling her mug of tea now, but the look on her face was almost peaceful. Her grandson was safe.

There was no doubt Henry was loved.

And then Matt returned and Meg glanced at his face

and saw there was more to come. He'd seemed preoccupied since he'd made his phone calls. He'd asked to use her computer, the internet, and he'd locked himself in her messy excuse for a study until dinner time. She'd thought, of course, he'd have to catch up on business.

Now, though…she turned from the sink and saw his face and knew it was more than business.

'I need to talk to you both,' he said, and she glanced at Peggy and saw the elderly woman brace. As if she, too, knew instinctively that something bad was coming.

Meg poured more tea for them all, slowly, sensing somehow they needed space for what was coming. And then they all sat down at her battered wooden table and Matt told them what Helen had told him. And what he'd learned.

He'd made the call to Steven Walker. Yes, he'd rung him at one in the morning but, dammit, this was his son. This was his kid's life. So he'd rung and found Steven had been doing his own investigation. He'd researched where Henry had been taken and he'd been horrified. He'd faced the options, he'd accepted responsibility and he'd made a decision.

'He doesn't necessarily want custody,' he told them. 'Although he'll accept it if necessary. He has kids from three relationships. He hardly wants more, but he sounds inherently decent. He had a relationship with Amanda that lasted for six months and then she broke it off and demanded he find himself another investment lawyer. He said she broke it off so abruptly he wondered why, and now he thinks maybe he was used. He's pretty angry about it but if the DNA test proves positive he wants Henry back in the US.'

'But—' Peggy was staring at him, appalled '—Henry doesn't even know him. He doesn't even know he exists.'

'That's not Steven's fault,' Matt said gently. 'Peggy, he sounds reasonable.'

'It's not reasonable to take him away from me.'

'Henry's an American citizen with an American father,' Matt told her. 'Steven says if he'd known about him he would have interjected well before this. I'm sorry, Peggy, but he says he'll apply to the courts if necessary. If the DNA test proves positive—and he believes it will—then Henry has to come home.'

'To live with him?'

'He doesn't necessarily want that, although he'll provide it if necessary. He'll provide accommodation, a nanny, boarding-school fees...'

'No!' Meg spoke before she could stop herself. 'He's better off here. With his gran. With me.'

'I don't think that can happen,' Matt said, still gently. 'Steven's named on the birth certificate. Henry hasn't been living with Peggy so there's no established alternative. That Amanda didn't tell him of Henry's existence doesn't make a difference to his rights now. We need to face it. I believe I'll have to take him back. Peggy, you might be able to persuade him to let you keep custody, but that argument will have to happen over there.'

Peggy's face was ashen. 'I won't let Henry go. I can't. And there's nowhere in the States I can go.'

'I've thought of that, too.'

Meg stared at him. His voice was calm, controlled, the complete opposite to the panic both she and Peggy were feeling. He'd had hours to think this through, she thought. He'd come to terms with it, and Henry was a colleague's child, nothing more. He was nothing to do with him.

And then she thought of the look on his face when he'd lifted a sleepy Henry and carried him to his bed. She thought, *No, Henry's much more.*

And his next words confirmed it.

'I have a plan,' he said, and she saw Peggy's look of despair take a tiny step back.

'A plan... So I can keep him.'

'I know you love him,' Matt said. 'And I also know you're an American citizen, as well. Your marriage gave you that. Steven's talking about setting up a home with a nanny, so why don't we simply arrange that for him? Make it easy for him to agree? What I'm proposing is that you swap Meg's beachside home for my beachside home.'

Peggy stared at him, wildly. 'What…? What…?'

And Meg thought, *What is he saying?*

'It's not so different,' Matt said, calmly now, as if he were talking about choices for what was for dinner. 'Meg offered you a home with her, and you accepted.'

'I want to live here,' Peggy said almost defiantly. 'We could be happy here.'

'And you could be happy at my house in the Hamptons. It's big, it has a great garden and it's right on the beach. There's a community there Henry could be part of. You've been on an island for years so you'd be less isolated there than you have been, but you could still have your privacy. There's fishing, boating, the ocean. I work in the city but I could come down at weekends to make sure things are okay, and yes, to see Henry because, to be honest, I've grown fond of him. His father could see him, too. And, Peggy, once you're in the States…the custody thing… Henry's kept all the letters you've ever sent him. He'll tell any court that you've rung him, that you've written, that you've been in contact with him all his life. If he's living safely in the States with his grandma, with me, I doubt Steven will even fight you for it. What he's doing is what he thinks is the right thing for a child he feels responsible for. Let's make it easy for him. Come and live with me.'

'You won't be there.' She seemed…gobsmacked. Too much was happening, too fast.

'I'll be in Manhattan working but I can be there often at weekends. And I'll always be in touch. I can be with you in a couple of hours if you need me.'

'But I don't know anything about you.' Once more Peggy's voice rose in a wail. 'I know nothing about this place you say we could live in. How do I know…anything?'

'Come and see.'

'I won't fly.' The panic in her voice was real and dreadful. 'Not again. Half an hour was awful. How can I do more? I can't take him. I won't.'

'Peggy, slow down and think.' Matt's voice seemed like that of someone accustomed to providing reason in the midst of crisis. 'My house can provide you with a wonderful beachside place to live, with as much privacy as you want, with the fishing and beachcombing you love and, most of all, with a solid, secure home for you and for Henry. Is there any reason why my home's any less of an option than Meg's?'

'But I know Rowan Bay,' Peggy wailed. 'And I know Meg. At least…I knew her grandmother. I'm going on trust.'

'Then I'm asking for you to trust me. For Henry's sake.'

Peggy was crying now, tears slipping down her wrinkled face. It was so unfair to land this on her. 'I can't. I won't fly. I won't.'

'Peggy, you don't need to fly tomorrow,' he said. 'Henry's been through enough and this isn't urgent. We need to get the DNA sorted and, as I said, Steven's reasonable. He's relieved Henry's off the island and he'll give us time. But I believe we need to face the fact that there's little choice.'

'There is,' Peggy said wildly, and she turned to Meg. 'You go.'

'What?' Meg stared at her, taken aback.

'I shouldn't ask you,' Peggy said. 'After all you've done for us. But I know you, or I feel like I know you. You're a Rowan Bay girl. You're a loner, the same as me. You love the sea and dogs and I know you care for Henry. I can see it. So you go. Go back with him. I'll stay here, care for Henry, let us both get our breath back. You go to this place he's talking about. If you think it's a place Henry and I can live then I'll…I'll get on a boat. There must be ships that'll take us there.'

'I can't move to America,' Meg said, stunned.

'I'm not asking you to,' Peggy said, swiping away tears, and Meg saw a hint of stubbornness, the inexorable strength that had let her live on a solitary island for all these years. 'You check it out and come back and tell me. If it's really, truly okay, then we can go.' She blinked away the rest of her tears and suddenly looked hopeful. 'Is that a plan? Meg? Would that work?'

She was going to America.

How had that happened?

Fast, that was how. She'd seen Peggy backed into a corner and she'd promised. Now Matt was on the internet, emailing Steven, and she was sitting on the deck overlooking the bay thinking what had she done?

The door opened behind her. She heard Matt's footsteps.

She didn't look up.

'Can I have half a step?'

She moved over, but grudgingly, not the least bit sure she wanted him sitting beside her.

She needed time to work things out. To figure what exactly she'd promised.

'Done,' he said gently and she flinched. Done what?

'You want to tell me?'

He cast her an amused glance. 'You think I'm being bossy?'

'You and Peggy… Organising my life… Yes, I think you're being bossy.'

'Everything's tentative,' he said. 'I've made plans but they can be changed if you want to pull out.'

'Like I can pull out. I'm heading to the States to do what? A real estate inspection?'

'You promised Peggy,' he said gently. 'I'll cover all costs. I'll make it right with Charlie, and, let's face it, it'll be a sight easier than having Peggy and Henry living with you for years.'

She turned to him then, incredulous. 'Is that what you think? That I want to be rid of them?'

'They're strangers.'

'They need me.'

'They're not your family.'

'No, but they could be.' And then she heard what she'd said. She heard the raw need that had suddenly surfaced and she bit her lip and turned away.

'Is that what you want?' Matt said, sounding puzzled. 'Family?'

'I wouldn't mind.' Why not say it? This house had echoed with emptiness since Grandpa had died. Even though her offer might have seemed generous, there'd been a part of her that had thought living with Peggy and her grandson might even be fun.

And he'd heard it. She could see it on his face. The porch light combined with the moonlight let her see him as clearly as he saw her. It let her see the gravity of his expression, those intelligent, searching eyes that seemed to see…more than she'd let on.

But did he see, she wondered, just how confined her circumstances had made her? A lifetime of caring had her trapped in a job, in a lifestyle she'd had no choice in. At twenty-eight, she'd spent her life fishing and caring, hardly moving from the confines of Rowan Bay. Now, deep in debt, she had little choice but to continue that lifestyle. She could clear her debt—just—by selling the house, but where did that leave her? She'd have nowhere to live, no career.

To have Peggy and Henry live with her… To have someone to come home to…

Oh, for heaven's sake, that made her feel needy. And vulnerable. She was neither of those things. She was tough as old boots. She'd heard Charlie describe her as such and she fought for that now. Meg O'Hara, the tough one.

But maybe Matt was seeing under the surface. Maybe he guessed.

'So here's a proposition,' he told her. 'While I've been on the phone to Steven I've been turning things over, looking at problems, searching for solutions. And, Meg, it might seem crazy but I have another proposition.'

'What?' It was hardly a graceful or grateful response but it was all she could come up with.

'Let's do what Peggy suggests,' he said. 'As soon as the DNA connection's confirmed, as soon as your cough's settled, let's you and me get on a plane and head back to the States. You can check out the house, look at it from all angles, think about it. But, Meg, maybe you could also look at it for you, too. Peggy's just a little bit…vague…and in a strange setting it might be worse. I'd like someone to take care of them. That person could be you.'

'Me…'

'They won't need all that much care,' he said hastily, as if trying to explain before she could refuse. 'Henry will be at school and Peggy will want to be independent. But it's a great place to live. If you wanted…there are charter companies down there, a lot less dodgy than Charlie's. You could get work with them. You could garden. You could fish. You could…' He hesitated. 'You could love Henry.'

'So you wouldn't have to?' It was out before she could stop it.

'I do love Henry.' He paused for a long moment and when he spoke again his voice had changed. 'I didn't know it for a while, but finally I'm starting to figure it out. Meg, my childhood's been bleak, solitary, not quite as bad as Henry's but almost. I don't…get close to people. I thought I was bringing him here to do him a favour but he's been

sitting in the corner of my office for years. He's become…
Yeah, I concede, he's become part of my life. Today, on
the chopper coming back here, I watched his face, I could
see the excitement. I could see the transformation. And
I looked around and saw you watching him. Caring for
him. I saw Peggy overcoming her terror of flying to be
with him. And then I thought, you know what, I want to
be in that equation, too. To love a kid… Surely that's a
privilege.'

'I guess it is.' Her words were a bit shaky. Wary. She
wasn't sure where this was going.

'And then I talked to Steven. His response was guarded
but it was definite. If this was his kid then he was ready to
do whatever it took to keep him safe. But then I thought,
I hate it that he has the right and I don't.'

'He has the right to provide boarding schools and
nannies…'

'That's what he's offering,' he said strongly. 'That's what
I'm trying to prevent. Steven doesn't know him. Henry
needs more than that.'

'So you're offering Peggy your home.'

'I am,' he said, strongly now. 'I believe a court could well
come down on Peggy's side if she's settled over there. But,
Meg, if Steven contests it, they might demand even more.
An old lady… Me at weekends… It might not be enough.'
He hesitated. 'Meg, if you come…there's more to my list
of things that you might do.'

'Housekeeper?' she said astringently. 'I can't see that
as a job description.'

'It wouldn't work,' he agreed. 'I can't see you changing careers to wash floors, and I already have a perfectly
good housekeeper. And I've been thinking of problems.
But there's another position going vacant.'

'You've said there are boat charter companies. Garden?
Fish? What else could I do? And what problems?'

'There'll be visa restrictions,' he conceded. 'You might

not be able to stay long term. But, if you were to come…if you were to see there could be a life there for you… I have this idea. It sounds crazy but I want you to think about it. It could be the solution to all our problems.'

'Which is?' To say she felt wary was an understatement. A huge understatement.

And she was right to be wary because his next statement floored her.

'Think this through,' he said, urgently now because maybe he could see by the expression on her face that she was already suspecting him of something dire. And here it came. 'Meg, I'm in the market for a wife and I think that wife could be you.'

CHAPTER TEN

IT WAS CLEARLY the most ridiculous thing she'd ever heard of.

She stared at him in astonishment, then rose and stared at him some more.

'Right,' she said at last, obviously deciding the whole proposition was ludicrous and acting accordingly. 'Did you take another of those travel sickness pills before the chopper ride? In rare cases they can cause hallucinations, so I'll give you the benefit of the doubt. I'll leave you to get over it. Goodnight, Matt.'

And she walked inside—or maybe bolted inside might be a better description. But then she closed the door carefully behind her, as if a sudden bang might unsettle a disordered mind even more.

Leaving him staring into the dark, unable to follow up with his very reasonable…reasoning.

What had he just said?

He didn't even know how the idea had come to him. He'd been thinking through the visa options and marriage had just appeared. Like a light bulb being turned on.

Meg didn't seem to think it was a light bulb. To her it was nuts.

Maybe he shouldn't have sprung it on her quite so soon.

Yeah. He knew that was right, but the more he thought about it, the more it seemed…reasonable?

Marriage had always been there, in the back of his mind, as an option he'd get to sooner or later. Probably later. He'd met some amazing women but there'd never been a woman he wanted to wake up beside, morning after morning.

To share his life with.

To be honest, he wasn't thinking of sharing his life now. He never had. Solitude had been his way of life for so long he couldn't imagine himself changing.

But now he had a vision in his head that refused to go away.

The big house at the Hamptons was a house he'd always loved. As a kid it had seemed magic.

Once upon a time his grandparents had employed a gardener, Peter, a gentle guy with a limp and a smile and five kids. Matt's nanny had liked Peter and she'd liked Peter's kids, so Matt remembered a couple of school breaks where the house had come alive with adventure, noise, chaos.

Matt's mother had finally arrived midbreak and put an abrupt end to it, but Matt still remembered that feeling of…home.

He was thinking of it now. A house with Peggy and Henry and Stretchie and Boof.

And Meg.

A family to come home to.

He saw himself arriving from Manhattan and being swept up in family, dogs, laughter.

And Meg's smile.

Meg.

There was the siren call.

It was too soon. Far too soon to think about marriage. He'd known her for less than a week.

But part of him didn't think it was ludicrous. To part of him it was making complete sense.

He'd terrified her with his impulsive proposal. He needed to give her space now, but he was hopeful. Calm thought would surely show her what could be good for them all. Yes, a major proposition as marriage needed to be considered from every angle. But it was sensible. Wasn't it?

He rose and stared out into the night and the more he thought about it, the more reasonable it seemed. Here, Meg had a lousy job and a load of debt. She'd admitted she was lonely. She'd opened her home to Peggy and Henry, and he could tell she was already opening her heart.

To him?

There was the rub. He didn't have a clue how she felt about him. But she'd admitted she also felt this…thing between them, this frisson of electricity that honestly he'd never felt before. Maybe it was because she was so far out of his orbit, almost another species from the glamorous women in his professional world. Or maybe it was the way she comforted Henry, she offered her home without a thought, the way Peggy instinctively trusted her.

Maybe it was the way Matt instinctively trusted her.

The way he wanted her.

And there was the bottom line, he thought, honesty surfacing. The idea of having a ready-made family at weekends was appealing. The idea of finding Meg in his bed was even more so.

'Yeah, back off,' he told himself. 'Let's put this as a proposition of sense, not of need.'

Need… There was an interesting word. It hovered uncertainly in his mind.

He didn't need anyone. He'd learned that a long time ago. So why did he hope…?

'Because of Henry,' he said out loud but Meg was there, front and foremost, and he knew he was a liar.

She lay in the dark in the bed she'd slept in for ever. She stared up at nothing in particular and she thought, *Matt just asked me to marry him.*

Just like that. Marriage.

She'd known him for how long? The man was clearly deluded.

Except he wasn't. The man was beautiful.

Was that a weird way to describe a guy? Maybe it was, but it was how she was starting to think of him. Physically he was gorgeous but that was only the start of it. The way he smiled at her... The way he held Henry... The way he cared... The way he'd held her back on the island...

The feel of his kiss...

Block that out, she told herself. Passion has nothing to do with sensible life decisions.

What he was suggesting was so far from sensible it was unthinkable.

Or was it?

Marriage to a guy she'd known for less than a week? How could that make sense?

But if it ended up being a feasible solution...

Suddenly she found herself drifting into the possibilities of maybe. What if?

This was fairy-tale stuff. A kid who left school at sixteen and caught fish for a living marrying a billionaire?

It was nonsense, but what if?

It'd be a Cinderella scenario, she told herself, and the story of Cinderella had always left her uneasy. What happened when the credits faded, the happy-ever-after disappeared from the screen and Cinders was left with an idle life in a world she wasn't born to?

But if she did let herself climb aboard that pumpkin coach... If she let herself be cared for by one Matt McLellan...

She didn't need to be cared for by anyone, she told herself. She was twenty-eight, independent, solid and... tough as old boots?

She was stuck in a lifestyle that was starting to feel more restrictive than an overtight corset. She was facing a life of either living in Rowan Bay while she paid down her debt or trying to make a living somewhere else. With what skills?

She thought of what she was doing now, taking parties of amateur fishermen out to sea, coping with seasickness, drunkenness, then crates of fish to be gutted because cleaning their fish was incorporated into the charter.

She didn't mind it too much. It was a living. But the

thought of Peggy and Henry living with her had offered a sliver of how things might be. Of a life less lonely. That sliver had gone now, except Matt had offered an alternative.

A voice was suddenly whispering in the back of her mind. She could just see. She didn't have to commit. Cinders had fallen into her prince's arms and the deed had been done, but it didn't have to be like that. Could she go to the States, do Peggy's real estate inspection, just try?

She heard Matt's footsteps coming down the hall, heading to the bedroom she'd designated for him. And suddenly a decision was made. Without giving herself time to think, she was out of bed, opening the door. 'Matt?'

He was right by her door. Close. Large.

The passage footlight was on, shining upward.

He was beautiful. He was right…there.

'Meg.' He sounded wary.

'It's an off-the-wall idea,' she said.

'It is,' he agreed. 'But it's just an idea.'

'We couldn't possibly agree to such a thing unless we got to know each other better.'

'I agree.'

It was a weird scenario. She was standing barefooted, clad in her flimsy nightgown. He was fully dressed in his new clothes, shaved now, contained, watchful.

Gorgeous.

She should back away.

She wasn't backing. This was the mature version of Cinderella, she told herself. She was twenty-eight and she was going for it.

'Matt?'

'Mmm?' He wasn't sure where to take this, she thought. He'd made the proposition and now…was he having second thoughts?

'You really are proposing marriage?'

'I'm saying we could think about it.'

'So I'm thinking.'

'That's good.'

'Matt…'

'Mmm?'

'You know when we stopped at the pharmacy for steroids for my cough?'

'I… Yes.'

'I didn't just buy steroids.'

'I see.' And suddenly the wariness was being edged out by laughter. 'You, too?'

'What do you mean, you, too?'

'Because while you were in the back waiting for your prescription to be filled, I was making my own purchase.'

'Oh.' She couldn't think what to say—or do—next.

'So now we seem to be equipped,' he said. 'Just in case.'

'I'm not agreeing to marriage. That'd be nuts.'

'It surely would. But getting to know each other better…' His hands came out and cupped her face. 'Meg, that'd be sensible.'

She didn't seem sensible. She seemed as if she were floating.

The feel of his hands… The warmth of his voice…

Oh, Cinders, she thought. *You might have been an idiot but I'm starting to figure you had no choice.*

'I won't pressure you,' Matt said, his voice serious again, and she found herself smiling.

'Suit yourself, Matt McLellan,' she told him. 'Because I believe I'm about to pressure you. You can't make a woman a proposition like that and then go calmly to bed.'

'I think I can,' he told her, and then, suddenly, his hands dropped from her face, his arms scooped under her, and she was lifted, held against him, and his laughter was all around them. Not out loud. Just there. Laughter and…love? 'I think I can,' he said again. 'It's just a matter of whose bed we go calmly to.'

'Forget the calm,' she managed. 'And your bed because it's bigger.'

* * *

It was a week before the results of Henry's DNA testing came through and it was a magic week.

Matt should be back in Manhattan. There was need for him to return but somehow the need to stay was greater.

It wasn't spoken pressure, though. For Matt it was the way Henry's eyes lit when he entered a room, the way Henry tentatively asked him if he could fish, the way he offered to show him what Meg had taught him.

It was the way Peggy deferred to him, depended on him, questioned him endlessly about what would happen. The way her voice wobbled as she bravely accepted her world had changed.

It was the way the two dogs bonded, tearing around the house like crazy things, annoying the chickens, bouncing as if the world was their constant delight.

But mostly it was the way Meg smiled at him. It was the way she folded into his body at night. The rightness of it.

The way her shabby, down-at-heel house felt like home.

Home seemed an insidious word, but more and more it centred around Meg. They didn't speak of marriage again—she backed away if he raised it and maybe she was right. No decision needed to be made yet. But suddenly Manhattan didn't seem as pressing. Staying with this makeshift family, being part of it, feeling as if he was making a difference in keeping Henry happy, in reassuring Peggy, in helping slash grass, collecting eggs, repairing a fence…

Lying with Meg. Feeling her curve against him. Being part of her.

Yes, it felt like home and when the results of the DNA came through—positive, as they'd all expected—he was even sorry.

But his plan meant this didn't end. It simply moved.

First things first—take Meg to McLellan Place. Show her how life could be.

Show her how a plan could become reality.

CHAPTER ELEVEN

IT WAS MEG'S first time in a plane and it left her stunned. Her bed, her seat, the service were all great. Her first-class pyjamas were pretty much the nicest pyjamas she'd ever worn and apparently she could keep them. She should be enjoying the whole experience.

She was lonely.

What had she expected? Maybe that they'd talk? Watch movies together? Just…share this fantastic experience.

Whatever, it wasn't happening. It was as if a switch had been flicked the moment Matt had stepped into the plane. 'Work's overwhelming,' he told her apologetically. 'I need to get a handle on what's happening before I land.'

A plane was obviously a place where he was accustomed to working. He surfaced for meals, he slept briefly, but for most of the time he used the plane's internet and 'got his handle'.

She peeked out of the windows—blinds were pulled because they messed with the screens of Matt and the other seasoned travellers around her—and marvelled at the world beneath her.

And wondered more and more what she was getting herself into.

Marriage? The idea was seeming more and more like a pipe dream. Every time she looked, Matt seemed a world away, deep in his life of high finance.

He'd been dramatically pulled from work, she told herself as the long plane trip finally reached its end. Maybe she needed to cut him some slack.

'We'll go straight down to McLellan Place,' Matt told her as they landed. 'I'm needed in the city but Peggy will be eager to hear from you. McLellan Place is where I hope you can all live.'

'Where Peggy and Henry can live,' she retorted. 'There's no *me* in this equation yet.'

'I hope I can persuade you otherwise.'

'Matt—'

'Wait and see,' he said simply, so she shut up as they were streamlined through the airport, then as a chauffeured car drove them through the city, toward the increasingly beautiful country to his beachside home.

But once again Matt wasn't with her. For most of the journey he was on the phone. 'Now I'm back I need to re-schedule urgent meetings.'

'You're going to dump me and run?'

'I'll spend tonight and maybe tomorrow with you and then maybe you can come back to Manhattan with me. I have an apartment there. You'll get to see the whole package.'

She fell silent, doubts crowding in from all sides.

Peggy and Henry were back in Rowan Bay, fishing, exploring, making themselves at home, giving themselves time to get to know each other and come to terms with their shared grief. Maureen had promised to keep an eye on them, which would involve at least half a dozen visits a day. Boof remained with them, as did Stretchie. 'We're going to check out a for-ever home for you,' Matt had told Henry, and Meg knew Henry was beginning to feel safe enough to be left.

Meg, on the other hand, wasn't feeling the least bit safe. In fact she was feeling so unsafe that, when they finally pulled up before the magnificent gates of McLellan Place, it was as much as she could do not to bolt.

There was a house just inside the gates, but the car didn't even slow. 'That's the gatehouse,' Matt said, dismissively.

'Right,' she said faintly, looking at the house that was far bigger and grander than hers. 'For what, someone to live in while they open and shut the gates?'

'The gates work automatically now. Our head gardener lives there.'

Head gardener. Right.

She had no more questions.

The driveway seemed to stretch for ever, meandering through private woods, then opening to gardens that welcomed them in. And finally she saw the house, long, low, gracious…mellowed with age. She counted five gables, two together and then three, with a vast stretch of what looked like a pavilion in between. An enormous vine—wisteria?—ran the entire length of the gables, its drooping autumnal leaves accentuating the gold hue of magnificent stone steps.

It looked like something Meg had seen in magazines in doctors' waiting rooms. Not in real life.

'You don't really live here,' she breathed.

'Mostly I live in Manhattan.'

'Then who…?'

'It stays pretty much empty,' he told her. 'My great-grandparents used it for entertaining, as did my grandparents. My parents never liked the seclusion so they planned to sell but the seclusion suits me. I bought it from them ten years ago.'

'You bought it from your parents…' She was struggling to get her head around the dynamics of his family. Of this place. Of wealth beyond her comprehension.

'I was sent here most holidays,' he said. 'I've grown fond of it.'

'I could grow fond of the gatehouse,' she said frankly. 'To grow fond of this house…'

'You don't like it?'

'It's like a palace.' She turned to him, feeling totally confused. *Bewildered* wasn't a big enough word. 'Matt, why on earth would you want to marry me?'

There was silence at that. The car had pulled to a halt in the vast circular driveway. The driver opened the doors for them to alight and occupied himself taking their luggage into the house. Meg could see a woman—a housekeeper?—ushering him in.

What nonsense was this? With this amount of wealth, with these supports, Peggy and Henry would be safe for ever. They certainly didn't need her.

'Meg, it's just a house,' Matt said. 'If you came, you'd make it a home.'

Home.

She thought of home as she'd known it, before the accident, before loss and grief had robbed it of its heart. Her parents and grandparents had made her house a home.

She glanced back toward the vast gates that had seamlessly closed behind them. They were so far away she could no longer see them.

She shivered.

'Give it a chance,' Matt told her. 'Didn't your parents tell you not to judge on appearances?'

'Their vision of appearances didn't stretch to this,' she breathed. 'This is movie stuff.'

'This is home.'

'Here? By yourself?'

'I hope not,' he said seriously and took her face in his hands and kissed her. 'We could be happy here, Meg.'

'Could we?'

She was shown to her bedroom—sumptuous enough to make her gasp. The housekeeper who'd greeted them formally, but who'd disappeared almost the moment they'd arrived, had said lunch would be at twelve. Meg showered and changed into her best trousers and shirt and she still felt…not dirty, just small. Then she made her way cautiously back to the dining room. Taking in the house as she went.

The living rooms and bedrooms, the gleaming bathrooms, the windows leading out to the sea without a trace of salt on them, the acres of lawn and garden…there must be an army of 'housekeepers' keeping this place functioning.

To say she was unnerved was an understatement.

Matt was on the phone when she reached the dining room. He raised his brows in apology and waved to the table.

She sat and she felt smaller. This table was ridiculously big.

Matt finally finished his call.

'Is everything okay? Is your bedroom comfortable?' he asked.

Of all the questions to ask. She had eight—eight!— pillows to choose from. How could she not be comfortable?

She ate the most beautiful salmon salad she'd ever tasted in her life. There were tiny lemon meringues for desert. And grapes. And wine.

She very carefully didn't touch the wine.

'Jet lag,' she said when Matt offered to fill her glass and he raised his brows.

'You slept on the plane. Under a down duvet. With three pillows.'

'That was because I couldn't choose from the pillow menu. I can't choose here.' She stared at him in bewilderment. 'Matt, with all this, you could have any wife you wanted.'

'I want you.'

'How can you want me? I'm a nothing.'

'How can you say you're a nothing? You're everything I've ever wanted in a partner. Brave, beautiful, smart, funny, independent…'

'Is it the independent thing that makes me suitable?' she ventured. The loneliness thing was starting to get to her.

'I don't want a wife who clings, if that's what you mean.'

'I don't cling. But if I needed to cling…'

'I'd be there for you.' And his voice—and his expression— said he was serious.

'Don't do that.' She was starting to recover. The feistiness she seemed to have been born with—or the feistiness she'd developed almost as a shield as she'd struggled to survive by fishing in a mostly guys' world—was coming to her aid. 'Matt, there is this…thing between us but it's called lust. We've been thrown into each other's company in a weird way and it's messed with your judgement.'

'My judgement's never let me down in the past.'

'Well, it might have let you down now. Especially if you've judged that Peggy and Henry could be happy here. They'd…I don't know…wallow.'

'Wallow?'

'Lose each other. Echo. This place is vast.'

'It doesn't need to be vast. There's a guest wing at the end I thought they could use, two bedrooms with a sitting room between. It's cosy.'

'I don't know if I agree with your definition of *cosy*.'

'And there's the sea. If you've finished your meringues…'

'I might never finish these meringues,' she admitted. The one she was currently attending was a perfect crisp shell, cracking to reveal a marshmallow centre and at its heart a scoop of the most delicious lemon curd she'd ever tasted. There were still ten…twelve…on the plate. 'If I don't eat them will they be fed to the compost?'

'I have no idea,' he said faintly.

'Really?' She took another, almost defensively.

'I'll give orders that they're to be served at supper, as well.'

'You're kidding. You'll give orders…'

'I'll ask nicely. My staff are accommodating.'

'I bet they are.' She shook her head. 'Matt, this place is out of this world.'

'It's special,' he agreed. 'I need to show you the beach. Would you like a swim?'

'A swim.' She considered. She glanced out of the dining room window at the outside pool, then across to what looked like a vast pond, and, in the distance, the beach.

'The house pool is heated but the beach is better. I know it's autumn but the water shouldn't be too cold. Not after the water you're used to.'

She finished her meringue and tried very hard not to be seduced by the zing of lemon, by the soft marshmallow, by the crisp outer shell... By the smile of the man watching her from the other side of the table. Who'd spent almost all of the last twenty-four hours on his laptop or on his phone.

'Will you come with me?'

'Yes.'

'Will you bring your phone?'

He glanced at his phone, lying on the table beside him, and then he looked at her. Decision time?

'I won't,' he said. Supreme sacrifice? 'We can walk to the beach or we can take the boat.'

'I'd like to walk,' she told him.

They walked around the cultivated shore path that bordered the pond and led to the sea. The path was a thing of beauty on its own, Meg thought, with coastal grasses, trees seemingly sculpted by the winds, vast rocks scattered as if the sea had thrown them there. It was only her knowledge of true wild seascapes that told her this was landscaping brilliance.

She'd donned her bathing gear under her jeans and T-shirt. She was a guest of Matt and she was heading for a swim. There was no reason why her knees were shaking.

It's jet lag, she told herself, but she knew it was no such thing.

'It's gorgeous,' she managed. She'd been walking for ten minutes with Matt striding silently beside her and she needed to say something. Anything.

'It is.' And she could hear the pride in his voice.

'That one man could own this... And hardly share...'

'I am offering to share,' he told her. 'That's why you're here.'

She shut up again.

And then they reached the beach and her world seemed to settle.

It was always like this. As a child she remembered getting home from school and racing down to the beach. Sometimes she'd swim or walk one of the legion of O'Hara dogs. But often she'd just sit, doodling in the sand, savouring the feel of the sun on her face…or simply being. The wash of the waves, the immensity of the ocean, the timelessness, soothed something inside her so deep, so intrinsic that she knew she could never leave the ocean.

That was why she couldn't sell her grandparents' house and walk away from her debts. Where else could she be by the ocean every day of her life? In the city, maybe, or a decent-sized tourist town? Sure, she could rent herself a bedsit, make herself a life. She could walk on the beach with other tourists.

It was totally selfish, this feeling that the ocean was hers.

'You love it, don't you?' Matt asked gently, and she could only nod.

She expected him to continue. She expected more pressure. Instead he said simply, 'Swim?'

And he kicked off his shoes, tugged off his shirt and trousers and headed for the sea.

She stayed for a moment, watching. He walked straight in and then dived. The waves here were small, the cove protected by two headlands. There was no sign of anyone, of anything. A private beach? She'd heard of such places.

Did he own all this?

He'd disappeared, sleek, smooth, sliding underwater, only the faintest break in the surface occurring when he needed to breathe.

She could see seagrasses from here. A sheltered rocky cove… It'd be home for so much.

What was she doing, standing gawping at a guy like Matt when she could be checking out seagrasses?

She gave herself a mental shake—which kind of didn't work because she was still thinking of Matt, of his gorgeous body, of the way he'd slid into that wave as if he'd been born to the sea…

But she had to ignore it. There was a whole new ocean world to explore.

And Matt McLellan was surely only an incidental part.

He had his life sorted. She just had to see it.

From the moment the idea had come into his head, there'd been not a single doubt that this was the right decision. Matt McLellan was known for decisiveness. It had never let him down in the past and it wasn't letting him down now. The path he saw in front of him was perfect.

He'd grown fond—okay, very fond—of the little boy who'd sat in his office, who'd spent so much time with him. The thought of Henry being an 'extra child' to a father who'd sounded responsible on the phone but not emotionally involved left him cold. Henry needed a family.

More than that, Peggy needed a home, and in the days since he'd met her he'd grown to like her. She loved her little grandson.

But Henry needed more. He needed a Meg. A woman who cared, who'd take over the reins as Peggy grew older. The three of them would love McLellan Place. It'd come to life again.

And Meg would be here.

That was the part of the equation that wasn't so straightforward. For her to stay seemed a viable solution to her problems and to his need to have someone here for Peggy and Henry. And yet it was much more than that.

He had to give her space. In business deals he knew when too much pressure threatened a deal and he could sense it now.

But hell, he wanted to pressure. Because this was perfect.

Meg was perfect?

A fisherwoman from Australia, wife to the heir to the McLellan fortune? His mother would have forty fits.

But at a deeper level his mother wouldn't care. Since when had she ever cared?

Meg would care. That was the thing. From the moment he'd met her, he'd known that caring was Meg's special skill. Her warmth, her humour, her passion... The generosity of her lovemaking. The way she held him...

That was the thing that had somehow slipped under his skin, into his heart? She smiled at him and he thought she didn't give a toss about who he was, how much he owned, what his family represented. She was simply Meg, holding Matt.

A huge part of him was telling him to march back up the beach right now, sweep her into his arms and carry her back to the house. Hold her. Claim her.

What was he, a Neanderthal? But that was how she made him feel, and when he saw her slip into the water to be with him, the urge was so great it took every ounce of his self-control to keep swimming.

The seagrasses here had held him fascinated for years and they should hold him fascinated now. They changed every time he visited. His attention should be on them because turning and taking Meg into his arms was *not* on the agenda.

Luckily, once he motioned to the grasses, she turned her attention downward.

She swam as well as he did—maybe better. Snorkels and masks would be good. He should have brought them with him, but yeah, he'd been distracted. Luckily Meg didn't seem to need them. She was using her arms to sweep forward underwater. Her copper curls wisped around her face. Her body, lithe, slim, beautiful in a simple black bathing costume, was entrancing.

And then she saw the turtles. Her arms stilled. She floated forward and he thought, *She has to breathe sometime...*

Usually the turtles held him entranced. These were little more than hatchlings, floating over and through the rafts of seagrasses, feeding on the tiny sea creatures or on the grass itself.

He'd seen them first when he was about the same age as Henry. They were almost unheard of at this latitude, but the protection of the bay and the warmth of the currents seemed to provide a haven where they flourished. They'd always held him entranced.

As they held Meg entranced. She floated, breathing only when she had to.

He remembered the last woman he'd brought here. Lauren was a high-flying lawyer, whip-smart, with an acerbic wit he found incredibly sexy. She was also beautiful. They'd dated for six months and he'd fleetingly thought maybe they could take things further.

But then he'd brought her here for a week's break.

He'd brought her to this beach and shown her the hatchlings. *How sweet*, she'd said, but she'd headed back to the beach almost straight away. *I'm not wasting tanning time on turtles, sweet as they are.*

Back at the house she'd explored the empty rooms and said, *Why don't we invite...?*

In comparison, Meg looked as if she could float for hours. It had to be Matt who finally broke the moment. He had business calls to make—of course. Promise or not, business called.

'I need to get back to the house,' he said as they trod water and Meg smiled happily at him.

'That's okay. You go back. I'll come when I'm ready.'

That was another eye-opener. What woman had ever said something like that to him?

She was independent. He liked that.

He needed that.

'But tell me about the turtles first,' she begged. 'Are

they Kemp's ridley?' Had she recognised the distinctive heart-shaped shell?

'They are.'

'These are practically hatchlings. Is this a nesting site? I thought the only nesting sites were in Mexico.'

She really did know her turtles!

'And here,' he said.

'I've never heard of them nesting anywhere else.'

'Nobody has,' he told her. 'That's a huge reason why I can't sell this place. Once out of my hands, who knows what will become of it? These are incredibly endangered. The environmental authorities know they nest here, but no one else. This place is an environmental haven and I'll protect it with every means at my disposal. That's the biggest reason I bought it when my parents wanted to sell.'

'So you don't really need a mansion?' she said, treading water, watching his face. 'You want a turtle nursery.'

'I don't want it turned into a resort, if that's what you mean. This place is special.'

And then he paused and thought, Why not say it?

'Meg… If you agree to come here… If you agree to marry me, then you'll be taking on that responsibility, too. You'll be guardian to the piping plovers, who also nest in the dunes, and to the turtle hatchlings. If I can't persuade you to marry me because of Henry and Peggy, how about plovers and turtles?'

It was a joke. Sort of. He expected her to smile. Instead she gave him a look that was puzzled. Questioning. He wasn't sure what the question was but she didn't take it further.

'Leave it, Matt,' she said simply. 'Go make those business calls and let me play with turtles.'

And before he could say anything else she duck-dived downward. She was back underwater and he was left to make his way home alone.

* * *

In the end she had a fabulous day, floating, swimming, sleeping on the sand. Eating on the terrace under the stars. Talking to Matt about the things she discovered he cared about—amazingly he left his phone inside. Abandoning her bedroom because who needed two?

They slept that night in the most luxurious bed she could imagine. She slept in the arms of a man she was starting to believe she loved.

His body was everything she'd ever dreamed of. His voice, his touch, his tenderness, his passion… It must be a dream, she told herself as they loved until exhaustion finally had them drifting to contented, sated sleep.

Yes, she'd been lonely, but if she could have him like this… She abandoned herself to the belief that maybe the dream could become reality.

But reality had a way of poking its nose in. In the small hours she woke and headed to the bathroom. His en suite bathroom was bigger than her Rowan Bay living room. The bath looked like a claw-footed, gleaming white island, surrounded by a sea of white marble. The shower could accommodate a small family. It was all glass and chrome. There were two enormous vanity basins. And walls of mirrors.

She headed back to bed shivering, and as she did she saw Matt's phone blinking on his bedside table. She'd figured it by now. Blinking meant work.

'Everyone has work,' she told herself as she headed across the white pile carpet and dived back into bed. 'And this is just a house, even if it is over the top.'

Matt stirred and reached out for her. His arms enfolded her and she felt herself drift back into the dreaminess of being held by such a man.

But it was a dream. The crazy bathroom was out there, reality, luxury she could scarcely imagine.

The phone was on the bedside table.

'It'll be okay if Matt's beside me,' she told herself as she drifted back to sleep. 'If Matt holds me...'

It would work, Matt thought as he lay in the dark and held the woman he'd hardly imagined could exist. This was his perfect woman. His perfect wife?

With Henry here, and Peggy and the dogs, maybe with children of their own, this place could come to life. It could be a living, laughing home. He'd come down at weekends and it'd welcome him. Meg would welcome him.

She could come to Manhattan if she wanted, he thought, but he wasn't sure how she'd fit there. The social side of his financial world wasn't particularly welcoming, and she'd be a fish out of water, but if she wanted...

He'd talk to her. In the morning.

Morning. He'd intended to head back to the city but he had the wisdom to realise he couldn't leave yet.

He'd sensed her unease. She was uncomfortable right now, stunned by the immensity of the place, its opulence, its sheer difference from the world she was used to. He'd be a fool if he hadn't figured it, and he'd be a fool if he messed things up now for want of trying.

What to do about it?

His phone lay on the bedside table, a tiny light winking, telling him that even though he'd worked today, messages were building up.

But Meg... The future...

He needed to stay for a couple more days, he decided. For now Meg needed to be his priority.

And wasn't that what he wanted? Just to hold her.

To hold on to the dream.

CHAPTER TWELVE

MATT HADN'T BEEN able to spare the days he'd spent taking Henry to Peggy, or the days he'd spent at Meg's. He rang Helen first thing and heard her astonishment.

'Two more days?'

'Three at the most,' he said placatingly. 'Then I'm back full-time.' His absence was causing huge problems but he needed Meg to decide this was a good place to live.

Not because of Henry, though. Meg was already agreeing that Peggy and Henry could be happy here. Her job as Peggy's envoy was done.

'Though they might be happier living somewhere like the gatehouse,' she ventured. 'This place echoes.'

'This place needs you,' he told her, but she looked doubtful.

But in typical Meg style, she set about enjoying herself. She swam with the turtles. She kayaked and she walked the beach. He had the groundsmen find fishing tackle so she could try her hand at fishing. He was with her as often as he could manage, but when he couldn't he had one of the gardeners make sure she wasn't alone. He saw her out of the windows making friends with them.

He watched her doing her best to feel at home.

The weather changed and the nights turned autumnal. Night dining on the terrace was no longer an option and Meg decreed she loathed the dining room.

She suggested they eat in what his grandfather used to call the snug. The room had been his grandfather's retreat when his grandmother's socialising went over the top. It had faded sofas, favourite paintings, an open fire, an over-sized television. They ate and he tried to make time to watch old movies with her. They talked. Sometimes they made it to bed and made love and sometimes they didn't make it that far.

She didn't complain, though, when he left her to make his calls, to work in his study.

She wasn't needy.

After three days he was feeling more and more that this was working. He was starting to feel as if he'd found a woman who could be part of his life for ever.

Problem sorted? Time to move on? His life needed to resume and the demands from Manhattan could no longer be ignored.

Meg's plan was that she'd stay for two weeks. At least, that had been her plan on coming here. *His* plan was that she'd stay for ever, but he had the sense not to push.

Thinking ahead, she'd need time to pack up her belongings at Rowan Bay. Maybe in a few weeks he could snatch a little more time off and go back to Australia with her. He could put Peggy and Henry onto a cruise liner and then bring Meg home for ever.

Home. For ever. The words felt good. No, they felt great. McLellan Place had never seemed so alive as it did now that Meg was here. But work was imperative. Besides, he needed to be honest about how their life long term would be.

'I do need to head back to Manhattan,' he told her. 'I can come back at the weekend. Would you like to come with me or will you stay here?'

The weather had turned warm again and they'd been lying on the beach, sharing a beach rug. There might just have been a little lovemaking involved. He'd had one of the gardeners set up a sunshade, which was just as well.

'Because there are places I have no intention of getting sunburned,' she'd retorted as she'd sunk into his arms. They'd fallen asleep after laughter and woken to bliss.

Now, though, the words had to be said. The real world was breaking in.

'Back to Manhattan,' she said sleepily, but he heard a note of caution in her voice.

'It's where I work.'

'That's surely too far to commute, nine to five.'

'My work's not nine to five.'

'So you actually live in Manhattan.'

'This is my home.'

'You're here at weekends.'

'Most weekends.' Some.

'And if Peggy and Henry come here…'

'Peggy's independent. Henry can go to the local school. I can put in place as many supports as they need.'

'And you say you want me, too.'

'I do.' And then he thought, Why wait for the champagne and roses, the perfect moment? He'd already raised it. Why not say it formally? 'Meg, you do know I'd like to marry you. It seemed sensible back in Australia. It seems even more sensible now. So… Meg O'Hara, will you marry me?'

What followed was a troubled silence. This wasn't going well, he thought, and he had the sense to realise it.

She sat up and tugged her T-shirt on, almost as if she needed to be dressed to say what had to be said.

'I told you that my boss's son asked me to marry him just before all this happened,' she said, almost casually.

'He's obviously a man of taste.' He wasn't sure where she was going. 'I can't fault him on reasoning.'

'Yeah, that's it.' Her gaze met his head-on, but her eyes seemed troubled. 'I told you his reasons. They were sensible. Just like yours, only different.'

'I'd like to think that difference is huge.'

'Yeah, I get a bigger house and I don't have to gut Graham's fish.' She shook her head. 'No, that's not fair. The truth is, Matt, that I've fallen for you. Hard. I think… I think… I could even love you.'

Love. That was a word to take his breath away.

Did he even know what it meant? He still wasn't sure but now wasn't the time to say it.

'Then what…?' he ventured.

'Because I want the fairy tale.' The words came out too fast, too loud, and she bit her lip, seeming to almost cringe as she heard them. 'No. That's not true. It's no fairy tale. My gran and grandpa had it and so did Mum and Dad. There were no mansions, no double washbasin made of marble, no walk-in his-and-hers dressing rooms, no acres of gardens and staff to match. But they used to hug. All the time. When Dad walked into the room, Mum's eyes used to light up. She'd just drop everything and hug.'

'Your dad was a fisherman, right?' he asked cautiously. 'I'd imagine he spent days at sea.'

'He did,' she conceded. 'And so did Grandpa. When they could, Mum and Grandma would go, too, but sometimes they couldn't. And that's what I've been thinking. I'm figuring that what you're proposing is like the old days, for me to be here keeping the candle burning for your return.'

It was. 'Is that selfish? You could have a great life here, Meg. A far easier life than the one you have in Rowan Bay.'

'I know that,' she said uneasily. 'Matt, these few days… they've been wonderful but I'm still… There are still things I need to know.' She closed her eyes for a moment and then she opened them, decision made. She pushed herself to her feet.

'Okay,' she conceded. 'When Dad was at sea Mum always knew exactly where he was, what he was doing. Take me to Manhattan and show me the other side of your life.'

The chopper took them back to Manhattan early the next morning. He'd normally head straight to the office, but he took Meg to his apartment first.

Which didn't go as well as he'd have liked.

Matt thought of the night he'd brought Henry back here. There'd been a choice then: hand Henry over to Social Services or take him home himself. He'd walked into his apartment with the bewildered, shocked Henry and he'd wished the place had seemed more homey. Now, as he ushered Meg through the ornate foyer into his elegant sitting room, he wished the same.

'It's just a place to crash,' he told her and wondered why he sounded apologetic. 'I need to get a decorator in, make it seem a bit more kid-friendly.'

'Can a decorator do that?' Meg crossed to the picture windows opening to vistas of New York. 'How? Replace your Pre-Raphaelite paintings with Pooh Bear and Eeyore?'

Pre-Raphaelite?

His grandfather had started Matt's art collection and Matt had added to it. Local dealers gave him a heads-up when good pieces came up for auction. They were a good investment. Impressive. Solid.

'Do you like them?' he asked cautiously, aware of his prejudiced surprise that she even knew the label.

'Nope.' She finished checking the paintings in the living room, glanced into the dining room to see more, and she shuddered.

'Or yes,' she conceded. 'They're brilliant, of course. But, Matt, they should be in a museum somewhere, not oppressing the bejeezers out of everyone who walks in here.'

Oppressing? He'd thought impressing more like.

'I'm sorry you disapprove.' He heard himself stiffening, ancestral pride doing a double take.

'I disapprove of so much money being tied up for one man to look at over his morning toast.'

'I eat my toast in the kitchen.'

'Bully for you. Are there Pre-Raphaelites there, too?'

'Dada,' he said, and she shot him a look of incredulity

and headed through to see. Satirical, nonsensical, the Dada paintings were part of a collection he'd begun himself.

'Oh, my.' Meg stopped before a picture of a pair of eyes somehow superimposed on a twisted teapot. 'This is just the thing to face after a hard night.'

'Maybe not,' he conceded. 'But I eat my breakfast fast.'

'I would, too, just to get out of here.'

'I'll replace it before Henry comes here,' he said defensively, and she turned and gave him a long, hard look.

'Do you like this stuff?'

'It's an excellent investment. I can't see Pooh and Eeyore fitting in here.'

'I can't see anyone but you fitting in here.'

'As I said, I'll get a designer in.'

'It doesn't need a designer,' she said bluntly. 'It needs someone to treat it as home. Look at that refrigerator. Have you ever seen a fridge as big as that without at least one grubby note attached saying there's a Save the Whale meeting at your neighbours' next Thursday? Or a change to garbage schedule? Or a card for a friend who's turned clairvoyant and you promised you'd spread the word to your other friends who drop in unannounced with a slab of beer to watch a footy game?' She looked at him a moment longer and then shook her head.

'Uh-oh. Matt, you don't have a clue about your neighbours, do you?'

'I... No.' He was at the apartment so little, and his entrance was private.

'And mates who watch footy here? No?' She sighed. 'Okay, bring in your designer but keep an open mind about the fridge. Maybe let Henry decorate it. Meanwhile, are you heading to the office?'

'I am,' he conceded, but the thought of leaving Meg by herself with the Dadas... He hadn't thought this through. 'What will you do?'

'Not sit here and let a teapot stare at me, that's for sure. I'll go explore.'

'I'll put the car at your disposal.'

'No, thanks.' She said it fast. 'Shanks' pony is great for seeing. So you'll be back for dinner?'

This wasn't the way to encourage thoughts of marriage, he conceded. He should have left her at McLellan Place.

'I'm meeting Steven Walker for lunch,' he told her and watched her expression change.

'Henry's father? Really?'

'Yeah.' He'd had a few calls with Steven. Things were slotting into place, but a formal meeting seemed appropriate.

'Would you like me to come with you?'

'I don't know.' He hesitated. 'Meg, until… Unless you commit to helping care for Henry, it might give the wrong impression. We don't want to come across as a ready-made family.'

'We certainly don't.' She eyed him cautiously.

'But if you'd like to meet Steven…'

'I would.'

'Then I'll send the car for you at one.'

'Tell me the address and I'll get there myself.' He saw her glance down at the clothes she was wearing—neat jeans and a white shirt. 'That settles what I'll do this morning. I obviously need some going-to-lunch-with-billionaires clothes.'

'Steven's not a billionaire.'

'You've looked him up, too? Okay, multimillionaire. Practically on the breadline. Regardless I'm not going to lunch looking like the poor relation.'

'Try Neiman Marcus,' he suggested. 'Or Bloomingdale's. I have accounts there. I'll give you my card.'

'You're kidding me, right? Is this a *Pretty Woman* moment?'

'I can afford—'

'I'm sure you can but so can I.' She grinned and stepped forward and kissed him, a proprietorial kiss, short and sweet and far too fast. When she stepped back she was still smiling.

'Believe it or not, I can dress myself,' she told him. 'Allow me some dignity. Do you have somewhere here I can check the internet? Of course you do. The security code I saw you punch in—is that all I need to get in and out of this apartment? Great. Okay, off you go and cope with the world's financial convolutions while I go find something to wear. I know what I think is more fun.'

Steven Walker was pretty much as Matt had expected. He was in his fifties, well built but bordering on pudgy. His Italian suit looked as if it had been made for him, his aura was one of wealth and privilege, and he spoke with care, as if whatever was said could be used against him. He greeted Matt as a business associate, and Matt could see the reservations behind the man's eyes.

That was okay. Matt had reservations, too. This was uncharted territory. Negotiating the fate of one small boy...

He'd chosen one of his favourite eateries, discreet, expensive, a restaurant with myriad 'rooms' where business could be talked without fear of being heard. Maybe that had been a mistake, though, he thought, as the waiter hovered and asked about the absent 'third person'. This wasn't business. Or was it?

Whatever, by the time they were through their first beer he was conscious of escalating tension. They'd been edging around the topic of Henry. Neither of them knew where to take this. To Matt it seemed as if they were marking time. Waiting?

And then Meg arrived and the sight of her seemed to settle something deep within. It was all he could do to keep it formal, not to step forward and take her into his arms.

She looked amazing.

He'd expected her to be wearing, what? Something vaguely corporate? Not so much. She'd headed out with the idea of shopping for a business-type lunch in Manhattan. What she'd come up with was pure Meg.

When he'd first seen her she'd been in filthy jeans, a battered oilskin and bare feet. What she was wearing now wasn't even close to what she'd been wearing then, nor to the shabby jeans and windcheaters she'd worn back at Rowan Bay, but she'd lost nothing of that original, indomitable Meg.

She was wearing black tights with ankle-length boots made of soft charcoal leather. Her crimson skirt was short, crisp, neat, showing off her gorgeous legs. A black vest lay beneath a beautiful embroidered jacket. The jacket was a little shorter than her vest, making the outfit look eye-catchingly chic. A faded leather bag—he recognised the brand and did a double take—hung casually from her arm.

To top it off, she'd obviously found time to have her copper curls shaped into a proper elfin trim.

She looked happy, buzzy from a successful shop? Her eyes were glowing. She smiled brightly at him, and as both men rose she turned that glowing smile onto Steven.

'You're Steven? Henry's dad? I'm so pleased to meet you.'

Steven put out a pudgy paw; he held Meg's hand a little too long, and it was as much as Matt could do not to swipe it away and say, 'She's mine.'

He didn't. They were much too civilised. They sat again, and Matt tried not to look at Meg while she beamed at the waiter and asked nicely for a soda water, while she made small talk with Steven—while she held him entranced.

Gorgeous didn't begin to cut it.

'We need to talk about Henry,' he managed as their food arrived—the restaurant's speciality, a seafood platter to be shared.

'Let's.' Meg selected a scallop with care and popped it into her mouth. 'Yum. Tell us, Steven, are you upset about what's happening? And how do you see the care of your son playing out?'

They were good questions. Great questions. They left Steven no choice but to put his cards on the table.

'It's been a shock,' Steven admitted. He was watching Meg select an oyster and once again Matt had that almost-primeval urge to slap him. 'I'll admit my first emotion was anger that Amanda didn't tell me. But there's nothing I can do about that now, and I'll do what's right by the boy. He's my son and I want him under my eye. I've been trying to decide what's right, and I believe I have it sorted.'

'Tell us,' Meg said, seemingly entranced, and Steven flushed with the warmth of her attention.

'I'm a wealthy man,' he told her. 'And what's happened isn't the boy's fault. He is my son. I've therefore decided that it's only fair that he'll inherit. I have six children already, from three wives, but I'm fair. My estate was to be split six ways. It'll now be split seven.'

'That's generous,' Meg told him with a sideways glance at Matt. 'But that's for when you're dead. What about now?'

'My current wife has enough on her hands with her… *our* two children,' Steven said smoothly, as if this was something that he'd worked out with care. 'And, of course, my children from previous marriages still have a call on me. My time's limited to attend to this boy's needs. As long as his grandmother moves here, I see no reason why he shouldn't stay with her. I've checked out McLellan Place on the web and he's a lucky child to be invited to live there. I'll pay for schooling, of course. He can go to the school I attended. It teaches boys to be boys—he can't do better.'

'Really,' Meg murmured. 'Boys will be boys, eh?'

'None of that "caring sharing" stuff,' Steven said, expanding on his theme. 'My son should be tough. Boarding school, of course. Not that you'd want him all the time. Boarding school's great until they turn into real human beings.'

Matt's hand slipped on his glass. He was gripping too hard. He carefully put it down. Smashing a glass would help nothing.

But Steven wasn't noticing tension. 'I'll cover any other costs he incurs, of course,' he said genially. 'After-school care, summer camps, that sort of thing. Oh, and of course, I'd like to meet him. Could his grandmother bring him into town, maybe once a month? Lunch? An hour or so? Kids aren't much company but you do need to make an effort.'

'You do,' Matt said. Tightly.

'So that's agreed?' The man seemed to relax, ground rules sorted. 'I can't help thinking Amanda used me, but I'll do what's right.'

'What's right,' Meg said thoughtfully and turned to Matt. 'An hour a month and funding. And no caring and sharing. Okay, Matt, your turn. What do you think's right for Henry?'

The seafood platter was excellent. The calamari was a little tougher than she liked, but then this place wouldn't be able to catch a squid a couple of hours before lunch.

She ate two calamari rings and another oyster while she waited for Matt's response. She knew this man by now. She could see tension in the set of his shoulders as he thought through Steven's...offer?

It was a crap offer but did he have a choice but to accept? Steven had the upper hand—there was nowhere for Matt to go.

This seemed like negotiating a business contract, Meg thought suddenly, and she didn't like the analogy.

Neither did Matt. She could see the tension on his face. She could see him thinking how to respond.

'Steven, what you're suggesting seems adequate,' he

said at last. He was speaking slowly, and she could see him thinking each word out before he spoke. 'This way he'll have three adults in his life, his father, his grandmother, and me. I admit, I'd still like to be involved. You know Amanda was on my staff? Henry's been in and out of my office since he was a toddler. I've grown fond of him.'

'I understand that,' Steven said. 'If he's a son of mine he'll be whip-smart. If I get him well educated he'll be a son to be proud of.'

'I think that, too,' Matt said smoothly. 'But then…you already have children and you're a busy man. You'd have trouble fitting him into your schedule.'

'I'll make the time,' Steven said. 'My wife won't like it but it's a duty.'

'Does it have to be?' Matt said, tentatively now. 'You're doing what's right, but there is an alternative. It's possibly too soon to commit to such a thing but if the placement I'm proposing works out… If you and your wife agree… There may be another way forward. You have six children and I have none. Steven, once you've checked us out thoroughly, and I know you'd want to do that, how would you feel about allowing us to adopt him?'

What?

Meg sat back in her chair and let the words sink in. Or tried to.

Adoption?

Where had that come from?

And he'd just said…*us*?

And it seemed Steven was as astounded as she was. 'You're kidding?' He stared at Matt as if he'd just said something crazy. 'You realise if you adopted him you'd be responsible? School fees, the lot. More, he'd end up with a claim on the McLellan estate.'

Here we go, Meg thought numbly. Money.

'I'm happy for that to happen,' Matt said smoothly. He'd put his proposition on the table. Now he sounded ready to negotiate the finer points. 'But the most important thing is surety for the boy. Peggy's elderly and edging on confused. Hopefully she'll be here for him for a few years yet, but, if not, this would give Henry the sense of belonging I think he needs.' He glanced across at Steven. 'Of course, you'd still like access, and it's important for Henry to know as much about his background as possible. A scheduled meeting with him once a month would still be an option.'

'Of course,' Steven said, and Meg watched him visibly warm to the idea. Ridding himself of a responsibility he'd never wanted in the first place. 'So he'd stay with you?'

'He'd stay at McLellan Place with Meg. I'd be there as much as I can.'

'With Meg?' He turned to Meg, bemused. 'This young lady? Where do you fit in?'

'Meg's Australian,' Matt said smoothly. 'Peggy's sent her as envoy to see for herself what we've arranged.' He hesitated but then obviously decided to say it. 'I'm trying to persuade Meg to move to McLellan Place, as well. As my wife.'

And just like that, Meg's shock turned to anger. What was he doing, saying such things to a guy she'd only just met? This was personal.

Plus…adoption. He hadn't even mentioned the option to her. He was talking of marriage and a child, and he hadn't even thought to talk about something so important?

'So there'd be a mom for Henry,' Steven said, his eyes alight with interest. 'Marriage, eh? The fast research I've done puts you as a confirmed bachelor. What's made you change your mind?'

'Meg has,' Matt said simply. 'With Meg at McLellan House, Henry would definitely be lucky.'

Lucky? Define *lucky*, Meg thought, thinking of that vast mansion, of the empty rooms, of Matt's apartment here, of the sterility, of the loneliness…

And then she thought, *Who am I thinking of as being lonely? Henry? Or Matt?*

Or me?

She was struggling to get her head around this. He'd proposed marriage. He'd create a family, for him to be part of at will?

'But you'd only be there at weekends,' she managed. She was blocking Steven out for the moment, focusing on the man in front of her. Marriage? Adoption? What was he promising Steven?

She was being blackmailed.

'My life is here in Manhattan, but yes, I'd be there whenever I can find time,' Matt told her.

And she thought, *He doesn't get it. He doesn't see.*

'Your life's in Manhattan?' She was having trouble getting her voice to produce more than a squeak.

'I have a business empire to run,' Matt said smoothly. He sounded back in control again, contract laid out; all she had to do was sign. 'I'll take care of Henry as well as I'm able but my financial empire is based here. That's who I am.'

'Bullshit.'

She said it far too loudly. The waiter, who'd surreptitiously arrived to check on drinks, stopped dead in the doorway. He checked the contents of their glasses from afar and disappeared fast.

This restaurant was obviously geared to respectful discretion. It probably wasn't used to having Australian fishing persons swearing at two financial giants.

These men were at the peak of their careers, she thought bleakly. They were powerful and ready to have every suggestion applauded by minions. So here she was, being blackmailed into being…a wife minion.

He hadn't talked to her about the adoption option. Why?

Because he'd decided to slot her into what he needed from her. Sharing? Not so much.

Enough. She wasn't tasting this seafood anyway. She rose and the men rose with her. Matt even had the decency to look worried. 'Is everything okay?'

'It's not okay,' she told him. She was trying not to let her voice wobble but she wasn't succeeding. 'Steven, I'd appreciate it if you could forget what Matt said about marriage. It's not going to happen. I came here to check that Henry would be cared for if he moved here and I know that'll happen. You guys sort the financials. Peggy will do the loving. And me? I'm heading back to my old life. Heaving craypots. Taking punters on fishing charters. I'd like to say that's who I am, but it's not true. It's what I do.'

'What are you saying?' Matt was looking at her in bewilderment. 'Meg, you could have a great life at McLellan Place.'

'I could, couldn't I?' she retorted. What she had to say shouldn't be said in front of Steven but what the heck? She was too angry to care.

'But where's what I *am* in that equation?' she demanded. 'Matt, crayfishing, fishing charters, they're what I do. They're not who I am. I'm a woman who was truly loved by my parents and by my grandparents. I'm a woman who's increasingly falling for one little boy. I'm also a woman who's watched Peggy agree to change her whole life because of love. That's what you're asking of me, too, Matt, and yes, I could do that. But here's the thing. McLellan Place, Henry, Peggy, me… We'd fit in around the edges of who you think you are. You call the shots and we jump to.'

'Meg—'

'Don't stop me.' Rejecting a man's marriage proposal in front of strangers was not the kindest thing to do, but then, had it been a marriage proposal? This was a business lunch. Matt was the one who'd linked marriage with adoption in front of Steven. He'd made it into a contract. It felt as if he was blackmailing her into agreeing—and it wasn't going to happen.

'Matt, you asked me to marry you and that's quite a coup for a woman like me,' she told him. 'But I'd be the wife who fitted around the edges of who you are and that's not what I want. I've seen my parents' marriage, and my grandparents'. They truly loved, and work had to fit around that. If I married you I'd be fitting around the edges of what really matters to you. And if you adopt Henry I'd see him fitting around your life in exactly the same way.'

'Meg!' Matt looked appalled, as well he might. Steven was practically goggling.

'It's okay,' she said, anger being superseded by a weariness that seemed bone deep. 'I understand, Matt, I truly do. You've made a great offer. I know you'll do what you're capable of for Henry, because you're an honourable man. But me… I want the fairy tale. I'll admit, I'm close to being head over heels in love with you and that feeling's only going to get deeper. But love doesn't work the way you see it. It's not something that's there for the weekends. It's for ever.'

'Meg, this is not the place. Could we talk about this later?'

'You've made it the place and there's not going to be a later,' she told him. She turned to Steven. 'It was good to meet you,' she said. 'You and Matt seem to have Henry's life sorted. I'll head back to Australia and tell Peggy that life at McLellan Place could be awesome. And it could be awesome, Matt, but it's not for me. If I said yes now, I'd be hauled even deeper into caring for Henry. Most of all, Matt McLellan, I'be hauled into loving you. I'd be hauled into needing to share your life. My parents had it. My grandparents had it and I'm willing to leave because I want it, too. I think I love you already, Matt McLellan, but I won't be a part-time wife.'

'That's not what I'm suggesting,' Matt said explosively.

'So what are you suggesting? Having a family… How do you see that changing your life?'

'It wouldn't need to. At least…'

'Least? Yep, you'd do the least possible to keep us all happy. We wouldn't be part of who you are.' She glanced at the still-goggling Steven and what she had to say firmed. 'Matt, I bet Steven married like that, and he's on his third wife. So here's the thing,' she said, desolation sweeping in to squash out the myriad emotions she was already dealing with. 'Love should change. It's changing me and it scares me. If I were to be your part-time wife I might just end up breaking my heart.'

She had two men looking at her as if she were speaking Swahili and she was close to tears. They didn't understand and she had to leave before she disintegrated.

She snagged her gorgeous new bag—ten bucks at the charity shop…who'd have thought it?—and tried desperately to sound sensible.

'I'll leave you to your very important discussion,' she told them. 'How to accommodate a child without letting him interfere with your lives. I'll head back to the apartment to fetch my stuff but then I'm leaving. I'll assure Peggy that McLellan Place is fine as a place to live but I'll also tell her…beware where she gives her heart. She's already given it to Henry and that's a safe bet because Henry loves her back. Peggy's preparing to cross the world for love, change her life, put everything she has on the line. I don't think either of you are capable of doing that.'

And then, because she couldn't help herself, she took a step forward, stood on her toes and kissed Matt. Lightly on the lips but moving away fast.

'I think… I hope there's a plane leaving this afternoon,'

she told him. 'If there is I'll be on it. No, don't leave, you two have important things to discuss and none of them involve me. Thanks for the compliment, Matt. Thanks for giving me an amazing few days. I'll remember them all my life. Goodbye…and good luck. Please, don't follow.'

And she swiped away an angry tear and headed out.

Steven's voice followed.

'They're all like that,' he was saying. 'Emotional creatures. Time of the month? Who knows? I've been married three times and I've never figured it out. But it's okay, I can approve your adoption without her. You don't really need to marry on Henry's account.'

He couldn't follow. He had enough sense to realise that following her and reasoning on a packed New York pavement was never going to work.

There was also the bill for the business lunch. Steven seemed to realise the gravity of the situation—maybe he was even enjoying it—but he wasn't about to let Matt go without paying his half. Meg therefore had a five-minute start on him, and the traffic closed in. By the time he got back to his apartment she'd used her headstart to good effect. Her things were gone. She was gone.

Doing a romantic rush to the airport wasn't his style but he found he had no choice. He checked the website and learned there was a flight leaving midafternoon. But she'd moved fast. By the time he reached the airport she was already through international security.

'The only way through is if you buy yourself a ticket,' the security guard said jovially, and Matt almost decided to take him up on it.

He didn't have his passport on him. He had nothing apart from the memories of Meg's pale face. Of a last kiss.

He was forced to stop and think. What had just happened?

He'd put a loaded gun to her head.

Had he no sense?

He'd told Steven he'd hoped they'd marry before she'd agreed. More, he'd somehow linked that proposal to Steven's agreement for Henry's care.

He'd spoken in anger and in haste, pushed by Steven's coldness. That haste had had him making assumptions.

He knew Meg was falling in love with him. She'd said so. She'd already offered to share her life with Henry. He'd just put everything together, too fast.

He was an astute businessman. He knew how to negotiate a contract and it wasn't by bullying. It had been anger with Steven that had had jolted him from being sensible, from taking things calmly.

Where to go from here?

He could head back to the office, work until tomorrow and then take a flight that'd have him with her with only a twenty-four-hour gap. Or he could hire his own jet.

But would it make a difference?

He stared at massive metal doors, shut tight. Meg would be boarding.

Had she used the open first-class ticket he'd bought her when she came? He hoped so. He'd given her the ticket so she didn't feel trapped.

And then he'd tried to trap her. Ready-made family. Ready-made wife.

Reality was setting in now, cold as the metal doors in front of him. Meg had talked of her work, the things she did to make a living.

They're what I do. They're not who I am.

Family? It wasn't what he did.

Loving? He obviously hadn't a clue how to do that, either.

He thought suddenly of a time long ago, his parents heading for vacation, and Matt desperate to go, too. He must have been…maybe five? So young it was just a blur. But when he'd seen his parents' suitcases in the hall he'd raced to get his backpack, and in a fit of inspiration he'd popped his toy squirrel—Eric—into his mother's capacious purse. Eric was precious. He had to be in the safest place possible.

And then…he remembered his mother telling him to be a big boy, he was staying home with nanny. There'd been a swift kiss from her, an appalled look from his father—yeah, he'd been sobbing—and they were gone.

His nanny at the time—Elspeth—had been one of the better ones, kind and almost as appalled as he'd been when he'd calmed down enough to realise that Eric had gone, too. She'd known how precious Eric was and she'd taken the almost-unbelievable step of bundling him into a cab and following his parents to the airport.

To metal doors like this one. To an official who'd said he'd see what he could do to get a message to them—but Eric was gone.

Six weeks later his parents had returned but Eric hadn't come home with them.

Home… Where was home anyway? Surely he needed to be over the concept by now?

His phone pinged in his jacket. He took it out and stared at the screen.

Helen. Work.

That's what I am.

'Anything else I can help you with, sir?' the security guard asked. Obviously a lone businessman staring blindly at a closed door needed to be moved on.

'I… No. Thank you.'

He'd been dumb. He'd pushed her too hard, too fast, but a part of him knew what had just happened was inevitable.

He'd tried to *do* family. Meg had told him that was impossible.

So now what?

He clicked Recall on his phone.

'Helen?'

He needed to get back to what he was.

Once again she was ensconced in first-class luxury. She'd considered trading her open ticket for economy but they wouldn't give her a refund and she'd decided, what the heck? A few more hours of luxury and then back to real life.

She'd just thrown away a life that was pure fantasy.

She donned her first-class pyjamas and the flight attendant was instantly on hand to offer to make up her bed. 'But wouldn't you like dinner first?' she asked. 'We can offer a seven-course degustation menu. And would madam like champagne?'

Madam wouldn't, and flight attendants were trained to read nuances. She offered to dim the lights and left Meg to sleep.

Meg shoved her pillow on top of her head and thought, *What have I done?*

She'd given up on Matt.

'Maybe I could have changed him,' she whispered to her pillow. 'Maybe if I married him he'd be a different person. He'd learn to be family.'

Right. She thought suddenly of advice her grandma had given her long ago. It was a joke. Sort of. *Brides can go into marriage thinking, Aisle, altar, hymn. It won't happen, Meg, love. Look long and hard before you leap.*

She hadn't looked long, but she had looked hard.

'He'd break my heart,' she whispered into her muffling pillow. 'I'd sit at that great mansion watching Henry grow up, watching Peggy grow old, waiting for snippets, flying visits from a man who says he loves me. I might even have to watch Henry turn into the same, a man who doesn't have a clue what love's about.

'I could teach them both.

'There you go again. Aisle. Altar. Hymn. Get a grip. You've made a wise decision. You know he'd break your heart.

'I know that,' she told the pillow. 'So why do I feel like my heart's already breaking?'

CHAPTER THIRTEEN

PEGGY AND HENRY arrived at McLellan Place two months later, and by Christmas they'd settled in. Peggy made a warm, if rather muddled, attempt at being all the family Henry needed. Matt put supports in place to keep them safe and content. Even though he'd thought he'd visit every couple of weeks, he found himself there almost every weekend, increasingly taking work with him so he could extend his stay.

Because Henry needed him? Maybe not, but he was always so joyful to see him that the effort to get there seemed minor.

Peggy and Henry fished, beachcombed, turned the place into a sort of home.

He'd talked Steven out of the idea of Henry following his father to boarding school. Instead he started at the local school and seemed to fit in.

Then Christmas.

Christmas for Matt was usually a duty to be got over as fast as possible. There'd be a McLellan family dinner at New York's latest on-trend restaurant, with assorted relations all trying to outdo each other by revealing how much insider gossip they'd gleaned about each other in the previous year.

This year he didn't hear any of it.

Somewhat reluctantly he'd invited his mother to McLellan Place, but of course, she declined. It was as if he'd invited her to share a bad smell.

'You have a child there now?' she said with disdain. 'The son of that sleazy Steven Walker? And the child's grandmother, too? What business is it of yours?'

He'd made it his business, but on Christmas Day the place still felt empty.

He thought, If Meg were here, she'd have hauled Christmas dinner into the snug. She might also have scorned the massive Christmas tree his staff had organised. Plus the turkey. The roasted bird was carried into the dining room and Henry stared at it in wonder, while Peggy snorted as she saw its size.

'We'll be eating leftovers for ever.'

'I like turkey sandwiches,' Matt said weakly.

'I bet it's wasted.' Peggy was getting more and more acerbic as she became secure. 'Like all these bedrooms. They're for show, that's what they are. No one's used the whole west wing since we've been here. Not that we're ungrateful,' she amended hurriedly. 'It's a lovely place to live.'

'I liked your island as much,' Henry told her as he gamely tackled his turkey. He'd settled well into living here, revelling in his grandma's devotion and Matt's frequent visits. 'My friend Robbie at school says this place is like an island. It's like everything is blocked out. Robbie says the spikes on our gates make his mum feel scared.' He surveyed the tiny indent they'd made in the giant bird with concern. 'Matt, I don't think I like turkey sandwiches.'

'Neither do I,' Peggy told him.

'But I do like Meg.' Henry suddenly sounded wistful. 'I wish she could have come for Christmas.' He brightened. 'I'm calling her this afternoon. I want to show her the pictures of the shells Grandma and I found.'

'You're calling Meg?' he said. Why did that make something in his chest lurch?

'At four o'clock,' Henry told him. 'Grandma said that'd be a good time.'

It'd be a good time for them, Matt thought. It'd be the morning after Christmas in Rowan Bay. They'd have missed Meg's Christmas.

Had Meg been alone for Christmas?

He thought of her in that ramshackle old house. It did have a shiny new roof—he'd organised it—but had she been alone? He kept remembering the words she'd used when she'd invited Peggy and Henry to share her home.

I'll get to come home after a day's charter and the lights will be on.

By bringing Henry here, he'd taken that from her.

When the adoption came through he'd be able to take Henry back for a visit, he thought, but then, it wouldn't make much difference. She'd still be alone.

Peggy and Henry went back to tackling their turkey but Matt had lost his appetite. He glanced around at the truly impressive dining room. The dining table was all elegance, crimson and gold, with the gleaming mahogany table surface shining through.

To give his staff their due, they'd also tried to make it child-friendly. The decorations contained strings of sparkly Santas, and the centrepiece was a revolving Santa's workshop, complete with beavering elves. The Christmas tree was tasteful, exquisite. The food arriving from the kitchen was amazing.

Christmas at its best? It still felt lonely.

'Do you remember the fish Meg cooked in seaweed?' Henry asked and Matt flinched. He remembered. If he could turn back time…

He couldn't. Meg had made her choice. She didn't want this lifestyle and he couldn't force her.

But if she was in Rowan Bay by herself… If she was as lonely as he was…

What the…? He wasn't lonely. What was he thinking?

But if there was a chance she'd changed her mind…

'Maybe I could talk to her, too,' he told Henry, trying to sound as if it didn't matter. He'd spoken to Meg since she'd left but the calls had been brief. Working out travel for Peggy and Henry. Organising her promised roof. Giving updates on Henry. Nothing personal.

'Do you want to say Happy Christmas?' Henry asked, and Matt nodded.

'I do.'

What else did he have to say?

Are you lonely? Will you change your mind?

He wouldn't say it, he thought, but he would say Happy Christmas and see where the conversation led.

It was eight in the morning, Boxing Day, and Meg's beach was packed with Nippers as far as the eye could see.

Nippers were kids who'd be Australia's next generation of lifeguards, or simply beach-safe adults. Rowan Bay kids loved the organisation and the training it embraced. Parents and grandparents loved it, too. As soon as Christmas was done, every kid within a coo-ee of Rowan Beach transformed into a yellow-and-red Nipper.

The wind had been forecast to blow from the west and strengthen, which meant the main Rowan Bay beach would be choppy. The beach in front of Meg's house was a sheltered easterly cove, so the entire function had thus been shifted and given an early start.

There was a row of portable toilets by the chook pen. A water tanker was hooked to a shower to allow kids to be sluiced. Rows of barbecues, manned by an army of parents wearing fundraising Nipper aprons, were producing breakfast, and the smell of bacon was drifting across the beach to where Meg was sitting in the shallows.

'Meg!' Maureen, her next-door neighbour, was wearing a pink swimming costume and a life vest. She'd been helping Meg supervise the splashing competition for the toddlers, and had taken a break for some much-needed morning coffee. Now she'd returned, holding Meg's phone. 'Your phone? Thought so. It's ringing. Your turn for a break.'

It'd be Henry. Drat, she'd almost missed him.

She loved their calls. Somehow it still seemed important that she be a part of his life. It still seemed important that Henry be part of hers.

They video-called most days, talking of nothing and everything. School. What he'd found on the beach. What sort of fish the guys she took out on the charters had caught that day. Even trivial stuff like the new type of chocolate-chip cookie Matt's cook had made.

'What's your cook's name?' Meg had asked and Henry had hesitated before answering.

'Her name's Esther but I'm not supposed to know,' he'd told her. 'Matt says don't disturb the staff. It's better that way.'

'Really?' That had been a gut clencher. If she were there…

She wasn't there. She'd walked away from being part of Henry's life, of Matt's life.

Her life was here and life was okay. She shook herself free of seawater and took the phone from Maureen.

'Henry?'

'It's Matt,' the voice on the other end of the line said. 'Happy Christmas.'

Matt. It was almost a month since she'd talked to him. It was almost—what?—ten minutes since she'd thought of him.

'H-happy Christmas.' He still had the power to take her breath away. 'I… Thank you.' And then her breath caught. This was Henry's phone. 'Is anything wrong?'

'Nothing's wrong,' he said quickly. 'Henry was about to phone when his new puppy escaped with the Christmas beanie Peggy's knitted for him. It has a red pompom on top and if that's not asking for trouble I don't know what is. Peggy and Henry are currently chasing one cocker spaniel puppy across the lawn. Stretchie's helping. I don't like the beanie's chances.'

'Oh…' she gasped and then choked on laughter. 'A puppy. What a gorgeous idea. Was that your Christmas gift to him?'

'It was,' he told her. 'Made more complicated by Henry's insistence that Christmas gifts aren't given until after Christmas pudding. It's very hard to hide a puppy until after pudding.'

'I bet it is. Well done, you. Did Esther help?'

'Esther?'

'Your cook,' she told him. 'Henry says she's great.'

'She did help,' he said cautiously. 'Henry told you about Esther?'

'He did, and also about your edict about not getting to know the staff. What's that about?' She was standing knee deep in the shallows, surveying her Nippers, and she was feeling strange. Commenting on Matt's lifestyle? She had no right, but strangely it felt appropriate.

'If you get to know the staff it hurts when they leave,' Matt said and that was enough to give her pause. To make her think.

'Is that what you learned?' she said. 'When you were a kid?'

'It doesn't… We weren't talking about me.'

'I guess that's not what you phoned to talk about,' she agreed. 'It doesn't fit inside the Matt McLellan boundaries.'

'Meg…'

'Sorry.' She sighed. 'That was uncalled for. It's not my business. You'd have thought I'd have learned by now. Are you having a good Christmas?'

'We are.'

'Who's there?'

'Peggy and Henry.'

'Not Steven?'

'He sent Henry a very expensive construction kit.'

'Bully for Steven. He gets boundaries, too.'

'Do you need to sound so cynical?'

She caught herself. 'Sorry. I don't mean to. It's just a different way of life from the one I'm used to.'

'So who did you share Christmas with?' he said, and she heard a trace of cynicism in *his* voice. Like 'pot calling the kettle black' cynicism.

'Lots of people,' she said diffidently.

'Really?'

And that had her arcing up. She knew criticism when she heard it.

'Really,' she snapped. 'I'm not dependent on Matt McLellan for company. Maureen came over for Christmas morning eggnog. Then we had a massive barbecue on the beach. Maureen's kids and grandkids. Two of the charter boat guys. Charlie's ex-wife and her new husband—she's done so much better than Charlie. Their kids. And food... The best seafood ever. You might have a professional cook, but we can catch crayfish half an hour from our front door. And pavlova. There are raspberries on Maureen's bushes and one of her kids has a cow. Fresh cream. Beat that, Matt McLellan.'

'I guess I can't,' he said weakly. 'It sounds great.'

'It was great.'

'So you're not lonely?'

'How can I be lonely?' She stood in the shallows and looked around her, at the community she loved, at the community she was part of.

'Matt, this is a video call,' she told him. 'Can you turn your camera on?'

And she flicked the video icon on her phone and turned the camera to the scene around her.

Maureen was in the water covered with toddlers. A bunch of learner bodyboarders were in the shallows. Older Nippers were organised into swimming races around buoys set further out. Mums and dads talked or snoozed on the beach. Boof was digging a hole to China with a couple of other dogs helping.

She turned her phone to show her feet in the water and she kicked, a splash that was pretty much defiance.

'These are my people,' she said. 'I'm having fun.'

'I didn't ask that, though,' Matt said slowly. 'Meg, I asked if you're lonely.'

Oh, help. Heaven preserve her from a perceptive male.

'I'm less lonely than I would be at McLellan Place,' she told him. 'Being a part-time wife.'

'Meg, I love you.'

There went her breath again. How was she expected to breathe when he said things like that?

I love you.

Why was he saying it now?

'How can you say that when you have all those boundaries?' she managed. 'You can't just love at weekends. It doesn't work like that.'

Silence.

He'd turned his camera on as well, and she could see him. It was almost like talking face-to-face. Matt was dressed for Christmas in winter, in a crimson sweater and classy trousers. His dark hair was neat, beautifully groomed.

She was dressed for messy Christmas in summer. Bikini. Salt water. Not a lot else.

She swiped a dripping curl from her forehead.

Matt looked… Matt looked.

Focus on boundaries, she told herself. She needed to think of them. She couldn't live with them, no matter how sexy this guy looked. No matter how much her heart lurched every time she saw him.

'Some boundaries are necessary,' Matt said at last. 'Meg, you know I'm happy to share. I wouldn't have boundaries with you.'

'But you'd keep those gates locked. You'd advise me not to get to know your cook.'

'It works.'

'Not for me it doesn't.' She turned her camera back to the splashy toddlers. 'This is fun. Where's the fun for you, Matt McLellan?'

'I want you.' It was a guttural response, almost primeval in its intensity. It made her take a step back. It almost made her click Disconnect.

Why? Because it evoked an answer in her that was stronger than any echo.

I want you.

She looked at her screen, into his dark, troubled eyes, and she thought it was just as well she was on the other side of the world. If he were here, if he were to take her into his arms…

He wouldn't. Or maybe he would, but only if it fitted into the time slots he had available.

'I know you do,' she managed at last. Maureen was looking up from where she was crouched in the shallows with their splashing toddlers. Seeing her distress? She needed to finish this conversation and get back to what really mattered. Rowan Bay Boxing Day. Community. Life.

'It's the best compliment I've ever been paid,' she whispered. 'You loving me. But it won't work. Not while you don't know your cook's name.'

'I do know her name.'

'You know what I mean.'

'Meg…'

'Give my love to Henry,' she said sadly. 'And to Peggy. Tell Henry I'll head inside and ring him at about seven tonight, your time. I need to see his puppy. Will you be staying with him for much longer?'

'Until New Year. Meg, what do you expect me to do? I can't—'

'I don't expect you to do anything,' she told him. 'I understand. There's nothing either of us can do. I love you, Matt, but there's the problem. You have your boundaries you can't cross, and I can't cross them, either.'

* * *

He stared at the blank screen. Then he swore and shoved the phone onto the table so hard it slid across the shining surface and landed on the floor beyond.

Then he thought, uh-oh, that was Henry's phone.

Thankfully, it wasn't broken.

If it'd been his, would he have cared?

Of course he would. His phone was his link to his world. Those days at sea when he'd been out of contact had been a disaster. At least one multimillion-dollar contract had fallen over because of it.

But he'd been with Meg.

He stared down at the blank screen of Henry's phone and the thing almost mocked him. Two minutes ago it had been filled with life, with laughter. With Meg.

If he'd used his own high-tech phone he could have recorded. He could be playing it back right now.

He could be showing himself pictures of a woman who was nothing to do with him, of a life he wasn't part of.

He stood, silent, letting his thoughts go where they willed.

Outside Henry and Peggy were engaged in a silly game with Stretchie and the yet-unnamed puppy. They were rolling on the grass.

It was December. The grass was wet. They'd be soaked.

Peggy wouldn't care. All she wanted was for her grandson to be happy. He watched her giggling with Henry, and he thought, *She's shed ten years.*

She'd abandoned her island. She'd abandoned her life to keep her grandson happy.

He'd asked Meg to do the same and she'd refused.

The screen was still blank. He closed his eyes and it was filled again, with Meg, with a beach crowded with kids, dogs, laughter. Life.

Meg.

Their conversation was being replayed. A repetitive loop.

And suddenly the loop seemed to tighten, focusing on two statements.

I asked if you're lonely.

I'm less lonely than I would be at McLellan Place. Being a part-time wife.

That was an admission, he thought. She *was* lonely.

So what? It didn't mean she was missing him.

But if it did? How could he persuade her…?

He couldn't. She'd made her decision. She couldn't fit into his lifestyle.

The thought of her was still with him, the sight of her splashing in the shallows.

Meg.

He wanted her.

The feeling was suddenly a hunger so vast he had to open his eyes and steady himself. His foundations seemed to be disappearing, leaving him foundering.

And it wasn't just Meg.

He stared back out of the window. It was almost dark and starting to rain, just drizzle but enough for sensible people to run for cover. Henry and Peggy hadn't noticed. They were entranced, having fun, not caring about minor details such as wet clothes.

Peggy… Seventy-six years old.

The only thing she'd care about was if she lost Henry, he thought. She'd do anything to prevent that, and he'd help her. Once the adoption went through they'd be safe together.

So he was fighting for Henry and Peggy.

What about Meg?

He thought back to what she'd said. *You have your boundaries.*

Who didn't? He had to have boundaries to survive.

Peggy didn't have boundaries.

And neither did Meg, he conceded. She'd opened her home, opened her heart to Peggy and Henry. He had no doubt that if Steven hadn't intervened that was where Peggy and Henry would be. Sharing Christmas at Rowan Bay.

That was where he wanted to be.

Not possible.

Why not?

For a million reasons, he thought.

Name them.

Right. First, Steven would never agree. Steven had met the idea of adoption with initial consent, but Matt knew that a part of his reaction to his small son was his need for public approval. The story of Amanda's death and Steven's surprise parentage had filtered through the circles they moved in. Denying responsibility didn't fit Steven's self-image. Nor would sending Henry to Australia. If it was hinted at, the adoption would be off.

It couldn't be done.

So... Taking Peggy and Henry to Rowan Bay was problematic.

But him?

Taking himself to Rowan Bay?

What would he do with himself? His business was here. His life was here.

And then he thought, *Is business what I do or what I am?*

It was Meg's question, an accusation, echoing back to haunt him.

He looked again at Peggy and Henry. They were self-contained, gloriously happy with their dogs and their new life. They'd been delighted to see him when he'd arrived last night, they'd been even more delighted when he'd said he was staying for a week, but they didn't need him. Neither of them had invited him outside with them. They'd be expecting him to return to his office, as he normally did when he was here.

They wouldn't expect him to roll on wet grass.

Even if he did…it wasn't who he was.

Who was he?

What was important to him?

It wasn't a question he'd ever asked himself.

So ask it now.

This place was important to him, he conceded, this sheltered headland, this untouched beach. He'd fight for it.

This house? He looked around at the glamorous interior and conceded…not so much.

Peggy and Henry?

He glanced again at the pair outside and thought, yes, they'd become part of who he was. He'd fight for them, with every means at his disposal.

And his business? The massive financial world he lived in? He'd been bred to it. Its care had been ingrained from such an early age that he'd never questioned it.

Why?

Was it what he *was*?

The McLellan's foundation did so much good. It employed so many. The thought of it crumbling was unthinkable.

It didn't impress Meg.

And there she was again, front and centre. Meg.

He couldn't go to her. She wouldn't stay with him.

And then he paused as he heard the thought bubble.

She wouldn't stay with him.

But he hadn't asked her to stay with him. He'd asked her to fit in around the edges of what he was.

Of what he did.

Maybe Meg could be a part of who he *was*?

He closed his eyes again, letting his thoughts drift, to Meg as he'd just seen her, to a laughing, beautiful woman who'd taken the life she'd been given and accepted it with love and courage.

She'd been falling in love with him. She'd said it, but she couldn't love within his boundaries.

His world was shifting. *Boundaries.* Where were they and what was he protecting?

Himself?

A sudden flash of insight had him remembering Nanny Elspeth and the gardener who'd been sacked when he was small. He remembered the grief, the emptiness.

'That's what you're afraid of.' He said it out loud.

But then he glanced outside again, at Peggy, who'd taken herself off to her island in her own emptiness.

And Henry…

My friend Robbie at school says this place is like an island.

His world felt as if it were shifting.

Boundaries…

The French doors were suddenly flung open and a soaking Peggy and Henry and two sodden dogs burst into the room. Water scattered all over the parquet floor.

His parents would have had kittens.

But they're boundaries, he told himself as Henry launched himself at him, bursting with excitement.

'I'm going to call her Puddles because she loves splashing,' he said excitedly. 'She likes getting her nose wet. I bet she loves the beach.'

He thought suddenly of the turtles, of the nesting sites. That was how they were protected, with boundaries.

Or you figured another way.

'We'll need to train her to protect the turtle nesting sites,' he found himself saying. 'And not to chase the birds. We'll need to watch her until she's trained.' And then he thought, *We?*

He couldn't train a dog at weekends.

How many boundaries needed to disappear?

'I'm good at watching,' Henry said happily. 'She's a smart dog.' And suddenly he wrapped his skinny, soggy arms around Matt's body and Matt found he was lifting one small boy into his arms and holding. Hugging. Feeling Henry's small body cradle to his, his face nestle into his neck.

Feeling boundaries start to crack.

And then it was done. Henry struggled to get down and whooped off toward the kitchen to tell Esther the news about Puddles's new name. Esther. Not 'the cook'.

Another boundary.

Matt looked up and found Peggy watching. Smiling.

'Feels good, doesn't it?' she asked and he thought he saw tears behind her smile.

'It surely does. Happy Christmas, Peggy. You might need to go dry off before you freeze to death.'

'I'd die happy,' she said and he knew she would.

'Peggy…'

'Mmm?'

'I know I said I'd stay until New Year.'

Her smile faltered a little and then recovered. 'You can't? It's okay. Henry and I are okay.'

'You are okay,' he told her. 'But I want you… I want *us* to be more okay. I'm thinking of taking a fast trip to Australia.'

'To find Meg?'

'To ask her to marry me,' he said, because why not lay it on the line?

'She wouldn't have you last time,' Peggy said simply and he thought how much did Peggy see? 'So what's changed?'

'I think I have.'

Her eyes searched his face and slowly her smile returned.

'Is that anything to do with the way Henry hugged you?'

'Sort of,' he told her and then, because it seemed important, he stepped forward and hugged her, too. An all-enveloping, lifting hug that made her squeal, that had Henry tearing back from the kitchen to see what was happening.

'You're cuddling Grandma,' he said in astonishment, and Matt set the blushing, giggling Peggy down and hugged Henry again for good measure.

'I'm practising,' he told Henry. 'I'd never figured out that hugs are important but now… Maybe they're the most important things in the world.'

'Puddles likes hugs,' Henry said. 'Though she chews my ear when I hug her tight.'

'You might need to put up with chewing for a hug,' Matt told him. 'A chewed ear seems a small price to pay. I'm about to confess that all sorts of things can disappear if a hug is the pay-off. Peggy…'

'You go get 'em,' Peggy said happily. 'You said you'd stay here until New Year? Henry and I can sacrifice that for a very big pay-off indeed.'

CHAPTER FOURTEEN

CHRISTMAS IN AUSTRALIA meant the start of summer holidays, and holidays meant Charlie's charters were booked solid. The weather was great and the fishing was perfect. Meg cleaned and gutted more fish than she could count.

Thursday morning's charter was due to leave at eight, late for a charter. The fishing was usually better at dawn but she wasn't complaining.

She and Boof arrived to find the jetty almost deserted. The rest of the boats were already out. Her boat was tied at the docks. She was a sturdier vessel than the not-lamented *Bertha*.

No one was queued and waiting.

Cancellation? Her heart sank. A cancellation meant no pay, but she headed into the office and found Charlie beaming.

'The punter's already on board.'

'Punter?' she said cautiously. 'One?'

'That's right.'

It had happened before—one cashed-up tourist wanting sole attention. Usually she steered clear. Being alone on a boat with someone she didn't know was risky.

'Why didn't you get one of the guys to take it?'

'Specific request for you,' Charlie told her. 'Repeat customer so it's okay. Enjoy yourself.'

'Charlie…' She glowered. 'If it's some sleaze, I'm getting right off.'

'Suit yourself,' he said happily. 'With the rate this guy's prepared to pay I might even be tempted to take the boat out myself. Go check him out and let me know.'

Right. She headed out into the morning sunshine

thinking at least it was a great day for being at sea, and with one customer there'd be fewer fish to clean.

She stepped on board—and Matt appeared from below.

Matt.

Boof went nuts.

Boof was far too well behaved to be permitted to go nuts. She should click her fingers, order him back to her side.

How could she do anything? Her heart seemed to have stopped.

Matt was catching Boof's paws as he jumped up. Fondling his ears.

He was dressed casually in neat chinos, boat shoes and an open-necked shirt.

Why did he look different?

To be honest she wasn't capable of wondering much at all. All she knew was that Matt was here and she was having trouble jump-starting her heart again.

'Happy New Year,' he told her, smiling straight at her.

'I… Happy New Year.'

'I wanted to come earlier but I had things to organise.'

'Really?'

'Really.'

'I… You've come all this way…' She was struggling here. 'Henry? Peggy?'

'They're still at McLellan Place. I'd have brought them but Steven still won't let Henry leave the country. Not until the adoption goes through.'

'You're still…adopting?' Each word seemed an effort.

'It's early days yet,' he told her. 'But as long as it's made clear publicly that Steven hasn't abandoned Henry, he's amenable. But meanwhile, Meg, I've paid for charter. You want to put to sea?'

She took three deep breaths and steadied.

'Where do you want to go?'

'Garnett Island,' he told her. 'I need to check my new investment.'

'You've bought it?' That was a squeak. 'From Peggy?'

'I have.'

'But why?'

'Let's go see,' he told her. 'We can talk about it later. It's a great day. Let's just enjoy it.'

'Matt…'

'There are lots of things we need to talk about,' he said, suddenly grave. 'There are so many things I messed up. I need time to explain, time to get things in perspective. If you'll trust me to go to sea with you… Meg, can we enjoy the morning and let things happen as they will? No rush. For now let's just be together and let the future take care of itself.'

There was little choice but to agree. In truth there was little to disagree about. He wanted to go to Garnett and she was being paid to take him. What was there in that to make her feel as if the world were holding its breath?

There were so many questions spinning in her head but there didn't seem any way she could get them out. Matt didn't seem to want to talk, so neither did she.

She stood at the wheel and he stood beside her. Not touching but close.

The day was calm and warm—he really was seeing Bass Strait at its best. Dolphins were treating their wake as their own personal surf, leaping in and out of the milky foam, ducking under the boat, charging ahead—like a guard of honour?

It was almost dreamlike. That Matt was here… She had no idea what was happening but the closer they got to Garnett, the more she felt that something had stilled within her, some emptiness was filling.

It had to be her imagination. There was a part of her that was fighting to keep her stupid heart under control.

He'd bought Garnett? So what? It wouldn't dent his wealth and it'd give Peggy independence. It was only sensible that he come and check it out, figure what to do with it.

With her. He'd asked for her.

Down, she told her heart. Stop jumping about like a puppy with a treat in store. She had to stay sensible.

Halfway out she produced her standard punter fare of cheese sandwiches and coffee. She stayed at the wheel, munching her sandwich, checking out a bunch of cormorants diving off one of the rocky outcrops.

'It's stunning,' Matt said softly. 'I never realised how beautiful. Last time I was here…'

'You were too busy working out how to stay alive,' she said dryly and he smiled.

'I didn't have to worry about that. You were showing us how to live.'

There was enough in that to take her breath away all over again. There was also enough there to make her focus—fiercely—on her cheese sandwich and not say anything at all.

Finally Garnett Island came into view. As far as she knew, no one had been near the place for months. There'd been a couple of decent storms since they'd last been here. Peggy's boat hadn't fared so well. It was still at its mooring, but it had started taking water and was now partly submerged.

'That'll be a job, getting rid of her,' Matt said.

'You'll replace her?'

'I can't stay on the island without a decent boat.'

What the…? 'You intend to stay on the island?'

'I hope so. It's a great place for a family holiday. And Peggy tells me it's a haven for sea creatures. I'm starting to think we might form a chain of wildlife sanctuaries. Small but many. Today, McLellan Place and Garnett Island. Tomorrow, the world.'

There was even more to take her breath away. Luckily she had stuff to do. It took skill to manoeuvre the boat safely into the only part of Peggy's jetty that was still available. Matt helped, stepping easily out of the boat, manoeuvring ropes, attaching them with skill.

This was a charter. He'd wanted to come here to see his purchase. She had to stay sensible.

'I'll stay with the boat,' she said and he grinned.

'You think I engineered this whole thing so I could sit up in Peggy's house by myself? In your dreams, Meg O'Hara. What you see before you is step one of the McLellan and O'Hara Master Plan, and that plan has Meg O'Hara right in the very middle. Take you away and the whole thing disintegrates. You want to see?' And he held out his hand to help her off the boat.

She stared at his hand in bewilderment.

No one helped her off her boat. For some reason that thought was front and centre. Not since she could remember. Even as a tiny kid she'd made that leap herself.

He held out his hand and she thought, *I can do it myself.*

But… The McLellan and O'Hara Master Plan. Not the McLellan Plan.

His hand was just there.

She reached out and took it. He tugged her upward and she came a little too fast. It turned into a hug, a gentle caress, and then he put her away, still holding her hand but taking it no further. As if there were things to be said. Things to be sorted.

'If we're going up to the house maybe we should take the sandwiches,' she ventured. 'The charter includes food for the day. Cheese sandwiches for morning tea, salad sandwiches for lunch, fruit cake for a midafternoon snack.'

'Food's been organised,' he said. 'It's in the house. Come and see.'

His hold on her hand firmed. Numbly, she allowed him to lead her along the overgrown path, up to the house.

Boof, delighted to be off the boat, hared away to rediscover what seemed a doggy paradise.

Last time Meg had been here this hadn't seemed a human paradise. It had looked sad.

Now, though, the little cottage almost gleamed a welcome. Loose tin on the roof had been nailed down. Someone had worked on the garden. A pile of weeds were heaped by the fence, as if waiting to be composted.

'We had to work fast,' Matt said placidly. 'Do you realise how hard it is to get things done in Australia between Christmas and New Year?'

'It's beach and sleep time here,' she managed, feeling stunned. 'But, Matt, why…?'

And then he opened the door to the cottage and she couldn't say another word.

Gone was the appalling settee with the broken springs, the threadbare rugs, the rickety furniture. Peggy had asked for the things she most valued to be taken off the island and Meg had expected to see the place stripped. Instead, the shabby furniture had been replaced by…gorgeous.

No, not gorgeous, she thought, as she stared in amazement around the little living room. By simple. By comfortable. By cosy.

The settee was big and squishy. The rug was thick and warm. Lamps were set on either side of the fireplace.

Some of Peggy's photographs had been returned to the mantle. Another photograph took pride of place, though. It was a picture taken by the reporter from Rowan Bay's local paper the day they were rescued.

Four people were climbing from the helicopter. Peggy was holding Henry. She was turning back to smile as Matt lifted Meg from the chopper.

It was an action photo but it was much more. It was four people who'd come together in the most extraordinary circumstances.

'I figure it's our first family photo,' Matt said tentatively. 'At least I hope it is.'

She stared at the photo and then she turned and stared at Matt.

He'd lost his assurance, she thought. His eyes held doubt. Hope. Fear?

'What's happening?' she managed.

'Meg, we have a chance to change our lives,' he said and he took her hands. The link was warm, strong, but still she felt the tremor of uncertainty. 'I've messed it up. I'm hoping with everything I have that I haven't messed it up for ever.'

How to answer that? She had to make her voice work. *Caution*, her sensible self was saying. *If it's more of the same, you have to find the strength to pull away.*

'You'd better… You'd better tell me.'

'First things first.' She was right, the look in his eyes was definitely anxious. 'I've resigned as chairman of McLellan Corporation.'

'You've resigned.'

'As of this week. My combined family's currently having forty fits. My cousins are vying for the job. I have the biggest pecuniary interest so I get the say. I'm actually thinking of appointing my secretary. Helen knows the company backward and she'll support what I plan.'

'What you plan?' Did she sound like a parrot? She couldn't care.

'Here's the thing,' he told her. 'Meg, after Christmas, after your phone call, after seeing you on the beach, I started thinking why am I doing…what I'm doing. The answer came back that I'm good at it. I'm good at moving and shaking. I'm good at making money. But you're right, it's what I do. I've never questioned what I am. So then I thought who am I? And the deeper question is, who do I want to be?'

'Which is?' She'd started to shake. Why? It was warm enough.

Someone must have been here this morning. There was a fire in the grate. She could see the table set in the kitchen. She could see a bottle of wine. Glasses.

To say she was discombobulated was an understatement. All she could do was feel the warmth of Matt's hold, and wait for him…to set her world right?

'That's where the adoption comes in,' he told her. 'I want to *be* Henry's dad. I want to *be* a part of his life.'

'That's…that's great?'

'And I want to care for Peggy. We've talked about it. We reckon if I'm Henry's dad, then Peggy can be my mother-in-law. It makes sense. We both like the idea.'

'I… Yeah.' She could see that.

'And I don't want to work in Manhattan any more. At least, not much. Meg, as soon as I started thinking past what I do, the "wants" and the "don't wants" started cascading. When I was fifteen my grandfather allocated me the office next to his. He introduced me to "our people". As a kid, as a college student, I'd use my over-the-top office to study, picking up knowledge of the company while I did. It seemed natural. It seemed what I was. It's only this jolt… It's only you, Meg O'Hara, who's made me see it's not who I am at all.'

'So…' Wow, she was struggling. 'You're adopting Henry—and Peggy? You're quitting work?'

'I'm not quitting work. I'm probably going to be busier than I've ever been. That's the next step. I asked myself what gives me the most satisfaction. And one of the things is my turtles.'

'Protecting them…'

'With my gates? No. I've figured another way. I'm throwing the gates open. Peggy concurs. She'll help me. We're starting to channel McLellan money into forming conservation areas. More, we'll make part of what we do education. McLellan Place is one of the best places in the world to bring school groups, to teach, to learn. And we can set up places all around the world.'

'W-we?'

'You and me,' he told her. 'This isn't who I want to be, Meg O'Hara. It's what I want us to be. Which is you and me and Peggy and Henry and Boof and Stretchie and Puddles and whoever else comes along. My family.'

'Family.' She felt dizzy. This was unreal. Crazy. She was frantically trying to make herself make sense.

'How can you bring school groups to Garnett?' she managed, which was ridiculous but her head was spinning in so many directions the dizziness was almost making her sway.

'We might have trouble bringing school groups here,' he conceded, and he smiled down at her, a wide, encompassing smile that made her heart turn over. 'It's definitely a conservation area but I'm thinking we might be a little bit selfish.'

'What…what do you mean?'

'Let me show you,' he said, and his dark eyes gleamed with laughter. And tenderness. And…something that made her feel as if she were melting.

And before she knew what he was about he'd swept her into his arms and carried her up the stairs.

There were three bedrooms up here: Peggy's, the little room she'd furnished for Henry and a spare. In the time she'd been here, Meg had investigated and seen a barren room with nothing to recommend it but sunbeams shining through a dormer window and a view almost to Tasmania.

But now the room had been transformed with soft rugs, chintz curtains, lamps. Centre stage was the most enormous bed she'd ever seen. Covered with a feather duvet, pillows, pillows and more pillows, it was the sort of bed you could invite a small army to share.

'Is it big enough?' Matt asked, sounding anxious, and she almost choked.

'How did you get this here?' she squeaked. 'How did you even get it up the stairs?'

'Helicopters,' he told her. 'And manpower and money. Wasn't it lucky there weren't any bush fires this week?'

'Matt, this must have cost you...'

'I don't care what it cost.' He set her down carefully, tenderly on her feet. 'As long as it gets me what I want.' And then he hesitated. 'No. That's wrong. As long as it lets me be...who I am.'

'Oh, Matt.' All she wanted was for him to hold her and never let her go but somehow she had to ask. The sensible part of her was still making its unwanted presence felt. 'So, Matt, who are you?'

'I'll tell you who I am,' he said softly, lovingly, and he took her into his arms again and tugged her against his chest. 'Right this minute? I'm a man who's totally, completely, awesomely, undeniably in love with Meg O'Hara. I feel like I'm part of her and that's my biggest thing. It's what I want to be. Meg, I've asked you to marry me before, but it was different. I'm asking you again now. Meg O'Hara, the thing I want to be more than anything in the world is to be married to you. To be allowed to love you, for now and for ever. I want to *be* loved by Meg and I want to *be* allowed to love her back. So, Meg O'Hara... For the third and best time... Will you marry me?'

And how was a woman to reply to that?

There was no choice because Matt was holding her. Matt was loving her.

Her Matt.

'I guess the answer has to be yes,' she whispered.

He set her back a little. 'That sounds like you're being forced.'

'Not forced,' she whispered. 'Never forced, my love.'

And then she thought, *I need to get this right. I need to say it like it is.*

'Matt, I will indeed marry you but I am being forced,' she admitted. 'Not by you, though. By me. I believe I fell in love with you the moment we met. We saved each other and we did so much more. We figured out who we are. So me… I'm the woman who loves Matt McLellan. I'm the woman who'll help you adopt Henry, who'll help care for Peggy. I'm the woman who'll egg you on to save turtles and whatever else we can save along the way. But more than that. I'm the woman who'll stay with you for ever, even if it means staying here for longer than Charlie's charter, trying out this ridiculous bed, even if we have to burn our boat again to do it. Forced? I can't deny what I am, Matt McLellan. I'm the woman who's head over heels in love with you for ever.'

And that was that. The doubts fell away. He was her man, she thought, and she was his woman. For ever and ever and ever.

And the gleam in Matt's lovely eyes said he knew it, too. Their world was starting anew.

'I have news for you,' Matt said as he gathered her into his arms again and carried her over to the preposterous bed. 'I warned Charlie that we may be quite some time. I'm not stupid. I've set up radio checks every night. I've also asked Maureen to take care of your chooks. We're stocked with human food and dog food. Apart from that… is there anything at all to stop us staying here?'

'For ever?' she breathed. 'I guess the world will break in soon enough.'

'But it'll be our world,' Matt said, and then he kissed her, tenderly, joyfully, wonderfully. 'It'll be our world for ever, my beautiful Meg. Starting now.'

* * * * *

HER FAVOURITE MAVERICK

CHRISTINE RIMMER

Thanks to the brilliant and beautiful Kimberly Fletcher,
who named the sweet white kitten in this story.
Kimberly suggested I call the kitten Opal—and I did.
I love that name so much! As a thank-you, I offered
to dedicate this book to Kimberly. She asked instead
that I give her a different kind of dedication…

Her Favourite Maverick is dedicated to Wildflower and
Miss Clack and to everyone who has survived cancer.
Kimberly would also like to dedicate this story to
those who live with a cancer survivor and to anyone
who has suffered the loss of a loved one to cancer.

Cancer touches all of us in one way or another.
Fight hard, reach out to those you love
and know that you are not alone.

Chapter One

As Sarah Turner emerged from the tiny back-room office of the former train depot, Vivienne Shuster Dalton glanced up from a worktable covered in fabric swatches, to-do lists, project folders and open sample books.

"There you are," said Viv.

"Just giving it all one more look." Sarah tried for a light tone, but going over the books yet another time hadn't changed a thing. The news was not good.

"Please tell us you've found a solution to our problem."

If only.

Viv's business partner, Caroline Ruth Clifton, stood across the worktable from her. Caroline turned her big dark eyes on Sarah and asked hopefully, "We can swing it, right?"

The answer was no.

And for Sarah, whether she was trying to claw her way up the food chain at the biggest accounting firm in Chicago or working in her dad's little office right here in Rust Creek Falls, Montana, her least favorite part of the job remained the same. She hated telling clients that they were in trouble—especially clients she liked and admired.

Viv and Caroline were a couple of dynamos. They'd even opened a second location down in Thunder Canyon, Montana. Caroline spent most of her time there.

And here in Rust Creek Falls, all the brides flocked to the old train depot to get Viv to create their perfect wedding.

Unfortunately, both the rustic train depot and Viv's primary local wedding venue—the brick freight house nearby—needed new roofs. All new. They couldn't just slap a fresh layer of shingles on. Both buildings required tear-outs and rebuilds. Plus, there were structural issues that would have to be addressed. Viv had collected bids. She knew what the work would cost.

It was a lot.

And the wedding planners had already stretched every penny to the limit.

Gently, Sarah laid it out. "I'm sorry. I've been over and over the numbers you gave me. The money just isn't there. You need a loan or an investor."

"A loan against what?" Viv was shaking her head. "The buildings and the land belong to Cole's family." Her husband, Cole Dalton, was a local rancher. Cole and his large extended family owned a lot of the land in the Rust Creek Falls Valley. "I can't take a loan against my in-laws' property. We're doing great, but, Sarah, you already know it's all on a shoestring—and frankly, I struck out on my own so that I could do this *my* way." Viv's big green eyes shone with sheer determination. "An investor is going to want a say in how we run things."

"Not necessarily. Some investors just want a percentage of—"

The little bell over the front door cut Sarah off mid-sentence.

"Good morning, ladies," boomed a deep male voice. The imposing figure in the open doorway swept off his black Stetson to reveal a thick head of silver hair. "Maximilian Crawford, at your service." The man plunked his big hat to his heart. Tall and powerfully built, with a handsome, lived-in face and a neatly trimmed goatee and mustache, the guy almost didn't seem real. He reminded Sarah of a character from one of those old-time TV Westerns. "I'm looking for Vivienne Dalton, the wedding planner," he announced.

"I'm Viv." Viv started to step out from behind the worktable.

But Maximilian was faster. In five giant strides, he was at her side. He took Viv's hand and kissed it. "Such a pleasure to meet you. I've heard great things." He turned to Caroline, kissed her hand and then took Sarah's and brushed his mustache across the back of it, too.

Viv, who'd looked slightly stunned when the older man bowed over her hand, recovered quickly and made introductions. "Maximilian, this is Caroline, my partner, and Sarah Turner, with Falls Mountain Accounting."

"So happy to meet you, all three of you—and please

call me Max. My sons and I have bought the Ambling A Ranch east of here. We're newly arrived from the Dallas area, but we have Crawford relatives here in Rust Creek Falls. We're putting down roots in your fine community."

"Welcome to town, Max." Viv cut to the point. "How can we help you?"

"I have an important job that needs doing. And, Vivienne, I know you are the one to tackle it."

"Well, if it's a wedding you're after, you've come to the right place. I take it you're the groom?"

Max threw back his silver head and let out a booming laugh. "Sorry, Viv. Not me. I've had enough of wedded bliss to last me three lifetimes. But my boys are another story. I've got six, each one better lookin' than the one before. Goodhearted, my boys, if a bit skittish on the subject of love and marriage. As we speak, all six are single." He shook a finger. "You ask me, that goes against the laws of God and man. It's about time my boys settled down."

Caroline wore a puzzled frown. "So, then, what you're saying is that all six of your sons are engaged?"

Max let out a low, rueful chuckle. "No, pretty lady. What I'm saying is that my boys need brides. And, Viv, that's where you come in. I want you and the lovely Caroline here to find each of my boys the perfect woman to marry—for a price, of course. A very nice price."

A silence followed. A long one. Sarah, who'd moved back from the worktable to let the wedding planners do their stuff, couldn't help wondering if maybe Max Crawford was a few bucking broncs short of a rodeo.

And judging by their carefully neutral expressions, Viv and Caroline also had their doubts.

However, the train depot roofs weren't going to replace themselves. Viv needed a large infusion of cash, stat. And if Max *was* for real, cash was exactly what he offered—too bad he was ordering up services Caroline and Viv didn't provide.

"But, Max," Viv said patiently, "we *plan* weddings. We aren't matchmakers."

"And why not? Matchmaking is an honest, time-honored practice. A lucrative one, too—at least it will be for you, with me as your client."

Viv slowly shook her head. "I'm so sorry. But we just don't—"

"A million," Max cut in, bringing a trio of stunned gasps from Viv, Caroline and Sarah, too. Max nodded at Viv. "You heard me right. A million dollars. You find my boys wives and the money is yours."

"Max." Viv let out a weak laugh. "That's just crazy."

"That's where you're wrong. I've made my fortune thinking outside the box. And that makes me living, breathing proof that anything can be achieved if you're willing to make your own rules."

Sarah took another step back from the worktable. She couldn't have disagreed more. Rules mattered. And as much as she would like for Max to be the solution to Viv's money troubles, fast-talking men were dangerous. Sarah had learned that sad lesson the hard way.

Viv wasn't going for it, either. "Are you asking us to set up six arranged marriages? No. Definitely not. Caroline and I could never do that."

"Arranged?" Max huffed out a breath. "No way.

My boys would never go for that. They'll choose their own brides. All I'm asking is that you find the perfect woman for each of them."

"Right," Viv scoffed. "Easy peasy."

"Love isn't something you can force." Caroline added her quiet voice to Viv's mocking one. "It really does have to develop naturally and—"

"Caroline, darlin'." Max patted her shoulder. "I couldn't agree with you more. We're on the same page. You won't be *arranging* anything. You won't need to. I've heard all about Rust Creek Falls. Love is everywhere you turn around here and the percentage of pretty women is satisfyingly high. You set my boys up and they are bound to fall."

Sarah took another step back. How could they believe a word the guy said? He talked too fast and he'd openly admitted that he made his own rules.

As if he'd sensed her retreat, the big man shifted his glance to Sarah. "So how 'bout you, darlin'?"

Sarah straightened her shoulders and hitched up her chin. "What about me?"

"Are you looking for the right guy to marry?"

She was looking for anything but. "Excuse me? You want to marry me off to one of your sons?"

"Sweet, sweet Sarah, just say yes." Max actually winked at her. "You won't regret it."

"Sorry, but I'm not on the, um, market."

"Got a sweetheart already, then?"

"No. I'm simply not interested."

Max heaved a big sigh. "That's a crying shame, and I mean that sincerely. You're a beautiful woman with a sharp brain, I can tell. You'd be just perfect for—"

"Dad. What are you up to now?" At the sound of another commanding male voice, Sarah whirled toward the open door.

"Patience, Logan," Max replied. "Just give your old man a few minutes more."

"They plan weddings here, Dad. You don't have a fiancée, so you don't need a wedding. Xander and I are getting tired of waiting in the truck."

Sarah tried not to stare. But really, who could blame her? The cowboy in the doorway was hot—tall and lean, with thick brown hair and a mouth that would have just about any girl thinking of long, scorching kisses.

At the moment, though, that gorgeous mouth was scowling at Max. "What's going on here?"

As he spoke, another fine-looking cowboy entered behind him. The second guy said, "Whatever you think you're pulling, Dad—don't."

Max only laughed. "Come on over here, boys. Let me introduce you to Viv, Caroline and Sarah." His big white teeth gleamed as his smile stretched wide again. "What did I tell you, ladies? Meet my oldest son, Logan, and third-born, Xander."

The first cowboy, Logan, flicked a glance in Sarah's direction—and froze. Now he was staring right at her. "Hello, Sarah," he said low. Intimately. As though they were the only two people in the room.

And then he was on the move again, coming straight for her. He stopped a foot away, right up in her space. The breath fled her lungs. The guy was even hotter up close. It should be illegal to have eyes so blue.

With a little shiver of unwelcome delight, she took

his offered hand. His big, warm fingers engulfed hers. More shivers skittered up her arm.

Absurd. Sarah Turner had no time for the shivers. Not anymore. No way was she letting a pair of bedroom eyes lead her astray again.

But Logan wasn't making it easy for her. He stared at her like she was the most beautiful creature he'd ever seen.

Why? She so didn't get it. She was not at her best and hadn't been for way too long now. A year and a half ago, she'd been hot…ish.

Now, though? She wore her hair in a ponytail to keep it out of the way and didn't bother with makeup beyond a swipe of mascara and maybe some lip gloss. On a good day, she made it all the way to dinnertime without getting spit-up on her shirt.

Max just kept talking. "Boys, Viv and Caroline here not only plan weddings, they also serve as the Rust Creek Falls dating service." Such a liar, that Max. He wouldn't know the truth if it bit him on the butt. "And Sarah is not only gorgeous—she's got a mind for figures, works as an accountant right in town. Falls Mountain Accounting, I believe. Have I got that right, Sarah?"

Logan still held her hand. She really ought to pull away. But she didn't. "I'm a CPA, yes," she said as she continued to stare into Logan's blue eyes.

"I think I need an accountant," said the killer-handsome cowboy in that deep, smooth voice of his, never once letting go of her gaze—or her hand. "And a dating service works for me. Sign me up. I'll take you, Sarah. To dinner. Tonight."

"Uh, yeah. Right." She laughed, playing it off, as her traitorous heart flipped cartwheels inside her chest.

Ridiculous. Impossible. She had no time for dates. If she had any extra time, she would spend it sleeping. And never again would she believe the lies of a handsome, smooth-talking man.

Max was still talking. "Sarah, Logan here is a self-made man. He grew up on our ranch in Texas, but he couldn't wait to get out on his own. Earned his fortune in Seattle, in real estate."

Logan chuckled. "Shut up, Dad."

Max didn't miss a beat. "Son, why don't you and Sarah go on into town? Take her to the donut shop. You can firm up your dinner plans over bear claws and coffee."

Sarah opened her mouth to give both father and son a firm no when a baby's cry from the back room did it for her.

"Huh?" Max blinked in surprise. "That sounds like a—"

"Excuse me." Sarah pulled her hand free of Logan's warm grip and managed a breezy smile. "My little girl wants her mother." Turning neatly on her heel, she headed for the back room.

Was she disappointed that a certain dreamboat of a man was bound to lose interest fast when faced with a crying baby?

A little, maybe. But not *that* disappointed.

Really, it was for the best.

Logan Crawford watched Sarah's bouncing ponytail as she trotted away from him. What was it about her?

Those big golden-brown eyes, all that shining bronze hair? That smile she had that was shy and devilish simultaneously? Damned if that smile didn't dare him to kiss her.

He would take that dare at the first opportunity.

Was she married?

He hadn't seen a ring—and yeah, the baby kind of gave him pause.

But not that much of a pause. He could work around the baby. As long as she was single, well, why shouldn't the two of them have a little fun? Nothing lasted forever and he liked it that way.

It was chemistry, pure and simple. Sexual attraction. And damn, it felt good.

His dad was still talking to the other two women, while Xander just stood there looking midway between vaguely intrigued and slightly annoyed by what they were saying.

Logan, on the other hand, felt downright invigorated. He hadn't felt like this in years. Maybe never. Lately, he'd been kind of off his game when it came to women. He just had no drive to hook up and hadn't been with anyone in months.

But everything had changed the minute he set eyes on Sarah.

Just let her be single. That was all he asked.

She emerged from the back room with a backpack-style diaper bag hanging off one shoulder, a giant leather tote dangling from one hand and a pouty-faced infant in a baby carrier on the other arm. "Sorry, everyone. We'll just be going."

Uh-uh. Not yet. In four strides, Logan reached her.

"Here. Let me help you." The baby stuck a fist in her mouth and stared up at him, wide-eyed.

"No, really." Sarah seemed flustered. Her cheeks had turned the sweetest shade of pink. "There's no need. I'm good."

He ignored her objections and eased the diaper bag off her shoulder. "What's her name?" He took hold of the tote. For a moment, she held on like she wouldn't let him take it.

But then she let go. "Sophia," she said. "Her name is Sophia."

"Pretty name. How old is she?" He wiggled his eyebrows at the baby, who had a pink cloth flower tied around her mostly bald head.

"Five months," said Sarah.

The baby took her slobbery hand out of her mouth long enough to announce, "Ah-da!" and stuck it right back in.

Behind him, his dad started flapping his jaws again, apologizing for trying to set them up. "I'm so sorry, Sarah. I didn't see a ring on your finger and I assumed—"

"You assumed right," Sarah responded coolly. "I'm not married."

Excellent. "But are you engaged?" Logan rattled off the pertinent questions. "Living with someone? Dating exclusively?"

"None of the above," she replied. "It's just me and Sophia." As if on cue, the little girl let out a goofy giggle around the fist in her mouth. Sarah added, delectably defiant, "Just us. And we like it that way."

So she's free. It was all Logan needed to know.

Unfortunately—and for no reason Logan could

understand—Max moved in next to him. "Son, Sarah has to go. Give her back her things."

Not happening. Not yet. "Give us a minute, would you, Dad?" He turned his back on his father and moved in closer to Sarah and little Sophia. That caused Sarah to retreat a step. Logan closed the distance. The process repeated—Sarah retreating, Logan eliminating the space she'd created—until they reached the door.

A glance over his shoulder revealed that Max had started talking to the wedding planners again. His dad and the blonde wedding planner shook hands. Logan made a mental note to find out what that was about as he turned his attention back to the irresistible brown-eyed girl.

She said, "I really do have to go."

Logan held on to her tote and diaper bag and started talking, pulling out all the stops, flirting shamelessly with both the woman and her baby. He made silly faces at Sophia as he coaxed information from Sarah, learning that she'd moved back to Rust Creek Falls a month before and had a cottage in town.

"Truly, Logan." Sarah's pretty white teeth nibbled nervously at her plump lower lip, driving him just a little bit crazy. He wanted to nibble on that lip himself. "I'm not interested in dating. I'm way too busy for anything like that."

He nodded. "I understand. Let me help you out to your car."

"No, that's not necessary."

"Yeah, it is. You've got too much to carry and I've got a couple of perfectly good free hands."

Her sweet mouth twisted with indecision—and then she gave up. "Well, um, okay. Thank you."

He walked her out to her white CR-V and waited while she strapped the baby's carrier in the back seat, handing her the giant bag and backpack when she was ready for them. She set them on the floor, shut the door and went around to the driver's door. Admiring the view, Logan followed after her.

"Well," she said with an overly bright smile as he held open the door for her. "Good luck, then—with the ranch and all."

"'Preciate that," he replied. She jumped in behind the wheel, her denim skirt riding up a little, giving him a perfect glimpse of one smooth, shapely thigh. "Drive safe," he said and shut the door.

She waved as she pulled out. He stood in the warm June sunlight, watching her drive away, thinking that he would be good for her, that she needed to get out and have some fun.

Sarah Turner deserved a little romance in her life and Logan Crawford was just the man to give her what she deserved.

Chapter Two

"Logan, it's a bad idea," his father said. "You need to forget about Sarah Turner."

It was past six that evening. Logan, his dad and Xander were out on the porch of the ranch house at the Ambling A enjoying a beer after spending a few hours plowing through the stacks of boxes that weren't going to unpack themselves. At some point, one of them needed to go inside and hustle up a meal. But for now, it was nice out and the beer was ice-cold and refreshing.

Logan stared off toward the snow-tipped mountains. The sky was cloudless, perfectly blue. "I like her, Dad. And it's not your call." He didn't point out that he was a grown-ass man and would do what he damn well wanted to do. Max ought to know that by now. "I'm curious, though. She's single, smart and pretty. She works for a living. She's got it all going on as far as I can see. What have you got against her?"

"Nothing," Max answered gruffly. "You're right. She seems like a fine person."

Xander rocked back in his chair and hoisted his boots up onto the porch rail. "So what's the problem then, Dad? I was standing right there when you struck that crazy deal with the wedding planners to find us all brides for a cool million bucks. To me, that means you want us all to get married. Whether that's ever gonna happen is another question entirely. But the way I see it, if Logan's found a girl already, you should count your blessings."

A million dollars to marry them off? Logan hadn't heard that part. Sometimes his dad came up with the wildest ideas. Logan had no plans to marry anybody. But that wasn't the point. He followed Xander's lead. "Yeah, Dad. You were eager enough to hook Sarah and me up until the baby started crying."

Max sipped his beer. "I do want you boys married. It's about damn time. But when kids are involved, well, things get too complicated." He pointed his longneck at Logan. "Take my word for it, son. You don't need that kind of trouble. Viv will find you someone perfect— someone sweet and pretty without a baby hanging off her hip."

"I'll say it again, Dad. *I* like Sarah and I'm going to move on that."

"I don't want you—"

"Stop. Listen. There is no problem here. You don't want me marrying Sarah Turner? Great. I'm not going to marry her—or anyone. The last thing I want right now is a wife, with or without a baby in the bargain, so you can save that million bucks. When my time comes to tie the knot—if it ever does—I'll find my own bride. I don't need anyone setting me up."

Xander recrossed his boots on the railing. "That's too bad. Because Dad's got that wedding planner setting us *all* up."

Logan leveled a warning look on his dad. "Are you listening? Because you ought to know your own sons better than that. I think I can speak for all six of us when I say that we're not letting anyone choose brides for us—not you, Dad, and not those two wedding planners back at the train depot."

"Nobody's choosing for you," Max insisted. "Viv and Caroline are just going to be introducing you to some lovely young single ladies. You should thank me for making it so easy for you to develop social connections in our new hometown."

Xander grunted. "Social connections? You're kind of scaring me now, Dad."

"I just don't get it," Logan said to Max. "For years, you've been going on about how marriage is a trap—and now suddenly you're shelling out a million bucks to make sure we've each got a wife?"

"Yeah." Xander scowled. "Seriously, Dad. You need to cut that crap out."

"Don't get on me, boys." Max assumed a wounded expression, but he didn't say he would give up his matchmaking scheme.

Not that Logan really expected him to. Unfortunately, once Maximilian Crawford got an idea in his head, telling him to cut it out wouldn't stop him.

They would have to warn their brothers that Max had brokered a marriage deal for all of them and they shouldn't be surprised to find a lot of "lovely single ladies" popping up every time they turned around.

Just then, a quad cab rolled into the yard. A tall, solidly built cowboy got out.

Max stood from his chair. "Nate Crawford. Thanks for coming."

The guy did have that Crawford look about him—strong and square-jawed. He joined them on the porch. Max offered him a beer. They made small talk for a few minutes.

Nate, Logan learned, was a mover and shaker in Rust Creek Falls. He owned controlling interest in the upscale hotel just south of town called Maverick Manor. Logan thought Nate seemed a little reserved. He couldn't tell for sure whether that was because Nate was just one of those self-contained types—or because Max's reputation had preceded him.

Logan loved his dad, but Max was no white knight. The man was a world-class manipulator and more than a bit of a scamp. Yeah, he'd made himself a fortune over the years—but there was no doubt he'd done more than one shady deal.

Yet people were drawn to him. Take Logan and his brothers. They were always complaining about Max's crazy schemes. Yet somehow Max had convinced each one of them to make this move to Montana.

For Logan, it was partly a matter of timing. He'd been between projects in Seattle and ready for a change. When Max had offered a stake in a Montana cattle ranch, Logan had packed his bags and headed for Big Sky Country.

If nothing else, he'd thought it would be good for him to get some time with his brothers. And yeah, he couldn't help wondering what wild scheme his dad might be cooking up now.

Never in a thousand years would Logan have guessed that Max had decided to marry them all off.

Max clapped Nate on the shoulder. "I really do appreciate your dropping by. Wanted to touch base, you know? Family does matter, after all. And now that me and the boys are settling in the area, we'd like to get to know you and everyone else in the family here."

"How about this?" Nate offered. "Saturday night. Dinner at Maverick Manor. The Rust Creek Falls Crawfords will all be there."

"That'll work," said Max. "My other four boys will be up from Texas with the breeding stock by then. Expect all seven of us."

"Looking forward to it." Nate raised his beer and Max tapped it with his.

The next morning at nine sharp, Logan paid a visit to Falls Mountain Accounting.

The door was unlocked, so he walked right in.

Inside, he found a deserted waiting room presided over by an empty front desk with a plaque on it that read, Florence Turner, Office Manager. The door with Sarah's name on it was wide open. No sign of his favorite accountant, though.

The door next to Sarah's was shut. The nameplate on that one read Mack Turner, Accountant. Something was going on inside that office. Faintly, Logan heard muffled moans and sighs.

A woman's voice cried softly, "Oh, yes. Yes, my darling. Yes, my love. Yes, yes, yes!"

Logan debated whether to turn and run—or stick around just to see who emerged from behind that door.

Wait a minute. What if it was Sarah carrying on in there?

It had damn well better not be.

He dropped into one of the waiting room chairs—and then couldn't sit still. Rising again, he tossed his hat on the chair and paced the room.

What was this he was feeling—like his skin was too tight and he wanted to punch someone?

Jealousy?

Not happening. Logan Crawford had never been the jealous type.

He was…curious, that's all, he reassured himself as he marched back to his chair, scooped up his hat and sat down again.

The sounds from behind the shut door reached a muted crescendo and finally stopped.

A few minutes later, a flushed, dewy-eyed older woman who looked quite a bit like Sarah emerged from Mack Turner's office. Her brown hair needed combing and her silky shirt was half-untucked.

"Oh!" Her blush deepened as she spotted Logan. "I, um…" She tugged in her shirt and patted at her hair. "I'm so sorry. Just, um, going over the calendar for the day. I'm Florence Turner."

Hiding his grin, he rose again. She marched straight for him, arm outstretched.

"Logan Crawford," he said as they shook.

"Please just call me Flo. I manage the office. We're a family business, just my husband, our daughter, Sarah, and me." Flo put extra heavy emphasis on the word *husband*. Apparently, she wanted to make it perfectly clear that whatever he'd heard going on behind Mack Turner's door was sanctioned by marriage. "Are you here to see Mack?"

"I'm waiting for Sarah."

"Oh! Did you have an appointment?"

"Not exactly." He tried a rueful smile.

"Well, I apologize for the mix-up, but Sarah has meetings with clients—all day, I think she said."

"Really? That's inconvenient." He patted his pockets. "I seem to have lost my phone." He'd left it in the truck, but Flo didn't need to know that.

"Oh, I'm so sorry," Sarah's mom said.

"Unfortunately, that means now I don't have Sarah's cell number…" Okay, yeah. He'd never had a cell number for her. But it was only a *little* lie.

And it worked like a charm. Flo whipped out Sarah's business card. It had her office, home and cell numbers on it.

"You're a lifesaver. Thank you."

"Any time, Logan—and you're more than welcome to use the phone on my desk."

"Uh, no. I need a coffee. I'll use the pay phone at the donut shop up the street."

That was another lie. He called her from his truck as soon as he was out of sight of Falls Mountain Accounting.

* * *

Sarah was with a client when the call came in from an unknown number. She let it go straight to voice mail. The day was a busy one, appointments stacked up one after the other.

When she finally checked messages in the late afternoon, she found one from Logan.

"Hello, Sarah. It's Logan Crawford. Call me back when you get a minute."

She played it through twice, sitting in her white CR-V with Sophia snoozing in the back seat. His voice, so calm and commanding, made her feel strangely breathless.

The truth was, she hadn't been able to stop thinking of him, of the way he'd looked at her, like she was the only person in the room, of the way he'd kept hold of her hand when there was no excuse for him to be holding it beyond the fact that he wanted to. She'd loved how he'd been so sweet to Sophia and that he'd insisted on carrying her diaper bag and tote out to the car.

Plus, well, he was way too good-looking and she hadn't been with a man in over a year.

The plan was to give up men, after all. At least for a decade or so—maybe longer.

And really, hadn't she made her unavailability perfectly clear to him?

Annoyed and flustered and oddly gleeful all at the same time, she called him back.

"Hello, Sarah."

"Hi, Logan. How did you get my number?"

"I stopped by your office. Your mom gave me your

card." Dear Lord in heaven, his voice. It was so smooth, like raw honey. She pictured it pouring from a mason jar, all sweet and thick and slow. And then he added, "Your mom and dad are obviously very happy together."

Sarah felt her face go hot. Stifling an embarrassed groan, she answered drily, "Yeah. I try to be out of the office as much as possible." Then she changed the subject. "Logan, I'm flattered you went to all that trouble just to get my number, but really, I meant what I said. I hardly have time to wash my hair lately. I'm not dating anyone, not even you."

"I get it. I called on business."

"Oh." Did she sound disappointed? Well, she wasn't. Not at all.

He said, "We're just getting moved in at the Ambling A and frankly, the accounts are a mess. We need a professional to get the books on track. We want to hire local. And that means Falls Mountain Accounting."

Her heart rate had accelerated at just the idea of being near him as she gathered the information to whip those books of his into order—but no. She needed to keep her distance from him, which meant he would have to work with her dad. "Did you meet with my dad yet? He's the best. I know you'll be happy you hired him."

"Sarah." He made her name into a gentle reproach. "Your dad seems to have his hands full—with your mom."

She did groan then. "I do not believe you said that." He didn't immediately respond and she suddenly had a burning need to speak, fill the silence between them. Bad idea. But she did it anyway. "They never used to be like that, I swear. I don't know what happened. I haven't asked. I doubt I ever will."

"I understand."

"Yeah," she grumbled. "Sure, you do." He made a soft, amused sort of sound. "Did you just chuckle, Logan? I swear to God I heard you chuckle."

His answer was actually more of a demand. "*You*, Sarah. I intend to hire *you*." He was just so…commanding. She'd never liked bossy men, but she found herself longing to make an exception in his case. In a strictly professional sense, of course.

And she might as well be honest—at least with herself. It was a definite ego boost to have this hot rancher so interested in her, even if she would never let it go anywhere.

Plus, well, he'd insisted he wanted to work with her. If she said no, he would go elsewhere. It wasn't good for business to turn away work.

"All right, Logan. Have it your way."

"I love it when you say yes. How about I meet you at your office?"

Her office, where there was no telling what her parents might be up to? "Er, no. I'll come out to the Ambling A."

"That's even better. I feel I should warn you, though, it's kind of a mess, old records all over the place. Some are on floppy disks, believe it or not. There are even some dusty, leather-bound ledgers that go back to the fifties."

"It will be fine, don't worry. Mostly, I need the current stuff."

"Well, I've got that, too."

She quoted her hourly rate.

"That works. Today?"

"Logan, it's almost five. I need to go home, feed my baby, maybe even stretch out on the sofa and veg out to the new season of *GLOW*."

"You're tired." He actually sounded as though he cared. "Tomorrow, then."

"All right. I have a nine o'clock that should go for an hour, two tops. After that, I'm flexible. Is it all right if I call you when I'm ready to head over to the Ambling A?"

"Works for me. Call me on this number."

She said goodbye and then sat behind the wheel for a moment, thinking how she would have to watch herself tomorrow, make sure she kept things strictly business. In the back seat, Sophia made a soft, happy sound in her sleep, and that had Sarah thinking how good Logan was with the baby.

Too good, really. The last thing she needed was him being charming and wonderful with Sophia. That could weaken her already shaky defenses.

Sarah bent her head over her phone again and texted her dearest friend since childhood, Lily Hunt.

Hey. You on the job at the Manor tomorrow?

Lily was an amazing cook and worked at Maverick Manor as a part-time chef.

Not tomorrow. Why?

Now, that was a long story. One she didn't really want to get into via text—or in a phone call *or* face-to-face. Because what was there to say, really? Nothing had happened between her and Logan and nothing was *going* to happen.

I have to go visit a new client, Logan Crawford. He and his dad and five brothers have bought the Ambling A. I think things will go more smoothly if I'm not trying to take care of Sophia while I'm setting up their accounts. So how 'bout a cushy babysitting gig at my house?

There. That sounded simple and reasonable without giving away too much. She hit Send.

And Lily took it at face value: You're on. Tell Sophia that Aunt Lily can't wait. When to when?

Be at my place at 8:30. I should be back by two or three.

I'll be there. But I want something from you in return.

What? You think I won't pay you?

Sarah, I know you'll pay me. You always do. If I didn't take the money, you would chase me up Pine Street waving a handful of bills.

Very funny.

These are my terms. Saturday at 6. Dinner at the Manor. You and me, my treat. A girls' night out. We deserve it. Get your mom to take Sophia. That's what grandmas do. Come on, it will be fun.

It did sound kind of fun. Sarah hadn't been out to dinner in so long, she couldn't remember the last time. And Lily didn't get out enough either, really.

Sarah, I meant it. Ask your mom.

Grinning, Sarah replied, Okay. I'll ask her.

Yes! See you tomorrow morning, 8:30 sharp. And don't put it off, call your mom now.

Sarah did call her mom. Flo answered on the first ring. "Honey, I'm so glad you called. Here you are back in town and we're all working together—and yet, somehow, we hardly see you. How's my sweet grandbaby?"

"Asleep at the moment."

"She is an angel—oh, and by the way," her mom began much too coyly, "a handsome cowboy showed up at the office this morning looking for you."

Who are you and what have you done with my real mother? Sarah thought but didn't ask. Florence Turner used to be quiet and unassuming. A nice person, but a grim one. Not anymore. When she wasn't disappearing into her husband's office for a quickie, Flo bounced around Falls Mountain Accounting full of energy and big smiles. It had been that way since Sarah moved home from Chicago a month ago. Who knew when it had started?

Sarah was afraid to ask.

Her mom prompted, "Did he call you?"

"Logan Crawford, you mean?"

"That's him."

"Yes, he called me."

"Honey, that is one fine-looking hunk of a man, a complete hottie, I don't mind telling you."

"Yeah, I've seen him. Thanks, Mom."

"You should snap that one up."

"Mom. He wants me to straighten out his accounts, that's all."

"Oh, I think he's hoping to have you *straighten out* a lot more than his accounts."

"Mom!"

"Sweetheart, don't be a prude. Life is beautiful and so are you. You deserve the best of everything—including a tall, hot cowboy with gorgeous blue eyes."

"Yes, well. I didn't call to talk about Logan. I was wondering if you would watch Sophia Saturday night. Lily and I want to get together for dinner."

"Honey, at last!"

"What do you mean by that?"

"You've been home for weeks and this is the first time you've asked me to take Sophia for you."

"Oh, well, I…" Sarah didn't know what to say. Her mom had offered, but it had never really been necessary.

"It's all right," Flo reassured her. "I'm just glad you've finally asked me—and yes, I would love to."

"Perfect." Sarah thanked her and ended the call before her mother could say another word about Logan Crawford and his hotness.

Armed with her laptop, her business tote and the steely determination not to be seduced by a sweet-talking cowboy, Sarah arrived at the Ambling A at eleven the next morning.

Logan was waiting for her on the long front porch

of the giant log-style house. He wore faded jeans that fit his strong legs much too perfectly and a dark blue shirt that clung to his lean chest and arms and brought out the color of his eyes. He dropped his hat on one of the porch chairs and came down the steps to open her car door for her.

"Where's Sophia?" he asked. She'd just picked up her laptop from the passenger seat. He reached in and took it from her, tucking it under his arm as he offered his hand to help her from her car.

She hardly required assistance to get out from behind the wheel and she really was trying not to let him get too close. But to refuse him just seemed rude.

"The baby?" he asked again as his warm, slightly rough fingers closed around hers. His touch felt way too good. She grabbed her giant leather tote with her free hand and hooked it over her shoulder.

"Sophia's at home today." She emerged from the car into the late-morning sunlight. "My friend Lily was free and agreed to babysit." They stared at each other.

His fine mouth twitched at one corner as he quelled a smile. "I'm disappointed. I was looking forward to another lively game of peekaboo."

Just like the other day at the train depot, she had to remind herself to ease her hand from his.

He led her inside, where there were moving boxes stacked in the front hall.

"It's a great house," she said, staring at the wide, rustic staircase that led up to a gallery-style landing on the second floor. "I vaguely remember the Abernathy family. They owned the place first and built the house, but they left a long time ago."

"We got a hell of a deal on the place from the last owners, I'll say that much." He put his hand on the fat newel post. "The house needs work, but we'll get around to that eventually. Right now, we're just trying to get everything unpacked—my dad and Xander and me. My other brothers will be showing up in the next couple of days. Then we'll be focused on buying more stock. The barn and stables need repair. Lot of ditches to burn and fences to mend. Fixing up the house is low on the list of priorities."

She should move things along, tell him she needed to get going on the work he had for her. But she was curious about him. "So, you're from Texas, I think your dad said?"

He nodded. "We had a ranch near Dallas. Me and my brothers grew up there."

"You *had* a ranch?"

"We put it on the market when we decided on the move here."

"So, you've always been a rancher, huh?"

He shook his head. "I went to college for a business degree and then moved to Seattle. Been there ever since."

"Seattle." She remembered then. "That's right. Your dad said you were in real estate."

"Property development, to be specific. I got there just in time for the boom years, and I did well. But then my dad got this wild hair to move to Montana, get us all together working a new spread. The timing was right for me. I'd been thinking that I was ready to try something different." He was looking at her so steadily. She liked having his gaze focused on her. She liked it way too much.

Then he asked, "How 'bout you? Where did you go to college? Have you always lived in Rust Creek Falls?"

His questions were perfectly reasonable.

Her response took her completely by surprise.

All of a sudden, her throat was too tight and there was pressure behind her eyes.

Really, what was the matter with her? Out of nowhere, she hovered on the verge of bursting into tears, right here in the front hall of the Ambling A ranch house with this too-handsome, charming man looking on.

Crying? Seriously? She wasn't a cryer. Crying was pointless and completely uncalled-for in this situation.

And yet still, she wanted to put her head in her hands and bawl like a baby over all the ways her life hadn't turned out as she'd planned, just stand here sobbing right in front of this superhot guy. A guy who seemed hell-bent on seducing an overworked, constantly exhausted single mom who wanted nothing more to do with the male of the species, thank you very much.

She gulped the ludicrous tears down and managed an answer. "I went to Northwestern and then I worked in Chicago for a while."

Now he was frowning at her, a worried sort of frown. Those eyes of his seemed to see way too much. "Sarah, are you okay?"

"I'm fine." She pasted on a wobbly smile. "Really. And don't you have a mountain of records and receipts to show me?"

He gave her a long look, a look both considering and concerned, as though he was trying to decide whether to push her to confess what was bothering her or back off. She breathed a sigh of relief when he said, "Right this way."

They went down a central hallway, past a big living room and a kitchen that could use a redo to an office at the back of the house.

By then, she'd pulled herself together. "You weren't kidding." She gave a low laugh as she approached the big mahogany desk that dominated the room, its surface piled with old ledgers, dusty CDs and floppies.

"Most of this is probably meaningless to us, I realize," he said, setting her laptop on a side chair.

She put her tote down beside it. "Yeah, it's doubtful I'll need any of the records generated by the former owners."

"If you don't need them, we can just toss them out."

"I *might* need them. I can't say until I look through all the current records. And *you* might want to look through it all later. You might find out you own something you didn't even know you bought."

"Even the floppies? They would need converting just to read them, wouldn't they?"

She shrugged. "Doesn't hurt to keep them for a while. If you decide at some point you want to go through them, we have a guy in Kalispell who will convert them for you."

"That sounds really exciting." He put on a dazed expression, even crossing his eyes. His playfulness made her grin and caused a flare of warmth in her belly. The man was way too appealing. But at least she was no longer about to cry and he'd stopped looking worried that she might have a meltdown right in front of him.

She said, "What I'll need to set you up are your current records, including whatever you've got up till now of the Ambling A's inventory, income and expenses."

"Income?" He chuckled. "Not hardly. Not yet."

"Well, okay then. Just your expenses and whatever inventory you have of machinery, equipment and livestock—including your best judgment of their value. I'll need the documents you received from the title company when you closed the sale. I'll put it all together using a basic accounting program that should be easy to keep current. That will be a few days to a week of work for me here at the ranch, if that's all right?"

"Sounds good to me." He had that look, like he was talking about a lot more than bookkeeping.

She pretended not to notice what a shameless flirt he was. "I'll be in and out because I need to keep up with my other clients, too. But if I do the work here, I can come right to you with any questions I have about the records you've given me. We can clear up any issues on the spot."

"Works for me." He said it in a low rumble that stirred a bunch of butterflies to life in her belly.

She tried valiantly to keep a professional tone as she rattled off more suggestions. "After you're all set up, you'll need someone to post transactions regularly. I have a couple of local people who can do that. Or you can just put in the time every week or so and do it yourself. I suggest you reconcile the bank balance and the general ledger at least once a month."

"Sure. And I'll hire whoever you suggest. What about tax time?" he asked.

"I'll be happy to do your taxes."

"Good." He arched an eyebrow and teased, "How 'bout an audit?"

She laughed. "Very funny. You know I can't audit my own work."

"Damn. Busted." He tipped his head to the side, his gaze lazy and warm. It felt so good just to have him looking at her, to be staring right back at him, thinking all kinds of naughty thoughts as she went through her stock suggestions for keeping accounts in order.

Really, this was getting out of control. They were more or less having sex with their eyes. If she didn't watch out, she would do something crazy, like throw herself into his arms and beg him to kiss her.

Uh-uh. It needed to stop.

"I should get to work," she said.

"Right." He pointed at the piled-high desk. "I think everything you need is there, including that big manila folder jammed with receipts, the inventory lists and the packet from the title company. You can tell the current stuff by the lack of dust."

"Okay, then." She moved behind the desk and pushed the records she would be using to one side. That left the piles of ledgers and old disks.

He got the message. "You need space to work."

"Do you have another desk you want me to use? A table works fine, too."

"The desk is yours for as long as you need it. I'll box up the old records, get them out of your way."

There were empty boxes waiting against one wall. Together, they started putting the ledgers in one box and piling the old disks in another.

She'd straightened from the boxes and was turning

to the desk to grab another handful of disks when she spotted Max leaning in the open doorway to the back hall. He looked like some old-time gunslinger in black jeans, black boots, a white shirt and a black Western-cut jacket.

"The lovely Sarah," the older man said. "What a surprise." Something in his tone made her uneasy, some faint edge of...what? Mistrust? Disapproval?

But why?

"Hi, Max." She gave him a big smile.

He didn't smile back or even give her a nod, but turned to Logan as though she wasn't even there. "Give me a few minutes?"

"Can't it wait? Sarah and I were just—"

"Go." Sarah faked an offhand tone. She felt completely dismissed by Max and that had her emotions seesawing again the way they had in the front all. There was absolutely no reason she should care if Logan's dad didn't like her. But she did care. There was a clutch in her throat and a burning behind her eyes as her totally inappropriate tears threatened to rise again. She waved Logan off. "Talk to your dad. I'll finish clearing the desk and get to work."

Impatient to return to his favorite accountant, Logan reluctantly followed Max out to the back porch.

The old man leaned on one of the posts that framed the steps down to the yard. He stared out at the ragged clumps of wild bunchgrass that extended to the back fence. Like too many fences on the property, it needed repair.

Logan braced a shoulder against the other post.

"Okay, Dad. What's so important we have to deal with it right this second?"

Max's gaze remained on the backyard. He took a long count of ten to answer. "I can see now why you suddenly decided we needed to get the books in order."

Why deny it? "You know I like Sarah. It shouldn't be a surprise—and we do need someone to set up a system to keep track of everything."

"You've got a fancy business degree. You can do all that yourself."

"Dad, I didn't come to Montana to take up book-keeping. Sarah is equipped to do it fast and efficiently."

Max slanted him a narrow look. "Maybe you don't trust your old dad. You think you need a professional to tell you that everything's on the up-and-up."

Logan snorted out a dry laugh. "Oh, come on. I wouldn't have signed on for this if I thought you were up to something you shouldn't be. Still, it never hurts to have a professional putting a good system in place, keeping everyone honest."

"So you're telling me she's only here for her book-keeping skills? You've got absolutely no interest in those big amber eyes and that pretty smile?"

This conversation was a complete waste of time—time he could be spending with the woman he couldn't stop thinking about. "I'm thirty-three years old," Logan said flatly, "long past the age I have to run my personal choices by you. I'll date who I want to date." *At least, I will if I can somehow convince Sarah to give me a shot.*

"A woman with a child, Logan. It's a bad idea. If it doesn't work out, the kids are always the ones who suffer."

Logan had had about enough. He straightened from

the porch post and turned to face his father directly. "What is it with you all of a sudden? Are you talking about Sheila?" Sheila was his mother. She'd left them when Logan was seven. It had taken him several years to accept that she was no mother to him in any way that mattered. Even saying her name made a bitter taste in his mouth. Max shot him a bleak glance, but then, without a word, he turned and stared off toward the fence again.

"You dragged me out here," Logan prodded. "Talk. I'm listening."

But Max only waved a dismissive hand and continued to stare at nothing. Fed up with him, Logan went back in the house.

When he entered the office, Sarah glanced up sharply from behind the desk. He didn't like the look on her face, a tense look, kind of teary-eyed, a look a lot like the one she'd had in the front hall earlier.

He pushed the door shut behind him. If Max had more to say, he could damn well knock. "What's wrong?"

She had her laptop open and the big packet of sale documents spread out in front of her. Shutting the laptop, she rose. "You know what? I should go." She swiftly lined up the stack of papers and closed the packet. "I know of a perfectly good bookkeeper in Kalispell. I'll text you his number."

"Sarah."

She didn't answer, just scooped up her laptop and took a step out from behind the desk. Logan stopped her by blocking her path, causing her to clutch the laptop to her chest and stare up at him defiantly. "Excuse me, please."

"Sarah."

She hitched up her pretty chin. "You are in my way."

"What's the matter?" It took everything he had not to touch her, not to grab her good and tight in his arms. "Talk to me."

Her soft lips trembled. "It's, um, quite obvious that your dad doesn't want me here."

"It's not about you, not really."

"Of course you would say that."

"Look. Sometimes I don't think *he* knows what he wants. He gets these wild ideas, that's all. You can't take him seriously. Bottom line, we need the accounts in order and that means we need *you*."

"But I just don't understand. It's like he thinks I'm after you or something, trying to trap you into—I don't know, putting a ring on my finger, I guess. And I'm not. I swear I'm not. I've got no interest in marriage. I don't want to trap anyone." She stared up at him through eyes swimming in barely held-back tears, so earnest, so very sincere. "Especially not, um, you."

He tried to tease her. "You know, if you keep talking that way, you're bound to hurt my feelings. I'm a very sensitive guy." And he did dare to touch her then. Clasping her shoulders, he held her gaze.

"I...oh, Logan." She looked absolutely miserable and he should probably just let her go. But he held on.

What *was* it that she did to him? He didn't get it. He felt like ten kinds of selfish jerk to be putting her through this. But still, he just stood there, hands holding her slim shoulders, keeping her in place.

Finally, she spoke again. "See, the thing is, it hasn't worked out for me, to get involved with a man. So I promised myself I wouldn't. Not for years. Maybe never.

And then you show up and, well, frankly, Logan, you really tempt me."

This was *bad* news? "Excellent."

"No. No, it's not. It's not excellent in the least. All it does is confuse me to feel this way about you. I don't need it, all this confusion. I'm already overworked and exhausted. The last thing I need is a sexy cowboy in the mix."

"Hold on," he said tenderly. "So then, what you're saying is you think I'm tempting and sexy?"

She huffed out a frustrated breath. "That is so not the point."

"Maybe not. But you can't blame me for being pleased to hear how you feel." He wanted to kiss her, just pull her close and put his mouth on hers. But he wasn't sure how she would react to that. She seemed really upset and he didn't want to make her any more so.

"It's all too much, don't you get it?" she cried. "I'm just plain on overload." And then, as if to illustrate her point, a single tear got away from her. It slipped over the dam of her lower eyelid and traced a gleaming trail down her cheek.

"Sarah. Damn it." He let her go, but only so he could get his hands on the laptop she clutched so tightly. When he tried to take it, she resisted. "It's okay," he coaxed. "Come on, now. Let go." And she did. When she gave in and released it, he plunked it down on the desk and took her shoulders again. "Sarah, don't cry."

Another tear escaped. And another after that. "Too late," she said in a tiny voice.

"Aw, Sarah…" He pulled her close and she let him,

collapsing against him, her soft arms sliding around his waist.

For a too-short span of perfect seconds, she clung to him. He breathed in the clean scent of her silky hair, wondered what she'd done to him, hoped that whatever it was, she would never stop.

But then she looked up again, her eyes wet and so sad, a tear dripping off the end of her pretty nose.

"Here," he said. "Sit down." He pushed her gently back into the old leather desk chair and looked around for a tissue. There weren't any.

She sniffled. "Give me my tote, please." He went around the desk to grab it from the chair where she'd left it and handed it to her. She pulled out a travel pack of tissues, took one and wiped the tears from her cheeks. "I'm a mess," she said.

"No." A hank of her hair had escaped from her ponytail. Gently, he guided it back behind the shell of her ear. Retreating, but only a little, he hitched a leg up on the corner of the desk. "You're tired and overworked. And completely gorgeous."

She gave a little snort-sniffle at that. "Yeah, right."

He put up a hand, like a witness about to swear to tell the truth and nothing but the truth. "You're gorgeous," he said again. "And I mean that sincerely."

She started to smile, but couldn't quite manage it. Her shoulders slumped. "I'm just so tired, you know? Tired of working nonstop and trying to be a decent mom to Sophia and really not doing either all that well. I don't get it, I really don't. How did everything go so wrong?"

He leaned closer. "What went wrong? Sarah, come

on. Tell me. I need to know everything that's bothering you."

She scoffed. "Why?"

"So I can try to make it better." He actually meant that, he realized as he said it. He wanted to be with her—for as long as it lasted. And during that time, he wanted to be good for her. When they parted, he wanted her to remember him as a good guy who had treated her well.

She shook her head slowly. "If you keep pushing, I'm just going to go ahead and unload it all on you. My whole life story, all the ways I messed up. It will be a lot. It will be a really bad case of extreme oversharing and you will wish you'd never asked."

"No, I won't."

She scoffed. "Yes, you will. Believe me. Let's talk about something else."

"Uh-uh. For you to talk to me about what made you cry is exactly what I want." And he did want it. He really did. "Tell me. Tell me everything."

She stared at him, considering. "You're sure?"

"I am. Talk to me, please."

"Logan, I—"

He stopped her with a shake of his head. "Tell me."

For a long moment, she just stared at him. And then, at last, she let it all out.

Chapter Three

"My parents used to be so different," Sarah began.

Logan thought of Flo Turner the day before, coming out of her husband's office with her shirt untucked, her hair sticking out on one side and a smile of complete satisfaction on her flushed face. "How so?"

"When I was growing up, they were both so gloomy, always bleak and determined."

"You're not serious."

"As an IRS audit," she sneered. "They got married because they 'had to.'" She air-quoted that. "Because I was on the way. And they stayed married out of a sense of duty—they actually used to say that, how they stayed together because it was their duty. They were so noble. I couldn't wait to get out of that house, to live my own life, make things happen, get out in the big world and have everything. Success. True love. A great marriage.

Kids. And a whole lot of fun. But somehow, once I was on my own, there just wasn't enough time for fun, you know?"

"Why not?"

"I'm really not sure. I guess, because the way they raised me did rub off on me at least a little. I was driven, a straight-A student. I got a scholarship to Northwestern and my parents covered everything the scholarship didn't. I had a full ride and was driven to get through college fast and get on with my life." She'd studied like crazy, she said, and spent all her free time building her résumé.

To get a head start on her accounting career, she began interning in her sophomore year. She'd crammed six years of college and work experience into four and passed the CPA exam at the very young age of twenty-two. By then, she was already working at Chicago's top accounting firm.

And up until then, she'd never had a serious boyfriend.

"I met Tuck Evans not long after I got my CPA license. He was so charming. He also had a good job and claimed to be crazy for me. He was my first and only love—or so I thought." They'd moved in together.

But two years later, Tuck was perfectly happy with the status quo. "He said he saw no reason for us to get married. He said that we had it all without the ring. To teach him a lesson, I moved out and waited for him to come crawling back to me." She fell silent.

He prompted, "And?"

"Didn't happen. Finally, I called him. He was sweet and good-natured as ever, saying how right I was to end it. Really, he said, it wasn't working out and we both knew it." She glared up at Logan defiantly. "I was such an idiot."

"No, you weren't. Tuck wasn't good enough for you. He did you a favor."

Sarah glared harder. Logan could see her sharp brain working, trying to find something objectionable about what he'd just said. She wanted a fight.

He wasn't going to give her one. "Go on," he said gently.

She blew out a breath—and continued. "The day after I called Tuck and he said how glad he was that he and I were over, I headed off for a big conference in Denver. When a handsome bachelor came on to me at the conference, I decided a rebound fling was just what I needed."

"This handsome bachelor got a name?"

"Mercer Smalls. Does it matter?"

"No," he said honestly. "You're right. His name doesn't matter." Except that Mercer Smalls was a ridiculous name for a man. But whatever the guy's name had been, Logan would have disliked him on principle. Not that he was actually in any position to judge. He'd enjoyed more than one fling himself. Way more. And a lot of one-night hookups, too.

"I spent the three nights of the conference with Mercer," she said. "When we parted, he promised to call, but he didn't."

"Good riddance." Logan kept his tone mild, but he had to grit his teeth to do it.

Sarah sighed. "I was philosophical about it. Those three nights with Mercer helped me realize that flings just aren't for me. I knew I wouldn't be doing that again." She fell silent.

He realized that he was maybe a little like her first boyfriend, Tuck. And like the guy at the conference, too. Out for a good time, not looking for anything too serious. She was making it painfully clear that having a fling with a guy wasn't for her—that right now, she didn't want a guy at all.

He should back off, walk away.

But the thing was, she really got to him. And he *would* do right by her, damn it. She needed fun—all the fun she'd never had yet. She needed a man who knew how to treat a woman like a queen. It might not be forever, but when it ended, she would be glad for what they'd shared. He could make certain of that, at least.

And the silence between them had stretched out too long.

He guessed. "Mercer Smalls is Sophia's father?"

She nodded. "I couldn't believe it when I found out I was pregnant. It wasn't like we hadn't used protection. We had. But the stick turned blue anyway."

"Does Mercer know?"

"Of course. I knew the city he lived in and the name of his firm, so I reached out to him. I didn't imagine he would go down on one knee or even that he might be the guy for me, but a man has a right to know when he's going to be a father."

"He absolutely does," Logan agreed. A man deserved to know about his child, to be a part of his kid's life— even if the man was a player named Mercer Smalls who'd said he would call and never did.

"But as it turned out," she said, "Mercer wasn't a bachelor, after all. He was married with children and wanted nothing to do with me or the baby I was going to have. I couldn't believe it," she muttered, her eyes full of shadows, her gaze far away. "My rebound fling was a cheating husband who denied his unborn child outright. He just wanted to sign off all responsibility for the baby and be left alone."

He thought of Sophia, with her goofy little grin and her baby sounds that seemed like real words to him. Mercer Smalls was ten kinds of douchebucket. And a damn fool, to boot. "You gave him what he asked for?"

"You bet I did. His loss, the schmuck."

"I'm guessing this is the part where you swore off men forever?"

"How did you know?" She troweled on the irony. "I decided I would forget men and love and all that. I would be a successful single mom—and, Logan, I tried. I really did."

But fighting her way up the corporate ladder in the big city wasn't compatible with tackling motherhood solo on a tight budget. "The cost of day care for an infant was through the roof and I just couldn't keep up the pace at work."

In the end, she'd accepted the inevitable and moved home to Rust Creek Falls. "It's great, it really is—or it should be." She swiped another tear away. "I've got this cute, cozy cottage my parents own and a job in the family business. I can take Sophia with me to work whenever I need to. I mean, things could be so much worse. My baby is the light of my life and my parents are here to help and support me. Right?"

He nodded on cue and then prompted, "But?"

"Well, you've heard about Homer Gilmore, haven't

you?" At his puzzled frown, she grinned through her tears. "Nobody's told you about Homer?"

When he shook his head, she launched into this story about a local eccentric who made moonshine that had everyone doing crazy stuff. A few years ago, at a wedding on the Fourth of July, Homer had spiked the wedding punch. People had danced in fountains, gotten in a whole bunch of crazy fights—and had sex. A lot of sex. So much sex that nine months after that wedding, Rust Creek Falls had actually experienced a baby boom.

"My point being," she said, "that sometimes I wonder if my mom and dad have somehow drunk the Homer Gilmore moonshine. I mean, you've been to the office. You've witnessed firsthand how they are now. Their marriage of grim duty has turned into something completely different. My mother and father have fallen in love."

And if Flo and Mack weren't doing it in the office, she said, they were suddenly heading out the door, going who-knew-where together.

"Not to visit clients, that's for sure," she grumbled. "So yeah. I'm back in my old hometown, still trying to be a good mom while putting in killer hours doing my best to catch up with the workload my parents are currently too busy *schtupping* to shoulder."

He looked at her sideways. "Did you just say *schtupping*?"

"*I did. And* I have no idea where that came from. I've never used that word before in my life." Her sweet mouth was trembling—and not with tears this time. She laughed out loud, tipping back in the chair, the sound free and open and so good to hear.

He just wanted to hold her, though he doubted she'd allow it.

Still, he had to try. Rising, he offered his hand. She put hers in it. He pulled her up and into his arms, guiding her head to rest on his shoulder.

They laughed together, holding on to each other, until he tugged on the end of her ponytail.

She looked up at him. "What?"

"Is that it? Is that everything?"

"Pretty much, yeah. I'm working nonstop and still somehow barely keeping up. I adore my baby, but I hate being constantly frazzled and frumpy."

He put a finger to her lips. They were so soft, those lips. He ached to kiss them. "You're not frumpy. Not in the least. You're beautiful and you're doing a great job and it's all going to work out."

She actually smiled at him. "I shouldn't believe a word you say. But you know what? I kind of love it. Because all this flattery and praise, well, I can use a little flattery at this point. I really, really can."

"Sarah." He touched her silky cheek. And she didn't even try to stop him.

She didn't stop him when he traced the perfect shape of her ear, either. Or when he put his finger under her pretty chin and lifted it a fraction higher. She smelled so good, like flowers and baby lotion and something else, some delicate spice.

And then she whispered his name so softly and just a little bit hesitantly, lifting her chin even higher, offering up those plump, tempting lips to him.

He took what she offered. Carefully, at first, not wanting to push her, he brushed his mouth back and forth across hers until she opened to him, her lips parting on a soft, hungry cry.

It was all the invitation he needed.

He went for it, settling his mouth more firmly on hers, smiling a little when she made a sweet humming sound.

Her body was pliant in his arms. Every inch of her felt just right, giving and womanly, soft where he was hard. He could kiss her forever.

But too soon, with a tiny moan, she lowered her chin and broke the perfect kiss. Suddenly shy, she pressed her face into the crook of his shoulder.

He kissed her temple, her hair, even gave a quick nip to her earlobe. That brought a giggle. She lifted her gaze to him again. They regarded each other. Her eyes were almost pure gold right now.

"Let me take you out," he said. "Friday night. There's this great little Italian place in Kalispell I discovered a week or so ago when I got tired of eating Xander's cooking."

"Really, Logan. Didn't you hear a word I said?"

"I heard *every* word. Let me take you out."

"I just can't."

He touched her chin again, ran his thumb back and forth across those perfect, kissable lips of hers. "*Can't* has got nothing to do with it. You know you *can*. All you have to do is say yes."

"You are the sweetest man."

Sweet? Had any woman ever called him that? Doubtful. And he wasn't sure he liked it all that much. But he'd take it if it got him what he wanted. What they *both* wanted. Because she was drawn to him as much as he was to her. If he'd had any doubts on that score, the kiss they'd just shared had ended them. "So that's a yes, right?"

Her head went from side to side, that ponytail swaying slowly. "I've got no time for fancy restaurants."

"The restaurant I'm thinking of is a great place, but not that fancy, I promise you."

She sighed. "Logan, I shouldn't have kissed you and nothing is going to happen between us."

What was it about this woman? He'd never worked so hard to get a girl to say yes—and not even a yes to spending the night in his bed. Uh-uh. So far, he couldn't even convince her to let him buy her dinner.

He should give up.

But she had those golden eyes and she smelled so good and, well, something about her had him willing to do whatever he had to do just to get the raw beginnings of a chance with her. "How 'bout a quiet evening at your house, just you and me and little Sophia? I'll bring takeout."

"Really, I—"

"*Yes.*" He said it firmly. "That's the word you're looking for. Three little letters. Just say it. Say it now."

"Oh, but I—"

"Yes. Come on, you can do it."

"Logan, you—"

"Yes."

"I—"

"Yes."

She bit her lower lip, adorably torn.

"Yes," he whispered yet again, holding her gaze nice and steady, keeping his tone gentle but firm.

And finally, she gave in and gave him what they both wanted. "Oh, all right. Friday night, takeout at my house. Yes."

The next day, Thursday, Logan's other four brothers arrived from Texas bringing a caravan of stock trailers full of horses and cattle. Sarah drove up not long after they all pulled in and Logan made the introductions.

Once she'd greeted them all, Sarah retreated to the office and got to work. That day and the next were busy ones at the ranch, what with getting the stock and the rest of the family settled in. Logan didn't have a lot of free time.

But for Sarah, he *made* time. He really liked the simple fact of her being there at the Ambling A, of knowing that he could see her whenever he had a spare minute or two. All he had to do was visit the office at the back of the house.

Both days, she brought Sophia with her. The baby slept in her carrier on the edge of the desk or rolled around in the collapsible play yard on the floor at Sarah's feet, making her cute little noises, staring up at a mobile of butterflies, birds and airplanes, happily gumming a series of rattles and rubber toys.

Logan checked in every two or three hours in case Sarah had questions. If Sophia was awake, he would spend a few minutes bent over the carrier or the play yard. The little girl made her goo-goo sounds at him and he answered each one with, "You're right" or "I agree completely" or "Yes, your mama is looking even more beautiful than usual today."

Sarah pretended to ignore him whenever he kidded

around with Sophia. She focused on her laptop, her slim fingers working the mouse, swiftly tapping the keys. But Logan didn't miss the slight flush to her cheeks or the smiles she tried so hard to hide.

If Sophia was fussy, he would pick her up and walk her around the office a little until she quieted. The first time that happened, Sarah said, "You don't have to hold her. She's fine, really. I usually wait a few minutes before I rush to calm her. Half the time, she settles down by herself."

He stroked the baby's wispy hair and kept walking back and forth. "Are you saying you don't *want* me to pick her up?"

"Of course not. You're sweet to do it. Hey, knock yourself out."

"Thanks." He grinned at the baby and she grinned right back. "Because Sophia and I, we have a good thing going on."

Sarah kept right on typing. "She has you wrapped around her teeny-tiny finger is what you mean."

"Exactly," he answered proudly. "And Sophia and I, we like it that way."

Once he'd had a little quality time with Sophia, Logan would answer any questions that Sarah had for him and then leave her to her work. It wasn't easy, keeping his visits to the office at a minimum and his hands to himself. Every time he went in there, he longed to move in behind her, bend close, breathe in the scent of her, maybe turn her chair around and steal a steamy kiss. But he needed to show her that he was capable of respecting her workspace.

By Friday afternoon, though, he was anticipating the coming evening like crazy.

He hoped that she was, too.

There was a white van parked at the curb in front of her Pine Street cottage when Sarah answered the door at seven Friday evening with Sophia in her arms.

"Cute house," said Logan, looking way too hot in dress jeans, a snow-white shirt and a leather jacket that probably cost more than a Ford Fiesta.

She saw over his shoulder that his fancy crew cab pickup was right behind the van—the van that had "Giordano's Catering for All Occasions" printed in flowing red script across the side. He was having dinner catered? That wasn't the deal. She was about to question him when Sophia seemed to recognize him.

The baby pulled her fist from her mouth and giggled out a nonsense word, "Adaduh," as her face lit up in a giant, toothless smile. Before Sarah could stop her, she swayed toward him, fat arms outstretched.

"Whoa," he said. "Okay." And he caught her neatly on one arm. "I've got you."

"Gack!" She patted his face with her little hand.

"She'll get drool on your jacket," Sarah warned.

"I don't care." He made a silly face at Sophia, who giggled in delight and patted his cheek some more.

A dark-haired woman emerged from the passenger side of the van and bustled up the front walk as the driver got out, went around and opened the van's rear doors.

"This is a lot more than takeout," Sarah chided.

"It'th better than takeout," he said with a lisp because

he was gumming Sophia's fingers. He caught the baby's hand and kissed her tiny fingertips. Sophia chortled as he suggested, "Wait and see."

Really, the guy was impossible.

The caterer introduced herself. "I'm Mia." The burly driver came up the steps behind her. "This is Dan." She asked where Sarah wanted them to set up.

Sarah led Mia and Dan into the dining alcove. "How can I help?" she asked.

Logan took her arm and pulled her over next to him. "Step back and let them work."

Mia and Dan swiftly set the table with white linen, fancy china, real silver and shining glassware. There were candles—tall, white ones in silver candlesticks. It was really beautiful.

Logan still held Sophia. The baby waved her arms and jabbered away as Mia and her assistant took the food into the kitchen. They put the salads and dessert in the fridge and set the rest out on the counter in chafing dishes to keep it warm.

"We'll serve ourselves," Logan said when the caterers were finished setting up.

Mia explained that she would be by around eleven the next morning to collect the dishes and everything else. "Just leave it all on the porch if you're not going to be here or if you plan to sleep late." She and her helper headed out the door. Sarah followed, thanked them again, and stood there in the doorway as the van started up and drove away.

She turned back to the man and the baby. He'd given Sophia the rubber frog Sarah had left on the coffee table. Sophia chewed on it contentedly, resting her head against his broad chest.

"You shouldn't have," said Sarah flatly.

"You love it," he replied.

And yeah, she kind of did.

Logan was getting downright attached to Sophia. She seemed to really like him, too. Yeah, she got drool on his jacket, but so what? She chewed on her rubber frog and occasionally glanced up at him. "Ack," she would say, or "Bah," like she was telling him something really important.

She was wearing pajamas, white ones with pink sheep printed on them, all ready for bed. Sarah said no way was she sitting down to that beautiful dinner while the baby was still awake.

When Sophia started to get fussy, Sarah took her. "You can hang your jacket on that rack by the door," she said, as she knelt to put the baby on a play mat on the living room floor, setting a mobile over her with little forest animals hanging from it. Sophia didn't even try to turn over as she often did when Sarah had her in the play yard at the ranch. She just gummed her frog and stared up at the slowly rotating bears and squirrels.

Logan caught Sarah's hand as she rose from the floor. He turned her around so they were facing each other. Back at the ranch earlier that day, she'd been wearing dress jeans and a pale green button-up. Now, she wore a silky bronze-colored shirt with a nice low neckline that clung to the rounded curves of her breasts. "I like this shirt." He liked her snug jeans, too, which were a little darker brown than the shirt. On her feet she wore flats in a leopard print.

"Thank you." She smiled at him. Slowly. All he wanted was to kiss her.

Somehow, he controlled himself. "You should give me a tour."

She pointed at the short hall a few feet away. "Two bedrooms and a bath through there." And she gestured past the dining area. "Kitchen through that arch there. It's small, but it's home." She gave a wry grin, a grin that enticed him because everything about her enticed him.

And he couldn't resist a moment longer. He reeled her in, caught her face between his hands and kissed her. She tasted so good and she kissed him back, shyly at first and then more deeply.

The feel of her against him was temptation personified. He wanted to take it further. But now was hardly the moment, with their dinner still uneaten and her baby staring up at them from the floor.

Reluctantly, he broke the kiss and pressed his forehead to hers. "I could get used to this."

She pulled back. He caught her fingers before she could fully escape him. They stood in the middle of her small living room, holding hands, regarding each other. "You're a very determined guy, Logan."

"You noticed, huh?"

She did that thing, catching her lower lip between her teeth. He loved when she did that. It also drove him just a little bit wild. He ached to bite that lip for her.

"You're here in my house," she said. "My baby has a crush on you. I don't believe this is happening. This is everything I promised myself I wasn't going to do again."

"It's just dinner," he reminded her—though it was a whole lot more than that. And both of them knew it.

But he would tell whatever little white lies he had to tell to get closer to her.

She glanced down at Sophia. He followed her gaze. The baby lay, her arms above her head, rubber frog abandoned, sound asleep, as the mobile of forest animals continued to turn slowly over her head.

"I'll just put her in her crib," Sarah whispered, easing her fingers from his grip and kneeling to gather the little girl into her arms. Sophia's tiny mouth stretched wide in a yawn, but she didn't open her eyes.

Sarah carried the baby down the short hall and Logan followed. She entered the room on the right. He remained in the open doorway as she laid Sophia in her crib and settled a light blanket over her.

When she turned and saw him standing there, he felt a little guilty for trailing after her. He was constantly pushing the boundaries with her and he knew he had to be careful not to go too far. Sarah just might send him packing.

But apparently, the sight of him in the doorway to her baby's bedroom didn't bother her. Those golden eyes were soft and accepting of his presence there.

She came to him. "Let's have dinner," she whispered. "I'm starving."

Sarah dished up the food as Logan lit the candles and opened the bottle of Chianti he'd ordered to go with the meal.

They sat down to eat. It was heaven, Sarah thought, even if it was exactly the kind of intimate evening she should never have let happen.

But still…

A beautiful meal and a nice glass of wine, a gorgeous man across the table from her. It really was a special treat. She hadn't had a single sip of anything with alcohol in it since the day the home pregnancy test came out positive. Not only was drinking bad for the baby, who had time for it? Not Sarah.

However, she'd stopped nursing two months ago. The stress in Chicago had been killing her and it was just too much, all that pumping to get enough milk for when Sophia was at day care. Sarah had given up the fight and switched to formula. It wasn't as good for her baby—or her wallet—but at least Sophia seemed to be doing fine on a bottle. She was even starting to eat pureed foods.

And if Sarah had a glass of wine or two tonight, her baby wouldn't suffer for it.

"Hey," said the killer-handsome guy across the table. "Hmm?"

"You're frowning. Something wrong with the wine?"

"No way." She raised her glass to him. "It's delicious. And the veal is amazing."

He seemed pleased. "Told you so."

The conversation flowed easily. They talked about her progress on the Ambling A accounts. Logan reported that his second-born brother, Hunter, and his six-year-old daughter, Wren, had moved into one of the three cottages on the property. Knox, fifth in the birth order, had claimed a second cottage. Finn and Wilder had taken rooms in the main house with Max, Logan and Xander.

"Six of you boys and Max, too," Sarah teased. "That's a lot of testosterone."

"We get along," he said. "Mostly. Dad can drive us all kind of crazy, but his heart's in the right place."

Was it? She didn't know what to think about Max. "If you say so. How did your brothers react to the news that Max has offered Viv and Caroline a million bucks to find you guys brides?"

He laughed. "They're used to his wild ideas and schemes. Mostly, we all told him to knock it off, that we could find our own brides when we were damn good and ready. But Dad won't give up. He's relentless when he's got a plan and more often than not, he makes his plans come together, no matter how out-there they might seem at first."

What was he telling her, exactly? She shouldn't even let herself try to figure out what he meant. But she did wonder.

Would he be going out with the women Viv and Caroline introduced him to? Did he actually expect he would end up married to one of them? He certainly couldn't mean *her*. She wasn't marrying anyone, thank you very much. And Max had made it more than clear that he didn't want Logan getting too close with the single mom from Falls Mountain Accounting.

Not that Logan seemed like the kind of guy who did things his father's way. And the simple fact that he was here, sitting across from her over this perfect meal he'd arranged, well, that said something, didn't it? He really did seem to like her and her little girl, too.

And what about those amazing kisses they'd shared—the ones she probably shouldn't have let happen? Was he going to go from kissing her so thrillingly to taking some other girl out next Friday night?

He gazed across the table at her, those superfine blue eyes full of humor—and other things, sexy things she also wasn't going to think about.

She held out her wineglass and he filled it again. "So, tell me about your life in Seattle."

He said he'd gone to the University of Washington and teamed up with college friends to start investing in real estate. The business had grown. He'd scored big with some large commercial properties. "I loved it," he said. "There's always something going on in Seattle. The nightlife is great and the work kept me interested. But I missed the wide-open spaces, I guess you could say."

"Any serious relationships?" she asked. Because why not? She wanted to know. And after her TMI crying jag at the ranch the other day, she figured she deserved to hear at least a little about his past loves.

"None," he said.

She laughed. "Did you really have to go into so much detail?"

He lifted one hard shoulder in a half shrug. "Okay, I've dated exclusively a few times. But I've never been married or engaged, never even lived with a woman."

She turned her wineglass slowly by the stem. "So, you're a player?"

"Smile when you say that."

She raised the wine to her lips and savored its rich

taste of earth and dark cherries. "Looks like Viv and Caroline will have their work cut out for them with you."

He gazed at her way too steadily. The look in his eyes caused a warm shiver to slide over her skin. "There's only one girl I'm interested in and I think you know that. I want to be with *you*, Sarah, and I'm hoping that you'll realize you like being with me, too."

She did realize it. She realized the hell out of it and that didn't ease her mind one bit—and what was she doing right now?

Exactly what she *shouldn't* be doing, staring at his mouth. Staring at those lips of his and remembering the delicious pleasure of his kiss.

Blinking, she refocused. Somehow, this meal seemed to be turning into a seduction. She couldn't allow that.

But the food was so good and the man across from her so very charming. Plus, as usual, she was exhausted. The delicious wine seemed to be going straight to her head, making her body feel loose and easy, giving everything a sort of hazy glow.

He asked her about the brushstrokes of different-colored paint on the wall next to the dining-room hutch and in the kitchen and the hallway and the baby's room, too.

She explained that she had plans to paint the cottage, to make it bright and cheery and really hers. "Unfortunately," she admitted with a resigned sigh, "painting my new place is low priority right now. Too many other things come first."

"Like?"

"Making a living and taking care of my baby. I've

got a million things to do if I ever get a free minute. Starting with sleeping. That would be a thrill."

When their plates were empty, Logan granted her a slow smile full of sexy devilment. "Ready for dessert?"

He insisted on serving her. It was chocolate semi-freddo, essentially a frozen mousse. And it was amazing. She ate it slowly, savoring every bite, trying to keep her moans of sheer delight to a minimum.

When she was done, Logan pushed back his chair. "I'll clean up and put everything out on the porch, all ready for Mia and Dan to pick up in the morning." He came to her side of the table and held out a hand to her.

She stared at that offered hand, a shiver of awareness warming her skin to have him so close. "Oh, no," she said.

"Oh, no what?"

She shifted her gaze up, into his waiting eyes. Really, she felt so good, easy and lazy with the wine and the wonderful food—and what was it she'd been about to say? She blinked and remembered. "You sit back down. I'll do it."

"Give me your hand." When she hesitated, he took it anyway and pulled her to her feet.

"Logan, seriously," she protested. "You provided this amazing dinner. The least I can do is clear the table."

"Uh-uh." He took her by the shoulders and turned her around. "Start walking."

"No, really, I—"

"Straight ahead." He guided her to the living room sofa, turned her around a second time and then gently pushed her down. "Relax. I've got this." He seemed determined.

And she *was* relaxed—more than relaxed. She felt downright lazy. "Go ahead." She waved him away. "Do all the work."

He bent close and pressed his lips to her forehead. "I will."

She watched him stride back to the table, admiring the width of his shoulders and his truly stellar behind. Really, did he have to be so good-looking both coming and going?

"Not fair," she muttered as her eyelids kept trying to droop shut and her body sagged against the armrest. She grabbed the throw pillow and stuck it under her head.

What could it hurt to shut her eyes? Not for long, of course. Just for a minute…

Chapter Four

Twenty minutes later, Logan had the table cleared, the leftovers transferred to plastic containers and stored in the fridge and everything else stacked and waiting on the front porch, ready for pickup the next day.

By then, Sarah was completely conked out on the sofa, looking so cute, with her head on a pillow, her lips softly parted, her feet still on the floor.

She stirred when he knelt to slide off her shoes. "Wha…? Logan?"

"Shh," he soothed her. "It's okay," he whispered. "Close your eyes."

"Hmm…" And she drifted back to dreamland again. He eased her feet up onto the cushions, settled the sofa blanket over her and placed a chaste kiss at her temple.

Should he grab his jacket and let himself quietly out the door?

Probably.

But what fun was that?

He took the easy chair across from the sofa, hooked one booted foot across the other knee and settled in to watch her sleeping.

What was it about her? he asked himself for the umpteenth time. He liked her. Too much? Maybe. But she had grit. He admired that. She was beautiful and smart with a wry sense of humor. And every time he kissed her, he wanted more.

More of the taste of those sweet lips of hers. More of her laughter and more of her sighs. More of all of her.

It surprised him, his own patience in this never-quite-happening seduction of her that he'd been knocking himself out to orchestrate—so far to minimal success.

There was just something about her. She gave him… *feelings*, which was emo and weird for him. But good. Somehow, it didn't bother him at all, having feelings for Sarah. She was so independent and determined, but so womanly, too. She tried to be tough, but she had a tender heart. He could sit here across from her in the easy chair all night, watching her sleep, wanting to sketch her.

Logan had always been good at drawing things. Give him a tablet full of paper and a pen or a pencil and he could spend hours doodling pictures of trees, houses, horses—you name it.

Early on, he'd discovered that women loved a cowboy with a little artistic talent. In high school and later, at UW, he would carry a sketchpad wherever he went. If he saw a woman he admired, he would draw a picture of her, which would get her attention and also bring other women flocking around him. If guys ribbed him about being an artsy-fartsy type, he would just shrug and say it worked great with the girls.

Nobody needed to know it went deeper. Drawing pictures of the things and the people around him focused him somehow, brought him a sense of peace within himself.

And he'd just happened to notice that Sarah had a small desk tucked into a corner of her kitchen. Would she be pissed at him if he looked in there for some paper and a pencil?

He got up to check and found just what he was looking for: a large spiral-bound notebook of unlined white paper. She also had several #2 pencils in the pen drawer, all of them sharpened to perfect points. No surprise there. He could have guessed that Sarah was a woman who kept her pencils sharp. He took two, just in case he broke the lead on one.

Back in the easy chair, he got down to it, quickly sketching his favorite accountant as she snoozed on the couch. He finished a first attempt of her, head-to-toe, her hands tucked under her chin on the pillow, the bottom half of her covered in the brown-and-white couch blanket that looked good with her hair and that silky shirt she was wearing. He could almost wish he had colored pencils or pastels to capture the colors of her, too.

He'd just started on a close-up of her face when whiny sounds erupted from the baby monitor on the hutch in the dining alcove.

"Ahduh. Unh. Ga?" Sophia was awake and if he didn't do something, Sarah would be, too.

Pencil and notebook still in hand, he scooped up the monitor as he passed it.

The door to the baby's room was shut. He pushed it open. Enough light bled in from the living room for him to see that she'd kicked off her blanket and grabbed hold of her own toes.

"Maaa?" She'd turned her head to look at him through the slats of her crib.

Laughing a little at the sight of her with her little hands clutching her feet, he switched on the table lamp and shut the door to mute the noises she was making.

"Duh," she said. "Uh?"

He dropped the pencil and notebook by the lamp, turned off the monitor and put it down on top of the pad.

Sophia let go of her feet and fisted her hands. She made a sound that was more of a cry than a nonsense word.

He went to her and scooped her up. "Hey. Hey, it's okay."

Her lower lip was quivering. And then she did start to cry. She smelled like a dirty diaper, which was probably the problem. It couldn't be that complicated to clean her up, could it?

The dresser a few feet from the crib had a pad on top and shelves above with stacks of diapers and wipes.

He could do this.

Sophia chewed on her hand and looked at him through big, blue tear-wet eyes.

"It's okay. We got this," he promised her as he laid

her down on the pad with its soft cotton cover printed with ladybugs and smiling green caterpillars.

Actually, it wasn't that difficult. Everything he needed was right there within reach. Sophia whimpered softly up at him as he worked, watching his every move as though she couldn't quite trust him to know what he was doing.

He couldn't blame her for having her doubts. His experience with babies was nil. When Hunter's little girl, Wren, was born, Logan had been busy making his mark in Seattle real estate. Yeah, he'd gone home to Texas maybe twice while his niece was still a baby. He'd done the classic uncle things—shaking a rattle over her crib, holding her while someone snapped a picture. That was it. Diaper changing never once came into play.

But he managed it with Sophia well enough. By the time he got her back into her pajamas, she'd stopped fussing.

He took her in his arms. "What'd I tell you? Stick with me, kid. Ready to go back to bed now?"

"Unh." Her lip started quivering all over again.

Sixty seconds later, she was making soft bleating sounds—not a full-out cry, but he had zero doubt she would get there if he didn't figure out what she needed very soon. He paced the small room, patting her back, trying to soothe her.

Maybe she was hungry.

He hated to open the door. Her cries were bound to wake Sarah—which would be good, wouldn't it?

Hell, yeah. Sarah would know what to do.

But she'd been sleeping so peacefully when he left

her. And she really could use a little rest. He didn't want to disturb her unless there was no other choice.

Advice from an expert. That was what he needed. Wren's mom had died shortly after her birth, leaving Hunter to raise his daughter on his own. Hunter had been a hands-on kind of dad.

As Logan paced the floor and did his best to soothe the baby, he dug his phone from his pocket and attempted to text his brother, which turned out to be a losing game with Sophia squirming in his arms.

He gave in and punched the call button.

Hunter answered on the first ring. "Logan. What?" By then, Sophia was steadily fussing. "Is that a baby? What are you doing with a baby?"

Logan continued to pace the floor and pat the baby as he briefly explained that Sarah was sleeping and he didn't want Sophia to wake her.

"Sarah. Sarah Turner, you mean? The woman you hired to set up the ranch accounts?"

"Right."

"You've got a thing going on with the accountant? Fast work, big brother."

"Hunter, focus. I need some help here. I changed Sophia's diaper, but she's still not settling down."

"You, of all people. Falling for the bean-counting single mom." Hunter chuckled.

"Think you're pretty funny, huh? The baby's crying and I need some help here."

Hunter got serious. "She could be sleepy."

"She *was* sleeping. She woke up."

"Uh, right. How old is she, exactly?"

"Who? Sarah?"

"The baby."

"Five months?"

"What? You're not sure?"

"I'm sure enough. Five months."

"Okay, so I see three options to start. Is she flushed and feverish?"

Sophia's cheeks were pink, but that could be from fussing. He felt her little forehead. "I don't think she has a fever."

"She's probably hungry, then. Or maybe teething." He said Logan should look in the freezer for a cold teething toy. As for something to eat, he should look for formula and follow the instructions on the packaging. "Or wait. Is Sarah nursing? I know zip about that. Wren was on formula from the first."

Was Sarah nursing? Logan didn't know, and that really bugged him. A guy should know if the woman he couldn't stop thinking about was nursing. Shouldn't he? "I've never seen her nurse the baby. But bottles. I've seen her feed Sophia with those."

"Are you in the kitchen? If there's formula, follow the directions on the packaging." Hunter added, almost to himself, "Or then again…"

Logan kept pacing, the phone tucked under his chin so he could use the hand that wasn't supporting the baby to stroke her back and hold her steady as she squirmed. He really didn't get what his brother was trying to tell him. "You're saying that I shouldn't look for formula, after all?"

"No. I was just thinking you could look for baby food, too. Sarah might be introducing her to solids at this point."

Sophia gave a loud cry that faded into a pained whine. She flopped her head down on Logan's shoulder with a sad little sigh.

"Logan? You okay?"

"Not exactly. If I go in the kitchen, Sarah will probably hear her fussing and wake up. The whole point is for Sarah *not* to wake up."

"Then put the baby in her crib and go to the kitchen without her."

"She's upset. I don't want to leave her alone."

"Yeah, I know. It's hard when they can't tell you what's bothering them. But I don't know what more to suggest. You've already changed her diaper and she doesn't have a fever. Your best bets are that she's hungry or teething."

"Gotcha. Gotta go."

Hunter was wishing him luck as Logan ended the call. He dropped the phone on top of the notebook next to the baby monitor. Then he carried Sophia back to her crib.

"I'm going to put you in your bed," he explained, as if she could understand actual words. "And then I will run and see what I can find to make you feel better. I'll be right back." He peeled her off his shoulder and gently laid her in the crib.

She let out a sharp cry and then a longer one, her little face scrunching up, her arms reaching for him.

"Right back. Promise." Before he could relent and pick her up again, he got out of there, shutting the door on Sophia's unhappy cries.

As he raced by the living room, he noted that at least

Sarah was still dead to the world. He really hoped he wouldn't end up having to wake her.

In the kitchen, he found powdered formula and some jars of pureed baby food in the cupboard. There were also a couple of plastic baby toys in the freezer. He decided to try the frozen toy pretzel first. Grabbing it, he rushed back to the baby's room, where Sophia was miserable, wailing now, her face scrunched up, beet red. He slid in and quickly shut the door behind him.

She continued to cry and he felt terrible. If the teething toy didn't work, he would have to get Sarah.

"It's okay. I'm here." Her crying stopped when he picked her up, but then started in again. "Come on. Try this." He touched the pretzel to her lips and a miracle happened. She took it in her mouth and even grabbed hold of it with her little hand.

A relieved sigh escaped her as she worked her gums on the frozen toy. She chewed the toy and regarded him so seriously, a last tear shining on her fat cheek, reminding him of her mother the other day, so sad over all the ways her life hadn't turned out as she'd planned.

He gently rubbed the tear away. "Feel better?"

"Unh."

"I'm going to take that as a yes."

He carried her over to the rocker in the corner and sat down. She gummed her pretzel and drooled on his shirt as he rocked her gently.

Eventually, she let go of the pretzel. It fell to his lap. That was when he realized she'd gone back to sleep.

He just sat there rocking her for a while longer because really, she was just the cutest thing, smacking her lips now and then as she slept, yawning once or twice.

When he finally got up and tucked her back in her crib, she didn't even stir.

Before he turned off the lamp, he grabbed the spiral-bound notebook he'd stolen from the kitchen desk and dashed off a few sketches of her all cozy and peaceful, looking like a little angel as she slept.

Sarah came awake slowly.

She was lying on the sofa with a blanket over her. The lamp in the corner, turned down low, cast a soft glow over the living room. Across the coffee table, in the easy chair, Logan snored softly, his drooping head braced on a hand. She sat up and squinted at the little clock on the side table.

It was after two in the morning. The baby monitor that had been on the hutch was now on the coffee table next to a plastic teething pretzel that she remembered putting in the freezer the afternoon before. The only reason she could think of for Logan to remove the toy from her freezer was to soothe Sophia's teething pain.

Also on the coffee table were a full-size notebook and two pencils, most likely from her desk in the kitchen. The open pad was turned away from her, the top pages turned back. He'd been drawing something, though from this angle, she couldn't see what.

Quietly, so as not to disturb him, she picked up the notebook and flipped through the pages.

There were eight drawings total, five of her and three of Sophia. Logan had been sketching pictures of her and her daughter as they slept. They were beautiful, those sketches. Who knew the guy had that sort of talent? She'd had no clue.

It felt a little strange to think of him watching her, drawing her without her knowledge. But it didn't bother her, not really. And that was strange in itself, that she didn't mind he'd done the sketches without her knowledge. She wasn't really that trusting of a person, especially when it came to Sophia. She had a hard time counting on anyone but herself. Yet she'd dropped right off to sleep last night and left him to take care of Sophia. She did trust him, at least a little. And she loved the drawings.

She wanted them—especially the ones of her little girl. Maybe if she asked him nicely, he would give them to her.

And maybe she was growing kind of attached to him already. *Fond* of him, even. On top of being so strongly attracted to him.

Not good. Not wise at all.

But right now, she was too tired to ponder where this thing between her and the gorgeous, surprisingly artistic, baby-soothing man sleeping in her easy chair might be going. She got up, covered him with the blanket, grabbed the baby monitor, switched off the lamp and headed for her bed.

Sarah woke to daylight, feeling more rested than she had in months.

She blinked in surprise when she saw the time. Past eight. Sophia often slept through the night lately, but never as late as eight in the morning.

The monitor by the bed was silent, the screen dark. She touched it and it lit up with an image of Sophia's empty crib.

Sarah's heart started racing with the beginnings of alarm—until she remembered the baby-soothing rancher she'd left sleeping in her easy chair last night.

As soon as she opened her bedroom door, she heard Logan's low laughter and her baby's happy cooing. She followed the sounds into the kitchen where he sat at the two-seater table with Sophia on his lap. He fed her baby cereal as she waved her arms and babbled out nonsense syllables.

A messy business, feeding Sophia.

Sarah leaned in the arch to the dining alcove. "I would bet you that more cereal has ended up on you and the baby than in her mouth."

With the back of his hand, he wiped a dab of the stuff off his beard-scruffy cheek. "I never take a bet I know I'll lose." And then his gaze wandered over her, down the length of her body and back to meet her waiting eyes again.

Her hair was a mess. She wore her old robe over sleep shorts and a T-shirt with a frayed neckline. And yet somehow, that lingering glance of his made her feel like the prettiest girl in Rust Creek Falls.

"Sleep well?" His voice was low and deliciously rough.

"I did, yeah." She must have gotten a good ten hours total. Because of him. "Thank you."

"Anytime." And he smiled at her.

She felt that smile of his as an explosion of warmth in the center of her chest.

Oh, this guy was dangerous. She could so easily get in over her head with him.

"Bacon and eggs?" she asked.

"I would love some."

A half hour later, he reluctantly headed for the door. She thanked him again for the beautiful evening and the priceless hours of glorious sleep.

"I'll call you," he promised as she ushered him out. She made a noncommittal noise in response and quickly shut the door.

In the living room, the pictures he'd drawn were still there on the coffee table. Apparently, he didn't want them. Which was great. Because she did. She would find frames for the ones of Sophia. And the ones of her, well, she would keep them as a reminder of him. Because he was a great guy and last night had been lovely.

But it was just too risky to go there. Her life now at least had a certain equilibrium. She couldn't afford to take chances with her heart.

He texted her that afternoon. I had a long talk with Sophia last night. She finally opened up to me and admitted that she wants us to spend more together.

Even feeling edgy and sad that she had to call a halt with him, she couldn't help smiling. Right. Sophia's a big talker. Too bad she doesn't use actual words yet.

I understand her. We communicate, Sophia and I. How about tonight? I'm supposed to go to this family thing. Come with me. Or if you want to go somewhere just the two of us, that's even better. I know a steak house in Kalispell. You're going to love it.

Her hopeless heart filled with longing—to spend another great evening with him. But that had to stop. Lucky for her, she already had a date with Lily for tonight. Sorry, I can't. It's a girls' night. Just my friend Lily and me.

Damn. Sunday? Come out to the ranch? Or maybe a picnic in Rust Creek Falls Park? Sophia would love it.

No, really. I can't. I'll see you Monday at the ranch. I still have a couple more days' work getting everything set up.

He didn't respond right away. But then, an hour later, her phone rang. She saw it was him and tried to hold strong, to let it go to voice mail. They could talk about it Monday. She could explain that it wasn't going to work, that she couldn't go out with him anymore.

But having it out with him Monday wouldn't be right, would it? She was going to the Ambling A to work. She needed to keep personal discussions out of the work environment.

Really, it had to be done now. She answered on the third ring. "Hi."

"What's going on, Sarah?" His voice was so careful. Flat. Controlled.

She needed to just do it. Get it over with. Move on. "I really can't do this, Logan. I can't go out with you again—I mean, I *won't* go out with you again. You're a wonderful man and I really like you, but it's not going to happen between us."

Dead silence from his end.

"Logan? Are you still there?"

"Yeah. And all right. I hear you. I'll see you Monday—and don't worry. You want it strictly business, so I'll give you what you want."

Chapter Five

Sarah's mom arrived right on time that night. She took Sophia into her arms and followed Sarah into the kitchen and then the baby's room as Sarah explained what to feed her, when to put her to bed and how the baby monitor worked.

"Amazing," declared her mother, thoroughly impressed. "Nowadays a baby monitor is a mini-security system. And the picture is so clear, honey."

Sarah still had trouble reconciling this pretty, confident, enthusiastic woman with the quiet, dutiful mouse of a mother who had raised her. "Yeah, well. As you can see, it's pretty simple. You shouldn't have any trouble with it."

Flo blew a gentle raspberry against Sophia's cheek and the baby giggled. Sarah watched them. Never in her life had she expected to see her mom blow a raspberry. It was all too strange and hard to believe.

"How's my girl?" Flo asked the baby.

Sophia giggled again and added, "Bah. Ga."

Sarah kind of tuned them out. She kept thinking about Logan, feeling heartsick about cutting things off with him.

She knew it was for the best.

But why did it have to hurt so much?

She'd only had the one evening with him. How could she have gotten so attached so fast?

"You seem kind of down, sweetheart. What's bothering you?" Flo asked as Sophia chortled in glee and bounced up and down in her grandma's arms. "Could this have anything to do with the fancy pickup that was parked in front of your house overnight last night?"

"Who told you that?"

"Honey, this isn't Chicago—it's Rust Creek Falls," her mom said as if that explained everything. And really, it kind of did.

In Rust Creek Falls, everybody pretty much knew everything about everyone else. They shared what they knew because they cared about their neighbors and also because it was a form of local entertainment to speculate about who was doing what—and with whom.

Sarah's mom regarded her with understanding, inviting her to share. And she really *wanted* to share…

But no. Uh-uh. Not happening. Bad idea.

It was over with Logan. Over without ever having really gotten started. There was nothing to talk about.

"Burdens are lighter when you share them," Flo advised with a radiant smile.

Say something. Anything. Just not about Logan.

"Actually, I, um, have noticed how well you and Dad seem to be getting along lately." Talk about an understatement. Sheesh. "And I've been kind of wondering what's happened between you two?"

She had been wondering, though she'd never planned to actually go there. Right now, though, even hearing about her parents' sex life would be preferable to discussing the man who'd become way too important to her way too fast.

"Oh, honey," said Flo. "I was beginning to think you'd never ask."

Beaming with pleasure, Sarah's mom told all. It had started with a routine visit to her new gynecologist and a pelvic exam that had led to a simple procedure that had changed everything for Flo and Mack.

"You see," said Flo, "as it turns out, I didn't heal properly after your birth, but I never realized that was the problem. It was just so painful to be intimate. And your father and I were hardly experienced. There was just that one time. Prom night. We got a little carried away. It was the first time for both of us.

"After that, we swore to wait. And then we learned you were coming and we got married earlier than we'd planned. We were just a couple of kids. What did we know? You arrived and your father went off to college. The next time we tried, well, it was awful for me. And no fun for him. We gave up, stopped trying—for years and years. Looking back, I can't believe we didn't at least try to figure out what might be wrong. But that's all changed now and I can't even describe how wonderful it is…"

There was more. Lots more. Stuff Sarah so didn't

need to hear. Some of it was kind of nice, though, about how her mom and dad had gotten counseling to increase their intimacy emotionally, too.

Eventually, when she'd heard way more than enough, she put up a hand. "So what you're saying is that you're happy together now, you and Dad?"

"Oh, sweetheart. Words cannot express."

"I'm glad, Mom." And she *was* happy for her parents. Plus, she'd managed to keep her mouth shut about Logan. "And look at the time! I really should get going."

"Have fun, darling. Say hi to Lily for me."

"Thanks, Mom. I will." Sarah kissed her baby and got out of there.

Maverick Manor had been built back in the eighties as a private home. Perched on a rise of land back from the highway, it was a giant log structure, one that had been enlarged even more when it became a hotel. Surrounded by manicured grounds, the place was rustic and luxurious at once. In the lobby with its vaulted, beamed ceiling, a giant mural depicted the early history of Rust Creek Falls and the pioneer families who had founded it.

When the hostess ushered Sarah into the dining room, Lily Hunt was waiting at a quiet corner table. They ordered their meal and a glass of house wine each.

Wine two nights in a row, Sarah thought. She was living the wild life, no doubt about it.

She studied her friend across the small table. Lily had striking red hair and gorgeous green eyes, yet most people in town considered her plain. She rarely wore makeup and kept her beautiful hair pulled smoothly back and anchored low at her nape. Some called her shy, but she wasn't, not really. Not with Sarah, anyway.

Once the waitress had served them their food, Lily said, "You mentioned the other day that you were working out at the Ambling A, setting up the books for Max Crawford and his sons…"

Sarah guessed where her friend was going. "You heard about the deal Max made with Viv and Caroline to find brides for Max's sons, didn't you?"

"Yep." Lily's smile bloomed slowly. "Me and everybody else in town."

"Why am I not the least surprised?"

Lily buttered her bread. "I also heard that Logan Crawford is completely smitten with a certain brilliant accountant, a beautiful single mom with an adorable little girl."

"Brilliant *and* beautiful, huh? You're flattering me. Why?"

"I only speak the truth." Lily was all innocence.

Sarah savored a bite of her petite filet and said nothing.

Lily leaned closer. "Tell me everything." Her green eyes gleamed with eager interest. "Hold nothing back."

After all that had happened since Lily babysat for her last Wednesday, Sarah could no longer pretend that nothing was going on between her and Logan.

She laid it all out. From her powerful attraction to Logan to Max's opposition to her as a possible match for his oldest son, to Logan's unflagging pursuit of her and their first "date" the night before.

"Logan's been nothing but wonderful," Sarah reported glumly. She explained that she'd ended it with him when he called that afternoon.

"I don't get it." Lily frowned. "Logan Crawford provides a sit-down catered dinner with all the trimmings, thrills you when he kisses you, takes care of Sophia both night and morning so you can get what you need the most—a good night's sleep. The man draws beautiful pictures of you and your baby. He doesn't leave you hanging but instead calls the next day to ask you out again. And yet you've decided it can't possibly work?"

Sarah loved Lily. But sometimes her friend was just way too logical. "I told you I've had it up to here with men and all the trouble they cause."

"So stay away from the jerks and troublemakers. But, Sarah, when a good one comes along you need to give the guy a chance."

"He's in his thirties. He's never been married. Yes, he's a great guy. But he's not interested in anything long-lasting."

"He *told* you that?"

"No. I just know it. I, well, I *sense* it."

Lily tipped her head to the side, frowning. "Suddenly, you're psychic?"

"Of course not. It's just that he told me he's never even lived with anyone. I seriously doubt he's suddenly decided he wants to try marriage, that's all."

"Where to even start with you? So he's in his thirties? It's a prime age for a guy to finally find the right woman. He's mature enough to know what he really wants—and anyway, what about you? Do *you* want to get married?"

"Did I say that? No, Lily. I don't want to get married. I'm not looking for a serious relationship. I honestly don't even want a date. I'm through with all that. I have Sophia and a job I'm good at and a cute little cottage that will be even cuter if I ever find the time and energy to fix it up a little."

"So then, be flexible."

Sarah slanted her friend a suspicious glance. "What, exactly, are you getting at?"

"Have a wonderful time with a terrific man for as long as it lasts. Because if you don't, Viv Dalton's dating service will be finding him someone who will."

Sarah sat up straighter. "That's okay with me."

"You don't mean that."

"Yes, I do." She tried really hard to tell herself that it wouldn't bother her in the least if Logan started seeing some other woman in town.

A murmur of voices rose from the far side of the big dining room.

Lily leaned in. "And speaking of the Crawford family…"

Sarah followed the direction of her friend's gaze and saw that the hostess was ushering in several new arrivals. They included Nate Crawford and his wife, Callie, a nurse at the local clinic. Nate's parents came in, too, as well as his pretty sister Natalie and his brothers and their wives.

And behind the local Crawfords came Max and six big men who looked a lot like him—including the tall, blue-eyed cowboy who made Sarah's heart beat faster and her cheeks feel much too warm. The Crawford clan took seats around a long table in the center of the room.

Lily whispered, "Max Crawford and sons, am I right?"

"How did you guess?" Sarah asked wryly.

"Everyone says they're all really good-looking." Her friend sipped more wine. "Everyone is right."

"Now that I think about it, Logan mentioned that there was some kind of family get-together tonight."

"A Crawford family reunion," said Lily. "Who's the cute little girl?" She gave a slight nod toward the blonde sprite who'd entered with Logan and his family.

"That would be Wren," said Sarah. "Her dad is Hunter Crawford. He's sitting to her left. Logan told me that Wren's mom died shortly after she was born."

"How sad." Lily was silent for a moment, kind of taking it all in. "Hmm…"

Sarah focused on her friend and tried really hard not to let her gaze stray to Logan. "Hmm, what?"

Lily tipped her head toward a table on the far side of the dining room. Viv and Caroline sat there, along with three other women who lived in town—single women, Sarah was reasonably sure. As Sarah watched, Viv turned in her chair and spoke to a woman at the next table over. Interestingly enough, that table was women-only, too.

Lily said, "Looks to me like Viv and Caroline's dating service is very much open for business."

Logan sat down at the table full of Crawfords, ordered a glass of eighteen-year-old Scotch and tried not to think about Sarah.

He noticed the wedding planners right away, as well as the pretty women at the table with them *and* at the next table over. Apparently, the wedding planners were already on the job providing potential brides for him and his brothers.

And his father, who had somehow ended up sitting next to him, was looking right at him. When Logan met Max's eyes, his dad winked at him. Logan gave his dad a flat stare—and then turned to face the other way.

Viv came over just to say hi. Max introduced her to Knox, Finn, Wilder and Hunter. She exchanged a few words with each of them, said hello to the local Crawfords and then rejoined the women.

Logan sat back and sipped his drink slowly as Nate Crawford explained how he and a few other movers and shakers in town had created Maverick Manor so that Rust Creek Falls would finally have a resort-style hotel.

When Nate finished his story, Finn, who was twenty-nine, fourth-born after Xander, got up and went over to where all the women sat. Viv introduced him to each of the women. He nodded and chatted them up a little before eventually wandering back to his seat. Wilder, last-born, rose a little later and strolled over to introduce himself, too. No way was Wilder ever going to let himself get tied down to one woman. But all the pretty ladies would have to find that out for themselves.

Logan's dad just couldn't leave it alone. As Wilder took his chair at the table again, Max leaned close and pitched his voice low for Logan's ears alone. "Yep. Lots of fine-looking women in this town. Take your pick, son. Viv will introduce you."

Logan didn't bother to answer. He just turned his head slowly and gave the old man another flat, bored stare.

Max got the message. He started yakking with Nate's dad, who was seated on his other side.

Logan was about to signal for a second Scotch when

he spotted Sarah and a red-haired woman sitting in a small, tucked-away corner of the dining room. He wasn't sure what made him turn halfway around in his chair and glance over there, but when he did, his eyes collided with hers.

She quickly looked away.

He should look away, too. But he didn't. Man, he had it bad. It hurt just to see her. And he was feeling sorry enough for himself at that moment to go ahead and indulge his pain by turning in his chair and staring.

Yeah, it was rude. But he didn't care.

Sarah wore a cream-colored sleeveless dress and her hair was down, soft and smooth on her shoulders. As he watched, the waitress appeared and set a check tray on the table between Sarah and her friend. The redhead whipped out her credit card. Sarah tried to argue, but it appeared that the redhead won. The waitress left to run the card. A few minutes later, she dropped off the tray again on her way to take an order at another table. The redhead signed the receipt and put her card away.

Any minute now, Sarah and her friend would get up and leave.

Today, she'd made it more than clear that she refused to get anything going with him. He needed to take a hint, order that second Scotch and let her go. He turned away.

And something inside him rebelled at the sheer wrongness of the two of them, so acutely aware of each other and trying so hard to pretend that they weren't.

Forget that noise. He couldn't let her go without at least saying hi.

Logan shoved back his chair.

Ignoring his dad's muttered, "Logan. Let it be," he pushed in his chair and turned for her table.

In three long strides, he was standing above her.

She put on a fake smile. "Logan, hi. This is my friend, Lily Hunt."

The redhead said, "Happy to meet you," and actually seemed to mean it. She got up. "I think it's time for me to go."

"Lily," Sarah protested. "Don't—"

Lily didn't let her finish. "Gotta go. Call me," she said and then she walked away.

Logan claimed the empty chair before Sarah could leap up and disappear.

"This is pointless," Sarah said—softly, in a tender, hopeful voice that belied her words. She had her hands folded together on the table.

When he put his palm over them, she didn't pull away.

In fact, she looked up at him, finally meeting his eyes.

Their gazes held.

The packed dining room and all the other people in it faded into the background. There was no one but the woman in the cream-colored dress sitting across the table from him, the connection he felt to her, the cool, smooth silk of her skin under his hand.

"How's Sophia?" he asked as he slipped his thumb in between her tightly clasped fingers.

A smile tried to pull at the corner of that tempting mouth. "Same as this morning. My mom's watching her."

"Does she miss me?"

A chuckle escaped her and a sweet flush stained her cheeks. "Stop…"

"You need to say that with more conviction—or not say it at all." He pretended to think about it. "Yeah. Say something like, 'Logan, I'm so glad you're here and I've changed my mind and would love to go out with you any time you say.'"

"I…"

"You…?" He succeeded in separating her hands and claimed one for himself, weaving their fingers together. They stared at each other across the table. Her fingers felt just right twined with his, and her cheeks had a beautiful, warm blush on them. He never wanted to let her go.

"Logan, I do like you. So much."

"Which is why you need to spend more time with me. And I don't mean as my accountant. I mean quality time. Personal time."

She drew in a slow, unsteady breath.

He knew then with absolute certainty that she was going to change her mind, tell him yes. Finally. At last.

Except that she was easing her hand free of his. "No. It can't go anywhere." She rose. "I meant what I said this afternoon. I would really appreciate it if you would please keep it business-only while I'm working for you at the ranch. And right now, I really do need to go."

Logan knew when he was beaten. She wasn't giving an inch and he needed to accept that. "All right. I'm through. See you Monday, Sarah. You can finish setting up the books. And that will be that."

With a tiny nod, she turned and walked away.

He rose and went back to join the family. The waitress brought him that second Scotch. He sipped it slowly and considered his options, of which there really was only one.

It was time to wise up, quit playing the fool. Sarah was never giving him a damn break and he needed to stop following her around like a lovesick calf.

A pretty blonde sitting with the other women at Viv Dalton's table gave him a friendly smile. He raised his glass to her and her smile got wider. She had dimples and big blue eyes.

What was that old song? *If you can't have the girl you want—want the girl you're with.*

Or something like that.

Chapter Six

The following Wednesday night, Logan took the blonde, whose name was Louise, out to that steak house he liked in Kalispell. Louise was a nice woman. As it turned out, she worked in Kalispell, teaching high school English. But she had her own little house in Rust Creek Falls inherited from a beloved aunt. She loved dancing, she said, especially line dancing.

Logan sat across from her and listened to her talk and wondered what it was about her.

Or more correctly, what it *wasn't* about her. She was pretty and friendly, intelligent and sweet. There was nothing *not* to like.

Except, well, he just didn't feel it. *Want the one you're with*, huh? Maybe. In some cases.

For him and Louise, though? Not so much.

Still, he nodded and smiled at her and tried to make all the right noises while his mind was filled with thoughts of Sarah.

She'd finished up at the ranch just that day. He wouldn't be seeing her again until tax time—except for now and then, the way people did in a small town. They would end up waving at each other as they passed on the street or maybe dropping by Buffalo Bart's Wings To Go at the same time.

"You're awfully quiet." Louise sent him another sweet, dimpled smile and sipped her white wine.

He was being a really bad date and he knew it. Sitting up a little straighter in his chair, he ordered his errant thoughts back to the here and now.

Later, when he took her home, Louise asked shyly, "Would you like to come in?"

He thanked her, said he had to be up before dawn and got the heck out of there.

Viv called him the next day. She said she'd talked to Louise, who'd reported that she really liked Logan but she just didn't feel that the "chemistry" was there. Logan had to agree.

He'd meant to tell Viv that he didn't need another date. But somehow, before he hung up, Viv had talked him into spending an evening with a girl named Genevieve Lawrence.

He and Genevieve met up on Friday night—in Kalispell again, at a cowboy bar she knew of. They danced and joked around. Genevieve knew ranch life and horses. She was a farrier by profession. They got along great, him and Genevieve.

But right away, Logan had that feeling, like she was

his sister or something. He could be best buds with Genevieve. But tangled sheets and hot nights with her to help him forget a certain amber-eyed accountant?

Never going to happen.

Plus, more than once between dances, Genevieve teased that he seemed like he was a million miles away.

And he kind of was. He was thinking of Sarah, and ordering himself to *stop* thinking of her. And then thinking of her anyway. Because dating other people didn't make him forget the woman he wanted. It just made him want her all the more.

At the end of that evening, Genevieve gave him a hug and whispered, "Whoever she is, don't be an idiot. Work it out with her."

It was great advice. Or it would have been, if only Sarah wanted to work it out with *him*.

When Viv called the next day, he explained that he really wasn't in the mood for dating. "So I won't be needing your, er, services anymore, thanks."

But evidently, Vivienne Dalton was downright determined to earn her million-dollar payout. Before he hung up, she'd convinced him to try a coffee date at Daisy's Donut Shop. "It's a half hour out of your life," promised Viv. "You get a coffee and a maple bar and if it goes nowhere, you're done."

Monday afternoon when Sarah dropped in at Falls Mountain Accounting, her mom was actually *not* behaving inappropriately behind the shut door of her father's office. Flo sat at her desk, her hair neatly combed, her shirt on straight. She was smiling, as she always did nowadays, typing away. The waiting area was empty.

"Hey, Mom."

Flo looked up from her desktop monitor with a welcoming smile. "Honey."

Sarah went on through to her own office and put the baby carrier, her backpack and laptop on her desk. In the carrier, Sophia was sleeping peacefully. Leaving the door open a crack so she would hear if the baby woke, Sarah returned to the main room, where her mom was now on the phone.

She picked up the stack of mail from the corner of Flo's desk and went through it, finding three envelopes addressed to her and setting the rest back down.

"Dad?" she asked as her mom hung up the phone.

Flo tipped her head toward Mack's shut door. "He's with a client."

"Okay, I'll be in my office if you—"

"Sweetheart." Her mom took off her black-framed reading glasses and dropped them on the desk. "I'm just going to ask."

Sarah had no idea what her mother could be getting at now. "Uh, sure. Ask."

"What went wrong between you and Logan Crawford?"

Just hearing his name hurt. Like a hard jab straight to the solar plexus.

"That face." Her mother made a circular gesture with her right hand, fingers spread wide. "That is not your happy face. Are you ever going to open up and talk to me?"

"I don't..." Her silly throat clutched and she hardswallowed. "I really don't want to talk about Logan."

"Oh, yes, you do. You're stubborn, that's all. You always have been. But here's what I know. A week ago last

Friday, Logan's pickup was parked in front of your house all night. Since then, well, *something* has gone wrong. The light has gone out of your eyes—don't argue. Your eyes are sad. They're full of woe. Then an hour ago, I drop by Daisy's for a cruller and a coffee and I see Logan sitting in the corner having donuts with some elegant-looking brunette. What *happened*, honey?"

"He was out with an elegant brunette?" God. That hurt so much—even though she knew very well she had no right at all to feel brokenhearted that he might be seeing someone else.

"Yes." Flo's tone had gentled. She gazed at Sarah with understanding now. "And yes, it was only coffee and a donut. I can't say beyond a shadow of a doubt that it absolutely was a date. But, well, sometimes a woman can just tell. You know?"

"No, Mom. I don't know."

"It's just that, the two of them together, well, there was a definite 'datish' feel about it."

"*Datish?* What does that even mean?"

"You *know* what I mean."

"I just said I didn't."

Flo waved her hand some more. "In any case, seeing your guy with another girl—"

"Mom, he is not my—"

"Yes, he is. If he wasn't your guy, you wouldn't be so crushed to learn that he had coffee with someone else." The phone rang.

"Aren't you going to get that?"

"Voice mail will get it. This is more important." They stared at each other through two more rings. As soon as the phone fell silent, Flo went right on. "Honey, I do understand your fears. You were always so sure of where you were going and how it would be for you. All your growing-up years, while your dad and I were stuck on a treadmill of unhappiness and emotional isolation, I just knew that for you, things would be different."

"You did?" Sarah felt misty-eyed that her mom had actually paid attention, had believed that Sarah would make a success of her life.

Flo nodded. "You had a plan and you were going to have it all—a high-powered job you loved, the right man at your side. And eventually, children to love and to cherish."

"Well, I do have Sophia, right? Things could be worse."

"But they could also be better, now, couldn't they? You haven't shared specific details with me, but here you are back at home, single with Sophia. It's patently obvious that things didn't work out according to your plan. You've been disappointed. Deeply so. But you can't just shut yourself off from your heart's desire because you've been let down a time or two. If you do that, you'll end up nothing short of dead inside. Take it from your mother who was dead inside herself for far too many years. Honey, you need to give that man a shot. If you don't, some other lucky girl is going to snap him right up."

That afternoon and through way too many hours of the night that followed, Sarah couldn't stop thinking about the things her mom had said.

In the morning, she had a nine o'clock appointment with a client out in the valley not all that far from the Ambling A. The meeting took a little over an hour.

When she finished, she secured Sophia's seat in the

back of her car, got in behind the wheel—and called Logan before she could think of all the reasons she shouldn't.

It rang twice. She was madly trying to decide whether to leave a message or just hang up when he answered. "Sarah?"

All he said was her name, but it was everything. Just to hear the slightly frantic edge to his always-smooth voice. As if he'd missed her. As if he was afraid she'd already hung up.

"Hey." Her mind went blank and her heart beat so fast she felt a little dizzy.

"Sarah." He said her name like it mattered. A whole lot.

And that gave her the courage to suggest a meeting. "I'm maybe five miles from the Ambling A and I was wondering if—"

"Yes. Meet me at the house. Come straight here."

She sucked in a deep breath and ordered her heart to slow the heck down. "Yeah?"

"I'll be waiting on the front porch."

Hope flaring in his chest and sweat running down his face, Logan stuck his phone back in his pocket. Luckily, he was within sprinting distance of the house.

"Gotta go." He jammed his pitchfork into the ground.

"What's up?" demanded Xander.

"Everything okay?" asked Hunter.

"Everything is great. Got a meeting with my favorite accountant," he called over his shoulder as he took off at a run, leaving Xander and Hunter staring after him, on their own to finish burning out the stopped-up ditch behind the main barn.

Entering the house through the back door, he hooked

his hat on a peg, toed off his dirty boots and then headed for the utility room, where he stripped off his shirt and used the deep sink there to wash away the smoke and grime.

Clean from the belt up, he raced upstairs to grab a fresh shirt and a pair of boots free of mud and cow dung. He was just stepping out the door, tucking his shirt in as he went, when Sarah's white Honda pulled up in front.

She got out before he could get there to open her door for her. God, she looked good in snug jeans, boots tooled with twining flowers and a white shirt, her thick hair swept up in the usual bouncing ponytail.

He skidded to a stop a foot away as she pulled open the back door and bent to unhook Sophia's seat.

"Here. Let me take her."

"Ga! Ba!" The baby waved both fat fists and smiled that gorgeous toothless smile at him as Sarah passed him the carrier.

"It's really good to see you, too," he said to Sophia.

"Pffffft," the little girl replied and then laughed that adorable baby laugh of hers.

Sarah anchored her baby pack on one shoulder. "I was wondering if we could talk?"

He almost had a heart attack from sheer gladness right then and there. "Absolutely. Let's go to the office."

In the office, Logan put Sophia's carrier on the desk.

Sarah dropped her pack beside the carrier, opened the front flap and pulled out a teething toy to keep the baby busy for a little while. She offered the toy and Sophia took it.

Pulse racing and a nervous knot in her stomach, hardly

knowing what she was going to say, Sarah turned to face the man she hadn't been able to stop thinking about.

How could such a hot guy just keep getting hotter? Surely that wasn't possible. Still, his eyes were bluer, even, than she remembered, his sexy mouth more tempting. His hair was wet, his shirt sticking to him a little, like he'd washed up quickly and hadn't really had time to dry himself off.

No doubt about it. He was, hands down, the best-looking man she'd ever seen. She wanted him so much. And she was so afraid it wouldn't work out.

But then he said, "Sarah," sweet and low and full of yearning.

The very same yearning she felt all through every part of her body.

And then he was reaching out. And she was reaching out.

She landed against his warm, hard chest with a tiny, hungry cry. His arms came around her and she tipped up her mouth to him.

His lips crashed down to meet hers. She sighed at that, at the perfection of being held by him, of having his mouth on hers. He smelled of soap and hay and something kind of smoky—and man. All man. So good. So right. So exactly what she needed.

She moaned low in her throat, her hands reaching, seeking, sliding over the hard, muscled planes of his chest and up to link around his neck.

He lifted his head, but only to slant that wonderful mouth the other way. His big hands roamed her back, pulling her closer, as though he could meld their two separate bodies into one.

And then from the doorway, a gravelly voice said, "Ahem. Hope I'm not interrupting."

With a gasp, Sarah broke the kiss.

She would have jumped back from Logan's embrace, except he didn't allow that. He cradled her close to him and said to his father, "Well, you *are* interrupting. Go away and close the door behind you."

"Aw, now." Max glanced down at his black boots and then up again with a rueful half smile. "I just need a minute or two."

"Whatever it is, it can wait."

"No, it can't. Come on, son. This won't take long."

Sarah felt awful and awkward and very unwelcome. It was disorienting—one minute swept away by the glory of a kiss and the next feeling somehow like an interloper in the Crawford house. "I should go."

Logan only held her tighter. "No way."

She couldn't stand this. Max in the doorway, refusing to leave them alone, Logan holding her too tightly, glaring at his dad.

"Really, Logan. Please. Let me go." She pushed more strongly at his chest and he finally released her.

Grabbing the baby carrier, she hitched the pack over her shoulder and turned for the door. Max stepped back. She swept past him and fled.

Max blocked the doorway again as soon as Sarah darted through it.

Logan barely held himself back from punching his own father right in the face. "Get out of my way, Dad."

Max didn't budge. "Now, son. You need to just let her go. She's not the one for you. She has a child and no man, which tells me things went bad with whoever that baby's daddy is. That's not a good sign. And beyond that, you never know. The father could show up any day now."

"You don't know what you're talking about. The father is out of the picture. Period. End of story."

"Well, whatever happened with the guy before you, I don't think I'm out of line in assuming it didn't end well. That means Sarah's been hurt and it won't be that easy to win her trust. I just don't get it. Why choose a woman with all that baggage? You're just asking for heartbreak."

Faintly, Logan heard the front door shut. "I don't know where you think you get off with this crap, but it's got to stop."

Max looked at him pleadingly. "Just give someone else a shot, that's all I'm saying."

"Pay attention, old man. Shut your mouth, open your eyes and use your ears for once. I've done it, let that wedding planner of yours set me up, gone out with the women she found for me. And you know what that's done for me? Not a thing—except to make me more certain that if there ever could be the one for me, Sarah's it."

"Now, that's not true."

"You're still not listening, Dad. It's a problem you have. Sarah is the one that I want. All your plotting and scheming isn't going to change that." Outside, he heard a car start up. He needed to go after her. "Move aside."

Max only braced his legs wide and folded his arms across his chest.

Fast losing patience, Logan made one more attempt to reason with the stubborn fool. "Okay. I get that whatever's eating you about Sarah is somehow related to what happened with Sheila way back when. You want to talk about that, fine, you talk about it. Just cut all the mystery and say right out what you're getting at. Because frankly, you're making no sense to me *or* to my brothers. For years, you've warned us off getting seriously involved with a woman. 'Have fun, boys,' you always said, 'but don't tie yourselves down.' And 'Marriage is like a walk in the park—Jurassic Park.'"

Max had the nerve to chuckle. "You have to admit, that was a good one."

"Not laughing." Logan glared at his father until Max's grin vanished. "What I want to know is why, out of the blue, you want all six of us married—just not with any woman who already has a child?"

"Think about it. It's not good for that baby, Logan. To get all attached to you and then to lose you. That's bad."

"Who says anyone's losing me?"

"You don't know what can happen."

"Nobody does. That's life. What I do know is that the way you just behaved with Sarah was rude. Unacceptable. Sarah's done nothing wrong and she's nothing like Sheila. Sarah would never turn her back on her own child the way Sheila did to us."

Max got the strangest look on his face. His straight shoulders slumped. All of a sudden, he looked every year of his age. "Maybe *I* did a few things wrong, too, you know? Maybe you and the other boys don't know the whole story of what happened with your mother."

"Maybe?" Logan got right up in his face over that one. "Dad, you are so far out of line, I don't know where to start with you."

"Son, I—"

"I'm not finished. If you haven't told us the whole story about Sheila, remedy that. Tell it. Do it now."

Max put up both hands and mumbled, "I'm only saying, if you really care about Sarah and her baby, you should do the right thing and walk away now."

"You're saying nothing and we both know it. And I am finished with listening to you tell me nothing. You keep that wedding planner off my back. You tell her I'm not going on any more dates with the women she's constantly calling to set me up with. I'm done dating women I don't want. I want Sarah. And right now, I'm going to do my level best to convince her to give me a real shot. Out of my way."

That time, Max didn't argue. He fell back and Logan headed for the door.

Outside, Logan found that Sarah's white CR-V was already long gone. At least he'd left his crew cab in front. He jumped in. Skidding and stirring up a mini-tornado's worth of dust, he headed for the highway.

He drove fast and recklessly all the way to town, not even knowing for sure if that was where she'd gone. It just seemed his best bet. If he didn't catch up with her, he would have to call her and he had a bad feeling that when he did, she wouldn't answer.

Damn the old man. This was all his fault. One minute, Logan had Sarah in his arms again and she was kissing him like she'd finally realized that she needed to give him a real, honest shot with her—and the next minute, his dad was there, acting like an ass, hinting of dark secrets, messing everything up.

If Max had ruined things for good with Sarah, there

was going to be big trouble as soon as Logan got back to the ranch.

He rolled into Rust Creek Falls on Sawmill Street and slowed down a little—after all, this was his town now. He didn't want to run any of his neighbors down. Plus, it would be hard reaching out to Sarah if the sheriff locked him up in jail. He rolled along at a sedate pace and then had to choose his first destination—her house on Pine or Falls Mountain Accounting on North Broomtail.

He slowed down at Pine—but he just had a feeling she'd gone to her office, so he rolled on by that turn, taking North Broomtail instead.

And he scored.

She was parked in front of her office, the back door open, bending to get Sophia's carrier out when he pulled his pickup in next to her.

Glancing back over her shoulder, she spotted him. Rising to her height, she turned. He jumped out and they faced off over the open car door.

"Sarah, I'm so sorry about my dad. You can't listen to—"

She put a finger to her lips and spoke softly. "Sophia's asleep."

He lowered the volume. "We need to talk. You know we do."

"Oh, Logan. I really don't—"

"*You* called *me*. You know you want to talk this through. Give me a break here. Don't change your mind. I missed you so damn much. Admit you missed me, too."

Her soft mouth hardened. "Yeah. Right. You missed me so much you were going out with someone else."

"Sarah…"

"Shh." She glanced up the street as a couple of older ladies came toward them on the sidewalk. They smiled and waved. He watched as Sarah forced her lips into an upward curve and waved back. Logan waved, too.

The ladies strolled on by, bending their heads close to speak in low voices, glancing more than once at Sarah and Logan.

Finally, the ladies moved on down the street and Sarah said, "Really, I don't—"

"I don't want anyone else," he vowed before she could finish telling him no all over again. "I only went out with those other women because you dumped me."

She scowled. "Dumped you? We had one date. You can't dump a person after just one date."

"Okay, so *dump* is the wrong word. You didn't dump me. You only said you didn't want to be with me and you wouldn't go out with me again. Fair enough?"

"I…" Her sleek brows drew together. "Wait a minute. Other *women*? There was more than just one?"

She hadn't known there were three dates?

He could punch his own face about now—trying so hard to explain himself and just making it worse. "Look. I was miserable. Viv Dalton kept calling. After the first one, I knew I wasn't interested and I told Viv I wasn't. But that woman is really determined and I was just sad, missing you, wanting you and trying to forget you. Those three dates did nothing for me. They didn't help me forget you. How could they when all I did was think about you?"

She was softening. He could see it in those golden-brown eyes, in the way she looked at him. Intense.

Reluctant—but expectant, too. "You, um, thought about me?"

"Only you. And I'm done. Finished with trying to forget you by wasting the time of nice women I'm not the least interested in."

"You are?"

"I am. I swear it to you—and I also promise that I'm not rushing you. I'm only hoping that maybe we could try again, take it slower, if you need it slower. Be…I don't know, be *friends*." He tried not to wince when he offered the friend zone. Being her friend wasn't going to satisfy him, no way. "Whatever you want. As long as we can see each other, be together, find out where this thing between us might go. That's all I want from you. It's all I'm asking."

Over the top of the open car door, Sarah stared at his impossibly handsome face.

Really, she didn't need any more convincing. He'd said he missed her, that he couldn't forget her. And she'd missed him, too. So very much.

No, she still didn't see him as the kind of guy who would sign on for forever with a single mom and her baby girl.

But the barriers between them were at least partly because of her. She was afraid to trust him. She'd had a little too much of men she couldn't count on and she was holding back, keeping him at a distance in order not to get hurt again.

But Logan was turning out to be so patient. He really did seem to want to be with her. He was kind and generous and he was crazy about Sophia.

Why not just go with it, for however long it lasted? So what if it didn't go on forever? Why shouldn't she just enjoy every minute she could have with him?

Sarah stepped back. His face fell in disappointment.

But then she pushed the door shut—not all the way. She left it open enough that she would hear if Sophia started fussing.

About then, Logan must have seen her decision in her eyes. "Sarah." He said her name low, with relief. And something bordering on joy.

She moved in close. He opened his arms. And she stepped right into them, laying her hands on his broad chest, feeling his heat and the beating of his strong heart under her palms. "I'm just…scared, you know?"

His eyes turned tender, soft as the summer sky. "I know. And that's okay. Just give me a chance, anyway. Give *us* a chance."

There was a giant lump in her throat. She swallowed it down. "Okay."

One corner of that fine mouth of his hitched up. "Okay…what?"

"Okay, let's give this thing between us a fighting chance."

"You mean it?"

"Yeah. Let's do this. Let's try."

"Sarah…"

For the longest, sweetest moment, they just stared at each other.

And then, at last, he gathered her close and he kissed her, a deep, dizzying, beautiful kiss. She let her hands glide up to encircle his neck and kissed him right back.

Someone was clapping behind her. Someone else

whistled. Logan lifted his head and said, "Get lost, you kids."

She glanced over her shoulder in time to see a couple of local boys run off down the street in the same direction the two older ladies had gone.

"All right," he said, putting a finger under her chin and guiding her face back around so she met those fine blue eyes of his. "Where were we?"

She grinned up at him. "Tonight?" she asked.

"Where and when?"

"My house. Six o'clock."

Chapter Seven

Sarah turned from Sophia's crib.

Logan was waiting in the open doorway.

He held out his hand. She went to him and he wrapped his arms loosely around her. "Well?" he whispered.

She put two fingers against his lips and mouthed, "Sound asleep."

He caught her hand. "Come on."

She turned off the light and silently shut the door behind them.

After one step, he stopped in the middle of her tiny hallway. "Wait."

She gazed up at him, confused. "What?"

"This." Pulling her close, he lowered his mouth to hers.

She giggled a little against his warm lips. And then she sighed in dizzy pleasure as he kissed her more deeply. It felt so fine, so absolutely right, to be held in those lean, strong arms of his, to have his lips moving on hers, his tongue exploring her mouth in the most delicious way.

When he lifted his head and gazed down at her, she saw his desire in his eyes. Her bedroom was two steps away. And all at once, what would happen between them tonight was breathtakingly, scarily real. Her heart rate kicked up a notch. She could feel her pulse beating in her neck. He regarded her without wavering, his eyes full of promises, his mouth a little swollen from that beautiful, lingering kiss they'd just shared.

"I haven't, um, been with anyone," she said, every nerve in her body hyperactive, quivering. "Not since that conference in Denver when I got pregnant with Sophia."

He put his hands on her shoulders, so gently, in reassurance. "You're not sure."

"I didn't say that."

He stroked his palms down her arms in a soothing caress. "How about we make popcorn, stream a movie or something?"

She stared up at him, studying him, memorizing him—the fine lines around his eyes, his square jaw, that mouth she couldn't wait to kiss again. His cheeks were smooth tonight, free of the usual sexy layer of scruff. It pleased her to picture him shaving, a towel wrapped around his lean waist, getting ready for his evening with her.

And her nerves? They were easing, settling. "Not a chance." She offered a hand and he took it, weaving his fingers together with hers. "This way," she said.

In her bedroom, she turned the lamp on low. The

baby monitor was already waiting in there, the screen dark until sound or movement activated it.

"So will it be that gray-blue or the bluish-green color?" He was staring at the paint colors she'd stroked on the white wall.

She stepped in close to him and got to work unbuttoning his dove-gray shirt. "I have to tell you, at this moment, paint colors don't interest me in the least."

Now he was looking directly at her again and it felt like just maybe he could see into her heart, see her tender, never-quite-realized hopes, her slightly tarnished dreams. "Gotcha." And he kissed her, another slow, deep one.

She sighed and melted into him, surrendering to the moment, letting him take the lead.

He claimed control so smoothly, easing her into the glory of right now, his lips moving against hers, his big hands skating over her, stroking her, quieting every worry. Banishing every fear.

She let him undress her. He did it slowly, with care, taking time to kiss her and touch her as he peeled away each separate item of clothing. Time kind of faded away, along with the last of her nervous fears. He laid her down on her bed and she gazed up at him, wondering at the perfection of this moment, the hazy, sweet beauty of it.

He took his phone from one pocket, a short chain of condoms from another and set them all on the night table by the lamp. After that, he took off his own clothes swiftly, revealing his body, so lean and sharply cut. Such a fine-looking man. Everywhere. In every way.

"Is this really happening?" she asked him when he came down to her.

"You'd better believe it." He pulled her close, skin to skin. "At last."

And he kissed her some more, kisses that managed both to soothe and excite her. He kissed her all over, whispering naughty things, his lips skimming down the side of her throat, pausing to press a deeper kiss in the curve where her neck met her shoulder, sucking at her skin in that tender spot, bringing the blood to the surface.

But not stopping there. Oh, no.

He went lower, lingering first at her breasts, making her moan for him, making her cry out his name.

Swept up in sensation, she forgot all about the ways her body had changed with pregnancy, the new softness at her belly, the white striations where her skin had made room for the baby within her—until he kissed them, brushing his lips over them, so sweet and slow. She lifted her head when he did that, blinking down at him, not really believing that any man would linger over stretch marks.

He glanced up and met her eyes. And he winked at her.

She laughed and let her head fall back against the pillow.

He continued his journey, dropping kisses on the crests of her hipbones, nibbling across her lower abdomen, eventually lifting her left thigh onto his shoulder so that he could slide underneath it and settle between her legs.

Intimate, arousing, perfect kisses followed. The man

knew what he was doing. He invaded her most secret places.

And she let him. She welcomed him, opening her legs wider, reaching down to spear her fingers in his thick, short hair, urging him on, begging for more, losing herself to the sheer pleasure of his mouth, of the things that he did with those big, knowing hands of his.

She went over the edge, losing herself completely, crying out his name.

And he? Well, he just went on kissing her, touching her, stroking her, luring her right to the edge again...

And on over for the second time.

By then, she was vanquished in the best way possible, limp and so satisfied. She simply lay there, sighing, as he eased out from between her open thighs, rose to his knees above her and reached for a condom.

"Hey." His voice was low, a little raspy, teasing and coaxing.

"Hmm?" She managed a lazy smile.

"You okay?"

"Oh, Logan. Yes, I am. No, wait. On second thought, 'okay' doesn't even come close. I'm much better than okay. I'm excellent. Satisfied. Perfectly content. And ready for more." She lifted a lazy arm and reached out to him.

He took her fingers, bent closer and pressed those wonderful lips of his to the back of her hand. "That's what I wanted to hear." He let go of her to suit up, the beautiful muscles of his arms and chest flexing and bunching as he did so.

Then he braced his hands on the mattress on either

side of her and lowered himself down to her, taking care not to put all his weight on her at once.

But she wanted that—all of him, pressing her down.

"Come here. Come closer." She took those broad, hard shoulders and pulled him down.

He gave in to her urging, settling on her carefully, taking her mouth again, kissing her slowly, tasting her own arousal, reminding her sharply of how much she wanted him, of his skill as a lover, which was absolutely stunning in the best sort of way.

She felt him, large and hard and ready. And she wanted him. All of him, with nothing held back.

Did she believe that her dreams would come true with him?

No.

Something had broken in her, after Tuck and then the disappointment of Mercer. It wasn't the men, really—how could it be? She hadn't understood Tuck at all. And Mercer, well, she hardly knew the guy.

No. It wasn't the men. It was about her, about her absolute belief in her plan for her future. She'd been so very sure she had it all figured out, that she wouldn't be like her parents, settling for a colorless, nothing life in her hometown. She would have everything—great success, true love and beautiful children in the big, exciting city, because she knew what she wanted and how to get it.

But what *had* she known, really?

Nothing, that's what. She'd gone forth in arrogance, ready to conquer the world. And nothing had worked out the way she'd intended.

So no. She wasn't thinking she would get forever with Logan. She wasn't counting on anything.

For her, it was all about right now, here in her bed, with this beautiful man. Having him in her arms, wanting her, holding her.

This moment was what mattered. It was way more than enough.

He was right there, pressing, hot and insistent, where she wanted him so very much. She eased her thighs wider, wrapped her legs around him.

He groaned her name as he filled her.

"Yes," she answered. "Oh, Logan, yes…"

And then they were moving, rocking together and her mind was a white-hot blank of pure pleasure. He made it last for the longest, sweetest time. She clung to him, feeling her body rise again. When she hit the crest, she cried out at the sheer joy of it.

He followed soon after, holding her so tight.

For a while, they just lay there, arms and legs entangled, whispering together, reveling in afterglow.

As for what would happen next, what the future might bring, none of that mattered. For now, for tonight, she belonged to Logan.

And he was hers.

Thursday was the Fourth of July.

They had breakfast together at the cottage—Sarah, Sophia and Logan. He filled more pages of her notebook with sketches of Sarah at the stove flipping pancakes and then of Sophia in her bouncy seat, laughing and waving her little arms.

In the late afternoon, Sarah dressed her baby in red,

white and blue, and the three of them joined their neighbors in Rust Creek Falls Park for a community barbecue. Sarah's parents were there and Lily was, too. They all sat together on a big blanket Sarah had brought. When it came time to eat, they shared a picnic table. Everybody wanted to hold the baby. Sophia loved the attention. She hardly fussed at all, even dropping off to sleep in her baby seat when she got tired.

Laura Crawford, Nate Crawford's mom, who was a fixture behind the counter at Crawford's General Store, stopped by to chat with Sarah's mom and dad. Sophia was awake again by then and Mrs. Crawford asked to hold her.

"She's such a good baby," the older woman said as Sophia grabbed her finger and tried to use it as a teething toy. Laura Crawford glanced at Logan. "And she has your eyes."

For a second, Sarah's skin felt too hot and her pulse started racing. She felt thoroughly dissed. Surely everyone in town knew that she was a single mom and that Logan Crawford—a relative of Laura's, after all—was not her baby daddy.

But Laura wasn't a mean person. Most likely, she just meant it in a teasing way, because Logan and Sophia both had blue eyes and Sarah and Logan were making no secret of their current coupled-up status.

And what did it matter what Laura Crawford actually thought? Sarah intended to enjoy every minute of her time with Logan. A random remark by Nate Crawford's mom wasn't going to make her feel bad about herself or her choices.

Clearly, Logan wasn't bothered in the least. He

grinned at Laura. "You noticed," he said, at which point Sophia decided she wanted him to hold her.

"Ah, da!" the baby crowed, reaching out her arms to Logan, falling toward him.

Logan jumped up to catch her as Mrs. Crawford reluctantly let her go. Once he had Sophia safely in his arms, she patted his cheek and babbled out more happy nonsense.

A little later, Flo and Mack said they were going on home. Flo volunteered to take Sophia. "Stay for the dancing," she told Sarah. "You can pick the baby up on your way home. Or if it gets too late, she can just stay with us. Come get her first thing in the morning."

"Thanks, Mom." Really, it was nice. To have her mom and dad close by—especially her mom and dad the way they were now, happy and kind of easygoing, fun to be around. Sarah was even starting to get used to her mother's new frankness about sex and relationships. If Flo and Mack would just quit exploring their new sexual freedom at the office, Sarah would have zero complaints when it came to her parents.

She handed over all the baby paraphernalia and promised to come pick Sophia up by ten thirty that night.

"Or in the morning," her mom offered again. "That's fine, too."

As the band started tuning up, Sarah, Logan and Lily sat and chatted. Logan's brothers Xander and Wilder joined them. They all joked about Max and his scheme to get his boys married off.

Xander said to Logan, "At least Dad seems to be making progress with you."

Sarah sighed. Xander so didn't get it. Max wanted Logan married, yeah—just not to her. She looked away and reminded herself that she had no business feeling hurt.

So what if Max didn't consider her a good match for Logan? It wasn't like she was picking out china patterns and dreaming of monogramming her towels with a capital *C*. She and Logan were going to take it day by day and she was perfectly happy about that.

"Hey." Logan leaned in close.

She turned to him. "Hmm?"

And he kissed her, right there under the darkening sky in front of everyone on the Fourth of July in Rust Creek Falls Park. It was a quick kiss, but tender. And so very sweet.

Whatever happened, however it ended, she would remember this moment, sitting on the red, white and blue quilt her grandmother had made years and years ago, Logan's warm lips brushing hers in affection and reassurance.

"Hey, guys. What's up?" Genevieve Lawrence, in a yellow dress and cowboy boots, dropped down on the blanket next to Xander. She gave Logan's brother a radiant smile and then turned to Logan. "So, I see you took my advice."

Sarah didn't know Genevieve well, but she knew that the pretty, outgoing blonde was a true craftswoman, a farrier who trimmed and shod horses' hooves for a living. "What advice?"

Logan leaned close again. "Date number two," he whispered.

"Ah." She asked again, "What advice?"

Genevieve pretended to smooth her flared skirt. "It's all good, I promise." She wiggled her eyebrows at Sarah. "Make him tell you when you're alone."

Right then, the band launched into Lady Antebellum's "American Honey."

Genevieve turned to Xander. "How 'bout a dance?"

Xander jumped up, offered his hand and led the energetic blonde to the portable dance floor set up under the trees just as the party lights strung from branch to branch came on over their heads.

A moment later, another girl wandered over. Sarah vaguely recognized her, but couldn't recall her name.

Not that it mattered. The girl asked Wilder to dance and off they went.

Lily watched them go, a wistful look on her face.

Sarah slid a glance at Logan. Their eyes met and it was as though he'd read her mind.

"Want to dance, Lily?"

Lily smoothed her pulled-back hair. "You should dance with Sarah."

He only gazed at Lily steadily and asked again, "Dance with me?"

Sarah said, "Looks like he's not takin' no for an answer, Lil."

"Oh, you two." Lily waved her hand in front of her face. But when Logan got up and held down his hand, she took it.

As they danced, Logan asked Sarah's friend about her job at Maverick Manor.

Lily said she loved to cook and she really wished she

could get more hours. "But as of now, I'm part-time. Hey. At least it's something."

Cole and Viv Dalton danced by. Viv smiled at Logan.

He nodded in response and glanced down at Sarah's friend again. "So, have you joined Viv Dalton's dating service yet?"

Lily scoffed. "Yeah. Like that's gonna happen."

"Why not? I can personally vouch for each of my brothers. They can be troublesome and maybe a little rough around the edges, but they're all good at heart, not to mention good-looking. One of them could be the guy for you."

"Seems to me they've got plenty of women to choose from already."

"Give it a chance, Lily. What have you got to lose? If nothing else, you might have a good time."

She frowned up at him, but her eyes gleamed with wry humor. "Logan Crawford, you are much too persuasive."

"Just think about it."

She shrugged. "Sure. I'll do that."

Did he believe her? Not really. And that created the strangest urge in him to keep pushing her—because he liked her and she mattered to Sarah and he really did think it would be good for her, to get out there and mix it up a little.

On the other hand, it was none of his damn business whether Lily Hunt went out with one of his brothers or not. He'd said more than enough about the wedding planner's dating pool.

When the dance ended, he and Lily rejoined Sarah on the blanket. Hunter and Wren wandered over and sat down with them. Max stopped by. Logan prepared to get tough on his dad if he gave Sarah any grief. But Max was on his best behavior, greeting both Sarah and Lily in an easy, friendly way, going on about how great it was to spend Independence Day with the good citizens of his new hometown.

The band started playing another slow one. Logan leaned close to Sarah and breathed in her delicate scent. "Let's dance."

"Yes." Her eyes shone so bright and he was the happiest man in Montana, just to be spending his Fourth of July at her side.

She gave him her hand. They rose together.

Max got up, too. "I think I'll go check in with Viv and Cole. Great to meet you, Lily." He aimed a too-wide smile at Logan. "We need you out at the Ambling A good and early tomorrow."

"I'll be there."

"Fences to mend, cattle to tend," Max added in a jovial tone that set Logan's teeth on edge.

He always did his share of the work and Max knew it, too. Ignoring the temptation to mutter something sarcastic, Logan led Sarah to the dance floor, where he wrapped his arms around her and didn't let go through that song and the next and the next after that.

A little later, they rolled up her grandmother's quilt and wandered over to Rust Creek, which meandered through the center of town. The local merchants association had arranged for a fireworks display right there at creekside. Everyone sat around on the grass and watched the bright explosions light up the night sky.

It was after eleven when the fireworks show ended.

Logan and Sarah strolled by her parents' house on the way to Sarah's place, just on the off-chance that her mom and dad might still be up. All the lights were off.

Sarah said it was fine. She would pick up Sophia in the morning. Holding hands, they strolled on to her cottage, where she hesitated before leading him up the front walk.

"I know you have to be up and working early," she said.

He had the quilt under one arm, but he pulled her close with the other hand. "Are you trying to get rid of me?"

She gazed up at him, her mouth so tempting, the moon reflected in her eyes. "No way."

"Good, then. I'll get up before dawn and sneak out. I promise not to wake you." He wrapped his free arm around her and claimed a quick, hard kiss.

Laughing softly, she led him up the walk.

Sarah woke at six fifteen the next morning.

Logan's side of the bed was empty. She slid her hand over there. The sheet was cool.

Longing warmed her belly and made her throat tight. Last night had been every bit as beautiful and fulfilling as the night before. He'd made love to her twice and she'd dropped off to sleep with a smile on her face.

Already, she was getting so attached to him. She should probably claim a little space between them, let a few days go by at least, before seeing him again.

But then she got up and went into the kitchen and found a drawing of a weathered fence, a barn in the background and a sign hooked to the fence that read, *See you tonight. 6 o'clock. I'll bring takeout.*

And her plans to get some distance? Gone like morning mist at sunrise.

Grinning to herself, she grabbed her phone and texted him.

There had better not be candles or fine china involved in your takeout plans this time. She paused without sending and frowned at the text box before adding, You know what? Forget takeout. I'll fix us something. She hit Send, figuring it would be a while before he had a chance to check his phone.

Not so.

He came right back with, I'll stop at Daisy's and get dessert.

That evening, he arrived right on time carrying a bakery box full of red velvet cupcakes with cream cheese frosting. Then he kept Sophia busy while Sarah got the dinner on. When they sat down to eat, he held Sophia in his lap. With one hand, he helped her keep hold of her bottle. With the other, he ate his chicken and oven-roasted potatoes.

Once Sophia was in bed, he led Sarah straight to her bedroom. He removed her clothes and his, too, in record time and then did a series of truly wonderful things to her body.

Later, after she'd turned off the lamp, as she drifted toward sleep, feeling so safe and satisfied and peaceful, her head on his chest and those hard arms around her, he said, "You need to choose your paint colors. I talked to the guy at the paint store in Kalispell. I can order the paint and he'll send it over with a couple of professional painters. They'll get the job done the way you want it."

She didn't know whether she felt bulldozed or taken

care of. "Logan, I don't want to spend my money on professional painters."

He smoothed a hand down her hair and pressed a kiss on the top of her head. "That's okay. I'm going to pay for the paint *and* the guys to do the painting."

She wiggled out of his grip, sat up and turned on the lamp. "No, you're not."

"Sarah," he chided gently. "Yes, it's true that now I spend my working days moving cattle and repairing farm equipment, but that's by choice."

"Back to the land and all that, huh?"

"Essentially, yeah. What I'm saying is I've got money to burn."

"Good for you, Mr. Moneybags. I don't."

"Exactly. So let me do this for you. Don't make a big issue of it."

"But it *is* an issue, Logan."

"It doesn't have to be."

She sat there and glared at him, more annoyed by the second. "How can you possibly be so wonderful and so pigheaded simultaneously?"

He pretended to give that some thought. "I'm getting the feeling the question is rhetorical."

"Let me make this achingly clear—no. You are not paying for the paint *or* the painters."

He studied her, his blue eyes narrowed. "You need it done. I want to do it for you. This shouldn't be a problem."

"Listen carefully. Thank you for the offer, but I will do this my way."

He didn't answer immediately, which gave her hope that he had finally let it go. And then he reached out, slid his big, rough hand up under her hair and hooked it around the back of her neck. A gentle tug and she was pressed up against him.

She glanced up to meet his eyes. And his mouth came down on hers. He kissed her slowly. By the time he lifted his head again she was feeling all fluttery inside.

"So what's the compromise?" he asked. "How about a painting party?"

She reached over and turned off the light. They settled back down, her head on his chest. She traced a heart on his shoulder. "Hmm. A painting party…"

"You like that?" He sounded way too pleased with himself. "We could at least get a room or two painted, depending on how many people we could get and how long we all worked."

"When would this painting party occur?"

"A week from tomorrow—or sooner, depending on when everyone can come? We could make a list of victims—I mean, volunteers. We'll paint and then feed everybody. I'm thinking pizza and Wings To Go, soft drinks, beer and wine."

"I'll buy my own paint and supplies."

"Hey, you're the boss."

"Yes, I am and you shouldn't forget it."

"I'll bring the food and drinks," he said. She would have argued, but he added, "Shh. Let me do that, at least."

"All right." She lifted up and kissed him. "Thank you."

The next day was Saturday. Well before dawn, she woke to an empty bed. But then a floorboard creaked and she saw him through the shadows. He was pulling on his jeans.

She sat up, flicked on the lamp and yawned. "Don't you take Saturday off?"

One shoulder lifted in a half shrug. "There's always work that needs doing around the Ambling A."

"You can't possibly be getting enough sleep."

He zipped his fly. A little thrill shivered through her when he looked up and met her eyes. Whatever this was between them, however long it lasted, it sure did feel good. "I set my own hours. Today, I'll only work until around three," he said, "and then I'll get a nap. I'm fine, believe me. I'll be back at six tonight."

She just sat there with the covers pulled up over her bare breasts, thinking he was the best-looking guy she'd ever seen. "I'll do something with the leftover chicken. I mean it, Logan. Don't bring anything. There are still some cupcakes left for dessert."

He'd picked up his shirt, but then he dropped it again and stalked to the bed. Spearing his fingers in her scrambled hair, he hauled her close and kissed her, a deep, slow kiss, morning breath be damned.

When he let her go, she laughed. She couldn't help it—really, she laughed a lot when he was around. "Did you hear what I said?"

"Every word."

Maybe. But that didn't mean he would do as she asked. "You are impossible."

"And you mean that in the *best* possible way, am I right?"

"Yeah, right." She admired the gorgeous musculature

of his back as he returned to the chair and scooped up his shirt again. Then she frowned. "Hold on a minute."

He turned as he was slipping his arms in the sleeves and she was presented with that amazing sculpted chest and corrugated belly. "Yeah?"

"I just remembered. I usually try not to schedule appointments on the weekends, but I have a quarterly report to go over with a shoe store owner in Kalispell. We were supposed to meet yesterday, but he asked if I could move our meeting to today. It could go as late as six or six thirty."

"No problem. I'll wait."

"What? Like on the front porch?" That didn't seem right.

He dropped to the chair and pulled on a sock. "Sarah, it's not a big deal." He put on the other sock and reached for a boot.

"No. Really. There's an extra house key in that little green bowl on the entry table. Take it. Let yourself in if I'm not here when you arrive."

"That works." He pulled on the other boot and stood to button his shirt and tuck it in. Then he came to her again, tipped up her chin and gave her another sweet kiss. "Lie down. Go back to sleep." He waited for her to stretch out under the covers and then tucked them in around her.

"Drive carefully," she whispered.

"I will." He turned off the light.

She listened to his quiet footfalls as he left the room. A minute later, she heard the soft click of the lock as he went out the front door and then, very faintly, his crew cab starting up and driving away.

For a while, she lay awake, staring into the shadows, thinking how she didn't want to start depending on him, couldn't afford to get overly involved with him. She wasn't ready to go risking her heart again.

And yet, she'd gone and given him a key to her house.

Chapter Eight

Logan worked alone that day setting posts to fence a pasture several miles from the ranch house. It was good, being out on his own. He got a lot done when there was no one else around to distract him with idle talk and suggestions about how this or that task should be done.

Being on his own also gave him time to think—about Sarah, about this thing they had going on between them.

When it came to Sarah, he didn't really know what exactly was happening to him.

There was just something about her. From the first moment he'd set eyes on her that day at the old train depot, he'd only wanted to get closer to her, get to know her better.

It wasn't like him. He adored women, but he'd always

been careful not to get attached to any of them, not to let them worm their way into his heart.

There had been some hard lessons in his childhood and those lessons had stuck.

Logan was seven years old when his mom abandoned her family to run off with her lover. Max had said really cruel things about her then, called her rotten names. He'd told Logan and his brothers to get used to her being gone because she'd deserted them without a backward glance and she was never coming home. He'd said that a man couldn't trust any woman, and it was better for all his boys that they were learning that lesson early.

At the time, Logan refused to believe that he would never see his mom again. How could he believe it? Until she vanished from their lives without a hint of warning, Sheila had been a good mom, gentle and understanding, always there when he or his brothers needed her. For years, into his middle teens, he refused to lose faith in her basic goodness, in the devotion he just knew she felt to him and to his brothers. No matter what his dad said, he was waiting for her to return.

But she never did. She never so much as reached out. Not a letter or a phone call. Nothing. Radio silence. Year after year after year.

On his fifteenth birthday, when once again she didn't call or even send a card, he finally got it. He accepted the hard truth. Max was right. Sheila was gone for good and he needed to stop waiting for her to change her mind and return to her family.

That day—the day he turned fifteen—he finally accepted the lesson Max had tried so hard to teach him. A guy needed to protect himself, because if you let her, a woman would rip your heart out and leave you with nothing, dead and empty inside.

By then, it didn't matter that logically he knew it was beyond wrong to blame all women because his mother had deserted her family. Logic didn't even figure into it. The lesson of self-protection had hardwired itself into his brain, wrapped itself like barbwire around his heart.

Of course, he knew that there had to be lots of women in the world who kept their promises and took care of their own above all. He just didn't see any reason to go looking for one of them. He liked life on his own.

And in the years that followed, Logan never allowed himself to get too close to anyone. He was more of an overnight meaningful relationship kind of guy, a guy who treated any woman he was with like a queen for as long as it lasted—which was never very long. He always made it clear to any woman who caught his eye that he wasn't a man she should pin her hopes on.

But with Sarah…

It was different with her from the first moment he saw her that day at the train depot. To him, there had seemed to be a glow around her. As though she had a light inside her, a beacon that drew him inexorably closer.

Part of her attraction at first was her very wariness with him. No need to protect himself when she was doing such a bang-up job of pushing him away.

She made it so clear that she didn't want anything from him, wouldn't accept anything from him and would never let him get too close to her. That deep reserve in her just made him want her more.

Because honestly, what man wouldn't want Sarah—

with that slow-blooming smile of hers, those golden-brown eyes, that long, thick hair streaked with bronze, her softly rounded curves and her scent of flowers and elusive spice?

He'd been miserable when she ended it before it ever really got started. And then, when she admitted she wanted to try again, he'd been over the damn moon.

And now, this morning, she'd given him a key.

A key, damn it. That should have been enough to have him backing out the door with his hands up, shaking his head, apologizing for giving her the wrong idea. That should have had him drawing the line, saying no, absolutely not. He wasn't a man who ever took a woman's key.

Which reminded him. He'd never had "the talk" with her, never said that he really liked her but she needed to know he wasn't looking for anything serious.

He'd never had the talk and he wasn't going to have the talk. If he did that, he knew exactly what she would say—goodbye. The last thing Sarah needed was reminding that what they had wasn't permanent. She already knew that.

Better than he did.

No, with Sarah, goodbye didn't work for him. He wasn't anywhere near ready to walk away from her.

Did he expect it to last with her?

He kept telling himself he didn't.

But all that day as he set posts for new fences, he couldn't stop thinking about her, about that smile she had that lit up her whole face, about the way she cared for Sophia, always putting the baby first, taking her everywhere, managing to run a business with Sophia in tow. Maybe that was what made Sophia such a happy, trusting little thing. Maybe even a baby knew when she could count on her mother absolutely.

And what about the way Sarah didn't want him to give her things or do things for her?

Well, that only made him want to do more, to give her more. He was having a great time just coming up with new ways to make her life a little easier, to bring a smile to that pretty face of hers, to make her laugh, make her sigh. He had this weird dedication to Sarah *and* to Sophia, to their well-being, their happiness.

Was he in too deep?

Definitely.

Would she mess him over?

God, he hoped not.

Because somehow, with Sarah, he seemed to have misplaced his hard-earned instinct for self-preservation.

Sarah didn't get home that night until ten minutes of seven. Logan's pickup was already there, parked at the curb. She turned into her narrow driveway and got out to open the door of the cottage's detached garage. But before she could do that, Logan emerged from the house.

"I'll get it," he called and jogged across her small plot of lawn to open the door for her.

She got back in behind the wheel and parked in the dim little space. Logan went around and got Sophia in her carrier out of the back seat as Sarah grabbed the diaper bag and tote and got out, too. He shut the garage door and they walked across the lawn and up the front steps together.

At the front door, he reached out and put his hand on her arm. "Before we go in…"

Warmth filled her, just from that simple touch. She slanted him a sideways look as Sophia let out a joyful crow of baby laughter, followed by a gleeful, "Ah, da, na!"

He glanced down at her and grinned. "I'm happy to see you, too, Soph. It's been hours."

The man was a menace—to her heart and her emotional equilibrium. Really, she needed to talk to him, tell him to be a little less wonderful, please. "Before we go in, what?" she asked. His blue gaze lifted to meet hers. Now he looked…guilty, maybe? Or at least marginally apprehensive. "What did you do, Logan?"

He made a throat-clearing sound and took his free hand from her arm to rub the back of his neck. "Well, it's like this…"

She tried really hard not to grin. Because she *shouldn't* be grinning. He'd done something he knew he probably shouldn't do, something that she would have vetoed if only he'd asked her first.

How did she know that? She had no idea. Just, sometimes, she could read him simply by looking at his face.

She forced a stern expression. "I'd better not find my house painted when I go inside."

Another happy giggle from Sophia. And from Logan, "Whoa." Now he looked hurt. "I wouldn't do that. We already agreed about that."

"Okay…" She spoke the word on a rising inflection and waited for him to explain himself.

"Well, see, it was like this. As I'm on my way back to town this afternoon, I see this kid by the side of the road, a little towheaded kid in busted out jeans and a straw hat. He's sitting in a folding chair with this big cardboard box beside him and a sign that says, Kittens Free to Good Home."

She knew what he'd done then. "Logan, tell me you didn't."

He put up his free hand and patted the air with it. "Look, if you don't like her, I'll take her to the ranch, okay?"

"It's a female kitten is what you're saying and it is in my house right now."

"See, Wren might want her. Or I'll keep her for myself if I have to."

"All these options you have for where you might have taken her. And yet, you brought her here."

"Yeah. But first, I stopped at the vet. I got lucky and they were still open. I bought everything she'll need. Food and bowls, litter, a litter box, a scooper thing, a scratching post, a few toys and a bed. The kid who gave her to me said she's ten weeks old and hasn't had any shots. So I had the vet give them to her—along with a checkup. She's a healthy little girl, no sign of fleas. And she'll need her next shots in three to four weeks."

"Thought of everything, did you?"

"Sarah." He'd adopted his most reasonable, placating tone. "Don't be mad, okay? I meant what I said. I don't expect you to keep her."

For some reason, she wanted to burst out laughing. He looked so worried and she was having way too much fun giving him a hard time about this.

And as for the kitten, the last thing she needed was another baby to care for. However…

"When I was a kid, I always wanted a cat," she heard herself saying.

His eyes went soft as the midsummer sky. "You did?"

"My parents didn't allow pets. As I mentioned that first day in the office at the Ambling A, my parents were different back then. But I'm not saying I'll keep her."

He put his hand to his heart. "What did I tell you? If you don't want her, I'll take her with me tomorrow when I go."

So then, he was staying overnight again? She had no urge to argue about that. In fact, she was glad. Probably gladder than she should let herself be. "Does this kitten have a name?"

"Not yet. I figured you would want to name her yourself—I mean, if you decide to keep her."

"How thoughtful of you."

Now he grinned. "Knock it off with the sarcasm. You just admitted you like cats. And I'm telling you, you're not going to be able to resist this one." And with that, he pushed open the door and signaled her in ahead of him.

She saw the tiny kitten immediately. All white, with a perfect pink nose and ears, and the prettiest, blue-opal eyes, she sat beneath the dining area table. "Oh, my God," Sarah heard herself whisper. "She's adorable."

Those gorgeous, wide eyes regarded her from that perfect little face.

Setting her laptop on the coffee table and letting the diaper bag slide to the carpet, Sarah dropped to a crouch. "Hey there." She held out her hand. "Come here, you little angel. Come on…"

The kitten dipped her head to the side, considering.

"Reow?" she said as though asking a question, but she didn't budge.

"Such a pretty girl." She coaxed, "Come on, come here…"

That did it. The kitten stood. Delicately, she stretched her front legs and widened her paws. White whiskers twitching, she yawned. And then finally, after a few extra seconds of ladylike hesitation, she strutted out from under the table. White tail high, she paraded across the dining room and straight for Sarah, stopping when she reached her to delicately sniff her outstretched fingers.

Sarah waited until the kitten dropped to her butt again before daring to reach out. The kitten was already purring. Sarah pulled her close. Cradling the little snowball against her heart, she stood.

From behind her, Logan chuckled. "So then, what's her name?"

"Opal," she said without turning, bending her head to nuzzle the kitten's wonderfully soft fur. "Opal, for those eyes."

"Thank you for Opal," Sarah said. It was a little past eleven that night. They were tucked up in bed together and had been for a couple of beautiful hours. Earlier, after sharing dinner, they'd made the calls to set up the painting party for next week. Sophia had been asleep since eight or so. With any luck, she wouldn't wake up until daylight.

As for the kitten in question, Opal was sleeping in her new bed in the laundry room with the litter box close by. Sarah had wanted to bring her to bed with them, but the vet had advised Logan that she should sleep in her own bed with easy access to her litter box until she got a little older.

Logan chuckled. The sound was a lovely rumble beneath Sarah's left ear because she was using his warm, hard chest for a pillow. "I knew you would want her." He eased his fingers into her hair and idly combed it outward over her shoulders and down her back. "And I've been thinking…"

She stacked her hands on his chest and rested her chin on them. "Uh-oh. What now?"

"You need an electric garage-door opener."

She lifted up enough to plant a kiss on his square, beard-scruffy jaw. "No, I do not."

"Yeah, you really do. And when winter comes, you know you'll thank me. You don't need to be staggering around on your icy driveway trying to get the garage door up."

"There will be staggering whether I have an electric opener or not. I still have to make it from the garage to the house."

"Right." He was frowning. "And you'll be carrying Sophia and a laptop in that giant bag of yours—and that diaper bag, too. It's too dangerous."

"Logan, let it be."

"A side door to the garage and an enclosed breezeway leading around to the back door would fix the problem. No matter how bad the weather gets, you and Sophia would be safe and protected."

"That's a major project, Logan."

"Just let me deal with it. It's not that big a thing."

It *was* a big thing. Really, he was relentless—and in the most wonderful way. "Stop. I mean it. Let it go."

He guided a lock of hair back over her shoulder with a slow, gentle touch. "Think about it."

She needed to change the subject, fast. And she knew exactly how to do it. They'd already made love twice.

Time to go for number three.

Lifting up again, she pressed her lips to his. He let out a low growl of pleasure as he opened for her. She eased her tongue in, sliding it slowly against his.

His arms banded around her, so hot and hard. "You're trying to distract me," he grumbled.

She caught his lower lip between her teeth and worried it a little. "Yes, I am. Is it working?"

"I still want you to have that garage-door opener." His voice was rough now, his breathing just a tad ragged.

She slid her hand down between them and encircled his hard length. He groaned aloud and she asked in a teasing purr, "Do I have your attention, Logan?"

He released a hard breath. "Sarah…" A harsh word escaped him.

"No. Garage. Door. Opener," she instructed, low and firmly, making each word a sentence. "Got that?"

"I do, yeah." Another groan escaped him. "I definitely do."

"Good, then." She captured his mouth as she stroked him, holding on tight, increasing the pressure, working her hand up and down on him—until he turned the tables, wrapping an arm around her and deftly flipping her over so that she was beneath him. He levered up and reached for a condom.

A moment later, she held him within her, all the way.

She stared up into his blue, blue eyes, feeling cherished. Happy. And so very aroused.

When he started to move, she forgot everything but the pleasure of the moment.

Who knew what would happen as the days went by? She didn't know and she really didn't care.

It didn't work to count on a man, not for her. She'd learned that the hard way.

So she wasn't counting on him. She was simply enjoying herself, having the best time, just being with him, being Sarah and Logan, together, for right now.

Sunday, Sarah had no appointments and Logan decided to take a day off.

He stayed for breakfast. Then he herded her and Sophia to his crew cab and drove them to Kalispell, where the paint store he'd chosen opened at ten.

They bought paint and painting supplies. He convinced her to go ahead and buy the paint for all the rooms, even though they would only be tackling Sophia's room and the kitchen during the painting party next week. The bill for all that was pretty steep, but she really did want to get it done.

Of course, he had to offer, "Change your mind. Let me take care of it." She just shook her head and handed the paint store guy her credit card.

Logan wanted to take them out to lunch, but Sophia was a little fussy and Sarah kind of wanted to get back and see how Opal was doing. They bought takeout from a Chinese place they both liked and returned to Rust Creek Falls. After lunch, while Sophia was napping, he suggested they paint one of the rooms.

She cast an anxious eye at the cans of paint and supplies taking up most of the space in her dining room. "I know nothing about painting and the more I think about it, the more I kind of have a bad feeling about this."

He reacted with an easy shrug. "Well, great. I'll call in the professionals."

"Don't even go there." She sent him her sternest frown. "We've been through that more than once and it's not happening."

"So, then, we paint."

"Ugh. You are way too upbeat about this."

He hooked an arm around her and gave her an encouraging squeeze. "Piece of cake, I promise you."

"Oh, like you're some kind of expert?"

"Well, I worked for a house painter part-time during college to earn extra cash and when I first got to Seattle, I flipped houses. To save money, I painted the interiors myself."

She gaped up at him. "It's kind of not fair how much you know about a bunch of random things."

"I'm a Renaissance man, no doubt about it." He kissed the tip of her nose. "Look. You said you don't need to do the ceilings or the trim, right?"

"Yeah. The white ceilings are fine. And the cream-colored trim still looks fresh. I think my mom said they had the place painted a couple of years back."

"So, it's going to be easy." He gave her a thoroughly self-confident smirk.

"You say that with such conviction."

"Because it's true. The trim takes the longest and we're not doing the trim."

"I'm kind of worried we don't have enough tape."

"No problem. We won't need to tape."

"That's crazy. We'll get paint on the trim."

"No, we won't. You can do the rolling and I'll use a brush to cut in—meaning frame everything out, do all the parts that are too tight for a roller…"

"But—"

"Shh. No buts. I've done a lot of cutting-in and I won't get paint on your trim."

He seemed so confident, she agreed to do it his way.

Lily showed up just after they'd finished pushing the living and dining room furniture away from the walls and covering everything with plastic drop cloths.

"I'm going to help," Lily declared. "I'll just run home and change." In no time, she was back wearing worn jeans and a frayed T-shirt. Logan gave her a quick lesson in how to use a roller and she went to work.

Then Sarah's mom showed up with a plastic container full of sugar cookies. They took a cookie break. Sophia woke up and started fussing, so Flo went and got her, fed her and changed her—and then stuck around to watch her and to keep Opal out of the paint trays.

At some point, Flo called a couple of her friends and Sarah's dad, too. They all came over to pitch in. As it turned out, Sarah's dad and one of Flo's friends both had painting experience. They joined Logan to do the detail work. The rest of them used the rollers.

By seven that night, they'd finished the living room, the dining room, Sarah's room, the hallway and the bath—everything but the two rooms slated for next Saturday's painting party. They even cleaned up, washing rollers and brushes, removing drop cloths and putting all the furniture back where it belonged.

Sarah's mom invited everyone to her house for slow-cooker pot roast. As a group, they walked over to Flo and Mack's house, with Flo pushing Sophia in her stroller.

On arrival, Flo served them all pot roast, with home-made ice cream for dessert. Sarah found it weirdly dis-orienting, eating dinner in her mother's dining room, everybody chattering and laughing, having a great time. It was so unlike the way things used to be when she was growing up.

That night, after Sophia was in bed, Sarah and Logan streamed a Western on her laptop. Opal joined them on the sofa, snuggling in close to Sarah. The room, now a soothing gray-green, looked amazing. Sarah spent more time staring around her in wonderment than she did watching the movie.

"I think you like the new paint," Logan said as the credits started rolling. She leaned forward to shut down the laptop on the coffee table in front of them. When she sat back, Logan wrapped his arm around her.

"I loved everything about today," she said with a sigh. Opal was curled up next to her in a fluffy white ball, sound asleep. Sarah scratched her head gently, sim-ply to hear her purr. "It was so nice how everybody just showed up—and then stayed to help get the job done. It was really so sweet of them."

"That's the deal around here, right? Everyone pitch-ing in, helping out."

"Yeah. I love that about Rust Creek Falls—but it was strange at my parents' today."

His arm around her tightened as he pulled her a little closer. "Why strange?"

"Well, it's just that when I was growing up, we hardly ever had people over. And the house was always deadly quiet. I felt so lonely. But now, today, everyone was talking over each other, laughing, having a great old time. My mom and dad looked so happy. Sometimes now, when I'm around them, I feel like I've dropped into an alternate universe. They aren't the Flo and Mack I used to know."

"But it's a good thing, isn't it, the way they've changed?"

She took his hand and laced their fingers together. "Yeah. It's definitely a good thing. I could really get used to this, to the way they are now. I feel…kind of close to them. And I love how they have my back now. I believe I can count on them now. Plus, I'm starting to look forward to being here for them as they're growing older." She leaned her head on his shoulder. "I mean, I dreaded coming home partly because I felt that I never had any real relationship with my parents. It was depressing just being around them, trying to do simple things like have an actual conversation with them. They were so closed-off and set in their ways. But since I've been back—well, you saw how they are with each other now."

He chuckled. "Yeah, no intimacy issues between Flo and Mack."

"Not anymore, that's for sure. It took some getting used to. But now, well, that's who they are and they're happy together. And I'm starting to be really glad about that."

He tugged on a lock of her hair. "So it's all working out."

"A lot better than I expected, yeah."

"Now, all you need is a decent TV."

She groaned and elbowed him in the side. "Don't even go there."

But he just kept on. "I'm thinking at least fifty inches. Flat screens are a steal lately. I can get one for practically nothing."

The guy was incorrigible. She leaned into him and kissed his cheek. "No. That is not happening."

He held her gaze. "I'm here all the time and I like being here."

"I like having you here."

"I also like big screens." He said it longingly.

She shouldn't let herself weaken. He did way too much for her already. But he was looking at her so wistfully, like Opal when she wanted her Fancy Feast. "It's a small living room," she said and then wanted to clap her hand over her mouth the minute she added, "Fifty inches is just too big."

One of his eyebrows inched toward his hairline. She'd just opened the door to a negotiation and he knew it, too. She could tell by that gleeful gleam in his eye. "Forty-three inches, then. That's thirty-seven and a half inches wide and just over twenty-one inches high."

She tried her best stern look—not that it ever did a bit of good with him. "I see you have all the stats on the fancy TVs."

"You know I do, baby. We can put it in that corner." He pointed at the arch to the dining area, on the right side nearest the hallway to the bedrooms. "It won't overwhelm the space, I promise you."

She was weakening. Because, really, why shouldn't he buy a nice TV? He said that money was no problem for him and she believed him. And if things didn't last between them, she could just insist that he take it back, keep it for himself.

If things didn't last...

She probably shouldn't let herself think that way. They had something special together and she was so happy.

But you just never knew in life. The whole point with her and Logan was to enjoy each other, take it one day at a time together.

He caught her chin and turned her face so that she met his eyes again. "Okay. What happened?"

"Nothing. Really."

"I was about to convince you we need to *compromise* and get a forty-three-inch TV and you suddenly got sad on me."

The man was way too perceptive. As a rule, she loved that about him. Except when he picked up on stuff there was no point in getting into.

She leaned in and kissed him, quick and hard. "I mean it. It's nothing—and okay."

His eyebrow rose again. "Okay, what?"

"Forty-three inches and not a fraction more."

He leaned even closer. His rough cheek touched her smooth one and his warm breath teased her ear. "Now, that's what I wanted to hear. Let's put Opal to bed."

"And then what?"

"I'm thinking that first we need a long, relaxing bath..."

They shared the bathtub and helped each other scrub off all the random dried paint spatters. Then they did other things. Sexy things.

By the time they were through in the tub, there was

water all over the bathroom floor. They used their bath towels to mop it up.

And then they went to bed—and right to sleep for the first time since he started spending his nights at her place. He wrapped himself around her, his front to her back. She smiled in contentment and closed her eyes...

And when she woke in the morning, he was already gone.

In the kitchen she found more sketches and a note.

I'll be back by three. I'll bring dinner—don't argue. Just takeout, I promise. And don't try to tell me it's too far to go for takeout. I'm going to Kalispell anyway. Hint: it's 43 inches and it has your name on it.

That night he set up the new TV. He'd even bought surround-sound speakers. She accused him of being extravagant.

"You're going to love it." He grabbed her hand, pulled her down into his lap and nuzzled her neck. "Now, how 'bout some popcorn?"

She popped up a big bowl of it and they watched a heist movie.

Later, in bed, he was playful, tender and demanding. Really, it was so good with him. Everything. All of it. The sex, definitely. But all the other stuff, too.

He was always looking for ways to please her, to help her, to make her life better somehow. And she liked just being with him, talking about nothing in particular. Or not even talking at all.

And Opal. That he'd given her Opal, well, that meant so much to her. The kitten was healthy, smart, affectionate and just too cute. It was as if he'd found that special something she hadn't even known she longed for, a childhood wish never realized and destined to remain unfulfilled.

Until now. Because of him.

He was so good with Sophia. Her daughter adored him.

That could be difficult if they broke up. Or was Sophia too young to miss him?

Yet again, she reminded herself not to think that way. No way was Logan considering breaking up with her any time soon. He was always saying how happy he was with her, how crazy he was for Sophia. And he proved the truth of his words in action every day. No, it probably wouldn't last forever, what Sarah had with him. But nothing ever did.

Life in Rust Creek Falls was turning out to be pretty good for her and her baby. And she needed to keep looking on the bright side of things.

The bright side most definitely included her relationship with Logan Crawford. She promised herself she would keep that firmly in mind, not let the hard lessons she'd learned from past disappointments ruin a really good thing.

For as long as it lasted, she would love every minute.

Chapter Nine

That Wednesday, Logan asked her to come on out to the ranch for a picnic dinner. Her last appointment ended early, so she arrived sooner than she'd said she would, at a little after five.

With Sophia asleep in her carrier on one arm and the always-present diaper bag slung on her other shoulder, she went up the front steps.

The door opened before she reached it.

"The lovely Sarah," said Max. "And her cute little baby." He stepped back and ushered her in.

"Where's Logan?" Sarah asked as Max shut the door behind her.

"He'll be down in a minute. Here, let me help you with that." He took the diaper bag off her shoulder and hung it on the coatrack, then he swept out a hand toward the arch that led to the living room. "Come on in. Have a seat."

She didn't trust him. But she couldn't run for cover every time Logan's dad glanced her way.

Head high, expression serene, Sarah went into the living room and took a seat on the leather sofa. She set the carrier on the cushion beside her.

Max took the big easy chair across from her. "I'm glad to have a moment with you, a little time to talk." He smiled that charming smile of his, but his eyes were cool. Calculating.

She sat up a little straighter. "Look, Max, I don't know what you're leading up to here, but—"

He cut her off with a wave of his hand. "It's simple, really. I just want to, er, touch base."

"Let me be blunt. You and I have nothing to talk about. But if you insist, I think it would better if we included Logan in whatever you're about to discuss with me."

"Now, Sarah, this is not a discussion. I only want to remind you that Logan is thirty-three and has never had a serious relationship. He's a bad bet. And for you, with a baby to think of, well, you have to see that it's unwise for you to get involved with him."

Okay, it was just possible that, given her own not-so-stellar experience with men and romance, she actually kind of agreed with Logan's dad—she'd even said as much to Lily that night at Maverick Manor. But her doubts about Logan were for her to deal with in her own mind and heart. She and Logan had an understanding. They wanted to be together for right now and that was working out beautifully for them. Max Crawford had no right to try to make her choices for her.

True, in the past, it had hurt her that Logan's dad seemed to view her as unsuitable for his oldest son simply because she had a baby. Up till now, she'd just wanted to escape, run away like a hurt child, when he treated her unkindly.

But this was becoming ridiculous. It was time she stood up to him.

Drawing her shoulders back, she folded her hands in her lap and said pleasantly, "So you're saying that Logan is a bad bet for me, but *not* for those other women you had Viv set him up with?"

Max blinked in surprise. Apparently, he hadn't expected a rational argument from her. "Ahem. You don't understand, Sarah."

"That's because you really aren't making any sense, Max."

"It's, um, for your own good and the good of your child. You should at least know the statistics on the situation."

He had statistics to convince her to walk away from Logan? Really? She asked politely, "What statistics?"

"Well, just that if a man of Logan's age hasn't been married or in a serious, committed relationship, his chances of ever getting married are very low—and if he does get married, it's not all that likely to be a marriage that lasts."

Did she believe him? Not one bit. "I have to tell you, Max. I think you just made up those 'statistics' to fit your weak argument. I mean, if Logan were over forty, yeah, I might agree. When a guy gets past forty and he's happily single, any woman could find herself wondering if he simply prefers the single life. That might make him a bad marriage bet. But a lot of men wait till their thirties to settle down, so in Logan's case, your argument doesn't apply—not that I'm hoping to settle down with Logan."

Max's eyes widened. "Er...you're not?"

"We enjoy each other's company and we're having a good time."

"I didn't, er, well..." Max was actually at a loss for words. It was a rare moment and Sarah let herself enjoy it.

"And also," she added, "if you really believe what you're telling me, that he's such a bad marriage bet, why set him up with some other poor girl when, according to your reasoning, he'll only break *her* heart in the end?"

Max hemmed and hawed. "Well, now, Sarah, I'm only trying to help you realize that—"

"What do you think you're doing, Dad?" Logan stood in the open arch to the entry hall. His hair was wet and his lean cheeks freshly shaved. The sight of him made Sarah's heart ache in the sweetest sort of way—and that ache scared her more than all of Max's disapproving glances, dire warnings and fake statistics.

Max jumped up. "Sarah and I were just having a little chat, that's all."

Logan came straight for her, stopping at the other end of the sofa. He gazed down at her with concern. "Whatever he said, don't believe a word of it."

Sophia spotted him then, gave a happy giggle and waved her hands. "Hey there, beautiful." He dropped to the sofa on the other side of the carrier and scooped her up against his broad chest.

"Ga, dah," she said and grabbed for his nose.

"Well." Max stared at the man and the baby. Sarah couldn't tell if he looked bemused—or crestfallen. "I'll leave you alone. Wonderful to see you, Sarah."

She forced a nod and a smile. "See you later, Max."

Logan shook his head as Max disappeared through the dining room and out the door to the kitchen. "What did he say?"

Sarah rose and picked up the empty carrier. "It doesn't matter."

"If he's upset you—"

"Logan, I'm not upset." It was true. She was pretty much over Max and his issues with her as a potential bride for his oldest son.

She *wasn't* a potential bride—not for Logan or anyone. And Max had done her no harm.

In fact, their little chat had been a good thing. It had served to remind her that she was single and planned on staying that way. She liked Logan—maybe too much. He was kind and so generous. He made her laugh and she loved being with him. And whenever he kissed her, she wanted him to kiss her again, to keep kissing her and touching her and doing all those wonderful things to her that made her feel desired and satisfied in all the best ways.

But he wouldn't break her heart. She wouldn't let him. What they had together was no lifetime commitment. She wasn't counting on anything. They were both having a wonderful time for as long as it lasted.

And, she promised herself, she was perfectly happy with that.

Logan kind of had a bad feeling about whatever had gone down between his dad and Sarah while he was in the shower.

But Sarah insisted it was nothing, so he didn't pressure her to share the gory details. Max wasn't going to change and if she'd come to grips with that and decided not to let the old man bother her, that was all to the good. He had plans for the afternoon and he felt relieved that his dad hadn't ruined Sarah's mood.

Logan had packed a simple picnic, with sandwiches, chips and dip, a bottle of wine and cookies from Daisy's for dessert. It was gorgeous out, with the temperature in the high seventies, not too much wind and the sky a pure, cloudless blue.

Sarah carried the basket of food. He took the baby, the diaper bag and the picnic blanket. They strolled along the dirt road past the barn and the horse pasture to a spot he'd chosen under the dappled shade of an old bur oak.

"It's pretty here," she remarked approvingly. They spread the blanket. He put Sophia down on it and Sarah gave her a toy to chew on. The baby made her happy nonsense sounds and stared up through the branches. She even managed to roll over and push up on her hands a couple of times.

He poured them wine in paper cups and they ate. When Sophia got fussy, Sarah gave her a bottle and they took turns helping her hold it. Sophia was getting better at controlling her own bottle every day, it seemed to him. She also had two teeth coming in on the bottom in front. He could see the white rims peeking out of her gums whenever she gave him one of her giant smiles.

Kids. Logan had never seen himself as a guy who wanted children—no more than he'd ever thought he might get married.

But now he'd met Sophia. And lately, kids seemed like a pretty good idea to him.

And marriage? Well, he was kind of changing his opinion on that, too. The more time he spent with Sarah, the more he started thinking that he wouldn't mind being married at all.

He even *wanted* to be married.

As long as he could claim Sarah as his bride.

He had that urge to go for it—right then and there. The urge to pop the question now, as they sat beneath the old oak eating their cookies, watching Sophia hold her own bottle. He wanted to grab Sarah's hand and tell her exactly how he felt about her, what he wanted with her. To say how good forever sounded as long as he could share it with her.

But then he tried to remember that she'd had a rough time of it, and she wasn't all that trusting when it came to the male species. He felt that he *knew* her, that he understood her in all the ways that really mattered. Sometimes, in the past few days, he kind of forgot that he hadn't known her all his life.

He had to keep reminding himself that they hadn't been together for any length of time at all— just a week and a day. No way that was long enough for her to come to trust him. Any sudden moves involving emotional intimacy could scare her right off.

He didn't blame her for being commitment-shy.

That guy she'd lived with, Tuck Evans, was just a stone idiot. Logan wouldn't mind meeting that fool out behind the local cowboy bar, the Ace in the Hole, and going a few rounds with him. Then he'd thank him for blowing it royally and giving Logan a chance to have Sarah for his own.

As for that Mercer dude, Logan wouldn't mind doing a lot worse than beating him up. That guy had cheated on his wife *and* turned his back on Sophia. There were no words bad enough for someone like that.

Their loss, my gain, Logan reminded himself.

"Got a little surprise for Sophia," he said, as they were packing up the remains of their picnic.

Sarah gave him the side-eye. "I get nervous when you talk like that."

He leaned toward her, pulling her close and claiming her sweet lips in a slow, lazy kiss. Sophia, on the blanket between them, giggled up at them and crowed, "Ah, da, ga!"

Logan ran the backs of his fingers down Sarah's velvety cheek. *This is happiness. Who knew?* "Come on. You're going to love it." He kissed her again, because once was never enough.

She picked up the baby. He pulled his phone from his pocket and zipped off a quick text to Xander.

Bring Petunia. Now.

"What was that about?" Sarah watched him suspiciously as he put on his hat, tossed the blanket over his shoulder and grabbed the empty carrier, the basket and the diaper bag.

"I told you. It's a surprise." He started back toward the house.

She straightened Sophia's little sun hat and fell in

step beside him. "Okay, I know you're up to something and I know that it's something I'm not going to like."

He chuckled. "Now, what kind of attitude is that?"

"The attitude of a woman who's seen the way you operate, Logan Crawford."

"You've got it all wrong."

"You're trying to tell me you're *not* up to something?" She was just too cute.

He would have thrown an arm around her if he didn't have his hands full of all the stuff they'd carried out there. "No."

She frowned. "So you're admitting that you are up to something?"

"That's right, I am—and like I said, you're gonna love it."

Right then, Xander appeared from behind the barn leading a palomino pony.

Sarah could not believe her eyes. "Oh, you didn't."

Logan beamed. "He's a rescue. A Shetland. Just ten hands high, about eight years old with a really sweet disposition. I can't wait to see her ride him."

Sarah stopped in her tracks. "Her? You mean Sophia? Logan, she'll be six months old next week. That's way too young to be riding a pony."

He stopped, too. At least he had the grace to look a little sheepish now. "Okay. I know she's too young. What I meant to say was, I can't wait to see her ride him *when* she's old enough."

When she's old enough...

Those words just made it all worse somehow.

Sophia wouldn't be old enough to ride that pony for years.

Years.

Sarah couldn't take on the cost and commitment of caring for a pony in the hopes that someday her little girl might want to ride him. And she couldn't accept the pony as a gift for Sophia and expect Logan to keep him here at the Ambling A for her.

She and Logan, well, they didn't *have* years. That had been brought sharply home to her not two hours ago, thanks to Logan's own father. The point was to enjoy every moment, live completely in the now and not expect anything. Not to start making starry-eyed plans for some lovely, coupled-up future.

Sarah had spent her whole life looking ahead. She'd planned and schemed and set goals and kept her eyes on the prize of a great career, a successful marriage—kids eventually, after she made partner and could afford really good childcare.

And what had she gotten for all her "looking ahead"?

Nothing she'd planned on, that was for certain.

"Sarah." Logan dropped everything right there at his feet in the road. He stepped over the picnic basket and moved in close, pulling her and Sophia toward him, wrapping his strong arms around both of them.

With a long sigh, she let her body sway against him.

Oh, it felt good, so very good, to lean on him.

But she really couldn't afford to lean on a man, to get her hopes up that she could trust him, that she could count on him—and take the chance of having those hopes crushed to bits. She'd had her hopes crushed way more than enough already, thank you.

"Hey," he whispered. "It's okay. I promise. If you don't want her to ride Petunia, she won't ride Petunia." Snuggled in between the two of them, Sophia cooed in contentment. Logan tipped Sarah's chin up. "I get it. I do. I didn't mean to scare you. Petunia needed a home and so I took him and I couldn't help thinking that someday he might be just right for Sophia. But that's all. It was just a thought and it doesn't have to mean anything, I promise. It's nothing on you. *I* took the pony and I am responsible for him."

She sucked in a deep breath and her racing heart slowed down a little. Out of the corner of her eye, she saw Xander about twenty yards away. He'd stopped in his tracks. Smart man. The pony waited right behind him, patiently nibbling the weeds that grew in the center of the dirt road.

Logan pressed his forehead to hers. "You all right?"

"Yeah. I, um, overreacted. Somewhat. I guess."

He pulled back enough that their eyes could meet. "Somewhat?" One corner of that beautiful mouth lifted in a half smile that coaxed her to smile, too. "You freaked."

And then she did smile. "Yeah. I kind of did."

"But you're over that? You're okay?"

"I am, yeah." She thought how amazing he was. She wished she was someone else, someone still capable of really going for it, opening her heart, trusting that everything would work out all right in the end.

But she was just Sarah, strong enough to go on, yet cautious to a fault when it came to trusting a man again. Even a wonderful man who seemed to want to give her the world.

"And I have to ask…"

"What?"

"Petunia?" she taunted. "Seriously?"

"Hey. He was already named. I didn't want him to suffer an identity crisis on top of everything else."

She knew she shouldn't ask. "So…Petunia has had a difficult past?"

"He had mud fever and cracked heels from being left out in the open in bad weather. The vet's receptionist found him wandering around in the park. No owner ever showed up to claim him."

"How did they know his name was Petunia?"

"He was wearing a frayed bridle with Petunia tooled into the cheekpiece."

"Poor guy."

"Yeah. Dr. Smith treated him. When no owner appeared to take him home, he was offered for sale."

"And you took him."

"I like a survivor. Petunia is my kind of guy." He skated a finger down the bridge of her nose as Sophia let out another of her happy sounds. "How about I introduce you?"

"Sure."

He let her go. She resisted the urge to huddle close a little longer, make him hold her and her baby some more. Xander started forward again, the stocky little pony following right along behind him.

When Xander reached them, Sarah passed Sophia to Logan and petted the pony. Petunia stood placidly as she stroked his nose. When she smoothed his thick mane, he gave a friendly nicker. He really did seem like an amiable creature.

Logan teased, "I think he's going to be so happy living in the backyard at your place."

She groaned. "Don't even kid about it."

"Your loss. Wren's already in love with him."

"Good. I'm sure she'll take wonderful care of him."

The pony was so gentle and easy-natured that Sarah gave in and let Logan set Sophia on his back just for a moment. Logan held the baby steady and Xander moved in close to the animal, taking the lead right up under Petunia's chin with one hand, soothing him with the other.

Sophia waved her fists and bounced in Logan's hold, trusting completely the strong hands that supported her. Sarah might have choked up just a little at the sight. She bent and dug her phone out of the front pocket of the diaper bag and snapped a couple of pictures. What proud mama wouldn't?

Leaning close as he handed Sophia back to her, Logan whispered, "What'd I tell you? Sophia loves her new pony."

Her heart just melted. She gazed up at him adoringly and let herself imagine that they would stay together, that one of her baby's first words would be *Dada*, and when Sophia said it, she would be reaching for Logan.

For a brief and beautiful moment, Sarah knew it would happen.

But really, who was she kidding? Life was a challenge and things didn't always work out as a woman hoped they might.

She wouldn't start counting on anything. Expecting a magical happily-ever-after just wasn't wise.

Saturday was the painting party.

Logan and Sarah welcomed the same crew as the week before, and also two of Logan's brothers, Knox and

Hunter. Hunter brought Wren, who was a sweet girly-girl. She carried Opal around with her and spent a lot of time with Sophia, handing her teething toys, thrilled to get a chance to give her a bottle.

With only two rooms to paint, they were finished in the early afternoon. After cleanup, everyone hung around to eat the wings and pizza Logan had ordered and wandered out to sit on the front porch or to gather under the big tree in the back.

Logan loved watching Sarah play hostess. She was so conscientious. She made sure to visit with everyone, to thank them for coming, to tell them how much she appreciated the help.

Once all the guests had left, he and Sarah straightened up the place and put the dishes in the dishwasher. Sophia was already asleep in her freshly painted room, which had been tackled first so it would have plenty of time to dry before her bedtime.

He and Sarah went to bed early and made slow, tender love.

Later, he held her as she slept and thought about all the things he wanted to say to her. He wanted to talk with her about the future—*their* future.

About where they might go, as a couple, from here.

No, they hadn't been together for that long. And she was skittish about making any real plans with him. He had a feeling his best move was *no* move, that he should just let her be for a while, enjoy this time with her, give her the space to come to fully trust him on her own.

But damn it, life was too short. Why waste a moment being cautious and careful when he knew what he wanted, when he was certain that, deep in her heart, she wanted the same thing?

Yeah, all right. She'd been disappointed more than once. He got that. But he hadn't disappointed her so far, now had he? And he *wouldn't* disappoint her. He would be there for her and for Sophia. Whatever happened, she could depend on him, through the good times and the bad. He aimed to prove that to her.

Yeah, it was a little crazy, how gone he was on her. But he knew what he had with her. He didn't question it. He knew it was real. After all the years of never letting himself get too close to anyone, he finally wanted it all. With Sarah.

It kind of scared him how important she'd become to him—both her and Sophia—and so swiftly, too. But being scared didn't bother him. He found fear exhilarating. He would bust right through it, overcome it to claim what he wanted.

Sarah, though, held back. She guarded her heart. She just couldn't let herself trust him, not in the deepest way.

And he wanted everything with her. He wanted it now, wanted to break through the barriers she put up to protect herself, and show her she didn't need protection—not against him.

She stirred in his embrace.

He smoothed her tangled hair, wrapped his arms a little closer around her. She settled.

And he started thinking that hanging back, waiting for her to decide it was okay to trust him, was no solution. Action was called for.

He needed to make a real move. The move had to make a clear statement of his intent, of his purpose, of what he held for her in his heart. He needed to prove to her that he wasn't going anywhere. To show her that she was his and he was hers, and she didn't need to be afraid anymore.

He pulled the covers a little closer around them and closed his eyes. As sleep crept up on him, he smiled to himself.

It was really so simple. He knew what to do.

Chapter Ten

"Sarah?" her mom called as she came in the door of Falls Mountain Accounting early Monday morning.

"Be right there." She glanced down at Sophia, who was sound asleep in the carrier. The baby didn't stir. Sarah hurried into her office, put the carrier on the desk, set her laptop beside it and then let the diaper bag slide to the floor.

She went on to her dad's office, where her father leaned back in his leather swivel chair, looking happy and relaxed in a way he never had while she was growing up. Her mom, in a silky blouse, high heels and a pencil skirt, had hitched a leg up on the corner of his desk. Flo Turner looked downright sexy, kind of lounging there, eyes twinkling, grinning like the cat that got two bowls of cream.

Mack gave a low, gravelly chuckle. Flo leaned close to him and whispered something in his ear before turning her glowing smile on Sarah. "Come in and sit down, honey. We need to talk, the three of us, before we open for the day."

For no logical reason, Sarah felt a prickle of unease tighten the muscles at the back of her neck. But her parents seemed happy and totally in love as usual, so what was there to be anxious about?

She entered the room and took one of the guest chairs. "Everything okay?"

Her mom and dad exchanged another way-too-intimate glance, after which her dad said, "We have some big news and we felt it was time to share it with you."

Big news?

The craziest thought occurred to her: Could her mom be pregnant? Growing up, she'd longed for a little brother or sister.

Her mom was only forty-four. Sarah had read somewhere that there were women who didn't reach menopause until their sixties. Was her mom one of those?

If so, well…

A new brother or sister…?

Given the way her parents carried on lately, a new baby Turner didn't seem completely out of the realm of possibility.

The more she considered it, the more she liked the idea—loved it, even.

It would be great. Sophia's new aunt or uncle would be a year or so younger. They would grow up together, do all those things that siblings do. Fight and make up, keep each other's secrets and have each other's backs.

Life. It never ceased to amaze.

Her dad said, "Your mother and I are planning a big change."

"A move," Flo added, excited and so pleased as Sarah felt her big smile fading. "A move to the Gulf. We want to mix it up in a big way. Go where it's warm, live near the ocean."

What?

Wait.

Her mom and dad were moving, going miles and miles away?

No...

It couldn't be. Not now.

Not when she'd just come to realize how happy she was to have them nearby, to know she could turn to them whenever things got rocky. She'd let herself picture them helping her raise Sophia. She'd imagined how she would be there to support them as they grew old.

Yes, all right. There had been that initial shock of coming home to find her dried-up, depressing parents had fallen in love with each other and couldn't stop going at it right here in the office.

But in the past couple of weeks, she'd grown used to the way they were now, even come to like how open and loving they'd become with each other. She enjoyed being around them.

And now they were *leaving*?

They seemed oblivious to her distress. They grinned at each other, so pleased with their big plans. Mack said, "Fishing charters. That's what we're thinking. But first, we'll find a nice little place, get settled in, take it easy, you know, just your mother and me."

Flo leaned toward Mack again. She touched his face, a tender caress. "Your dad never wanted to be an accountant. Did you know that, sweetheart? This was your grandfather's office and it was always just assumed that Mack would enter the family business."

"I had hopes I would maybe try something different," Sarah's dad said gruffly. "I wanted a job where I could work outdoors."

"But then I got pregnant with you," said her mother. "We had to be responsible. And we were."

"So responsible," her dad echoed sadly, the lines in his face etching deeper as the corners of his mouth turned down.

"And I know, I know, we've spoken of all of this, of the bleak years." Her mom looked sad, too, for a moment. But then she brightened right up again. "What matters is that those days are behind us. You turned out amazing—our baby, all grown up now, with a baby of your own, so capable and smart, taking care of yourself and doing a great job of it. Your father and I feel it's okay now for us to move on, to make a change."

Mack caught Flo's hand and pressed his lips to it. "We're going to live the life we've both been longing for."

"At last." Her mom turned to beam at her again. "Honey, the office will be yours."

"And there's plenty of money," said her dad.

Flo laughed. "My parents and your Turner grandparents were big savers. We inherited a lot. And the business has done well. All these years, we never spent a penny we didn't have to spend."

"And we've invested wisely," added Mack.

"We have a hefty retirement," Flo said, "so we're all set. The cottage, our house, the business and a nice chunk of cash will all be yours. You'll have no problem hiring an office manager—and another accountant, if you think that's the way to go. And I know you've been resisting day care, but Just Us Kids is right here in town and it's excellent. They take babies. And you can definitely afford it, so just consider that, won't you?" Before Sarah could speak, she continued right on. "Of course, we plan to return often to be with you and our darling Sophia."

"However…" Mack sat forward in his chair and braced his forearms on the desk. "We *have* been thinking about Chicago."

"Yes," Flo chimed in. "We mustn't forget Chicago."

Sarah had no idea what they were talking about now. "Uh. We mustn't?"

Her mom plunked her hand over her heart. "Honey, when you decided to come home to live, we did offer to pitch in so that you could keep your high-powered job and your life in the city. You refused to take our money."

"Mom. You'd already put me through college. You paid for everything my scholarship didn't cover. I've got a degree from Northwestern and I have no loans to repay. It was enough. More than enough."

Her mom made a tutting sound. "Having Sophia was just such a challenge, we understood that. What I'm saying is, we probably should have pushed you harder to take what we offered and keep on with your original plans—and since then, it has occurred to us that maybe what you really want is to return to your life in Chicago. But you insisted on coming home and, well, of course we do love that you're here."

"We should have questioned you further as to what course you really wanted." Mack frowned regretfully. "But we didn't. And that's why we're offering again now. If you want that big-city life you always yearned for when you were growing up, we want you to have it. There should be more than enough money, especially if you sell the properties and the business, for you to make that happen comfortably, without all the stress and pressure you were under before."

"Whatever your dream is, you will be living it," said Flo. "I admit, it has seemed to me that you're making a good life for yourself here. And things do appear to be going so well with you and Logan…"

"But we realize," Mack jumped in, "that we might only be hoping you're happy here because Rust Creek Falls is our hometown and of course we would love to return here whenever the mood strikes and have you and our granddaughter right here waiting for us."

"That's simply not fair," said her mom. "We can just as well come and visit you and Sophia in Chicago. So we want you to know that however you choose to go forward, we will support you one hundred percent."

"Absolutely," Mack agreed. "Whatever you want to do next, we will help make it happen."

Both of them stared at her expectantly.

Sarah realized they were waiting for her to say something.

Well, she had plenty to say. Yeah, okay. They were being sweet and understanding and so very generous.

But it didn't matter.

She wanted to yell at them that their plans were utterly foolish, wildly irresponsible, to argue that they had no right to go pulling up stakes and running off to the Gulf, because…fishing charters? Seriously?

She wanted to beg them to change their minds and stay.

But none of those reactions would be right or fair or kind of her.

In all those unhappy years while she was growing up, she wasn't the only one who'd suffered. Her parents had suffered, too, locked into what they saw as their duty, every day gray and uninspired, a challenge to get through.

And now they'd changed everything. They'd found their happiness. And they had a dream they longed to pursue. She got that, about having dreams—even if her own dreams hadn't turned out the way she'd planned.

Their dreams were all new and shiny. And she wanted them to have those dreams. She wanted them to have it all.

"Honey?" Her mom was starting to look worried now.

"Just tell us," said her dad, "if there's something we're missing. If you have objections, we want to know."

"No." She gave them her brightest smile. "No objections."

"You're sure?" asked her mother.

"I am positive." Surprisingly, she sounded convincing even to her own ears. "And I'm happy for you two. I really am." Well, at least that was true. She was so glad for them, for what they'd found together after all these years. If only she and Logan might…

No. Really, she was fine on her own. *Better* on her own. It just didn't work for her, to go counting on a man, to start hoping for what wasn't meant to be.

Sometimes she worried that she might be getting too attached to him, that she shouldn't let him spend so much time with Sophia, who might suffer when the relationship ended. Really, though, he was so good with her.

And why would Sophia suffer if Logan left? She was just a baby, after all. Sophia required a steady, loving presence in her life, someone to count on now and all through her growing-up years. Other people—Sophia's father, her grandparents, Sarah's boyfriend, neighbors, babysitters—everyone else might come and go. But Sarah would be there for Sophia, always.

As for herself and her own relationship with Logan, well, maybe she was getting in too deep. Maybe she needed to think about having a talk with him, reminding them both that they shouldn't get serious, that this was just for now and it was absolutely perfect and not everything had to turn into a lifetime of love.

But oh, it did *feel* serious. And, well, she loved how serious it felt. She didn't really know what to do about that. Maybe they actually could have forever together.

Or maybe, once again, she was making plans for a future that would never come true.

What she needed was *not* to get all tied up in knots over her own current happiness with Logan. He was a good man and she would enjoy every moment they had together, with no expectations as to what might happen next.

"And Chicago?" asked her dad.

She shook herself and focused on the subject at hand. "No. I don't want to go back, I really don't. I'm staying here."

"Sweetheart…" Her mom jumped off the desk and held out her arms.

Sarah rose. Her dad got up and joined them in a family hug. It was so bizarre, group-hugging with her parents, of all people. It made her feel loved and cherished—and lonely already that they would be leaving.

"When will you go?" she asked as they stepped apart.

"It's a process," said Mack.

"We're eager to get started." Her mom looked down-right starry-eyed. "We want to get moving on it right away."

"I completely understand."

"We're going to sign over the business and the properties and give you the money we talked about," Flo announced. "We were hoping we could all three go together to see Ben as soon as possible." Ben Dalton was the family's attorney. He had an office right in town. "We want to get everything in your name so you can start the transition—hire your office manager, whom I will be happy to train, and get you ready to run the business on your own. And then we're buying a motor home."

"We're flexible," her dad insisted. "We'll be here for you for as long as you need us."

Her mom practically glowed in her excitement—to be on the way south, to start living their great adventure. "However long it takes to get everything worked out, that's fine with us. The truth is you're carrying most of the workload here already. Falls Mountain Accounting *should* be yours, anyway."

"You're ten times the accountant I ever was," her dad said wryly. "You've been here a couple of months and you've already enlarged our client list, streamlined the office procedures and bolstered the bottom line."

"There will be our house to deal with, packing stuff up, clearing it out a little," her mom chattered on. "You might want to move to the bigger place and sell the cottage. Or rent it. Or sell the house and—"

"Flo." Mack wrapped an arm around her. When she glanced up at him, he brushed a kiss on her forehead. "None of that has to be decided today."

Her mom gazed at him adoringly. "Of course, darling. You're right." She gave Sarah a rueful glance. "Sorry, honey. I got carried away."

"No problem." Except for how much she would miss them and how sad and lost she felt at the prospect of them living so far away. "I promise to consider all the options carefully."

"We know you will, sweetheart. And as for your father and me, if possible, we're hoping to be on our way south sometime in August."

Quietly, Logan shut the door to Sophia's room.

In two steps, he reached the arch that led into the dining room. At the sight of Sarah, he hung back to enjoy the view. She sat on the sofa with Opal in her lap. Even all the way across the room, he could hear that kitten purring.

Sarah scratched Opal's chin and the purring got louder. "What are you looking at?" she asked without glancing up.

"A pretty woman and a dinky white motorboat of a cat."

That got him a grin. "She's a happy baby."

He wanted to linger there, leaning on the door frame, just looking at her. And he also had the urge to go and get the spiral notebook from the kitchen. He wanted to capture the way her slim, pretty hands stroked Opal's soft, white fur.

Most of all, he wanted to go to her, sit beside her, put his arm around her and steal a kiss.

The prospect of getting close won out. He crossed the room, sat down next to her and drew her nice and snug against his side.

When she glanced up, he took her mouth.

It never got old, kissing Sarah. She smelled like heaven and she tasted even better. He nipped at her upper lip. She let out a sigh and he deepened the kiss— for a moment.

Not too long. If he kept kissing her, he would want more than kisses.

But a little later for that.

He lifted away and gazed down at her. "Something on your mind?"

A tiny frown marred the smooth skin of her forehead. She confessed, "Got some big news from the parents today. They're leaving everything—this house, their house, the business—to me and moving to the Gulf of Mexico."

"Wow."

A chuckle escaped her. It wasn't a very happy sound. "No kidding."

"When?"

"As soon as possible. A month or so."

He ran a finger down the side of her throat and then couldn't resist bending close again, sticking out his tongue, tasting her there. She tasted so good, like everything he wanted, like hope and forever. "You don't want them to go." He breathed the words against her silky, fragrant skin.

She caught his face between her hands and pushed away enough that she could look in his eyes. "How did you know that?"

"Easy. You didn't tell me they were leaving until I asked. If you weren't conflicted about them going, you would have said something earlier."

She searched his face. "You're way too observant."

"I get a big thrill out of observing you." He moved in close again and kissed her soft cheek. "Did you ask them to consider staying here in town?"

"No. And I'm not going to, either." She idly stroked the hair at his temple with the tips of her fingers. He loved the feel of her hands on him. "They can't wait to be on their way. And I want them to have what they want. They did everything they were supposed to do for years. It's time they got their chance to be free."

"But what about you?"

"I'll get over myself, believe me. Sophia and I will be fine."

Sophia and I. He wasn't included. She and Sophia were a family of two.

He wanted his chance to hear her say that the *three* of them would be fine, to consider them a unit. A family. Together. And he intended to *make* his chance. The sooner the better. "Let's go out."

She shook her head, laughing. "Sophia's already in bed in case you didn't notice when you put her there."

"I mean tomorrow night or the next one. I'll bet Lily would watch her, or your mom."

She skated a finger along the line of his jaw and he realized he was happy in the best kind of way, all easy and comfortable inside his own skin, just to be sitting here on the sofa with Sarah, Opal purring away on her lap.

"I'll try my mom first," she said. "She loves looking after Sophia and she mentioned today that she hoped to get more time with her before she and my dad ride off into the sunset in the fancy new Winnebago they're planning on buying."

"So that's a yes?"

"Mmm-hmm. I'll check with her, find out which evening's best."

"It's not even eight. There's still time to call. Do it now so I can make the reservation."

"Let me guess." Those golden-brown eyes twinkled at him. "You know this great little restaurant in Kalispell…"

"That's right." He leaned in close again to nip his way up the side of her neck and then nibble her earlobe for good measure. "Dinner at Giordano's because it's *our* place, our Italian restaurant."

"'Our place' that we've never been to together," she teased.

"A mere oversight which we are about to remedy. And we'll go dancing afterward, though I'll admit I'm not sure where to go for dancing around here."

"Well, I know where to go. The Ace in the Hole."

He scoffed at that. "From what I've heard, the Ace is a

cowboy bar with peanut shells on the floor and country-western on the jukebox."

"That's right," she said. "When I was a little girl, I always wanted to go to the Ace. You know, have a burger, beg quarters from my parents and play the jukebox. But my parents never went out anywhere—not even for a burger at the Ace."

"You were deprived of an important cultural experience. Is that what you're telling me?"

"That's it exactly. And for some reason I still don't really understand, as I got a little older, I didn't just go there myself or drag Lily there. I was like that as a kid, serious and quiet. I had trouble getting out there and doing the things I longed to do. I kind of lived in the future, planning for college and my life in the big city where I would make everything come together, make all of my dreams finally come true." She looked so sad then. But before he could figure out what to do about that, she brightened. "But then it happened. I did get my chance."

"For a burger at the Ace?"

"That's right." She laughed, a low, husky sound, and her eyes turned more golden than brown as she explained, "I was seventeen, in my senior year of high school and one of the Dalton boys invited me to go."

He wasn't sure he liked that faraway look she had. "Should I be jealous? Which Dalton boy?"

"No, you shouldn't. And which one doesn't matter. He never asked me out again."

"Good," he said gruffly, followed up with a muttered, "What an idiot."

"My point, Logan, is that I loved it. Loved the Ace.

It was noisy and there was lots of laughter. Music was playing and everyone was talking too loud. A couple of drunk cowboys even got in a fight, so there was excitement, too. There was everything I never had at home. I remember sitting there across from the Dalton boy whose first name you don't need to know and thinking that the Ace was the best and I wanted to come back every chance I got."

"And did you?"

She shook her head. "It just never happened. And then I left for Illinois in the fall."

"You haven't been there since that one date when you were seventeen, you mean?"

"That's right."

He captured her hand and kissed the tips of her fingers. "I'll take you."

She put her lips to his ear and whispered, "It can be *our* honky-tonk saloon where we make all our most precious romantic memories as we're two-stepping to country standards, peanut shells crunching underfoot. I take it you haven't been there even once yet?"

"Nope."

"Well, then, we're going to remedy that oversight after dinner at Giordano's."

"You're on." He tugged on her ponytail. "Are all accountants as romantic as you?"

"Nope." She kissed him, a quick press of her soft lips to his. "I'm special."

"Oh, yes, you are." He pulled her close and claimed a deeper, longer kiss, gathering her so tightly to him that Opal let out a tiny meow of annoyance at being jostled. The kitten jumped to the floor. When he lifted his head, Sarah's golden eyes were low and lazy, full of promise and desire. "Call your mom," he ordered gruffly. "Do it now."

Logan made the Giordano's reservation for seven Wednesday night. They got a quiet corner table, as he'd requested. He ordered a bottle of wine to go with the meal and the food was amazing as always. Even on a Wednesday night, most of the tables were full.

He hardly noticed the other customers, though. All his attention was on the beautiful bean counter across from him.

She wore a sleeveless turquoise dress, the sexy kind, with spaghetti straps. The dress clung to her curves on top. It had a flirty layered skirt that was going to swing out like the petals of a blooming flower later at the Ace when they danced together. Her gold-streaked brown hair was loose and wavy on her shapely bare shoulders.

He wanted to sketch her in that dress. And he would later, back at her cottage, when they were alone. If he got too eager to get her out of that dress, well, he would sketch it from memory as soon as he had the chance.

More than once during dinner, he almost made his move. But the moment just never seemed quite right. They joked about which Rust Creek Falls bachelorette Viv Dalton had most recently set up with which of his brothers. They spoke of the new office manager she and her mom had just hired. Flo had started training the new employee that morning. They laughed about how the work out at the Ambling A seemed downright endless. The barn needed more repairs and the fence-building went on and on.

For dessert, they had the chocolate semifreddo again, same as that first night when he'd had their meal catered at her house. She joked that it was "their dessert" and now he could never have it with anyone else but her.

He raised his coffee cup to her. "You. Me. Semifreddo. Forever."

She gazed at him across the small table, her eyes so soft, her skin like cream, her lush mouth begging for his kiss.

It was the exact right moment.

But he decided to wait.

Was he maybe a little freaked out about how to do what he planned—and when? Was he putting way too much emphasis on finding just the right moment?

Maybe.

But he wanted it to be perfect. In future years, he wanted her to remember the moment with joy and admiration for how he'd picked just the right time.

It was almost nine when they left Giordano's. They got in his crew cab and he leaned across the console for a kiss.

And wouldn't you know? One kiss was never enough.

They ended up canoodling like a couple of sex-starved kids for the next half hour or so, steaming up the windows, hands all over each other. Like they didn't have a comfortable bed to go to in the privacy of her cottage.

She'd unbuttoned his shirt and he'd pulled the top of that pretty dress down and bared her gorgeous breasts before they stopped—and that was only because he whacked his elbow on the steering wheel and they both started laughing at the craziness of them going at it right there in his truck at the curb in front of Giordano's. Anybody might see what they were up to.

Probably some innocent passerby *had* seen.

He buttoned and tucked in his shirt and she pulled her dress back up, after which she flipped down the visor and combed her hair in the mirror on the back. She looked so tempting, tipping her head this way and that, smoothing the unruly strands. He couldn't stop himself from reaching for her again.

She allowed him one long, hot kiss—and then she put her hands on his chest and pushed enough to break the connection. "The Ace," she instructed sternly. And then a giggle escaped her, which kind of ruined the effect. "We need to get going. Now."

The Ace in the Hole was a rambling wooden structure on Sawmill Street with a big dirt parking lot behind it and a wide front porch where cowboys gathered to drink their beer away from the music, to talk about horses and spot the pretty women as they came up the steps to go in.

Beyond the double doors, there was the long bar, a row of booths, a stage and a dance floor surrounded by smaller tables.

Sarah gazed out across the dance floor. "So romantic." She leaned close and brushed a kiss against his cheek. "Thanks for bringing me." The way she looked at him right then, her big eyes gleaming, mouth soft with a tender smile—made him feel about ten feet tall.

He got them each a beer and they took a booth. Tonight, a local band had the stage. They played cover versions of familiar country songs.

"Let's dance," she said, smiling, a little flushed, her

eyes full of stars to be here at this cowboy bar where she hadn't been since she was seventeen.

They danced every song—fast ones and slow ones, never once returning to the booth.

The whole time, he was waiting as he'd been waiting all evening—for just the right moment. He might have done it there, on the dance floor of the cowboy bar she'd found so thrilling when she was a kid.

But no.

Private was better, he decided at last. He would wait until they got back to the cottage.

Around eleven, as they swayed together, their arms around each other, to Brad Paisley's "We Danced," she lifted her head from his shoulder and let out a giggle. She seemed thoroughly pleased with herself.

"What?" he demanded.

"Nothing—except it's official. I've danced at the Ace with the hottest guy in town. I never thought it would happen, but look at me now."

"You are so beautiful." Words did not do her justice. He dipped his head and kissed her, one of those kisses that starts out gentle and worshipful, but then kind of spins out of control.

She was the one who pulled away. "I'm thinking we probably ought to go soon," she whispered, sweetly breathless.

"I'm thinking you're right."

They left when the song ended.

At the cottage, Flo reported that Sophia had been an angel. "She had her bottle and ate her mashed peas and then some applesauce and went down at eight thirty. I haven't heard a peep from her since." They thanked her for babysitting.

Flo kissed Sarah's cheek. "Anytime," she said as she went out the door.

And finally, it was just Logan and Sarah, with the baby sound asleep. She scooped the snoozing Opal off the sofa and put her in her bed in the laundry room.

When she came back, he did what came naturally, pulling her into his arms and lowering his mouth to hers, walking her backward slowly as he kissed her.

In the bedroom, he almost guided her down to the bed.

But no. It was time.

Past time—to make his move. Say his piece. Ask her the most important question of all.

She gazed up at him, kind of bemused. Wondering. "What is it? There's something on your mind."

He took the ring from his pocket. She gasped. He was smiling as he dropped to one knee. "Sarah," he said.

And that was as far as he got.

Because she covered her mouth with her hands and cried, "No!"

Chapter Eleven

Logan felt as though she'd walloped him a good one—just drawn back her little fist and sent it flying in a roundhouse punch. He reeled. "What? Wait…"

"Logan. Get up. Don't do this, okay?" She actually offered him her hand, like he needed help to get up off the floor.

He rose without touching her and put the ring back in his pocket. He had no idea where this was going—except it was nowhere good, that was for sure.

She backed up until her knees touched the bed and then she kind of crumpled onto the edge of the mattress. He watched her hard-swallow. She didn't look well—her face was dead white with two spots of hectic color, one high on each cheek.

"Uh, sit down," she said and nervously patted the space beside her.

He shook his head. "I think I'll stand."

She stared up at him, begging him with her eyes—but for what? "I'm so sorry." She spoke in a ragged voice. "This isn't—I mean, I just can't, Logan. You're the most incredible man and I'm wild for you, you know I am. But I couldn't say yes to marriage. I just couldn't. Please try to understand. This thing with us, it's just for now and we both know that. We have to remember that."

"No." He shut his eyes, drew in a slow, careful breath. "No, I don't know that. I'm not going anywhere. Never. I want to be right here, with you."

"But it's not going to last. We're just, I mean, well, living in the moment, having fun, enjoying the ride. And it's beautiful, what we have together. Why ruin it with expectations that will break my heart and could hurt my daughter when they don't pan out?"

How could she think that? "You're wrong."

"No. I'm not wrong. I'm realistic. Nothing ever really does last, you know?"

"No, Sarah. I don't know." He also didn't know what to do next, how to reach her, how to recover from this. But then it came to him that he had to go all the way now, to say it out loud, to give her his truth. It was all that he had. "I love you, Sarah Turner. I want to marry you."

She let out another cry and clapped her hands to her ears this time. Her eyes glittered with moisture. A tear got away from her and carved a shining trail down her cheek.

He tried reassurance. "You don't have to be afraid. I'm not going to stop loving you. Not ever. This is for real. I swear it to you."

"You say that now—"

"Because it's true. Because what we have, what I feel for you, I've never felt before. I trust what we have. I love you. I love Sophia. I want to take care of you, of both of you. I want to be here when Sophia says her first real word, when she takes her first step. I want to be here for all the days we're given, you and me. This is where I'm happy. This is where it all makes sense. With you, with Sophia. The three of us. A family."

"I can't," she said again. "I just can't. I can't do that. It's one thing for us to take it a day at a time. To enjoy what we have while it lasts. But marriage? Logan, that's not what this is about."

"Yeah, it is."

"No. It's not." She said it so firmly, her shoulders drawn back now, her expression bleak, closed down.

He kept trying to reach her. "It's so simple. It's just you and me doing what people do when they love each other, starting to build a life together. Making it work."

"Your father hates me."

Really? She was going to go there? Patiently, he answered her, "No, he does not hate you. My mother broke his heart and ran off with her lover, abandoning him and me and my brothers. We never heard from her again."

She gasped. He saw sympathy in her eyes. "That's horrible."

"Yeah. It was pretty bad for all of us. And that's why he is the way he is. He's a lonely old man with some weird ideas about love and marriage. You're too smart to let Max Crawford chase you away."

"It's not only your dad. It's, well…" She blew out a breath, folded her hands and then twisted them in her lap. "Love just never works out for me."

"That's faulty reasoning, Sarah. You know it is. There was what? That idiot Tuck who didn't know the best thing that ever happened to him when he had it? Good riddance. And that Mercer guy? That wasn't love anyway, was it?"

Her eyes reproached him. "You're making fun of me."

"No, I'm not. I'm just saying that whatever you're really scared of, I don't think it's anything you've brought up so far."

"I, well, it's only… Logan, what if a year goes by and you realize you made a mistake?"

"That's not going to happen. I know what's in my heart. You're the one for me. That's never going to change."

"But, Logan, what if your feelings did change? What if we, you and me, didn't work out after a year or two or three? Think back. Try to remember how it was for you when your mother deserted you."

"I know exactly how it was, which is all the more reason I will never desert you."

She just couldn't believe him. "In a couple of years, Sophia will be old enough to suffer when you leave us."

"You're not listening. If you say yes to me, I will never leave you."

She only shook her head and went right on with her argument. "My daughter would count on you to be there and you would be gone. She would suffer because of my bad choices. It's just better not to go there. It's just better to leave things as they are."

He stood over her, burning to get closer, to reach down and take her hand, pull her up into his arms that ached to hold her. But she looked so fragile sitting there, as though his very touch would shatter her.

"I'm so sorry," she whispered on a broken husk of breath. "I'm so sorry but I can't. It's not possible. Not for me."

He didn't know how to answer her. Because words weren't making a damn bit of difference. He could stand here and argue with her all night long.

And where would that get them? What would that fix?

"Just tell me what you're really afraid of." He was actually pleading now. Imagine that. Logan Crawford, whose heart had always been untouchable, pleading with a woman just for a chance. "I can't fix this if I don't know what's broken."

"But that's it," she cried. "It's nothing you can fix. Nothing anyone can fix. I can't let myself count on you—on anyone, not really. I have to look out for my daughter and my heart. I have to be strong, be the mom and the breadwinner, the decision-maker and the protector, too. I don't have the trust in me to let someone else do any of that, not anymore. It doesn't matter how I feel about you, or how much I care. If I can't give my trust, well, it's not going to work."

Trust. There it was. The thing she feared to give. The real problem.

She couldn't—*wouldn't*—allow herself to trust in him.

How the hell was he supposed to break through something like that?

What a spectacular irony. He'd finally found the one

woman he wanted to spend a lifetime with. And she couldn't let herself believe in him.

Where did that leave them?

His heart felt so empty, hollowed out. What now?

Should he back off, forget about forever and try to convince her to simply go on as they were?

Really, it was so achingly clear to him now: he'd messed up. Jumped the gun, made his move too soon. He should have kept his damn mouth shut, not crossed this particular line until she'd had more time to see that it was safe to believe in him.

He'd rushed it. He got that.

And it really didn't look like there was any way for him to recover from this disaster.

Shoving his hands in his pockets, he made a last-ditch attempt to salvage some small shred of hope. "So then, I have to know. I want you to tell me. Is it that you need more time?"

She gazed up at him, a desolate look on her unforgettable face. "No." The single word came at him like a knife blade, shining and deadly, flying straight for his heart.

He made himself clarify. "Never. You're saying never."

She nodded and whispered, "I am so sorry."

Well, okay. That was about as clear as it could get. She hadn't hedged. She'd given him zero hope that he could ever change her mind.

And now she was watching his face, reading him. "You're leaving," she said.

Before he could answer, the baby monitor on the dresser erupted with a sharp little cry.

They both froze, waiting for Sophia to fuss a little and then go back to sleep.

Not this time, though. Sophia cried out again. And again. Each cry was more insistent.

Sarah started to rise.

"I'll get her," he said.

"No, really, it's—"

He cut her off. "Let me tell her goodbye. Give me that, at least."

She pressed her lips together and dipped her head in a nod.

He turned for the baby's room.

Sarah watched him go.

Dear Lord, what was the matter with her? She loved him. She did. And he'd never been anything but trustworthy with her, with Sophia.

And yet, she just couldn't do it, couldn't put her future in his hands, couldn't let herself believe that he would never break her heart, never change his mind after she'd given him everything, never turn his back on her and her child.

Sophia's wailing stopped.

Sarah heard Logan's voice, a little muffled from the other room, but crystal clear on the monitor. "Hey there, gorgeous. It's all right. I've got you. I'm right here."

The camera had come on. It used infrared technology so that even in Sophia's darkened room, she could see the tall figure standing by the crib with her baby in his arms.

"Ah, da!" cried Sophia. With a heavy sigh, she laid her head against Logan's chest. "Da…"

"I think we've got a wet diaper here, don't we?"

"Unngh."

The camera tracked him as he carried Sophia to the changing area. Handing her a giraffe teething ring to chew on, he quickly and expertly put on a fresh diaper. "There now. All better."

"Pa. Da." Clutching the ring in one tiny fist, she reached out her arms to him.

He scooped her up against his chest again and carried her to the rocker in the corner. "We'll just sit here and rock a little while, okay?"

"Angh." She stuck the teething ring in her mouth.

He cradled her in both arms and slowly rocked. "I wanted to talk to you, anyway." The baby sighed and stared up at him. "Sophia, I have to go now. I am so sorry, but I won't be back. I want you to know, though, that I would stay if I could. I would be your 'da' forever and ever. I would watch you grow up, teach you how to ride a bike and how to pitch a softball, help you with your homework, chase all the boys away until the right one came along…"

Sarah's eyes blurred with tears. On the monitor, Sophia gazed up at Logan so solemnly, as though she understood every word he said.

He fell silent. For a while, he just cradled her, rocking, looking down at her as she stared up at him. Slowly, her eyes fluttered shut. She let go of the toy. He caught it and set it on the little table beside the rocker.

Several more minutes passed. In her bedroom, Sarah watched on the monitor as Logan bent close to brush the lightest of kisses across her daughter's forehead.

He whispered something more, but she couldn't make out the words.

And then, moving slowly so as not to disturb the little girl in his arms, he rose and carried her to the crib. Carefully, he put her back down again, pulling the blanket up to tuck in gently around her. He leaned down for a last light kiss.

A moment later, he came and stood in the open door to Sarah's room. "She's sleeping now. I'm going."

Sarah didn't know what else to do, so she got up and followed him to the front door. He pulled it open. The night air was cool, the dark street deserted.

He stuck his hand in his pocket. She looked down and saw he was holding out the house key she'd given him. She took it. "Goodbye, Sarah."

She wanted to reach for him, grab him close. She wanted to *not* let him go.

But she only stood there, the key clutched tight in her hand. She made herself say it. "Goodbye, Logan."

He turned, went out the door and down the steps to where his crew cab waited.

She couldn't bear to watch him drive away, so she shut the door and kind of fell back against it, her knees suddenly weak and wobbly. Outside, she heard the truck start up, pull away from the curb and head off down the street.

The big, black eye of his fancy TV stared at her disapprovingly. She should have given it back to him. That had been her plan when she allowed him to bring it here—to return it to him when their time together ended.

Sarah shut her eyes. A sound escaped her—something

midway between a crazy-woman laugh and a broken sob. As if the TV even mattered. If he wanted it, he would come back and get it.

But she knew he wouldn't. He would want her to have it.

And he wouldn't want to see her or talk to her.

Ever again.

Chapter Twelve

Somehow, Sarah got through the next day. And the next.

It wasn't easy. She had this horrible hollow feeling—like her heart had gone missing from her chest.

But she knew it had been the right thing to tell him no. To break it off. The longer she had with him, the more painful it would have been to lose him in the end.

She managed to avoid her parents for those first two days, taking all of her appointments away from the office, being too busy to talk when her mom called on Friday.

Friday night was really tough. Sophia was fussier than usual. It wasn't a cold or an ear infection or the pain of teething. Sarah thought the baby seemed sad. And Opal kind of drooped around the house like her little kitty heart was broken.

It couldn't be true that her baby *and* her kitten missed

Logan as much as she did. Sophia was too young to even know he'd gone missing—wasn't she? And Opal was a cat, for crying out loud. Cats got attached to their place, their surroundings. Plus, if Opal had a favorite human, it was Sarah, hands down. She'd been Sarah's cat from the first. The kitten sat in her lap while they watched TV and came crying to her when the kibble bowl was empty.

No. Sarah knew what was really going on. She was projecting her own misery and loss onto her baby and Opal. She needed to stop that right now. She'd done the right thing and this aching, endless emptiness inside her would go away.

Eventually.

That night after Sophia finally went to sleep, Sarah sat on the sofa with her phone in her hands and studied the pictures of Logan, Sophia and Petunia that she'd taken that day they had their picnic at the Ambling A. She went through the notebook of Logan's sketches. It hurt so much to look at them. She'd been planning to frame some of them and put them up around the cottage.

But she didn't know if she could ever bear to do that now. Those sketches were a testimony to all she would never have, all she'd made herself say no to.

All she had to learn to let go.

Saturday morning, her mom appeared on her doorstep. "Okay," said Flo. "What is going on with you?"

When Sarah tried to protest that she was fine, her mom kind of pushed her way in the door, shut it behind her, took Sophia right out of her arms and said, "Pour me some coffee. We need to talk."

They sat in the kitchen where the morning sun streamed cheerfully in the window above the sink and the walls were the beautiful, buttery yellow Sarah had chosen herself—and that Logan had made happen. Every wall in her house was now the color she wanted it to be.

Because of Logan. Because he'd kept after her until she finally agreed to the painting party—and then, when she did agree, he'd taken her out to buy the paint and then worked for two days painting and also supervising the volunteer crew.

If not for Logan, she'd still be living in a house with off-white walls and random brushstrokes of color here and there, promising herself that one of these days she would get around to making the place feel more like her home.

Flo put Sophia in her bouncy seat and gave her a set of fat, plastic keys to chew on. Then she sat at the table across from Sarah and took a sip of her coffee. "It's Logan, right?"

"Mom, I don't think we—"

"He's not here and he hasn't been for days."

"How do you know that?"

"Sweetheart, it's Rust Creek Falls. Everybody knows that. No one's seen that fancy pickup of his out in front since Wednesday night."

"Mom, I really don't want to talk about it."

"But you *need* to talk about it. Now, tell me what happened."

"I, um…" Her throat locked up, her nose started running and suddenly there were tears streaming down her cheeks. "Mom, he proposed. He proposed to me and I sent him away."

Flo got up again. She grabbed the box of tissues from over on the counter and set them in Sarah's lap, bending close to hug her right there in her chair. "Mop up, honey. We need to talk." Flo sat down again and sipped her coffee, waiting.

Sarah blew her nose and dried her cheeks.

"Tell me," her mom demanded.

With a big sigh and another sad little sob, Sarah started talking. She told her mom pretty much everything, all about how beautiful and perfect Wednesday night had been—until Logan tried to propose.

Once she started talking, she couldn't stop. She spilled it all, about her disappointments with Tuck and the sheer rat-crappiness of Mercer Smalls, how she just couldn't trust a man anymore and so she knew it was the best thing, to end it with Logan now.

When she finally fell silent, she glanced over and saw that Sophia had fallen asleep in her bouncy chair, her little head drooping to the side, the plastic keys fallen to the floor, where Opal batted at them and then jumped back when they skittered across the tile.

Her mom got up and poured them each more coffee, put the pot back on the warmer and then resumed her seat. "Before we get into everything you've just told me, I have to ask. Are you upset over your dad and me leaving? Is that bothering you? Do you want us to stay?"

Sarah opened her mouth to insist that she didn't, no way, no how.

But before she got the words out, her mom shook her head. "Tell me the truth, honey. Please."

Sarah dabbed at her eyes to mop up the last of her tears. "Okay, it's a factor, that you're going. I will miss you. I mean, all those years growing up, it was like we were strangers sharing a house. And now, it's so different. You and Dad are helpful and fun. You've become the parents I always wished for and it's been so great having you nearby. But no. I don't want you to stay. If you stayed, you wouldn't be getting your dream and I want that, Mom. I want you and Dad to finally live the life you never let yourselves live before."

"But if you need us—"

"You're a phone call away. If I needed you, you would be back in a flash."

"But do you need us to *be* here, day-to-day? Do you need us close by?"

Sarah leaned forward and took her mom's hand between both of hers. "No. You and Dad are going. It's settled. I'm good with it, I promise you."

Her mom pulled her hand free of Sarah's hold, only to reach out and fondly smooth Sarah's hair. "And what about *your* dream, sweetheart?"

"Um. Yeah, well. That's life, you know."

Flo let out a wry laugh. "Honey, you grew up a lonely child in a silent house with unhappy parents. Then you set out to conquer Chicago. You worked so hard, got so far. But sometimes in life, our big plans don't turn out the way we want them to. You had to come home. I know it hasn't been easy for you, with so much on your shoulders. But the past few weeks, you've seemed to thrive. You're really good at running the business. I think you've been happy, especially since you've been with Logan. You've been sprucing up the cottage, settling in beautifully here with a little help from your friends and neighbors. It seems to me you've been having a pretty fine time in your old hometown."

Sarah sat back in her chair and eyed her mother warily. "You've become so upbeat and hopeful. Sometimes it's just exhausting."

Her mother laughed some more. "Well, honey, now think about. Ask yourself, is it maybe just possible that you came home in defeat only to discover that you can have your dream here? Is it possible that taking over the family business is more satisfying work for you than killing yourself at that giant firm in the big city? Is it possible you *like* running your own show, being your own boss? And as for Logan, well, the two of you seem to me like a great match. Didn't he offer you exactly what you've longed for—a good life with the right man, a father for your child?"

"Mom, it didn't work out, okay?"

"But it could." Flo leaned in again. "If you'll just let it."

Sarah glared at her. "Look. You want me to say it?"

Flo sat up straight again and smiled way too sweetly. "I do, yes. I absolutely do."

"Okay, Mom. I'll say it." Sarah sniffed and brushed another random tear away. "I freaked out. That's the truth. He went down on one knee to offer me just what I'd given up on, what I've always wanted most and have learned to accept that I'll never have. And when he pulled out that ring, well, I choked, okay? I just couldn't do it, couldn't reach out and take it." Sarah put her hands to the sides of her head because right at that moment it kind of felt like her brain was about to explode. "I blew it. I really did. I threw away my own dream. I turned away the man I love. I freaked out and now it's too late."

"Oh, sweetheart," said her mother. "As long you're still breathing, it's never too late."

Logan had taken to sleeping out under the stars.

After all, there were a lot of fences to fix on the Ambling A. He was taking care of that—and avoiding any contact with other human beings in the bargain.

The morning after it ended with Sarah, he'd had an argument with his father over nothing in particular. Really, he picked a fight because he blamed Max, at least partly, for the way it had all gone wrong with Sarah.

Then, that same day at breakfast, his brothers were yammering on about some discovery they'd made— an old, locked diary with a jewel-encrusted letter *A* on the front. They'd found it right there in the ranch house under a rotted floorboard and they were all trotting out theories as to who might have hidden it and what might be inside.

Logan could not have cared less about some old, tattered relic that had nothing to do with him or any of them, either. He yelled at them to shut the hell up about it.

Then Wilder made the mistake of asking him what his damn problem was. He'd lit into his youngest brother. They'd almost come to blows.

That did it. Logan realized he would just as soon not have anything to do with his family right now—or with anyone else, for that matter. He'd considered leaving for good, packing up his things and heading back to Seattle.

But the big city didn't thrill him any more than dealing with his family did. Nothing thrilled him. He was fresh out of enthusiasm for anything and everything. Until he could figure out what move to make next, he just wanted to be left alone.

So he'd loaded up his pickup with fence posts and barbwire and headed out across the land. He had a sleeping bag and plenty of canned food. For five full days he worked on the fences, brought in strays, dug out clogged ditches and didn't speak to a single person.

Eventually, he would have to return to the ranch house, have a hot meal, a bath and a shave. But not for a while yet. Not until he could look at his father without wanting to punch his lights out, not until his heart stopped aching.

Come to think of it, it could be a long time before he had a damn shower. Because the ache in his heart showed no signs of abating anytime soon.

On Tuesday, three days after her talk with her mother, Sarah had yet to do anything about how much she missed Logan.

Yeah, she got it. She did. She'd finally had a chance at what she really wanted with a man—and she'd thrown her chance away. It was up to her to go to him, tell him how totally she'd messed up and beg him to give her just one more shot.

But she didn't do it. She felt…immobilized somehow. She visited clients, cared for her baby, cuddled her cat. Inside, though, she was empty and frozen and so very sad.

Tuesday evening, as Opal jumped around the kitchen floor chasing shadows and Sophia sat chewing her rubber pretzel and giggling dreamily at the mobile of dancing ladybugs hooked to her bouncy seat, Sarah stood at the refrigerator with the door wide open.

She stared inside at food she had no interest in eating and tried to decide what to fix for dinner. Really, she wasn't hungry. There was a half a box of Cheez-Its on the counter. She could eat that—yeah. Perfect. Cheez-Its for dinner, and maybe a glass of wine or ten. Once she put Sophia to bed, she could cry for a while. That would be constructive.

The knock on the front door surprised her. Would it be her mom again or maybe Lily, somebody who loved her coming to tell her to snap out of it?

She almost didn't answer it. Really, she didn't want to talk to anyone right now and she couldn't figure out why anyone would want to give a pep talk to an emotional coward like her, anyway.

But then whoever it was knocked again. She shut the fridge door and went to get it.

"Hello, Sarah," Max Crawford said when she opened the door. He actually had his black hat in his hands. "I wonder if you would give me a few minutes of your time."

Her best option was obvious. She should slam the door in his overbearing, judgmental face.

Instead, she just sneered. "Didn't you get the memo? Logan and I broke up. You got what you wanted. There is absolutely no reason for you to be darkening my door."

"Please," he said, all somber and serious—and way too sincere. "A few minutes, that's all I'm asking for. Just hear me out."

Oh, she wanted to shove that door shut so fast and so hard...

But she didn't. Partly because she was too tired and sad to give him the angry, self-righteous rejection he deserved. And also because she couldn't help but be curious as to what Logan's rapscallion dad had to say now.

She stepped back and gestured him inside. "Have a seat."

He crossed the threshold and sat on the sofa. "Thank you."

She took the easy chair across from him. "Okay. What?"

Carefully, he set his hat on the cushion beside him. "Logan's out on the far reaches of the Ambling A. He took a sleeping bag, a truck-bed full of barbwire and fence posts, a shovel or two and a bunch of canned goods. He hasn't been back to the house since last Thursday."

Alarm had her heart racing and her palms going sweaty. "You're saying he's disappeared?"

"No, he's mending fences and bringing in strays. We been out, me and the boys, checking on him from a distance because he wants nothing to do with any of us. Sarah, you broke my boy's heart."

She saw red. She would have raised her voice good and loud, given him a very large piece of her mind, if it hadn't been for the innocent baby in the other room who would be frightened if her mother started screaming like a crazy woman.

With deadly softness, she reminded him, "Well, I guess you're pretty happy then, since that was what you wanted all along."

"I was wrong," said Max. "I was all wrong."

That set her back a little. She blinked and stared. "What did you say?"

"I just need you to know that I am so sorry, Sarah, for any trouble I have caused between you and Logan. I truly apologize for my behavior. I'm a guilty old man with too many secrets. I see—and I always saw—that you are a fine woman. And my son does love you. He loves you so much. I get it now, I do. Trying to chase you off was wrong. I never should have done that, and that I did it had nothing to do with you. It was a knee-jerk reaction born of my own bad deeds in the past."

Okay, now she was really curious. "Exactly what bad deeds, Max?"

He picked up his hat and tapped it on his knee. "Well, Sarah, at this time, I'm not at liberty to say."

She snort-laughed at that one. "Of course, you're not."

He had the nerve to chuckle. "Sarah, I just want you to know that I am finished trying to come between you and Logan. When you two work it out, I will be there for both of you, supporting you in every way I can."

"*When* we work it out?"

"That's what I said."

"You have no way of knowing that we will work it out."

"My son is long-gone in love with you. His heart may be broken, but he has not given up on you. He's just licking his wounds for a while, until he's ready to try again." Max rose. "He took his phone with him when he left, so if you were to call in order to put him out of his misery, chances are you would get through." He went to the door.

She followed him—until he stopped suddenly and turned back to face her. For several seconds they just stood there, regarding each other.

Sarah broke the silence. "You know where he is, right? You could take me to him?"

"Yes, ma'am."

"I'll be at the Ambling A ranch house at eight tomorrow morning."

The lines around Max's eyes deepened with his devilish grin. "Now that is what I was hoping you might say."

Sarah decided against Cheez-Its and wine for dinner—not because she knew she should eat something more substantial, but because she was so nervous about what might happen tomorrow that she couldn't eat at all.

She fed Sophia, gave her a bath and put her down to sleep at a little after eight. Then she sat in the living room with a pencil and a scratch pad trying to organize her thoughts for tomorrow. She wanted to have something really meaningful and persuasive to say when she finally saw Logan again, something to convince him that she truly did love him, that he could trust her with his heart. She needed just the right words, words that would reassure him, make him believe that if he said yes to her, she would not disappoint him ever again.

It was almost nine when she heard the truck pull up out in front.

An odd little shiver went through her and she rose to peer out the window behind the sofa.

It was Logan's crew cab, all covered in dust and dried mud, with a big roll of barbwire sticking up out of the bed.

With a cry, she threw down the scratch pad and ran to the door, flinging it open just as he got out of the truck. She stepped out on the porch and then kind of froze there as his long strides took him around the front of the truck and up the front walk.

He looked so good, in a nice, blue shirt and dark-wash jeans, clean-shaven, his hair still damp. He must have come in from the wild, talked to his dad, had a shower and a shave.

Her heart was going so fast she kind of worried it might beat its way right out of her chest, just go jittering off up Pine Street and vanish forever from her sight.

He stopped at the foot of the steps. "Sarah," he said. That was it. That was everything. Really, how did he do it? He could put a whole world of meaning into just saying her name.

"Yes," she said.

"Sarah." And he came up the steps.

"Yes!" She threw herself into his waiting arms. "All the yeses. All the time. Forever, Logan. I'm sorry I was so scared. I'm sorry I blew it. I choked in the worst kind of way. But I'm over that. I want a life with you. I want our forever. I want it, I do."

His Adam's apple bounced as he gulped. "You mean that?" His eyes gleamed down at her, full of hope and promise and so much love.

"I do. Oh, yes, I do. I love you, Logan. I've missed you so much. If you give me one more chance now, I will never let you down again."

"Yeah," he said, one side of that fine mouth quirking up in a pleased smile. "That's what I'm talking about." And he kissed her, a long kiss, full of all the glory and wonder and desire she'd been missing so desperately since she sent him away.

She melted into him, happier than she'd ever been in her whole life up till now.

And when he lifted his head he said, "Give me your hand." He pulled the ring from his pocket and slipped it on.

"It's so beautiful." And it was, emerald-cut with smaller diamonds along the gleaming platinum band. "I love it." She cast her gaze up to him again. "I love *you*."

"And I love you. So much. Sarah…" He grabbed her close for another kiss and another after that.

Then someone whistled. They looked out at the street to see one of the neighborhood kids jumping on his bike, speeding off, laughing as he went.

Sarah caught Logan's hand and pulled him inside. He shoved the door shut and grabbed her close again.

She said, "Your dad came to see me today."

"I know. He told me."

"I was coming after you tomorrow."

"He told me that, too. I couldn't wait. So here I am."

She lifted a hand and pressed it to his warm, freshly shaven cheek. "Oh, I am so glad. I want to—"

A cry from the monitor on the coffee table cut her off.

"I'll go get her," said Logan. They shared a long look. He knew the drill, after all. If they just waited, the baby might go back to sleep. "I need to see her," he said. "I need to tell her I'm here now and I'm not going away again."

Sarah blinked back happy tears. "Yeah. Go ahead."

Logan yanked her close and kissed her hard—and then turned for the short hall to the baby's room.

"Reow?" Opal sat beneath the dining room table. Delicately, she lifted a paw and spent a moment grooming it. Then she stretched and strutted over to where Sarah stood by the door.

Sarah scooped her up and kissed her on the crown of her head between her two perfect pink ears. "Logan's home," she whispered.

Opal started purring.

In the baby's room, Logan turned the lamp on low and went to the crib.

Sophia let out the sweetest sound at the sight of him—something midway between a laugh and a cry. She waved her hands wildly. "Ah!" she crowed. "Da!"

"How's my favorite baby girl?" he asked as he gathered her into his arms.

Much later, in bed after a more intimate reunion, Logan and Sarah made plans.

They would live in town—at the cottage for now, and eventually in the larger house where she'd grown up. Before they moved, Logan was going to get that garage-door opener installed and hire some guys to build the breezeway from the garage to the back door. They would keep the cottage for Flo and Mack so they would have their own place in their hometown any time they wanted a break from their adventures in the Gulf.

Neither Logan nor Sarah wanted to wait to get married. Her parents would be leaving soon and Sarah insisted the wedding had to happen before they headed south.

"How about Monday?" she suggested.

He blinked at her in surprise. "Monday as in a week from yesterday?"

"Yep. That's the one. We'll get the license tomorrow and I'll call Viv, explain what I want and see if she can make it happen."

"Sarah, don't most brides take months, even a year, to plan a wedding?"

She laughed and kissed him. "They do, but Viv Dalton is a miracle worker. Just you wait and see."

Epilogue

The following Monday at six in the evening, Mack Turner walked Sarah down the aisle Viv had created within a magical cascade of fairy lights in the center of the dance floor at the Ace in the Hole.

Monday, after all, was relatively quiet at the Ace and that meant the owner had been willing to close for a wedding—but really, since everyone in town was invited and most of them showed up, the Ace wasn't closed at all. The place was packed.

The tables were decked out in yellow-and-white checkered cloths with wildflower centerpieces and candles shimmering in mercury glass holders. Sarah wore a floor-length strapless lace gown that she and Lily had found in a Kalispell wedding boutique. Her white cowboy hat had a long, filmy veil attached to the band. The flouncy, full skirt of her dress was perfect for dancing.

And they did dance. Starting with the first dance. Logan and Sarah held Sophia between them and swayed slowly to Keith Urban's "Making Memories of Us."

They served burgers for dinner and there was plenty of beer and soft drinks for all. Sarah's mom took Sophia home at a little after eight, where a nice girl from up the street was waiting to babysit so that Flo could return to the wedding celebration.

By eleven, a lot of the guests had gone home. But most of the younger men and women were still there when Sarah jumped up on the bar brandishing her wildflower bouquet. Lily caught it with a yelp of pure surprise.

"You're next!" Sarah called to her lifelong friend.

Lily laughed and shook her head. She didn't believe it. But Sarah just *knew*. If she could find the only man for her right here in her hometown, certainly Lily could do the same.

Logan was waiting when Sarah climbed down off the bar. He swept her into his arms and out onto the dance floor. They two-stepped through three numbers and then the music slowed. He pulled her nice and close.

"Why the Ace of all places?" he whispered in her ear.

"You love it."

"I do, yeah—but why did you choose it?"

She gazed up at him, golden-brown eyes gleaming, as they swayed to the music. "I guess because the Ace has always meant romance and possibility to me. I love it here. There's music, people talking and laughing. Everybody's having fun. Truthfully, I can't think of a more perfect setting for us to say 'I do.'"

Right then, Cole and Viv Dalton danced by. Viv and Sarah shared a smile. At the edge of the dance floor, Max was watching, looking way too pleased with himself.

Sarah smoothed the collar of Logan's white dress shirt. "Your dad is such a character. I mean, just look at him, grinning like that. What is he thinking?"

"You really don't know?"

"Not a clue."

Logan nuzzled her silky cheek. "He's thinking, *One down, five to go.*"

Sarah threw back her head and laughed as Logan pulled her closer. "What?" she demanded.

"This." And he claimed her lips in a slow, sweet kiss.

* * * * *

COMING SOON!

We really hope you enjoyed reading this book. If you're looking for more romance, be sure to head to the shops when new books are available on

Thursday 11th July

To see which titles are coming soon, please visit

millsandboon.co.uk/nextmonth

MILLS & BOON

Coming next month

FALLING FOR THE PREGNANT HEIRESS
Susan Meier

"It kills me how you cannot understand that if I left you, your brother would be furious."

"He will be on his honeymoon."

Trent groaned. Always practical Sabrina would be the death of him. "He'll hear about this sometime and when he does all he'll see is that you were in a life crisis and I abandoned you."

"This isn't a crisis. It's a situation."

He gaped at her. "Does everything have to be so logical for you? Can you just once get mad? That man, Pierre—" he said the name with a disdain that rolled off his tongue like fiery darts "—didn't deserve the time he got with you."

No man really deserved her. She was soft and sweet. But hardened by a childhood with a father who expected her to be a perfect little doll. The man she finally let loose with, was honest with, had to be someone special. Someone who would see she deserved to be treated with kindness and love.

Not merely passion.

And right now the feelings he had for her were nothing but passion. He was angry, but she was gorgeous, sexy. He could picture every move of making love to her. He could almost see her reactions. Hear her coos and sighs of delight.

He scrubbed his hand across his mouth. It sounded as if he wanted to be that man. And he had to admit he liked the heat that raced through his veins when he thought about keeping her in his life, but that was wrong. He was a man made to be single, to enjoy life, to forge his own path. She was pregnant with another man's child, a woman who would need stability to bring order to her world right now.

And if both of those weren't enough, she was the sister of his best friend, which made her strictly hands-off.

Continue reading
FALLING FOR THE PREGNANT HEIRESS
Susan Meier

Available next month
www.millsandboon.co.uk

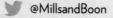